FAIRY TALE FATALE
BEARLY GOLD

A "Goldilocks and the Three Bears"
Reimagining

N. D. Jones

KUUMBA PUBLISHING
CREATIVE MINDS
PASSIONATE HEARTS

Kuumba Publishing
1325 Bedford Avenue
#32374
Pikesville, MD
kuumbapublishing.com

Book Layout & Design ©2017 - BookDesignTemplates.com

Editor: Chris at Hidden Gems
Cover Design: Fantasia Cover Designs
Jwahir and the Three Bears Coloring Pages: Ika Sirana

Bearly Gold/N.D. Jones. -- 1st ed.
ISBN-13: 979-8-9871464-4-6

Content Warnings: on-page sex between consenting adults, on-page/implied child death, implied child sexual assault, talk of/threatening child physical assault, talk of suicide, talk of drug use, talk of sex slaves

Dedication

Shirley Anita Chisholm
November 30, 1924–January 1, 2005
Politician, Educator, Author

"I want history to remember me . . . not as the first black woman to have made a bid for the presidency of the United States, but as a black woman who lived in the 20th century and who dared to be herself. I want to be remembered as a catalyst for change in America."

1: This Won't End Well

2122
The State of Namju
Fuxing City

"I'm not leaving my children here to die."

Fayola watched as Dr. Teresa Pérez-Soto stomped past her and back into Peace Blossoms Orphanage. Or rather, she inwardly sighed at the doctor's pointless theatrics as the woman reentered the two-story medical clinic. The sign on the brick building read: Peace Blossoms Clinic for Children. Someone, perhaps one of the youths Dr. Pérez-Soto claimed as her own, had used red spray paint to write *Orphanage* overtop of the last three words.

Clinic or orphanage, biological or adopted children, it doesn't matter. My mission is clear. Extract Dr. Pérez-Soto and return her to her worried brother. A straightforward mission. My last. Finally.

Fayola scanned the area. Small, local businesses lined both sides of the abandoned street. Like the clinic, an old-fashioned sign affixed to the front of each business drew the eye to big,

white letters outlined in black. One or more familiar pictorials—
a bear paw, an elephant trunk, and a human hand—appeared under the name of each business.

*The clinic's sign has all three images. Dr. Pérez-Soto services
every kind of child in this country.*

Twisted metal gates and broken glass from storefront windows
littered the sidewalk in front of many businesses with paw and
hand pictorials.

*The calm stillness of this street won't last. I can feel the vibra-
tions. Their marching is like a building earthquake deep in Earth
Pact's core. The regiments will converge on this part of the city
in an hour. That'll be more than enough time to complete the extraction part of my mission. Whether she wants to or not, Dr. Pérez-Soto will be leaving with me.*

Fayola tried the knob to the clinic, shaking her head when the
door did not open. Did the doctor think her temper tantrum and a
locked door would have her taking to the sky and failing to complete her mission?

Bam. Smash. Hinges snapped; the wooden door cracked in
fours and crashed to the floor.

Stepping on pieces of the ruined door, Fayola strolled inside
the clinic. Shafts of light from outside lit the foyer, bouncing off
candle wax stuck to the floor and the face of a frowning Dr. Pérez-
Soto.

"You broke my door."

With the tip of her booted foot, Fayola pushed one of the
chunks of wood out of her way. "Inconsequential."

"It isn't." Light brown eyes lowered to Fayola's glove-covered
hands before settling on her black boots. "Did you do that with
your hands or feet?"

"Inconsequential. We have less than an hour. Pack a bag and
say your goodbyes."

"I told you, I'm not going anywhere."

Fayola stepped farther into the clinic. The foyer led to stairs to the right and two closed doors to the left. Although she could not hear the children, she could smell blood from a recent injury in the air.

For the second time in less than ten minutes, the doctor turned her back on her. Long dark hair trailed to wide hips and over a pink and white dress the same color as the blooms of the fifty-foot peace blossom tree she landed on upon arriving in northern Fuxing City. The tree had afforded her a safe location for reconnaissance. As always, her mission intel had been correct. Regiments from the Sunhung and Taepo herds were on the move.

Fayola had seen the civil war's destruction; dead bodies left for ravager birds to pick over, buildings leveled to their rocky foundation, and crop fields burned to inedible ash.

No matter the place, war looks, smells, and sounds the same. Wars also wreak the same turmoil. Grief and heartache. Starvation and desperation.

A door from a room to Fayola's left opened. A six- or seven-year-old girl, human, from the fragrant berry scent of her, peeked around the door. Rubbing golden-brown eyes and shuffling tiny feet, she approached Dr. Pérez-Soto. Wrapping thin arms around one of Dr. Pérez-Soto's legs, the child buried a face as round as a ripe plum against the doctor's thigh. "I'm hungry."

One after the other, more children emerged from the open door, piling out and surrounding Dr. Pérez-Soto.

Orphans. Something else war leaves behind. Twenty-one of them, but not all are human. The first one out appears to be the youngest. The oldest are those twin girls holding hands. Fifteen or so. Bear shifters like Dr. Pérez-Soto. They share her almond-shaped eyes and straight dark hair. Those physical traits are typical of bear shifters from this region. But the twins' skin has a warm undertone to Dr. Pérez-Soto's coolness, neither of which changes how their blood would taste going down.

Fayola checked her tactical watch—a gift from Jelani. *Fifty-five minutes before they converge on this small city.* "Since the children are here now, the farewells can come first, then the packing. For your comfort, I suggest changing into pants."

"Do you have no heart?"

"What I have is a mission to complete." Fayola waved her hand at the gathered children, who watched her with a mix of curiosity and dread. "They are not my mission. You are. Come morning, nothing on this street will be left standing."

"Or alive."

Fayola took the two words as a rhetorical statement, as much as she did Dr. Pérez-Soto's attempt at guilt. Neither altered her mission parameters, so she set her watch for thirty minutes and took up position at the foot of the stairs.

"That's it? You have nothing else to say?" To her credit, Dr. Pérez-Soto did not argue her point—fruitless though it was—in front of the children. "Go through my office and back upstairs."

"But—" the twins began.

"Do as I say. It will be fine."

The twin with a healing cut across her forehead turned to Fayola. "Which kind are you?"

Fayola understood her question, despite having been stated with a vagueness typical of youth. "Inconsequential."

The girl nodded; her eyes filled with a world-weary maturity unbecoming of a person so young. "We prayed for a Dela Eden."

Dela Eden. I can't be that for these children. They aren't my mission, and one soldier is not enough to save twenty-two people.

"What's a Dela Eden?" the youngest child asked.

"A savior, but it doesn't matter." The twin with the scar took hold of the little girl's hand. "She isn't one. Not ours anyway." She led the girl back into the room they'd exited. Their retreat was followed by the other children. Not one of them looked back, accepting life's cruel fate with a grace she'd never seen in adults, much less in children.

No, not grace. Hopelessness.

"I guess this is supposed to be a rescue mission." Dr. Pérez-Soto closed her office door after the last child entered. She then leaned against the door, too arrogant or foolish to realize her stubborn posture held neither bite nor sway. "The kind you are doesn't matter. Your human form is about five-six. No bulk or fat. Nothing about your human body is impressive. But . . ."

Fayola only half listened to Dr. Pérez-Soto. If talking made it easier for her to accept the inevitable, Fayola wouldn't interrupt. Still, her silence did not mean she had to grant the woman her full attention.

Dr. Pérez-Soto pushed from the door but maintained the distance between them. "I've seen your people in flight. You're fast but also large enough to carry two or three adults. I bet you could even hold heavy bears on your back."

"No."

"No, you're not strong enough to carry two big bear shifters like me?"

"First, Dr. Pérez-Soto, you're a sun bear. One seventy at most. Not big by any bear shifter standard. Two, it doesn't matter how much weight I can carry because I have no intention of—"

"One seven-year-old and two ten-year-olds. That's it. Combined, they weigh less than I do."

"The pact is for your rescue only. That's my mission."

"Then change the mission. They're children. Innocents caught in a bloody, vicious war. Pacts don't matter here."

"Pacts matter everywhere."

"You're wrong." Dr. Pérez-Soto pointed a steady finger at Fayola. "You and me. We can create our own pact. Right here. Right now. You take the three youngest to safety. Save them.

Don't shake your head, damn you. I'm not finished. I haven't told you what I'm willing to offer in exchange."

"You have nothing I am permitted to take."

"Which isn't the same as me having nothing you want." Dr. Pérez-Soto stalked toward Fayola as if she were a predator ready to seize perceived prey.

Fayola allowed the movement and the foolish thought.

"I'm sure it was my CEO brother who formed a pact with your nation. Rescue, hostage recovery, counterinsurgency. That's what your people do. Dangerous missions in exchange for blood donation centers." Dr. Pérez-Soto stopped in front of Fayola. One hand went to her curvaceous hip, the other to hair she flipped over her shoulder—revealing a thick, pulsing vein. "To my knowledge, there are no bird beak pictorials in this entire country. No pictorial, no blood centers for shifters like you. No blood pact."

Fayola waited for the inevitable offer. Her stomach growled like a lion neither of them could shift into.

At the loud sound, the forty-five-year-old doctor's full lips lifted, and twinkling eyes brightened.

She eschews the value of pacts. But it's the blood pacts the Wake has with other countries that have kept us from taking what we want, when we want, and from whom we want.

Tilting her head to the side, Dr. Pérez-Soto proved herself both a self-sacrificing physician and a burdensome final mission. "Sun bears fall within your preferred blood type group. Therefore, I offer myself to you freely in exchange for my children's lives. That's all I ask. My blood for their safety. That will be our pact."

A rush of burning hunger twisted her insides, sparking a need forever close to the surface. Fayola could take the offer. Indeed, Dr. Pérez-Soto wasn't the first to suggest an illegal pact.

Fayola pressed her nose to Dr. Pérez-Soto's neck, smelling the rich flavor of her blood. She licked her. *Salty.* "I could claim everything you offer and then go on my way, not taking a single child with me."

"You wouldn't." Dr. Pérez-Soto tried to pull away, but Fayola wrapped an arm around her waist and yanked her close.

"I'm an impundulu. The power of lightning lives in my body, and the blood of birds and bears sustain me. But it wouldn't do for the Wake to eat until gorged. To hunt our food source to extinction. You die. We die. So pacts exist to protect us both. We honor our pacts. Always."

"Let me go."

"Why? This is what you wanted. My beak around your neck—squeezing but not eating from you until you are no more than a corpse primed for draining. Or would you prefer to feel me drink from you while you squirm in my arms as I sink my sharp eyeteeth into your unmarred neck?"

To press her point, Fayola revealed eyeteeth no impundulu could use to drink blood. But the myth persisted.

"You're unconscionable."

"Yet it was you who attempted to use your sweet-smelling blood to lure me from my sworn duty." Fayola licked Dr. Pérez-Soto's neck again because she enjoyed the shiver of fear the action evoked. "I cannot save them, Doctor, and neither can you."

Dr. Pérez-Soto struggled against Fayola's hold, so she released the woman. Sun bears were notorious for their small bodies and short tempers. If she goaded her longer, she would have a four-foot-long black bear with a ridiculously long tongue incapable of speech in front of her. As it was, Dr. Pérez-Soto hadn't used her normal-sized human tongue to say anything of worth from the moment she'd answered the clinic's door to find Fayola on the other side.

"If I break my vow as a diello, why would you then trust me to uphold my side of the pact once you're dead and I've slaked my hunger on your warm blood?"

Dr. Pérez-Soto stumbled backward. Her gaze was unwavering, but there was dawning realization in her eyes.

"You came here on a humanitarian mission—a little bear in an unstable nation ruled by elephant shifters."

"You think me stupid? Naïve?" The last two words were spat like a wad of tasteless tobacco. "I've done good work here. You speak of your high-and-mighty pact with my brother"—she flung her hands outward—"well, this is my pact right here. Caring for these children. Making sure they are fed and clothed."

"Honorable but ultimately futile." Fayola rechecked her watch. *Twenty minutes.* "You've resorted to burning candles because the government turned off the electricity to force people out of areas controlled by the opposition. You've permitted the children to seek whatever they and you require from the abandoned stores. Not without injury, though. But surviving isn't living. It's merely a stubborn postponement of death. Now pack your things so we can be on our way."

"You're heartless."

"If it makes you feel better to think of me as the villain, then I'm heartless. Once you finish wallowing in that characterization, stop and feel."

Raising hands at eye level, Dr. Pérez-Soto flexed her fingers. "Feel?"

"With your feet."

Dr. Pérez-Soto turned away from Fayola and toward the open doorway. In the short time Fayola had wasted indulging the doctor's bout of irrationalism wrapped in guilt, the sun had begun to set. She neither knew nor cared who had referred to the female as *stupid* and *naïve* for leaving the safety of her country to offer medical aid to children in a nation more concerned with avenging perceived wrongs than protecting its citizens.

Every battle can't be won. No more than every wound can be healed.

Dr. Pérez-Soto planted herself south of the broken door chunks.

Fayola knew the second the doctor grasped the magnitude of the situation—her loud gasp reverberated between them.

Slowly, as if walking in a pit of poisonous snakes, Dr. Pérez-Soto moved away from the entryway. "I can feel them coming this way. Two or three dozen." She sank to her knees, falling like a bird's egg from a nest—cracking but not shattering on impact. "So many of them. I thought we would be safe here after everyone fled. There's nothing here. No strategic advantage to claim this city."

Fayola grabbed Dr. Pérez-Soto's elbow and helped the woman to her feet. "My mission is your extraction from Fuxing City and safe return to Delcanos."

"Are Namju citizens still trying to cross into Delcanos? When the first wave left this neighborhood, seeking refugee status in the border nations, I gathered the children and went with them. I headed straight for the Namju-Delcanos border. But the border guards wouldn't admit the children. They didn't care that I was a Delcanos citizen and the children's doctor."

Of course they didn't. Leaders of the three countries bordering Namju may sympathize with the plight of its citizens, but none will risk being drawn into a war by opening their border to refugees. Conflict resolution support has been ignored. This civil war is far from over.

When she failed to respond, the doctor pushed on—talking fast. "New pact. I'll go quietly. No more fussing. I'll go. Take me to the Namju-Delcanos border. For an impundulu, it would be a ten-minute flight. Twenty minutes round trip.

"I'm sorry. Sorry for minimizing your adherence to pact law."

"You still are. I'm not supposed to be in this country. I can't be seen by Namju soldiers, much less confront them. You're a doctor, so you know basic mathematics. I'm a single impundulu."

"You're a diello, which means you're close to retirement, although you look a decade younger than me. For you to have earned that rank at such a young age tells me a lot about you; mainly, you're seasoned and skilled and as close to a Dela Eden as my children will get." Dr. Pérez-Soto dropped to her knees again, clasping her hands together—not in prayer to her god but in supplication to . . . Fayola. "Please, Diello Fayola. Please. Please."

She glared at the pleading female, whose eyes had gone misty and face red.

The office door opened again. Out came the same little girl from earlier—not rubbing her eyes or shuffling her feet, but walking with an adultlike purpose across the foyer and straight to Fayola. Small hands grabbed her legs and eyes a lighter shade of golden-brown than her hair peered up at Fayola. "I don't believe Mei lien. You are our Dela Eden."

Dr. Pérez-Soto jumped to her feet. "Yes, yes she is, Jwahir."

Fayola looked from little Jwahir to a grinning Dr. Pérez-Soto. "You haven't won."

"I'll let the children know I'll be leaving but that you'll return to watch over them until the danger passes."

"I said—"

"Yes, yes . . ." The sun bear darted toward her office, telling Jwahir to, "Hold your Dela Eden's hand. I bet she'd like that."

"This isn't part of my miss—"

Small fingers slid against tough leather gloves. "Thank you, Dela Eden."

Fayola swore under her breath. *This won't end well . . . for them or for me.*

2: Brave Yet Foolish Words

"Mei lien," Fayola yelled the second she rounded the corner onto a street she shouldn't be seeing again, much less to a girl whose safety wasn't her sanctioned mission, "get everyone out here. Now!"

Twenty-one children rushed from the clinic—wide-eyed and open-mouthed.

"What is that?" Huan, Mei lien's sister, asked.

Fayola pushed her burden down the street, moving quicker than she would be able once it was filled with children.

"A truck, obviously," a boy about the twins' age of fifteen said. Then, pushing limp black bangs out of his eyes, his lips turned upward. "One of her. A lot of us. How, this side of the tusk, did you think she was going to get all of us out of here?"

"Shut up, Peng. I wasn't talking to you."

"Doesn't matter. It was a dumb thing to say."

"Don't call me dumb, or I'll—"

Exiting the clinic, Mei lien shoved the quarreling teens' shoulders on her way past them. "Both of you are dummies. Shut up before Diello Fayola changes her mind about saving us."

"Dela Eden," Jwahir said. The little girl, dressed in loose-fitting sweatpants, white scuffed tennis shoes, and a fairy graphic tee under an unzipped jacket rolled up at her wrists, plodded her way around the teenagers and to the edge of the sidewalk. "Not Diello Fayola."

Mei lien snatched Jwahir from the edge of the sidewalk when she would've stepped in front of the 3,500-pound pickup truck.

Sucking in deep breaths, Fayola stopped the truck in front of the waiting children. She didn't have to tell them what to do, but she did say, "The three smallest up front and between the twins. Seat belts on and mouths closed."

They obeyed without question and with haste. She appreciated both.

Fayola knew this would be the easiest part of her illegal pact.

"This is a tree, not Delcanos," Dr. Pérez-Soto had complained.

With her long, pointy beak, Fayola had gestured to a thick branch. She'd waited for the sun bear to settle safely against it before projecting words into her mind.

A tall tree with lots of thick green leaves. No one will be able to see you, from the air or ground, unless you want to make yourself known. Don't.

"I'm not stupid."

So you keep saying. But I'm the one with questionable intellect for accepting the terms of your pact. I don't have time to fly you all the way to Delcanos, not if I want to give myself a modicum of a chance of getting those children out of the regiments' path.

"Which means me waiting in this peace blossom tree until you return for me."

Fayola had flown away, cursing the weak part of her that had caved with Jwahir's first touch.

Now she ran at top speed through the streets of Fuxing City, pushing an overloaded pickup truck.

For the first time in my life, I wish I'd learned how to drive. Not that the borrowed truck would've turned on with a thumbprint not programmed to its security system. An electric jump may have gotten it started, though. If I survive, I'll take Jelani up on his driving lessons offer.

Fayola ran from one mile to the next. From one neighborhood to the next. *Keep to the side streets and off the main roads. If I do, we might have a chance of escaping the city unseen.*

"You're breathing really hard." Peng leaned forward.

"Hold on to the side wall, and don't fall out. If you do, I won't stop to pick you up."

"Got it. Here."

Fayola stared at the boy.

"Right, right. You can't push with one hand."

Despite her warning, Peng leaned halfway out of the truck, his offering extended. "Open up, and I'll pour."

Fayola parted her lips, lapping at the bottled water like it was fresh blood. Some of it dribbled down her chin and onto her black jacket, but enough had coated her tongue and slid down her throat that the little stars she'd begun to see faded to dull lights.

Muscles cramped and sweat blurred her vision. Fingers digging into the tailgate, Fayola gritted her teeth and focused on keeping her legs in constant motion.

The alarm on her watch went off thirty minutes earlier. Although she'd placed miles between them and the clinic, her trajectory had taken them closer to a small Taepo herd already stationed on the border between Fuxing City and the nation of Delcanos.

A Sunhung herd is stationed to the south, while the arriving regiments are moving in from the east and west. Over is easier than through, but that isn't an option with this cargo.

Fayola didn't fool herself. No matter how many miles she ran without glimpsing the enemy, she knew this mission would end one way.

With most of the children and me dead. My final mission indeed.

2099

Twenty-Three Years Earlier
The United Wake of Benekal
Kettle of Aradi City

"Is there something wrong with your legs? If so, you should have told me before we left home. I believe I still have your baby stroller in storage."

Annoyed by her father's sarcasm, Fayola slowed her pace even more.

"Petulance. Today of all days, Fay?"

"I've only just turned fifteen. It isn't fair. The others have had months to get used to the idea."

"Such is the fate of those born at the end of the year."

Her father, Raicho, grasped her hand, shifting them to the right side of the sidewalk, so others could pass.

She didn't know how many children born during her birth year lived in the kettle in Aradi City, no more than she knew the count of fifteen-year-olds in other kettles throughout the Wake. What she did know was that their lives, like hers, would soon belong to The United Wake of Benekal Impundulu Military.

Fifteen-year-olds and their parents filed down the street that would take them to the city's center.

Fayola's gaze found a familiar face that strolled up the street. Her neighbor, Jelani, always held his head high and shoulders straight. If not for how his arm swayed, slightly grazing his mother's with each step, his anxiety would've gone unnoticed.

Jelani doesn't want to go either, but he's also not complaining. Instead, he's walking into his unavoidable fate with dignity.

Jelani nodded to Raicho as he passed, acknowledging his elder but ignoring her. It wasn't a slight but a nonverbal cue for her to follow his lead. More, Jelani's dignified acceptance reminded Fayola that her duty to her father, kettle, and Wake began the moment the sun rose, heralding a day unlike any she'd experienced.

The last day of the year but the first day of my new life. I'm not ready.

With one hand going around her waist, Raicho leapt up and to the right. They landed on the cantilever canopy secured to the side of a building. They weren't high off the ground—maybe twenty feet—but that didn't stop Fayola from staring up at her father with a daughter's awe.

"Don't look at me like that. Once you've gone through basic training, you'll be able to do the same and more."

"I don't want—"

"We all serve the Wake. None of us are exempt from military service."

"I know but—"

"You're afraid. So was I." The arm around her waist tightened, drawing her closer to his side. "You don't want to leave me and home. I felt the same when it was my time to drink from the Tree of Karasi. Service. Pact."

"I know, Dad." Fayola's forehead fell against Raicho's strong, broad chest. The scent of him—Beechwood honey—clung to his long-sleeved shirt. She breathed him in, not too proud to relish these last minutes of childhood. "Decades," she sniffled against his chest.

"I know. It took me three and a half of them before I fulfilled my sworn duty."

"I'll complete mine in two and a half."

She thought he would chuckle in that warm, loving way of his when she said or did something outrageous. He didn't. Instead, he hugged her to him and whispered in her ear, "A high bar. That route back home won't be easy."

"I know."

Raicho laughed, a rumble of sound against her cheek. "No, my brave lightning bird, you have no idea. But you will learn." He kissed her cheek—his day-old beard scratchy, his touch affectionate but too brief. "Service but also safety. Twenty-five years or longer, it doesn't matter. I'll be here when you return home. Now come before those tears I see you fighting to keep from falling undo us both."

Turning his back to her, Raicho bent to one knee.

Fayola grinned. She'd turned fifteen last week. Jelani and other neighborhood friends had attended her birthday party. She'd bestowed him with the first slice of her cake—as much an honor as it was an acknowledgment of their affection. But Fayola and Jelani had no more time for youthful flirting, no more than either of them was considered a child. Adulthood at fifteen.

Fayola wasn't ready. She had protested the closer this day drew.

I'm still not ready. But I'm out of time.

"Hop on."

Fayola claimed the spot on Raicho's back she knew well. She held on tight with legs around his waist and arms around his neck.

Jumping to the ground, Raicho took off up the street. Darting around people and vehicles, he leapt on canopies and roofs of short buildings—turning a solemn walk into an exciting father-daughter outing she would cherish during their years apart.

Fayola laughed and laughed, holding on to her good cheer, even after they reached the center of the city.

A 125-foot ancient tree—the Tree of Karasi—had been planted by the founders of Aradi City. A canopy of flowers formed an elegant weeping effect of perpetually gold, white, green, and red flowers on branches that spilled downward. Each flower color represented the four types of impundulu.

The colors of our lightning. Will mine be green like Dad's?

Fayola had seen the same kind of ancient tree in other kettles, so it took little to imagine similar gatherings occurring Wake-wide.

A twenty-two-foot-high, forty-eight-foot-deep wall surrounded the fountain into which the tree had been planted.

Raicho landed on the wall. "We have to part now."

Fayola knew. She also knew only inductees and the diello assigned to them were permitted on the wall during this annual event.

"I'm proud of you, my sweet Fay. Wherever you go in this big world, no matter who you help or try to save, during times of challenge and triumph, know I love you. No lightning bolt I've ever generated was more important than the one I formed to create the egg that would grow into my most precious blood pact."

Raicho retrieved something from his pants pocket, pressed the item into her hand, then closed her fingers around the circular flat object.

Without looking, Fayola shoved it into her pants pocket. "Thank you, Dad. See you soon."

Raicho smiled—big, wide, but also a little sad. "Yes, my Fay, see you soon."

Fayola watched as her father jumped from the wall to join the throng of parents and loved ones on the ground. Now wasn't the time to pull out her father's gift, so she pushed her way past the weeping branches until she stood directly under them.

Her peers circled the massive structure. She searched for Jelani in the crowd but couldn't find him. But she could see him in her mind's eye—brows drawn, hands fisted, and body taut.

"This tree," a female voice above her boomed, "represents the pact we impundulu made with ourselves over two thousand years ago."

Fayola couldn't see the source of the voice, but it came from the direction of the tree.

"Diello Madana." The girl to her right pointed to an area of a cluster of branches. "She's there . . . I think," the girl whispered.

"Your eyesight is better than mine because all I see are branches and blooms."

"Your vision is fine. You just have to watch for subtle movements." She pointed again. "There. Did you see that?"

"Not even a little. As I said, your eyesight is better than mine. I'm Fayola."

"I'm Durah. Is that guy who keeps staring at you your boyfriend?" Durah lifted her hand to point again but quickly lowered it when the voice spoke.

"Everyone must eat to survive. That is an undeniable fact of life. Yet our survival, our predatory instincts, need not result in the loss of lives."

Fayola searched the crowd again, smiling when she finally found Jelani standing between two males. Compared to their tall, wide-shouldered forms, Jelani appeared more like prey than the predator they all were.

"Where are you going?" Durah asked. "Diello Madana is speaking. It's impolite to . . ."

Quickly but quietly, Fayola maneuvered around her fellow kettle members. *I can listen and move at the same time. Besides, Diello Madana hasn't said anything I haven't already learned in school.* She squeezed past a girl on tiptoe who still couldn't see around the two taller girls in front of her, no matter which way she shifted.

"For the past fifteen years, the government has financed every aspect of your life—every meal you've consumed, every book you've read, every home you've lived in, every center of learning you've attended."

Crouching, in case her movement caught Diello Madana's attention, Fayola made her way to the left side of the wall. *I don't know how Durah spotted Jelani, but I'm glad she did. I'll have to introduce them later and thank her.*

Fayola tugged on a pant leg.

A male, who wasn't Jelani, stared down at her with an arched eyebrow and lips curled into a smile. "Who are you, and what are you doing down there?" He lowered himself to her crouched position. "You're trouble, aren't you?"

"No, I'm Fayola, and I'm here for him." She nodded in Jelani's direction. "But you have tree trunks for legs, so it was hard to get around you without knocking you into the pit."

"It's a fountain, and my legs aren't that big."

"It's a pit of blood everyone thinks is special."

"That's because it is special."

Fayola snapped her mouth shut, having already formulated a response before realizing the words hadn't been spoken by the boy beside her.

Those nearest her parted to the left and right, leaving ample space to close the final distance between herself and Jelani. Yet, within seconds, the clear view she had of him disappeared like a door slammed in her face.

This door, however, had a name. Fayola met the ruby eyes of Diello Madana. The female wore no definable expression, nothing so telling as a frown or glare. But she'd halted her speech and revealed herself sooner than Fayola assumed she had intended.

She stood to her full height of five-three. Not nearly as tall as the diello, but consequences for one's actions should never be taken in a submissive position. Her father had reinforced that lesson every time she did something worthy of a scold.

Fayola had never met Diello Madana. She imagined a six-and-a-half-foot muscular female with red-tipped brown braids down to her knees would be impossible to forget. She wore civilian clothing—a fitted sleeveless dark green dress that would've made for a classy outfit choice if not for her black paratrooper-style boots.

She could crush every bone in my body with those massive arms. That kind of fitness does not come from drinking blood.

"You've interrupted a sacred ceremony."

The thought of replying did not enter Fayola's mind. Diello Madana had not spoken with the expectation of having a conversation. Fayola may have displayed terrible manners, but she understood the importance of hierarchy.

"You're Raicho's fledgling." Long, thick fingers grasped Fayola's chin, slowly moving her head to the right then to the left. "You're here, so hardly a fledgling anymore. You have his large, bright eyes but also his daring. It will be my job to hone that natural tendency into a trait useful to our military. So tell me, daughter of Raicho, what was so important you left your side of the wall to travel to this one?"

She tracked my movement the entire time. But I couldn't see her, not even with Durah's help. To keep my promise to Dad, I have much to learn.

"Friendship," she answered.

"Ah, friendship." Diello Madana lowered her hand from Fayola's chin, and she feared she would ask her to call her friend forward. "Friendship is a good reason indeed. A young impundulu willing to risk the wrath of a diello to reach her friend's side is admirable but ultimately unwise. It is my job to teach you . . .

to teach all of you how to determine and weigh risks versus benefits. You, daughter of Raicho, risked much but gained nothing but my attention. Am I correct?"

Fayola disliked the spotlight. She had spent all her school years avoiding activities that would have her before a crowd. But there she stood with over a hundred sets of eyes on her. Some were friends and classmates, but most were strangers.

She shoved her hands into her pants pockets. The right settled on her father's gift—warm and sure against her fingers. "I am Retired Diello Raicho of the Covert Pursuits Special Forces Unit's daughter." She spoke clearly and loudly, so all could hear. "But I am first and foremost Fayola. When I awoke this morning, my mind revolted against coming here. My body rejected attempts to get out of bed. My heart clenched from the pain of knowing tomorrow I would awake in a place far away from my father. I sought comfort, Diello Madana, as much as I wanted to offer the same to my friend. Please accept my apology for interrupting the induction ceremony." Fayola pulled hands from her pockets and lowered her head. "I will accept any punishment you deem fit."

"Any? Hmm, brave yet foolish words. You have much to learn." Fingers touched her chin again. "An adult, yes, but still quite young. Raise your head, Fayola, and be the first to drink from the Tree of Karasi. An uncalculated benefit for your risk." Diello Madana's laughter rippled out of her and through the weeping branches like a gentle breeze over a still ocean. "I think it is me who's learned a lesson this induction day. Fine, then, no more long-winded speeches about history and tradition."

Diello Madana plucked a red leaf from the tree, handing it to Fayola.

She accepted the offering with a respect for the ceremony she hadn't shown earlier. Engorged veins in the heart-shaped leaf added weight to the appendage. Despite receiving permission to drink first, Fayola waited for the others.

A kettle can never be a single impundulu, no more than one kettle can form a Wake.

"I see Raicho has taught you well. The group before the individual. Go, Fayola, and stand beside your friend."

Jelani welcomed her with a roll of his eyes and an arm around her shoulders. "This has to be a Fayola record," he whispered in her ear. "You stay finding ways to get into trouble."

"It's your fault."

"I didn't ask you to come over here." The arm around her shoulders lowered to her hand, lacing their fingers. "But I'm glad you did because now we can do this together."

"Drink," Diello Madana ordered. "Drink from the fountain that holds the blood from countless successful pacts. This will be your last free meal until you've fulfilled your service to the Wake. Your kettle has fed you for fifteen years. It is now your time to feed the kettle."

Jelani squeezed her hand—the rough skin from his calluses a contrast to his soft smile. "Are you ready?"

Fayola wasn't, but she nodded, lifted the leaf to her mouth and accepted her new role as provider for her kettle.

As always, the blood tasted just right, a rich, bold flavor that came from one source.

Bears. Yum.

3: I'm An Impundulu, Not a Simple Bird

2122
The State of Namju

"Why are we slowing down?" Peng reached for Fayola, but she shook her head. "Don't do that. You need more water."

Water wasn't the liquid she required, just as the truck no longer served her purpose.

With a final shove, she stopped the truck behind one of several stout brick buildings in the vacant business park.

Mei lien, Huan, and Jwahir jumped out of the truck. Before she could stop her, Jwahir ran up to Fayola, wrapping arms around her legs. "You look tired."

"Yeah, she's tired." Peng leapt from the truck, landing on stocky legs and big feet she could imagine shifting into an elephant form capable of smashing bones to dust. "Too tired. You need to rest."

Mei lien approached, dark eyes raking over Fayola. "He's right." Those same dark eyes revealed an understanding Fayola appreciated. "But she can't rest, and neither can we."

"But—"

"Peng, this is as far as she can take us. Isn't that right, Diello Fayola?"

Fayola waved the rest of the children out of the truck, encouraging them, with a nod of her head, to huddle against the wall and out of sight. Ignoring a clinging Jwahir, Fayola pointed to her right. "We're about two miles from the Namju-Tikala border. If you keep to this road, following the business park until it lets out onto nothing but paved land, but with no buildings, you'll run into the border. This route won't put you on the opposite side of a border barrier."

A human boy with shaggy blond hair and eyes the color of moss stepped around Huan and closer to Fayola. "Dr. Pérez-Soto said she would take us to Delcanos. That, if we went with her, we would have a better life. She said she would find us new homes and parents. What's in Tikala for us?"

Huan raised her hand, as if to smack the boy in the back of his head, but stopped and turned toward . . .

Thump. Thump. Thump.

The sound of marching.

Fayola set Jwahir away from her, annoyed at the sense of guilt she felt at the girl's hurt expression.

"Tikala may not be Delcanos, but it also isn't Namju." Retrieving an item from her pants pocket, she handed it to Mei lien the same way it had been gifted to her. "Someone very special gave this to me. It has kept me safe since I was your age."

"Okay, but—"

"Give this to whichever border guard tries to prevent you all from entering Tikala. Tell the guard this medal represents Diello Fayola's blood pact with the twenty-one of you."

"But we gave you no blood." Unlike Fayola, who hadn't dared to look at her father's gift in his presence, lest she burst into tears,

Mei lien opened her palm, revealing Fayola's most precious possession. "We gave you nothing in exchange. We have no true blood pact."

At once, and to Fayola's impatience, the children complained in unison. Then, like Peng and the shaggy-haired human boy, some rolled up jacket sleeves and extended their wrist to Fayola.

"Put your arms down. I'm not one of those vampires from old movies and books. That's not how it works."

"Maybe not." Peng moved forward. "You still need blood."

The children nodded, more concerned with Fayola than those who approached.

"As I said, it doesn't work that way. Even if it did, I would never take blood from children. You'll need every bit of your strength to make it from here to the border."

"Yeah, but—"

"No more interruptions from any of you. No matter the kind, a pact is about survival and hope for a safe and happy future. I gave my father's lishan medal to Mei lien. I'm asking you all to get it safely to Tikala."

"Your father is in Tikala?" Mei lien asked.

"No, but Tikala has many pacts with my Wake. Give the medal to any border guard, and your safe passage into the country will be assured. From there, give them Dr. Pérez-Soto's name. She will take care of you, as she promised. That is her pact with you all. Mine is to clear your path to the border."

Thump. Thump.

As she'd done in the clinic, Jwahir grasped Fayola's hand. "Can a tired bird beat big bears and elephants?"

A rote answer came to mind. *I'm an impundulu, not a simple bird.* But, as Fayola looked at the faces that stared at her with a trust forged on the quiet, dark road between a clinic turned orphanage and an abandoned business park on the outskirts of Fuxing City, the shallow reply withered on her lips.

The truth, even when distasteful, went down easier than bravado. But Fayola would not deny the children their much-needed hope.

"I am lightning and will. Daring and stubbornness. I am—"

"Dela Eden." Jwahir grinned at her, and Fayola so wanted to be the children's savior.

But Diello Madana had taught Fayola how to weigh risks against benefits.

"Everyone ten and older will shift. The younger shifter children and humans will ride on the backs of their elephant friends. You'll travel faster and expend less energy in your animal form. Come on. Quickly now before the patrolling soldiers we hear get closer."

The business park was the last hiding place for immigrants who planned to make a run for the border. Tikala may not have a border barrier like Delcanos, but the nation's government was no less intolerant of illegal border crossings.

The older shifter children undressed as swiftly as they could manage and then changed into their animal form.

"Here." Mei lien tucked Fayola's medal in Jwahir's jacket pocket, zipping and securing it inside. "Keep it safe for me, okay?"

"Yup, I got it. Our pact with Dela Eden."

"That's right."

"Mei lien, you and Huan will take point," Fayola told the teen who, if Mei lien were an impundulu, she would be proud to serve as her diello basic training instructor.

Lifting Jwahir, Fayola placed her on Peng's back—a solidly built five-hundred-pound young elephant with two upper incisors that weighed half the size of an adult male's. Even still, at fifty pounds, his tusks could do much damage to an enemy.

His elephant form will be even more magnificent when he becomes a man.

"Peng will take the rear. Shift, Mei lien. Let me see if your bear is as lovely as your sister's."

Dropping to her knees, Mei lien wasted no time beginning the change. Like all the children, their animal form reflected their human age. However, none were as large or as imposing as an adult. They would not win a battle against a full-grown shifter, but they could survive a mad dash to the border if they worked together and Fayola accomplished her part of their pact.

A human body breaking apart, bone by bone, stretched and realigned, skin teared and organs shifted, enlarged. The sight, like the experience, turned the stomach and challenged the mind.

Not magic or a vindictive god's curse, but nature. Biology.

Beautiful. Mei lien is a stunning black bear. Long black fur, like her human hair. Fayola ran her fingers over the white patch of fur on Mei lien's chest. *Crescent-shaped like Huan's. Identical twins in both forms. If anyone can keep this group together, this young bear can.*

"Do your best, and I will do mine."

For long seconds, no one moved, not even Fayola.

Thump. Thump. Thump.

Almost no one.

What an idiot I am. I created a pact with children. Not even a blood pact but a vow that yields nothing for my kettle or Wake. A vow born of weakness. But a vow all the same. I will not fail them, no matter the cost.

"Remember what I told you. Follow this road to the border. I'll make sure Dr. Pérez-Soto retrieves you from the immigration intake center."

Following orders like the soldiers they weren't, the children turned away. Elephants, bears, and three human children.

And me. A vampiric bird with no taste for elephant blood.

Thump. Thump.

I guess I'll acquire one today.

2100
Twenty-Two Years Earlier
The United Wake of Benekal
Fort Kumelo City
Ngina Tower

"Staring at your hands won't produce lightning, Cadet Fayola."

"I know, but I was—"

"Trying my patience with your continued lack of progress." Diello Madana's eyes shifted from basic brown to ruby red in a literal blink. Sparks of lightning began at her irises, spread to the corners of her eyes, then traveled, like a snake cutting a path through a desert, down her cheeks and neck. The red lightning disappeared under her black T-shirt but reemerged when it slithered past the short sleeves to her biceps. Down arms and onto her wrists the lightning traveled, stopping for a second in the palm of her hands, only to continue to each digit, setting them ablaze with sparks of vibrant red.

Fayola shoved her hands in her pants pockets. The right found the lishan medal she always kept on her person. *Dad's gift and Jelani are all I have of home. I understand compulsory military service, but I didn't think basic training would be this difficult or that I would be this homesick.*

"Tell me about this tower."

Fayola glanced over her shoulder, convinced Diello Madana had spoken to one of the members of her training kettle.

Jelani, Durah, and Kwame stood twenty feet behind her, wearing the same uniform as Fayola: black boots, tactical pants, and short-sleeved shirt. They'd abandoned their black and gray battle dress uniform shirts at the base of the tower. Considering Diello Madana had done the same before running up the tower steps—three at a time, no less, Fayola assumed they wouldn't incur her wrath for their lack of uniform compliance.

"Not them, you. I've brought this training kettle to Ngina Tower for the past two months. You've been at the fort for twice that long. Surely a cadet who receives a perfect score on every academic assessment, thus far, must know the history of every building in this fort city. But you can begin with this tower."

After a week of training in the rain and marching through mud puddles, Fayola lifted her sweaty, sticky face to the sky, grateful for the sun, if not the heat and mosquitoes.

"Ngina means one who serves. Unfortunately, we don't know the precise year this castle tower was built because this territory was a spoil of war."

Wiping sweat from her forehead with the heel of her hand, Fayola lowered her eyes but not to Diello Madana. "This castle tower is one hundred and twenty-eight feet high." She moved to a section of the battlements with arrow loops. "Horseshoe shaped to resist siege weapons on the side. Rectangular back serves as a fighting platform on top." She pointed to the tower at the entry-way to the fort to her right. "Round towers offer more resistance to siege weapons like projectiles." Swinging her hand to the left, she pointed to Daisha Tower, officers' living quarters. "Daisha means the one who is alive. The tower was renamed, as every building in this conquered city was, after a regiment leader.

Daisha is a wall tower. Good for providing flanking fire from projectile weapons."

"Excellent. What else?"

Fayola closed her eyes again, finding it too easy to envision how this ancient city had fallen. "You've told us, many times, that over is easier than through. The bear herd which once called this city home must've thought the same."

"True. Hence so many towers."

"But we are more than our wings."

"Also true."

Fayola didn't hear, or even sense the movement, but she felt Diello Madana beside her when she hadn't been a second earlier. Opening her eyes, she watched first- and second-year cadets enter and exit academic buildings and living quarters, climb rock walls and swim in the Kumelo River to the safety rope and back. The entire west side of the fort consisted of physical training facilities. However, the roof of Ngina Tower served a less physically challenging kind of training.

Not training at all, but a reminder. Fayola placed her right hand back into her pants pocket, fingering her medal again. "I can see the entire fort from here, but also the spires from the tallest skyscrapers in the surrounding three-city area."

"Can you see Aradi City from here?"

"You know I can't."

"No, you cannot. Your life is bigger than that city and your kettle. You are now responsible for everything you can see and even more that you cannot."

"I know."

"If you did, you would focus less on Raicho's lishan medal in your pocket and more on learning the skills and knowledge necessary to earn your own. For thirty-five years, your father served our Wake with honor. Once your homesickness fades, you will do the same."

"The Wake before the individual."

"Yes."

"Sometimes through is a better option than over."

A strong hand patted Fayola's back, and a loud familiar laugh drove deep into her eardrum. "Considering first-year cadets aren't permitted to shift, much less fly, your only choice is through. The bear matriarch made a grave miscalculation. She cast her eyes to the sky, spent years planning to defend against aerial attacks only to be caught off guard when we stormed the city from the ground. Our ancestors left nothing standing except these old towers of stone. A false sense of protection . . . of preparedness."

Diello Madana spun on her booted feet, marching away, but Fayola lingered at the battlements.

Food at a high cost. That was life before pacts. Even back then, no impundulu escaped military service. No one wants us in their country without an established pact with the Wake.

Fayola removed her hand from her pants pocket, unsurprised Diello Madana had glimpsed the medal without Fayola's knowledge.

I told Dad I would do my best. But I've only put in enough effort to not embarrass myself and besmudge his reputation. That attitude isn't fair to my training kettle. The Wake before the individual. The missions won't matter, only what accomplishing them will mean for the Wake and me. The better a soldier I become, the easier the missions will be, and the quicker I'll be able to return home.

"Come, Cadet Fayola, the raging sun makes me question my refusal to cut these braids. The sooner you show me Raicho's green lightning, the quicker we can escape this blasted tower wall."

Knowing Diello Madana would drag them to this wall tomorrow to reinforce a point made a dozen times over, Fayola turned away from the sight below. A few strides had her filling the vacant space between Jelani and Durah. Neither of them looked at her, but she felt their support all the same.

Despite the strict nature of basic training, Diello Madana had granted the first-year cadets under her command the privilege of forming their training kettle. Durah had all but adopted Fayola since the day they met on the wall around The Tree of Karasi, while Kwame, the tall male who had stood between Fayola and her goal of reaching Jelani, had made an affable fourth.

"Performance anxiety will get you and your kettle killed." Diello Madana's eyes sparked crimson again. "It's not about whether you can generate lightning; you can. You're an impundulu. What I want to see, and what you will learn, all of you, is how to command it with potency and precision. Now, lift your hands, palms up, and show me the color of your lightning. Your training can't truly begin until you generate your first true spark."

Taking a deep breath, Fayola released it slowly. In through her nose and out through her mouth. In through her nose and out through her mouth.

Again.

Again.

"Teach me how to make lightning," Fayola had asked Raicho.

At ten, she'd made the same request of her father over the years. However, instead of answering, Raicho led her into his bedroom on that day, where he retrieved a circular, silver jewelry box from atop his dresser.

"Come sit with me." He'd patted the spot beside him on his bed.

Fayola jumped on the bed, sprawling across it as if it belonged to her. "What's that?"

Opening the hinged box, Raicho let Fayola peer inside. More than three dozen flat, circular green medals the size of a half zara coin was piled atop the white satiny material that lined the box's interior.

Without thinking, Fayola had reached for one of the medals but paused, looking up at her father for permission.

"It's fine. One day, these will be yours, as will everything else I own."

She hadn't liked the casual way her father had mentioned his death. But impundulus lived long lives, and he'd already survived forty special forces missions. So Fayola plucked a medal from the pile, sat up in bed, and held the medal up to the light that streamed in through the open balcony doors.

"These are my lishan medals. I was granted one after each successful mission."

"The color of your lightning." A single bolt of lightning bisected the medal. The United Wake of Benekal was pressed into a raised script around the medal's edge.

"Will my lightning be green like yours?" Inspecting a handful of medals, Fayola saw little other than the year under a lightning bolt that distinguished one from the other.

"It is believed, by some, that our lightning color is a manifestation of our character."

"What does green mean?"

Raicho searched through the medals, handing Fayola one he'd retrieved from the bottom of the silver jewelry box. "This is the last one I earned. Look at the date."

"Cool. It's the same year I hatched."

Raicho had nodded, a calm expression that belied how much he'd wanted to become a father. She hadn't heard of his desire from family and friends, but from a father unashamed to embrace and share his emotions.

"Green lightning is thought to mean equilibrium, renewal, and rebirth. Those with red lightning are often viewed as pioneers, leaders, ambitious, and determined."

"What about white and gold?"

"Growth, creativity, and openness for white."

"And gold?"

Raicho had kissed Fayola's forehead before collecting his lishan medals and returning them to his jewelry box and dresser. "I will not rush you into adulthood. You have only five years left before the Wake will expect much of you. Enjoy your childhood, Fay. Learning how to shift and generate lightning will come. When it does, you'll use it more often than you want and not always in the way you like. You'll do both, though, because nothing is more important than the maintenance of the Wake."

Scrambling from the bed, she'd sidled up next to him. "You're more important to me than the Wake. That won't ever change."

Raicho had only grinned down at her.

At the time, Fayola thought she understood his response as one of agreement. Now, as she permitted thoughts of service to the kettle and Wake to drift over her, she could see the sadness behind her father's smile she'd missed as a child.

Warmth began under her skin like a heat flash during a shower, forcing the memory away and her back to the present. In less time than it took for her to recall where she was and why, the heat turned hot. Boiling.

Fayola fell to her knees, gasping for air but swallowing heat and pain.

"Breathe through it, Cadet."

She tried, but damn, her insides felt like a raging forest fire—an unforgiving devourer of everything in its heated path.

"Come on, take control."

Take control. Take control. I can do this. I can . . . Fayola threw her head back on a scream, flung her arms into the air . . . and let go. She let it all go.

The heat.

The pain.

The hole in her heart.

"That's it. Keep your focus. Don't let it rage out of control." Diello Madana chuckled. "Not green like Raicho's lightning but a gorgeous gold."

"What does gold mean, Dad? You forgot to tell me about gold."

"Oh, yes." Raicho had bent to a knee, and Fayola hopped onto his back. "I'm hungry. Lunch first."

"Unfair."

"Unfair, huh? Fine. Let's see. Golds have high ideals, are wise, and experience much success in life. They triumph where others struggle and sometimes fail."

"I like that one."

"Of course you do. Know this, Fay, the color of our lightning means little without a good cause to justify its use. This truth will become murky when you are in service to the Wake. You may even forget. However, when it matters the most, you'll remember. When you do, you'll use your lightning, regardless of its color, for something or someone greater than a blood pact."

4: All Lightning but No Bite

2122

The State of Namju

"Where could they have gone?"

Breezy's ass hurt from sitting atop Zhang for so long. Sure, Zhang could've made him walk the patrol, but elephants were made for riding and bears for being carried around like the kings and queens they were. Chuckling, Breezy knew it best to keep his opinions to himself.

"Come on, man," Breezy complained. "Get off the damn mobile already. We got an hour left in our shift."

Their border patrol consisted of twenty soldiers—ten bear shifters and an equal number of elephant shifters. No humans, unfortunately. Breezy liked humans because they had a knack for inventing the best weapons.

What they lack in physical might, they make up for with ingenuity.

"Yeah, yeah, understood, ma'am. We're on it." Captain Seifu jammed his mobile into one of his side pants pockets. "New mission."

Breezy and the others groaned. "Come on, man. Our shift is almost over. My ass hurts, and I'm tired as fuck. All I want to do is go home, soak my balls and then crash for the next eight hours."

"Too bad. We've got a mission."

Ren, the newest member of their patrol unit, shook a cigarette free from its pack. He slid it between his lips then, because the man had a memory the size of an ant, patted all his pockets in search of his lighter.

"Here." Breezy tossed Ren his mini multitool. "You need to quit."

"Mind your damn business, but thanks for the lighter. I assume it's here mixed in with all this other shit. Got it." Ren formed circles of smoke, a man content with his nicotine addiction. He tossed the multitool back to him. "Except for the soaking balls part, I'm with Breezy. We've been out here for ten straight hours. Quiet. Everyone knows we got these borders sewn up tighter than an elephant's asshole."

Breezy laughed. "I do like you, newbie."

"Shut up. All of you. That was Matriarch Moshi. Three of her squads arrived at the children's clinic in Fuxing. It was empty."

"So?" Ren took a deep drag from his cigarette, damn near finishing the smoke in a few pulls. "How is that our problem?"

"Moshi beat the Taepo squads there. Competition is a bitch in this war."

Flicking his cigarette to the ground, Ren readjusted himself in his saddle. "I still don't get what that has to do with us."

"The doctor and kids were gone. Moshi's squads got out of there before the enemy arrived. No point fighting over MIA goods."

"Wait," Breezy said, his sleepy brain slow but catching up. "Moshi thinks the doc and kids are out here somewhere?"

"Yeah, here or at one of the other borders. She already contacted those border patrols. Nothing yet. The Tikala border is the softest target, though, for unskilled border crossers."

"If I had a smoke for every broken pact, I'd be—"

"What?" Breezy asked Ren. "Rich in smokes? Don't be stupid. Supply and demand, that's what it boils down to. We have a demand."

"Moshi wants us to make sure those kids don't leave Namju."

Ren snorted in a way Breezy knew he wouldn't have if Matriarch Moshi stood in front of him instead of Captain Seifu. "Then she should've gotten to the clinic sooner. If she had, we wouldn't have to stomp around in the dark looking for a bunch of brats."

Seifu nodded in the direction of the old business park less than a half klick up the road. Their patrol covered a two-mile radius from the business park in front of them to the Namju-Tikala border behind them. "We'll begin there, then circle back to the border. If we stay on our side, those Tikala border guards can't say or do shit about our tactics. We deal with our people the way we see fit."

"That's Moshi's orders, huh?" Bai, a 1,200-pound brown bear shifter with a slow drawl but a quick gun finger, scratched his scruffy chin. "Any elephant shifters in the bunch? I don't give a shit about humans, especially if they're young and scrawny, but we could use more strong calves."

"Her orders are to find and detain them if they are in this area. I didn't ask those kinds of details, and she didn't supply them. Who they are and how they'll be used is above our pay grades, so let's get to it, men."

Taking point, as usual, Breezy and Zhang headed for the business park. He didn't think they would cross paths with the kids, but he unholstered his handgun and positioned it above the flashlight in his left hand.

The others followed, spreading out the length of the two-lane highway. Zhang and the other elephant shifters were more than 6,000 pounds of muscle and might. Breezy had the displeasure of fighting the Taepo herd. One of the big bastards had dislocated his shoulder and broken a leg. If not for Zhang stepping between them, Breezy would have been roadkill. But compared to serving on the front line, border patrol was like a beach vacation.

Breezy shifted his gun and flashlight to the left and right. Rounding the corner of one of the buildings—a long rectangular structure with dust and dirt covering the windows—he thought he spotted movement one building down.

He shifted the flashlight to his left, holding that arm outward while keeping his right gun hand trained in front. *If I really did see someone, I don't want to make myself an easy target.*

"See something?" Captain Seifu asked from behind him.

"I'm not sure. Maybe."

"Okay, Kang and I will go take a look." Captain Seifu tapped Kang's thick neck, confirming the decision with him.

One big ear flapped backward, a nonverbal cue that bear riders understood as agreement.

"Watch our backs." Seifu and Kang made their way toward where Breezy thought he'd seen a flash of movement. All he saw now was stillness punctuated by silence.

Ren sidled up next to him. "Seeing things again. You aren't even drunk this time. You really do need to take your ass home and sleep off this long patrol."

"Maybe." *But I could've sworn I'd seen something. Not big like the guys and me. But larger than a kid.* "We should go after them."

"If something was wrong, the captain would've hollered."

"What if he can't?"

"Yeah, okay. You think one of those brats from Soto's clinic is tough enough to take on Seifu and Kang and win? If you do, you have bear shit for brains. Relax. Give them time to check out those buildings down there. After that, Seifu can report to Moshi that there ain't shit out here but—"

Bang. Bang.

"Nothing out here, huh."

Captain Seifu barreled toward them. Gun in one hand, the other arm hung like a kite in a windless sky.

Breezy and Zhang charged toward their captain. "What? What is it? Where's Kang?"

Mouth open and gulping air, Seifu pointed with his gun behind him. "Saw a truck hidden between two buildings back there. Someone knocked me off Kang. Fast. Sharp. A knife got me. Broke a bone."

Breezy lowered his eyes to Seifu's arm. A nasty-looking gash ran from shoulder to wrist. "Someone with a knife did that?" He couldn't see how, especially the break, while moving as quickly as Seifu claimed. "But it cut through three layers of protective uniform. That looks deep."

Blood spilled like a faucet left to run during a wintery blast.

Ren jumped from his mount. "Fuck, that looks bad. We need to—"

"Find who is out there."

"Yeah, I know, Captain, but . . ."

Leaning on Ren but firm in his words, Seifu gritted, "Two teams. One head to the border. Kemba, Harun, Yan, and Lai." Seifu winced but stayed focused. "Aguer and Chen, you go too. The rest of us are team two. We'll deal with whoever is hunting us. We end the threat and, hopefully, save what's left of Kang."

"Hunting us?" *No one hunts the Sunhung herd. We're the predators out here.* "The Taepo herd are—"

"Big and mean," Captain Seifu said and breathed out, slumping more against Ren with each passing second. "Not fast and stealthy, like who attacked me."

Breezy tracked the team of six as they rode in the direction that would take them back to the front of the business park instead of following the path Seifu had come.

"That doesn't look like no knife wound to me." Hassani slid from Derbie. He examined Seifu's arm with a veteran soldier's critical gaze. "You're here, but Kang isn't. He ran after your attacker so you could get away, right?"

"Yeah, but he should be back by now. That's the drill. Get separated, rendezvous back with the squad."

Hassani leaned in close, sniffing Seifu's arm.

Breezy had no idea what the man was doing but standing around there, waiting for Kang to return or for Seifu's attacker to strike again, made him fidgety.

Hassani's head snapped up, eyes wide and neck doing a good imitation of an owl—turning this way and that.

Breezy scanned the area too. "What did you see, man? Talk to us."

"Not what I saw. Smelled."

"On my arm?" Seifu allowed Ren to help him onto Zhang and behind Breezy. "I can still shoot."

"If what I think is out there is," Hassani said, "it's going to take all of us to bring it down."

Breezy didn't understand. From the furrowed brows of the others, neither did they.

"You guys don't know shit. Leave Namju for once in your fucking lives. Knives don't leave singe marks on clothing and skin. And knives sure as fuck don't smell like honey."

"You mean . . .?" Breezy glanced around, heart suddenly in his throat. "Bird?"

"Not a damn bird. A bloodsucking impundulu. Every one of those feathered bastards receives extensive military training. They do nothing but fight and eat. You saw that thing because it wanted you to."

As if an invisible puppeteer controlled them, they tilted their heads back, eyes going to the black, cloudless sky.

Nothing. No impundulu. No thunder. No lightn—

Rumble. Rumble.

Flash. Flash. Flash.

Lightning split the night sky like a rock splintering a windshield on impact.

Breezy gulped.

Ren and Hassani vaulted onto their mounts.

They took off, following the boom of thunder and the crackle of lightning.

Rumble. Flash.

Breezy charged forward, ears ringing and flashlight pointless in the suddenly bright sky.

Thunder deafened.

Golden thunderbolts raged.

Breezy jerked forward when Zhang skidded to a halt, damn near causing Seifu to fall. But, thankfully, his captain's one good arm had a firm hold around Breezy's waist.

Lightning blazed around them, smashing onto concrete and bringing team two up short.

"Does anyone have eyes on the impundulu?" Seifu yelled.

Guns out and pointed toward the sky, no one responded, which was answer enough.

"Shit," Seifu swore. "Somebody gotta have eyes on that feathered menace."

As if offended, the impundulu let loose a fresh shower of lightning bolts. They came from every direction, making it difficult to pinpoint the source.

"This isn't good." Hassani unleashed rounds behind them and in front. "Whatever impundulu is out here with us is highly skilled."

"No shit," Ren said, lowering his gun to his lap instead of wasting bullets firing at a ghost. "What tipped you off?"

"We don't have time for this." Seifu's grip tightened around Breezy's waist. "Let's get going, men. I want to test a theory."

Following their captain's order, they started off again. Unfortunately, they didn't get far before another barrage of lightning peppered the ground in front of them.

They stopped.

"Yeah, it's as I thought. Not just skilled, Hassani, but smart too. Strategic."

Blood from Seifu's arm had stained Breezy's BDU pants. But he didn't care, not as long as the man still lived. Breezy had already lost family and friends to this war; he did not want to add more faces to his nightmares.

"What are you thinking?" Hassani asked Seifu.

"I'm thinking this impundulu wants to only do enough to keep us from reaching the border. Which means it's here because of a blood pact."

"Nah, not a blood pact." Hassani let loose more pointless rounds in the quiet sky. "Isn't that right," he yelled into the darkness. "You aren't here on a blood pact mission. I know your kind. Seen you fight. Kill. Ruthless feathered bastards, the lot of you."

Breezy bristled at the insult, recalling the last time they'd upset the impundulu. Yet, as his eyes shot to the sky expecting another barrage of gold thunderbolts, all remained still and quiet. Finally, he lowered his gaze to Hassani, still not liking the man's decision to taunt their unseen enemy.

"Your people don't care who you must kill if it means a successful mission." Hassani snorted. "Nah, not a blood pact. Something else." Hassani nudged Derbie forward.

No one followed them.

"Let's see what happens," Seifu whispered. "He's right about the impundulu. It didn't have to reveal itself, but it did, which means it's protecting someone."

"The kids Matriarch Moshi is looking for?"

"Maybe, but I can't see one of those bloodsuckers giving a shit about orphans other than as a midnight snack."

"I'm right here, little birdie." Hassani held his hands up and out to the side—his gun silent, while the man was not. "A bear atop an elephant. Funny, right? You won't ever get a better target. Take the shot." He thumped his chest. "Right here. Come on, beakface, I'm right fucking here."

Ren swore, but no one else spoke or moved.

Then Hassani laughed—a mocking sound that would piss Breezy off if it had been intended for him. "Yeah, that's what I thought. You're not here on a blood pact mission. You've gone rogue. I bet your Wake will pluck every feather from your disobeying body before throwing you in a frying pan for killing someone not part of a sanctioned mission." Hassani thumped his chest again. "Prove me wrong. Strike me here."

Seifu cough-laughed behind Breezy. "That boar is one crazy son of a sow."

"Told you, Captain," Hassani yelled back. "No blood pact. All lightning but no bite."

Doesn't that make the impundulu more dangerous? I mean, if there are no mission parameters to control its actions, couldn't that mean it will do anything it wants? "Who would know or care how we died?" Breezy asked, challenging Hassani's assumption that a rogue impundulu soldier was less dangerous to their mortality than one in Namju on a sanctioned mission.

"What are you saying?" Seifu adjusted his broken arm, growling in pain when he used Breezy's back to keep the appendage steady.

"If that thing out there has really gone rogue, how can we trust it won't try to kill us? Maybe those earlier lightning strikes were warnings."

"You think it'll let me live?"

"Don't you? I mean, why would it do that? It could've killed you, right?"

The older man cleared his throat as if his pride had gotten lodged in his larynx. "Yeah, it could've. Get Hassani's ass back here for me."

"Yes, sir. Hey," Breezy yelled, "regroup."

"But—"

"Captain's orders."

If an elephant could look relieved, Derbie's rare blue eyes expressed the same feeling as Breezy.

"I had it, Captain."

"You didn't have shit. I had Breezy call you back here before that thing changed its mind. So before you start foaming at the mouth, thinking me a coward, remember there is a whole world of hurt between health and death."

Hassani's gaze dropped to Seifu's injured arm. "Yeah, I get that, but what about team one? You just gonna let that thing go after them?"

Ren opened his mouth to say something but slammed it shut at the sound of shouting.

They turned to see Kang, in human form, limp toward them. "W-wait, w-wait. Shit. Shit, that hurts." He fell.

"Go, get him."

"Yes, sir." Mostafa hauled ass toward Kang. Jumping off Tsou, a few feet from Kang, Mostafa helped the thirty-year-old man to his bare feet. "Are you all right?"

"She zapped the shift out of me." Kang touched his chest, hands trembling and red, like every bit of skin Breezy could see. "My heart is racing so fast. It feels like it's going to explode."

Breezy, Zhang, and the others approached.

"She?" Seifu asked.

"I think. Can't be sure because the attack was from behind. But the hands felt small and soft, like a female's. Small and soft before she pumped my hide full of lightning."

Breezy slid from Zhang, removed his jacket, and handed it to Kang. "We didn't see lightning coming from where you'd run off to."

Licking cracked lips, Kang winced as he slid first one arm then the second into Breezy's jacket. "Concentrated lightning. So much, it forced my shift and left me unconscious."

"Like I said, that impundulu is more afraid of being punished by her Wake for killing us than she is of our patrol unit." Hassani's deep, confident voice sounded more like premature vindication than a soldier assessing the current reality. "We need to press our advantage."

"We don't have an advantage." Breezy returned to Zhang, worried that a wilting Captain Seifu would come face-to-face with the ground.

"Breezy's right," Seifu said, lifting his head and looking from Tsou to Hassani, whose eyes had gone bloodshot red. "Still, I'm not about to let some feathered freak come into our country and do whatever in the hell she wants. Blood pact or rogue mission, this border is ours to control, and she can't have it. Not one fucking inch of it."

"That's what I'm talking about." Hassani pumped his gun hand. "What's the plan?"

"Not a good one for us. Just keep her ass here. Distract her. Keep her from going after team one." Seifu rubbed his injured arm. "It might also mean ending up like Kang or me. Ren, get on the horn. Call Kemba. Tell him they need to reach the border double-time. If she's here with us and is protecting those kids Matriarch Moshi wants so badly, that means she thinks they have enough lead time to outrun our patrol. Team one will prove that bitch wrong. Call him. Now!"

5: If We Took a Stand

2122
Six Months Earlier
The United Wake of Benekal
Kettle of Silesse City

"What are you doing?" Fayola asked Jelani as she dropped her comfy cotton robe at the foot of the bed, leaving her in a functional but not particularly sexy bra and panties. Both were a rich purple, though, a color that complemented her deep winter skin tone.

"Reading."

"Yes, at my desk and on my computer."

Jelani tapped the laptop screen with his index finger. Broad, bare back to her, his focus remained fixed on whatever he'd been doing while she showered. "I'm reading your email."

"When did you become *that* guy?"

Fayola meant it as a joke, but the look Jelani shot her over his shoulder didn't contain an ounce of humor. She flopped onto the side of the bed, with a silent regret at having left her email open.

"I wasn't snooping. My computer is downstairs, and yours is right here. This was sent yesterday. Marked as a priority. You haven't replied."

"Strangely enough, inaction is both a decision and a response. I thought we were going out. Instead, you're still in your boxers and socks."

He tapped the screen again, then closed the laptop with a gentleness she appreciated. Then, turning and straddling the chair, he faced her.

The view from the front outdid the one from the back. From any angle, Jelani was an attractive man. His wide prominent nose ended at full lips perfect for late-night kisses and early morning conversations.

Not that I'm interested in talking about that inconsequential email. Jelani clearly is, which means we'll be late for brunch with Durah and Kwame.

Donning her robe again to have a conversation that would take time but go nowhere, Fayola inwardly smiled at Jelani's slow, appreciative approval of a body he knew almost as well as she did.

If we're going to be late meeting our friends, there is a better alternative than talking.

He licked his lips as if tasting the residue of ripe blood. But Jelani plowed forward because nothing short of a battle or Fayola's sensual touch could discourage him away from his intention. "You don't blow off the Rashidi Tribunal."

Sitting cross-legged in the center of her bed, Fayola resigned herself to having this conversation. "I didn't. I replied to the first two requests politely but firmly with a: 'No, thank you.' You did the same. As did Durah and Kwame."

"We did, yeah, but this is different. One perfunctory request to extend military service is the norm. Of course, we all knew it would come when we neared retirement, but I don't know anyone who has received three requests, much less one written by a member of the tribunal."

Fayola hadn't either. The special attention left her feeling leery instead of honored. "You read the email; it's vague."

"It is. I don't like it."

"We agree then, good." Pleased the conversation hadn't taken as long as she'd thought, Fayola reached for her robe's sash, entertaining the idea of a quickie.

"They may have targeted you because of your proposal." Foregoing the chair, Jelani joined her on the bed. "Why aren't you more concerned?"

"I wrote the proposal two years ago. They returned it with *rejected* stamped in bold red letters. They actually took the time to have someone, probably some unfortunate administrative assistant, print out my paper and mail it to me."

"I remember. That was messed up. Before that day, I couldn't remember the last time we received physical mail." Jelani's big, warm hands took hold of hers. "An asshole move, but one likely driven by the contents in your proposal."

"Data is data. Facts are neutral."

He shook his head. "Facts are an indictment. If not for Belay Njeri assigning you the task of writing the proposal for your unit, you wouldn't have. My commanding officer assigned Arbery to write our unit's proposal." Kissing the knuckles of both hands, he released them, only to lean forward and plant a brief kiss on her lips. "He followed orders, of course, but he wrote fluff. He wrote content the tribunal wanted to hear, steering clear of writing anything that challenged current, or even past, policies and practices."

"I couldn't do that."

"You could have, but you wouldn't because that's not who you are."

Fayola understood Jelani's statement wasn't his own indictment of her personal code of honor but an acknowledgment. "They chose to ignore the details of my proposal, which is their right. When it comes to extending my military service, choosing not to do so is *my* right. I won't be bullied into changing my mind—not even by the tribunal."

Fayola returned Jelani's kiss, but her mind whirled with thoughts she'd buried after reading the third military service extension request. "Do you really think their persistence is connected to my proposal?"

"Honestly, I don't know. What I do know is that your proposal was well researched. The issue crosses borders and cultures. Few nations have gone untouched, their citizens both victims and victimizers. The Wake is among the rare exceptions, but you raised critical concerns about how easily that could change."

Fayola rolled onto her side, curling in a ball as if she were one of the thousands of frightened, brutalized children she'd written about in her proposal. "If we took a stand, we could make a difference in the lives of so many. There is nothing inconsequential about the breadth and depth of our might and influence. For once, we should use them for non-self-serving reasons."

"Doing the right thing because it's the right thing to do?" Jelani snuggled down beside her, pulling her into him and holding her close. "That's not our way. Well . . . it is but only for our own kind. We subsist on the blood of others, Fay. Our very existence is self-serving."

"Which is why we should give back without expectation of receiving something in return."

"A goodwill pact." He sniffed her neck, a deep, pleased inhalation that curled her toes and heated her core. "We don't do those. However, I think we can agree that your proposal put you on the tribunal's radar."

"Which doesn't explain why they keep sending me extension requests."

"It doesn't, but you should reply to the latest email. You only have one more mission left. You don't want to give the tribunal any reason to make your life difficult. Or worse."

Worse. No, I refuse to extend my service. Not by a year or a month. Not even by a damn hour.

Jelani rolled atop Fayola, kissing her neck and stroking her hip. "I'm suddenly in the mood for more than brunch."

"Good. So am I."

The State of Namju
Namju-Tikala Border

Fayola had wasted too much time with the soldiers at the business park. Worse, they had figured out her plan sooner than she'd anticipated.

She laid down lightning as she retreated on foot, not yet daring to take to the sky.

The longer they believe I'm at the business park with them, the more time I'll have to reach the other group without fear of being flanked by the Sunhung patrollers. But my focus is divided, and my lightning is less precise. It won't take them long to realize the lightning is coming from a distance farther away.

Fayola's legs warmed as she ran, beginning her transformation but not into her complete avian form. The following stride had impundulu magic pulsing through her lower body, heating her skin, loosening her limbs, and transforming clothing, shoes, and normal human legs and feet. Smooth black feathers sprouted over lean, muscular thighs. The lower part of her legs shifted into a bird's sturdy tarsus, ending in taloned feet.

Fayola stumbled as her lower body changed, but she did not fall.

I have too much ground to cover but not enough time to reach the children before those patrollers do. I need to finish my shift without crashing to the pavement and losing precious time.

With the first wave of magical heat coursing through her body, heralding her shift, Fayola had ceased her distance lightning attacks. Doing both simultaneously would yield little but frustration and failure. So, Fayola concentrated on bringing her hybrid form forth.

"We call it magic," Diello Madana had once told Fayola, "for lack of a better word to describe what we are capable of doing. We can control our body's temperature. Heat us up to shift. Cool us down to transform back into our human form. Clothing and limited items—gun, knife, your father's lishan medal, for example—can be summoned during your transformation. You'll never be naked, after a shift, or empty-handed and vulnerable. Magic. Impundulu magic. Now, let's practice shifting from human to hybrid."

Narrow, black feathers rippled up her body—over hips, chest, shoulders, and arms. Hands stretched, fingers elongated, and nails grew into sharp, deadly points. Wings pushed through her back, tearing skin and breaking bones. For disturbing seconds, skeletal protrusions hung from her body. Then, generating more heat and sending it to her wings, black and white feathers soon appeared—primaries and then secondaries, followed by marginal coverts, alula, and scapular feathers. Flowing from shoulders to knees, feathers formed and thickened.

Fayola leapt into the sky, careful to keep low but grateful for the extra speed her wings afforded her. A large impundulu, high in the sky, would serve up an easier target than a hybrid one flying at truck height.

Her short bang-swept hairstyle grew into black feathers with white tips. Growing up and out but also down, feathers covered her forehead, narrowing into a beak-like shield overtop her nose.

Flying at top speed, Fayola bolted through the sky. Eyes and ears alert, she searched for the inevitable. It didn't take long.

Gunshots boomed.

Men yelled.

Children screamed.

Fayola willed her wings to flap faster, harder. They couldn't. They didn't.

"I said stop."

Fayola lifted higher in the sky as she drew closer to the sound of yelling . . . and crying.

More gunfire rang out, heating her blood and sharpening her intent.

Bang. Bang.

"Let that be a lesson to you; I said stop."

More crying erupted just as one of the screaming voices went silent.

Fayola rushed toward the border. Her keen eyesight spotted six Sunhung soldiers. Three rode elephants.

Those elephants are larger than the one I disabled earlier. I should've fed from him, but that would've meant transforming, forcing my beak through his tough hide and then praying his disgusting blood would stay down. I didn't have time then, do I now?

Fayola didn't think she did, although her complete impundulu form was faster and stronger than her hybrid body. She also did not want to frighten the children with her complete bird form. Fayola should not care what they thought of her. But, listening to their terrified wails as they raced to the border barrier, she found the thought of the children shrieking at her true nature as distasteful as consuming an elephant's blood.

Fayola shifted into her complete impundulu form: an eight-foot, two-hundred-pound black and white bird with a thick, long beak and tail, and partially webbed toes with sharp talons.

I might horrify the children but being alive and frightened is better than being cold and dead.

Fayola flapped her large wings. With a thirty-foot wingspan, she could generate deadly lightning and deafening thunder.

I can't do either. Not here. Not unless these soldiers leave me with no better options.

Fayola swooped toward the men, knocking them off their mounts.

Mei lien and the other children had stopped a couple hundred feet from the border. None of them were in their animal form, and they formed a huddle around something . . . someone she could not see.

A bullet slammed into Fayola. Two. Three. More.

She rushed at the shooting bears, smacking them aside with her wings. They crumpled to the ground but staggered back to their feet—bleeding from heads and arms but still in the fight.

The three elephant shifters charged her, forcing Fayola to retreat to the sky.

Bright white lights, from the border towers, were turned in her direction—taking away the advantage the night sky afforded a black bird.

Get up. Fayola spoke in the children's minds—exerting energy she did not have to spare. *Get up and get to the barrier entry point. If you don't, we'll all die.*

Fayola didn't wait for a response. Having a group of weeping children, a flying impundulu, and shooting bears at the Tikala border had created a public scene that went against all of her specialized training.

Tikala guards leveled rifles at everyone not on their side of the border.

Flapping her wings, she released her lightning, striking the tower lights beamed at her.

Still, the children hadn't moved.

Bang. Bang. Bang.

Fayola dodged the bullets.

Bang. Bang. Bang.

"Stand down, or we'll turn our weapons on those kids."

There will be nothing to stop me from killing all of you if you do.

Fayola flew toward the children. So fast. She had always been swift. But not today. Not when her speed mattered the most.

Bang. Bang.

The shaggy-haired boy, whose name she hadn't bothered to learn, no more than she had the names of most of Dr. Pérez-Soto's "children," collapsed to the ground. Blood oozed from two wounds—head and chest.

The first shot killed him. The second was meant as a message to me.

The children screamed and cried, but the brutal murder had forced them into motion again. They ran for the border, leaving behind more than one victim of the Sunhung soldiers' heartlessness.

Fayola finally understood why the children had stopped . . . who they had been huddling around. A naked boy with long black hair stared at her—unseeing. Dead.

Peng.

Fayola landed beside him. The young elephant shifter had offered her cold water and warm blood. She'd taken the former but denied the latter. Yet it still spilled. Not for a pact of protection but because death was the most heinous cost of war.

Wasted blood. A wasted life.

Bullets slammed into her back, not sinking in, the way they had the children at her taloned feet, but still painful.

Spreading wings to their full width, Fayola flew low and directly behind the running children. Then, using her body as a shield, she urged them forward.

Jwahir stumbled and fell.

With a beak made as much for killing prey as it was for carrying nestlings, Fayola snatched up the three youngest children by their jacket collars.

They sniffled and cried, but they didn't scream or fight to free themselves from her grasp.

"Dela Eden, I knew you would come." Jwahir petted the side of her long beak as if she wasn't a bloodthirsty predator.

Heavy padded feet hit the ground behind her, and she knew the elephants were on the move.

She couldn't ask the children to shift. At such a young age, they were incapable of transforming on the move and quickly. So, she settled for shielding them as best she could while using the wind generated by her wings to push them along.

I'm Diello Fayola of The United Wake of Benekal. She forced the words into the Tikala border guards' minds. They had their weapons trained on the children, which she could not have. *I seek sanctuary in your nation. For these children and me. Blood pact.*

"You have to get here first," one of the guards yelled over the barrage of gunfire chasing Fayola and her charges. "We can offer no aid until you cross onto our land."

Meaning, no gun support unless the Sunhung try to cross into Tikala, which they are too smart to do. The soldiers will make their stand here. On the ground. Their preferred field of combat. Not mine.

Fayola flapped her wings hard, generating lightning in her feathers but not releasing it.

"We're almost there," Huan gasped out. "Come on. Come on. We can do this."

The children ran faster, putting their all into the last, critical leg of the journey.

Fayola felt warmth course through her that had nothing to do with impundulu magic. Pride. No adult could ask more from children. But all too often, they expected too much.

Four elephants pounded past Fayola and the children. Then, less than fifty feet in front of the border barrier, the elephant shifters stopped, planting themselves in their direct path.

Fayola flung her lightning at the wall of elephants, knocking them back but not down.

To her right, a metal gate with barbed wires opened. Four Tikala border guards, armed with automatic rifles, stood near the entrance and on their side of the border.

That's our invitation. They won't leave their border open for long. To your right, she told the children. *That's where you're going. No matter what you hear, do not stop running. Do not turn around.*

"But—" Jwahir began.

Our pact. This is our pact. Your safety.

Fayola had already lost two of the children. She'd known they wouldn't all survive. But seeing that truth in eyes that had once sparkled with life hurt her soul and enraged her spirit.

Returning the young ones to the ground, Fayola used one wing to push the children to the right while using the other to snap out lightning bolts.

Like an archer, Fayola aimed and fired.

The children didn't disappoint her. Mei lien and Huan led them toward the open gate.

"Hurry up," a Tikala guard ordered. "Faster. Faster."

Sometimes through is better than over. Fayola powered into the elephant shifters, infusing lightning strikes into her attack.

They were big and strong. Nothing about elephants was easy, not the tusks used to knock the breath out of her nor the trunks that smashed into her face.

Two sets of furry bear paws shoved her to the ground.

Fayola rolled, avoiding being stomped.

Bears and elephants towered over her as bullets had her scrambling away.

"Told you team one would get her ass."

More bullets knocked Fayola backward, keeping her on the ground. She risked a glance at the children. They were nearly to the gate. But two of the recently arrived elephants and their riders moved to intercept.

Fayola recognized one of the men. She had grazed him with a nonlethal bolt. Now he rode with another male toward her charges—a gun in a hand she should've claimed.

Three bears rushed Fayola, tackling her to the ground and ripping into her with sharp claws.

Lightning surged through her wings, shocking the bears and sending them flying.

Shaking off the attack, they charged her again.

Fayola leapt into the sky.

"Ruuuun," Mei lien shouted.

"That's right, kids. Run, run. Come on. You're almost here."

Fayola soared through the sky under a barrage of bullet fire. The bears were good shots, and she was a big target.

I don't want to kill them. I just need to—

Bang. Bang.

Fayola's head jerked back.

A child screamed. "Nooo, Dela Eden."

Equilibrium abandoned her, and she spiraled out of control, crashing to the ground. Blood flowed like a river seeking an ocean from her left eye. But the pain . . . the sharp, stinging pain doubled her over.

The bears attacked.

Jwahir continued to scream as Fayola took a beating.

The twins didn't scream her name, but they offered pleas on her behalf. "Stop. Stop. You're going to kill her. Please, stop."

"Come here," one of the Sunhung soldiers said. "You little brats. We're taking you to Matriarch Moshi. She wants you, and she's gonna have you."

Fayola didn't know if the pain would've been worse or less if the bullet wasn't lodged in her eyeball.

She rolled onto her side, using her wings as a shield as she struggled through nausea and pain.

Deep breaths, Fay. You don't have time for the pain. You'll lose them all if you give in to your screaming body.

An elephant kicked her in the back, as a punter would a football, sending Fayola skidding. Her body howled from the brutal impact. But the attack put distance between Fayola and her assailants.

"Get up," the Jelani in her mind told her. *"Get your feathered ass up and complete your mission."*

But I can't see, Fayola responded to herself. *I can't fly with one functioning eye.*

"Then don't fly. Eat."

Fayola could hear the approaching soldiers' laughter as clearly as she could detect Jwahir's ragged sniffles.

I might die, but I won't do it on my knees.

"Well, well, look who's up. You were wrong, Hassani; impundulu aren't hard to kill."

"She ain't dead yet, Ren. Brag after you've put another bullet in her bird brain."

Fayola's chin slumped to her chest. She couldn't see a damn thing out of her left eye while using her right made her dizzy.

She listened, tracking the bears and elephants. Fayola didn't question her next actions. She stopped thinking about the retribution from her Wake. She even set aside her incomplete blood pact with Dr. Pérez-Soto's brother.

She gave neither any space in her heart and mind. Instead, they floated away, freeing yet damning.

Lightning formed in her damaged eye, setting blood and bullet ablaze with gold sparks.

The soldiers laughed again—mocking but more unseeing than she.

"Dela Eden, we believe in you," one of the children shrieked, giving her the last boost she needed to see her vow through to the electrifying end.

She flung her wings wide, smashing into the closest enemies and knocking them to the ground. Fayola ran toward the sound of scuffling, and she knew the children fought. Lightning built in her wings with each whipping movement. It built and built, the potency intensifying the longer she held it in her wings.

"Don't let them stop you," the Jelani in her mind told her. *"Give them what they deserve."*

Fayola released her power in gold, deadly arcs of sizzling lightning. Over and again, she sent bolts at her enemies, striking them down.

A bullet scored her side, but she kept moving. Fayola didn't require sight, not when bear blood was in the air.

She flew in the direction of the delicious scent. *Crash.* Fayola had let the bear shifter live. The last time she'd used her lightning to knock him off his elephant mount. This time . . .

Taking from him what that Ren soldier had stolen from her, Fayola plucked out the downed soldier's eye. Uninterested in consuming the eyeball, she tossed it aside. It was a mere access point to what she truly wanted.

The man hollered but began to transform underneath her.

Fayola dug her long, sharp beak into his vacant eye socket, opened her beak and coated her tongue in fresh, warm blood.

The man screamed and bucked.

Fayola drank, strengthening her lightning and fueling an even greater hunger lust.

Swinging out with her wings, she clipped the two closest elephants.

They crashed to the ground, a rumble incapable of rivaling her growling stomach.

Run to the guards. Let them take care of you.

Once they were on the Tikala side of the border barrier, Fayola would no longer have to worry about their safety. Even if she died there, unable to return for Dr. Pérez-Soto, she did not worry.

She's a bear shifter. If I don't return for her, she'll climb down the tree to safety. She's survived this long in a war-torn country; I don't doubt she can make her way to Delcanos safely, even without my help.

Fayola opened her right eye, seeing double, but her binocular vision was better than it had been before she drank from the dead bear shifter.

"You fucking bitch. You killed Sei—"

Fayola flew at the cursing soldier, slicing him from ear to ear. Licking the blood from her talons, she savored the taste. She would need more bear blood to heal from her wounds, though.

No amount of blood will purge my guilt over those boys' deaths.

She raked her long beak down an elephant's side. Blood spurted. She attacked again, avoiding his tusks and slashing out with talons and beak. More blood flowed, splattering her feathers and splashing into her mouth.

Disgusting. But I'll take it. Make all of you cowards bleed.

The bullet in her eye shifted, radiating skull-splitting, stomach-churning pain. Fayola stumbled backward.

An elephant attacked, goring her side and tossing her into a circle of black bears. They had all shifted, and now they surrounded her.

Tired. Weak. I hurt everywhere, and they're going to kill me.

The bears attacked. Fayola did not know how many. All of them, perhaps. Strong and vicious, claws slashed, and paws pounded.

Fayola tucked her body into a tight ball, wrapped her wide, long wings around herself, and endured the assault. Gathering her waning strength, she heated her core hotter than ever before.

I won't allow my death to weigh on those children's conscience. They deserve the happy life Dr. Pérez-Soto promised them. And Jelani . . . Dad . . . I must survive for them too.

Sparks formed in her racing heart, blazing with heat and power.

And for myself. I'm not ready to die.

The attacks intensified. Kicks joined punches. Mighty bear paws gripped her wings and yanked. Feathers were torn, and wing bones were broken.

Still, her heat intensified, transforming hurt and hunger into electrical currents of anger and survival.

And grew.

And grew.

Boom. Boom.

Thunder beat against the sky in time with the bears' unrelenting paws.

Boom. Boom.

And grew.

And grew.

I won't die here. Not on the ground. And damn sure not at the paws of bears. They are food. My. Food.

Eyes popped open, and wings snapped out. Lightning roared from Fayola like a dragon spewing fire.

Roar after roar, her lightning surged from her body, filled her mouth, trickled from her eyes and nose, coated her talons and ignited her wings.

Flash. Flash. Flash.

Get.

Flash.

Off.

Flash. Flash.

Meeeee!

Flash. Flash. Flash. Flash.

Electrical currents drew Fayola to her taloned feet, her body a fuse box of sparking danger.

Hungry. So hungry. Need to eat. Feed.

Fayola caught a fleeing bear with her electrified wing. Drew him in close, shocked his system repeatedly, and then . . . and then . . . stabbed her beak in his heaving chest and drank his blood.

Drank. Drank.

Not enough. Still hungry.

Stepping back, she let the bear fall at her feet. His death wouldn't absolve her of Peng's death.

Lifting into the air, but barely able to see, Fayola flew toward the sound of crying and the pull of a vow that had become the bloodiest of pacts.

Jwahir. Your name means golden lady. Gold, like my lightning. But you're just a little girl, not yet a woman. So don't cry, golden lady. Don't cry.

6: Our Cub Comes Before Anyone Else's

The United States of Delcanos
Los Sanvo City

"She isn't a wounded kitten you found on the side of the road."

Teresa Pérez-Soto grabbed a fistful of her husband's sweatshirt and not so much pulled him away from the closed motel room door, as hoped he would comply with her tugging. A six-seven black bear in human form moved under no one's will but his own, which didn't prevent Teresa from yanking Castel as hard as she could.

"All right, all right. Stop all that. I'm coming." As if creating distance between them and the motel room had been his idea, Castel stomped past Teresa, down the steps and to his white SUV with custom finished gold rims. Crossing long arms over his chest, Castel leaned against the side of his truck. Dark brown eyes glared down at her as if she had created the situation.

"I'm the victim here, if you've forgotten."

He scoffed, and his eyes narrowed. "I told you Namju was too hot. You wouldn't listen."

"But the kids—"

"Would've still been there when things cooled down. The Sunhung and Taepo herds are brutal on their best day and crazy on their worst." Castel sighed, dropping his arms only to enfold Teresa in them. "I was the one who went a little crazy when I could no longer reach you."

"We lost power. No landlines and no way to charge my mobile."

"The civil war has been all over the news. I was scared out of my damn mind. I told you it was too risky."

Castel had but . . . "Civil wars leave so many children abandoned and desperate. They needed someone, and I was that person. I'm sorry. I know you were worried. Apparently, so was Javier."

Big arms tightened around her shoulders, a belated comfort for them both. "Your brother threw his weight and money around, as usual. I didn't think he would go so far as initiating a blood pact with the Wake, though."

Wake. The four-letter word brought them full circle.

Castel's arms loosened, then fell away. His movements ushered the return of her frowning husband.

Teresa joined Castel, leaning against the side of his truck. Her gaze rose to the second floor of the two-story red brick motel. The sun had risen an hour earlier, shedding light on a highway motel on the outskirts of Los Sanvo and the reality of a new day.

"She saved my life."

"Which is the only reason I let you talk me into getting her a motel room after meeting the two of you here."

"She and a Tikala border guard found me on a road." Teresa shook her head, still shocked at the sight of Diello Fayola's animal form. She had crash-landed in front of her, displacing the rider and knocking Teresa to the dusty ground. "She returned for me. Despite her injuries, despite having to rely on a stranger to serve as her eyes, she came back for me."

"I'm grateful. I am." Castel faced Teresa. Arms moved to the truck's roof, effectively caging her between him and his vehicle. "Truly, I am grateful. But everything that made that woman hard to kill . . . I mean, she has a fucking crushed bullet in her eye. I thought they were myths, you know?"

"That impundulus are impervious to bullets and knives? Well, more resilient than impervious, I guess."

Castel nodded. "She is hurt beyond the eye wound. When that border patrolman called me, I thought . . . I thought . . ." He looked away. The jaw she loved to kiss tightened, and hands that were always so gentle with her and Pablo slammed against the truck's roof. "Then you got on the mobile and my world righted itself again."

"She could have brought me directly home after she found me. But, instead, she permitted me to return with her and the guard to Tikala so I could check on the children. Even if I wanted to stay there and let her figure out her own way home, she wouldn't have left me in Tikala. 'My mission isn't complete,' she told me. Which meant permitting her to fly me to Delcanos." Teresa pointed to the motel, not that Castel required a reminder. "This was a better option than having her fly me to our home or even to Javier's company's headquarters. She's going to need help getting home."

"What she needs is blood." A steady finger tilted her chin up. "When she wakes, she'll want blood. I don't want to be anywhere near here when that happens. We haven't had our own breakfast yet. I damn sure won't be hers."

Teresa recalled Fayola's words. *"Would you prefer to feel me drink from you while you squirm in my arms as I sink my sharp eyeteeth into your unmarred neck?"* Worse, she remembered the feel of her tongue licking her neck the way children did a lollipop—with greedy anticipation. Her entire body shivered at the horrific thought.

"That impundulu is dangerous. If even a third of the story the children told you about her fight at the border is true, her only off switch is death or a successful mission. What do you think will happen if she learns the full truth?"

Teresa's gaze shot to the motel again. She had closed the curtains, hoping the darkness would minimize Diello Fayola's discomfort when she awoke. Under different circumstances . . . very different circumstances, Teresa imagined they could have become friends. But then she recalled how the children had rushed to Diello Fayola's side at the immigration detention center, clinging to her and crying. The impundulu had accepted their affection, with neither reluctance nor reciprocity but with angry eyes. The damaged one dripped blood lightning.

Never friends. But I would prefer not to become her enemy.

"We need to work with the Tikala authorities to claim legal possession of the children." Castel thumped the roof of his vehicle again. "That process will be a huge pain in the ass."

"Or we could cut our losses."

"After everything you've been through?"

A minivan pulled into a parking spot one row in front of them. Within seconds, a group of five exited—two forty-something women and three teenage boys. Stretching and chatting, they retrieved backpacks and a large red cooler with a white lid and durable-looking wheels.

"I got it, Mom." The teenager with a bad case of acne and a voice somewhere between awkward pubescent and untried young man freed his mother of her burden. Picking up and carrying the cooler, the boy marched toward the motel. "Which one, again?" he yelled.

Smiling at her son's back, the woman hiked her backpack over a shoulder, gripped the same kind of keycard Teresa had in her pants pocket, and then locked the older model minivan with an old-school fob she couldn't see, but the beep was unmistakable. "Room 108. That thing has wheels for a reason, Urban." The mother laughed. "I'm still not letting you drive before you get your learner's permit."

"Then I'll just have to keep showing you how responsible I am." The teen turned, his grin full of a little boy's hope and a grown man's innocent desire.

Teresa and Castel tabled their discussion. Instead, they leaned against the SUV until the motel room door closed behind the last boy—a kid with wraparound sunglasses and a swagger that reminded Teresa why she preferred dealing with children from places like Namju.

"We'll figure something out," Teresa said the moment the motel room door closed, leaving them alone in the parking lot. "I've invested a lot of time with this group. I would hate for it all to have been for nothing." Teresa wouldn't mention the stupid decision she'd made that could have resulted in her death if not for Diello Fayola's unexpected appearance at the clinic. "They don't have anyone else. Tikala's government already has its hands full with Namju refugees. Their detention centers aren't meant to house children beyond a week or two."

Teresa pushed from the SUV. An idea had formed that would leave one final positive impression on the honorable Diello Fayola.

"Where are you going?"

Castel would follow, so she ignored his grumbles and growls.

"As crazy as it may seem, Diello Fayola did us a favor."

"How?" Two strides to her five had Castel at her side. "Besides saving your ass, I mean? I assume you mean in another way.

Pablo missed you, by the way. All of your travels might pay for his medical bills and our home, but a cub needs his mama."

Teresa stumbled on a flat surface and her guilt. A hand to her elbow steadied her. "Thanks."

"I didn't mention Pablo to upset you, but we have to keep in mind why we started all of this. Our cub comes before anyone else's."

"I know."

They stopped at the stairs that would take them to the second floor. Ironically, it placed them in front of the room with the family of five. The same young teen with the too-confident swagger stared at them through the sole window in the room. Even inside, he still wore his sunglasses. Unlike the older teen, likely his brother, he radiated caution beyond his years.

The teen nodded to Teresa and Castel. For unnerving seconds, she felt as if the boy saw into her soul—the rotten and the selfish. Then he snapped the curtains closed, breaking the trance.

"This group will be the last," Teresa promised her husband, shaking off the strange sensation the human teen evoked. "Diello Fayola vouched for me with the Tikala border guards. She told them I was the children's guardian. That should be enough for social services to place them in my temporary custody."

"That's not exactly how it works, which is why we find homes for the children in their native country. It's simpler that way. Why are you going up the stairs?"

"There is one thing I think I should do before we leave her here by herself." At the top of the landing, Teresa turned in the direction of Diello Fayola's room. "I know having the children released into my custody is more complicated than what I just said. But do you really think an overworked and underpaid social worker will question a pediatrician who not only risked her life to save war-orphaned children but who also received the blessing of an impundulu? The bird shifters may be feared by many, but they are respected by even more."

"You want to leverage their reputation?" Castel stepped in front of her when she pulled out the keycard. Castel's right hand was outstretched, while his left rose to his lips, shushing her. "Her reputation as a diello?" he whispered.

Teresa nodded, having forgotten she had been the one to discourage their conversation in front of the door earlier. Impundulus might have excellent sight, but that did not mean their ears weren't also acute.

As if to prove her point, a strangely familiar voice spoke in her head.

I was told you promised to find the children good homes. Your pact . . . your vow, Dr. Pérez-Soto.

Teresa pointed to her temple but also used her fingers to imitate the movement of lips.

"Telepathy?" Castel mouthed.

Teresa shifted closer to the door, grateful her burly husband moved aside without fuss. She had slid the keycard back into her pants pocket, no longer needing it to speak to Diello Fayola.

Teresa directed her words to the door in a normal volume, now certain Diello Fayola could hear them on the other side. "I will keep my promise."

Make sure you do.

Teresa chose not to take the four words as a threat. "How are you feeling?"

Inconsequential.

She almost laughed. "Fine. Is there anything we can do for you before we leave?"

Teresa wondered if she would blow her off with another one-word reply. But the voice in her head softened, sounding even more fatigued than seconds earlier.

Tell me the shaggy-haired human boy's name.

Teresa had high hopes for him and Peng, especially for big, strong Peng. But the Sunhung soldiers had ruined her plans. More of the children had survived than she dared to hope. Still, if any of them had to die, Teresa would trade little Jwahir for the strapping, twelve-year-old blond.

Back at the clinic, I couldn't very well ask the Wake soldier to fly the biggest and strongest kids to safety without her questioning my motive. So deciding on the smallest kids was the right call to make. Few people, even a hardened soldier like Diello Fayola, can resist an adorable kid. And few are cuter than little Jwahir.

"Orion. His name is Orion Ridley."

The sudden silence felt worse than the diello's intrusive voice.

Castel tapped the screen of his mobile unit, reminding her Pablo didn't do well when left too long with a babysitter, not even when the babysitter was his uncle.

Tell me all their names.

Speeding through them, Teresa obliged, not liking Diello Fayola's interest when she had none before.

Good. Thank you. One favor, Dr. Pérez-Soto.

"Of course. What do you need?"

Diello Fayola rambled off an international number, which Teresa relayed to Castel.

Impundulus were not mind readers, but Diello Fayola had requested of Teresa the very thing she had returned to the motel room to offer.

Tell her I'm fine but that I need a pickup. This hotel address will be all she requires.

"Do you want me to tell her to bring blood?"

Inconsequential.

Even with a door between them, Teresa knew the impundulu needed food more than she did pride. But the woman was stubborn and Castel impatient, so Teresa made the call and delivered Diello Fayola's message.

"We can go now," Castel said in her ear, pocketing his mobile. "She's a big bird. She'll be fine."

Teresa agreed with Castel. She also hoped to never lay eyes on Diello Fayola again.

7: I'll Take the Forty Ops

2105
Seventeen Years Earlier
The United Wake of Benekal
Mokal City Kettle

"You look really nice." Jelani cleared his throat, and Fayola wished she could vanquish her self-consciousness just as easily. "I mean, you look beautiful. Really, really beautiful."

Kwame shoved Jelani's back, ending the sweet but awkward moment. "Wipe the drool from your mouth, stop eye fucking your girlfriend and follow the hostess to our table so I can order and eat."

"I wasn't eye fu—"

Durah grabbed Fayola's hand as if she were her date instead of Jelani. "You kind of were, but we get it." Her friend smiled at her, granting Fayola a wink then a whistle. "She is adorable, whenever we can get her to wear something other than her uniform or jeans and sneakers."

Fayola yanked her hand free. "That's pretty much what we all wear." *I won't lie, though, at least not to myself. Jelani in a suit is more delectable than frozen blood custard ice cream after one of Diello Madana's six-hour endurance flights. I do love how he looks after spending time in his barber's chair. A fresh shave and short curly hair with a tapered fade on the sides. Yum.*

Afraid her own eyes revealed the same thoughts as Jelani's, Fayola turned away from her friends and toward the direction the host had gone.

"Enjoy your meal," the hostess said. "I'm leaving you in Poet's excellent hands." The sixty-something woman smiled with rote professionalism that still left room for sincerity.

Their waiter, a man with a receding hairline but a full beard, stood beside a table for four.

Dipping her head in thanks, Fayola sat in the chair Jelani pulled out for her.

"Mine is right here," Kwame singsonged, tapping the back of the chair opposite Fayola's. "Gender equality and all that."

Like them all, Kwame had dressed for the social outing. He may not have worn a suit and tie like Jelani, but his dress pants and vest were a departure from his standard attire. Just as Fayola and Durah rarely had reason to wear makeup, pretty clothing, and cute shoes.

Cute but also uncomfortable. I understand Diello Madana's wardrobe choice from induction day much better now. Boots with a dress. Cute but also practical.

Jelani ignored Durah's protest of: "I can get my own chair but thanks." With a smirk Fayola knew well, Jelani pushed Kwame aside and pulled his chair from the table. "I'll hold it for you while you sit."

Never one to back away from a challenge, the six-two Kwame sat, allowing the five-ten Jelani to be the last man standing. Well, not including their waiter, who smiled at the exchange the way a patient father would his own young adult children.

"As Lexie said, I'm Poet, and I'll be your waiter. Welcome to Open Air Sweets." Poet nodded to the sky to his left.

Located on the thirtieth floor of Open Air Hotel, a popular chain of restaurants, Open Air Sweets specialized in combining impundulus' main food with tasty international desserts.

Fayola smiled, already enjoying herself. She listened as Poet described the Dessert of the Day—a sticky toffee pudding topped with warm toffee sauce mixed with organic brown bear blood.

She had no idea how blood from a brown bear could be organic, but the dessert sounded delicious. So too did the *alfajores*, a shortbread cookie with a sweet layer of dulce de leche cooked with sweetened milk and blood from a lactating sun bear. But it was the gooey, chocolatey brownie bites with a cup of warm sloth bear blood for dipping that watered Fayola's mouth.

"So, a round of brownie bites for everyone. Toffee pudding for the ladies." Poet nodded to Jelani. "Cardamom buns for the gentleman. And, for the other gentleman, crème brûlée. Very good."

Poet swept from their table with the confidence of a man used to being correct and the authority to excuse his mistakes when he wasn't.

Fayola felt Jelani's hand settle on her thigh while she watched his other hand reach for his glass of water.

Durah ran a finger around the rim of her own glass of water. "Is this a celebration or a farewell?"

Kwame shrugged, reminding her of the fifteen-year-old he had been when they met. "I guess it depends on what our decision will be."

At twenty-one, they were bigger and stronger than they were the day of their induction into the military. Basic training had turned them into soldiers. But their time with the Mokal City

Police Department had made them both enforcers of laws and friends of the kettle.

The hand softly, slowly rubbing her thigh stilled. "One year of basic training, then five compulsory years as a community police officer." Jelani finished his water, accepting a refill when Poet returned with their desserts.

For five minutes, they tabled their discussion, digging into their sweet, bear blood treats.

"So good," Fayola moaned. The brownie bites were a perfect size, while the blood was so fresh she could've sworn they had an open-veined bear in the kitchen. Licking her lips, Fayola moaned again.

Jelani's hand on her thigh tightened, and she sobered at his hungry look.

Returning his heated gaze, Fayola dreaded the thought of them going their separate ways. But she had a promise to keep to her father and to herself.

Jelani must follow his own path. I can't keep him with me, no matter how much I want us to stay together.

Kwame dropped his spoon into his empty bowl and sighed, pleased with his dessert as a human child having finished off the last spoonful of a pint of their favorite ice cream. "I'm getting three of those to go. Now," his hands clapped together with a loud *smack*, drawing attention from other diners, "about Durah's question. We've completed our five mandatory years as local officers. We could stay. Move up the ranks here or in another kettle's police department. Thirty-five years, then a lifetime pension. We could also transfer to one of the military's armed forces divisions. Forty years military service, then all-expenses-paid retirement. Or . . ."

The two-letter word hung between them, as she imagined the same decision had for every impundulu who had reached this milestone.

Two soft lips kissed Fayola's cheek. "We all know Fay's decision. It was made before we left home, and it hasn't changed."

"Don't," she said with the same petal softness as the red and gold ranunculus corsage Jelani had slipped onto her wrist earlier in the evening. "Your future shouldn't be based on a clingy fifteen-year-old daddy's girl's naïve promise."

Jelani kissed her cheek again, lingering a touch too long for the public display of affection. "Just because my choice coincides with yours, that doesn't mean my decision is about you."

"It is about her." Kwame threw his white napkin at Jelani, who caught it without taking his eyes off of Fayola.

"I'm sure most people would agree with you, but Fay knows me better than that."

I do, but we've done everything together ever since basic training. We even included the same top three cities in our placement application to the Wake Armed Police. So, too, did Durah and Kwame. Something other than luck had our first choice of Mokal City approved. But this decision is so much more than a five-year obligation.

Durah stole one of Fayola's brownie bites, tossing it into her mouth and chewing with a grin that dared Fayola to object. "We're friends. Aradi City kettle wherever we go. You aren't the only one who wants a quick way out of service. Guaranteed decades in local or national armed service, or forty successful special ops missions. I'll take the forty ops."

Kwame grabbed Fayola's last brownie bite, popping it into his big mouth before she could protest. "Me too. Everyone's not cut out for law enforcement. I would rather serve sweet treats, like Poet, to a playful brat like me, than spend three or four decades patrolling the streets and skies of a kettle or being deployed from one hot spot to another."

Jelani relaxed in his chair, eyed his own empty dessert dish, and then ordered another round of brownie bites for the table. "We serve because it's the way of our people. Natural-born predators. While I can appreciate the idea of freedom of choice, I'd rather argue against conscription from outside of a prison cell."

"Choosing to join a special ops unit is the most dangerous of the three options," Fayola said, feeling a need to remind them.

Her friends snorted as if the truth of her words held no more weight than the amount of bear blood a brownie bite could absorb.

"We want to go home too, Fay." Jelani brought her hand to lips she loved against hers and kissed her palm. "In a country that allows no choice when it comes to military service, we are given this single opportunity. We have power over this tiny part of our military lives. We get to choose. I choose special ops, you, and our little kettle of friends. Together, we'll get through those forty missions in record time."

Every mission would not be successful, but Fayola refused to lessen Jelani's declaration by stating the obvious.

Durah snatched another one of Fayola's brownie bites, but she caught her wrist before she could make her escape.

"You have an entire plate. Why are you stealing mine?"

"With the way you were looking at Jelani, I assumed you preferred his chocolate goodness to your brownies."

"You thought wrong."

"She did?"

Kwame laughed. "I guess you don't look as good in that suit as you think, peacock."

"Shut up."

"Make me." Kwame shoved his brownie bites into his mouth, downed his glass of bear blood, then pushed from the table with speed rivaled only by Jelani, who'd rounded the table before Fayola realized he no longer sat beside her.

"I'll make you, all right." Jelani grinned at Fayola over his shoulder, his charm as undeniable as his attractiveness. Then, just as quickly, he tackled Kwame.

Off the roof they went.

No banister or dwarf wall. Nothing but . . . well, open air, the true defining feature of the eatery.

"They're such children."

Fayola agreed with Durah but . . . "Race you." She rushed from her chair like a lioness chasing after an antelope.

"Cheater," Durah yelled, her mouth full of commandeered brownies.

Fayola dove off the roof, shifting into her bird form just as Jelani and Kwame soared past her like arrows freed from a quiver. She followed, leaving Durah to catch up.

When she did, her friend tapped her with her black wing. *"You're it, woodcock."* Durah darted out of reach, laughing in Fayola's head.

She sped, not after Durah, but Jelani.

"Hey, I wasn't the one who called you a slow woodcock. So why are you chasing me?"

Because you are all that made the last six years bearable. Kwame was right. Military service is not for everyone, but we do what we must. When I'm an elder, I will look back on my time in service to the Wake as the fleeting moment of responsibility it was. Fleeting but essential to the continuation of our culture. Those forty missions will be a means to an end, inconsequential except for the speediest route home.

Fayola voiced none of those thoughts to Jelani. They all carried their own burdens and fears. Being twenty-one only meant their hearts and minds were fertile grounds for future scars and pain.

Raicho had shared none of his stories from his time in the Covert Pursuits Special Forces Unit despite Fayola's request for her father to, "Tell me everything, Dad. How many people did you save? Were you ever scared?"

As the next phase of her military service loomed before her, Fayola feared she would come to know the answer to the one question she'd never asked Raicho: How many people have you killed and hurt to complete your missions?

But, as she chased after Jelani, more disturbing questions slithered from the depths of her young soul: Did you ever question the morality of any of your missions? Did innocents ever die because of your actions? Did you ever save someone guilty of harming others? What regrets plague your waking mind and seep into your dreams?

Crashing into Jelani, Fayola fell several feet before righting herself. *"You're it."*

Jelani's laughter rippled through her mind. *"Only you could turn careless flying into a game advantage. Fine, I'm it, but I'm going to make you pay until you scream my name."*

"Don't start that shit. Durah and I want to keep down our desserts." A flash of white lightning sparked beside Jelani. *"Take that, you horny peacock."*

Jelani nuzzled her neck, sending flutters through a body already warm from her transformation. *"I booked us a room for the night in the hotel. After I kick Kwame's ass, we can order more dessert then escape to our room."* Snapping out a wing, Jelani sent a red lightning bolt near Kwame. *"Sound good?"*

"It does. By the way," she returned his nuzzle, *"I like you way better than brownie bites."*

"How much better?"

She shoved away from him with a playful hiss of lightning. *"A little. Just a little more."*

Green sparks rained down on them like the first snow of winter. *"There's no way anyone would put the two of you in the same unit."* Durah lit up the sky with lightning the same rich green of emeralds found in the foothills of the Gazali Mountains in eastern Benekal.

"Jealous?" Fayola asked, already knowing her friend's answer.

"Not even a little."

Kwame charged Fayola and Jelani. *"You know what else Open Air Sweets is known for?"* White lightning struck Fayola's side, knocking her away from Jelani. *"Air battles after dessert."*

Human bodies leapt from the rooftop but impundulu forms surged upward, bringing booming thunder and blazing lightning.

Red, green, white, and gold lightning crackled and popped, brightening the night sky.

Fayola attacked friends and strangers alike, conjuring bolt after bolt. She hurled them with the same precision as the ones that slammed into her.

They played as if they were all *It*. As if their very existence did not depend on blood sacrifice. As if peace between the Wake and the world wasn't held together by mutually beneficial pacts that could unravel if the right thread were pulled.

Jelani's wing grazed hers, a gesture of affection that had Fayola tracking him with golden eyes. He circled her, dancing in the air like the peacock Kwame accused him of being.

"You're so silly."

"I'm more than that." His wing slid along her side just as his human hand had glided up and down her thigh.

"Mmm, what else are you?" Jelani's answer didn't matter, especially not with how wonderfully his wing stroked her body.

"When we're in our room and sated, I'll confess all."

"Sated from each other or from Open Air's sweet treats?"

"Both."

Fayola liked Jelani's answer but not the impatience his teasing touches evoked. *"Let's go."* She flew toward the rooftop, calculating the time it would take for them to receive their carryout order, to ditch their friends, and for them to be wrapped around each other behind a locked hotel room door.

Too long.

Fayola flew faster.

Jelani followed.

2122

The United States of Delcanos

Los Sanvo City, Telaro

Fayola should have sensed something before a warm, steady hand curled around her nape and lifted. Perhaps the opening of the door. Maybe the sound of footsteps. If nothing else, Fayola should have smelled the sweet scent of blood and chocolate. But she did not.

What she did sense, however, far too late to defend herself, if he meant her harm, was . . . *him.*

Safety. Trust. Home.

Jelani's big hand cradled Fayola's nape, supporting her weight between solid and gentle fingers. "You don't have to do anything other than drink."

The familiar cool of a steel straw settled against puffy, dry lips.

"Come on, Fay, drink for me. I brought your favorite ration."

Doing what she hadn't yesterday, Fayola followed orders as given, although Durah hadn't followed hers.

"Her name is Durah," she'd told Dr. Pérez-Soto. "Tell her my pickup will be her first civilian mission. She is to come alone. Emphasize that part of the message."

I should've known she would call Jelani and Kwame. I wish she hadn't, though. I don't want any blowback to hit them.

"You're almost finished with the first B-ration. Good. Keep going."

To stave off Jelani's worry, Fayola kept her eyes closed. She curled into him, grateful for his presence despite her desire to keep him far away from the inevitable blowback of her failed mission.

The reusable straw slipped from between her lips only to reappear, seconds later, in another B-ration.

"A half gallon should be enough to get you out of this bed and into the bathroom. I want you naked and under solar lighting, so I can thoroughly examine you before heading home."

"Are Durah and Kwame outside?"

"Durah is patrolling the sky, and Kwame is guarding the door." Jelani shifted until he sat against the headboard with her back pressed to his chest. "Why haven't you opened your eyes?"

"I'm hungry." Ordinarily, a twelve-ounce bag of blood would curb her hunger for three to five hours. Instead, the two she'd had coated her sticky tongue and soothed her dry throat but left her craving more.

"Is there a threat I need to know about?" Jelani helped her wrap her hand around another B-ration.

Fayola understood Jelani's concern. While they rarely discussed their solo missions until they were over, they provided an estimated time of completion as a concession to their relationship and peace of mind. As a general rule for any special operations mission, four hours beyond the estimated completion window were grounds for concern. While unsure of the exact time, Fayola estimated at least twenty-four hours had passed since her planned check-in time. As a result, she missed checking in with Jelani and Belay Njeri, commander of the Rescue and Recovery Unit.

"No threat. Thank you for coming."

A soothing thumb stroked her cheek, reminding Fayola of a truth that bound them on a level more profound than the ritual of marriage. Impundulus no more needed a legal pact to solidify their commitment to their loved one than they required the genetic material of another to become a parent.

"I love you, Fay."

Jelani had said the same the first time they'd stayed at the Open-Air Hotel in Mokal City. His confession had been the worst-kept secret.

Fayola turned in his embrace, wanting to see him but afraid her wound had worsened. "I love you too." She opened her eyes. Pain, like a knife slicing through flesh, had her slamming her left eye shut. The other remained open. Barely. She blinked, working to clear her right eye of the cloudy film that had formed.

"Was that a bullet?"

They were war-hardened soldiers, so Jelani's voice should not have squeaked upon seeing her wounded eye, no more than Fayola should have felt utterly safe at the gentle hands moving her onto her back.

Taking his time, Jelani peeled each item of clothing from Fayola.

He's removed my clothes many times but never under such circumstances and never with controlled caution and clinical-like care.

Even with both eyes closed, when he turned on the overhead light, she squinted at the abrupt change from hiding darkness to revealing light.

Jelani swore. His words were coarse but the hands examining her body felt like fingers wrapped in cotton. "How many?" he asked. His voice was low, but his tone was as deadly as the talons he used against prey.

Fayola couldn't determine if he wanted to know how many times she'd been shot or the number of enemies she'd fought. Neither answer would change Fayola's medical condition or Jelani's unvoiced and pointless wish that he had been with her in Namju.

I wish he had been there too. Not for my sake but for Peng's and Orion's.

"I need to get you out of here and to the hospital." Jelani helped Fayola back into her clothing even slower than he'd removed them. Impundulus' bodies might be durable, but that did not mean they could not be hurt. She'd felt every single bullet. Their impact was equivalent to hitting the ground from a thirty-foot fall—painful and bruising but not fatal.

"Here, drink up. I need you strong for the flight."

Fayola accepted another B-ration.

My body will heal. We both know it will. This isn't the first time I've been hurt. But my eye? I could've removed the bullet. I probably should have, but I couldn't be certain what would happen if I did.

Fayola reached for her left eye, but Jelani caught her hand between his.

"Don't. You've left it alone this long, there's no point in messing with it now. A doctor will know what to do."

Fayola didn't think, even with her impundulu physiology, that her eye or her eyesight were salvageable. But she pushed the depressing thought away while embracing the bag of chocolate flavored blood Jelani handed her.

"We have a lot to discuss." Hoisting her into his arms, Jelani scanned the motel room. Then, satisfied he'd left nothing behind, not even the empty bags of blood he'd returned to his backpack, he granted her a tight smile.

Fayola watched him through a right eye that opened a fraction, like parting drapes a few inches to let in a sliver of light. She hadn't wanted Durah to call Jelani and Kwame. The repercussions would be hers alone. Neither of them would like whatever penalty the Rashidi Tribunal would hand down, but Fayola was prepared to pay the price for her pact with the orphans.

Yes, they had much to discuss, all of which would change their post-military plans.

Jelani, Durah, Kwame, and me. Durah finished her forty missions first. She was the first of us to earn her freedom and return home only a month ago. I would've been the second. But, after what I've done, I can't go home. Not with honor. Not with Jelani.

Fayola closed her eye. The pain of how thoroughly she'd ruined over two decades of retirement planning sliced through her more potent than any bolt she'd leveled against the Sunhung soldiers.

"I'll take care of you."

Fayola knew Jelani would do his best.

"It'll be fine. You're safe now."

Safe, yes, but nothing is okay. Nothing will be fine after I report the details of my mission to Belay Njeri. She'll have no choice but to turn me over to authorities for my crimes. After that . . . shit, I'm not ready to think about how the Rashidi Tribunal will respond. For now, I'll embrace the delusion that all will be fine.

Fayola wrapped arms around Jelani's neck. Ignored fears heating her insides like logs set aflame, she repeated the one truth that had been a staple in her life. "I love you. No matter where I am or for how long, you will have my love and devotion."

8: I Won't Give You More

2123
Six Months Later
The United Wake of Benekal
Fort Kumelo City
The United Wake of Benekal Military Courthouse

Of the many times Fayola had dreamed of reuniting with Raicho, none of those imaginings involved a court-martial. Yet there they both were—in the same state, city, and room for the first time in twenty-three years. Despite everything—Fayola's shame and dishonor—she couldn't help but stare at her father.

He'd changed in the intervening years, as had she. Older but not old. Raicho's thick, ropelike twists fell to a lean waist where he'd tucked his light blue dress shirt into dark blue dress pants with the same military neatness as her own white shirt. Suit jacket fisted in one hand, the other slammed the door of the attorney-client conference room behind the retreating MPs.

Raicho observed Fayola with dark eyes. Inch by inch, he scanned her—from hair she loved for him to braid but that she'd cut short more out of lack of hairstyling skill than compliance to military grooming and appearance standards, to shifting dampener cuffs tightened around wrists that had only ever known a father's tender touch. His foot tapped like a doomsday countdown clock.

Unable to stomach the emotion she saw in his eyes, she permitted her own to drift down and away.

"I'm angry."

"I know. I'm sorry. I didn't mean to—"

Like a window opening to a warm breeze, Raicho rushed across the room, enveloping her in a tight embrace. "My precious lightning bird, I'm not upset with you."

Fayola wanted to weep. A thirty-eight-year-old woman shouldn't take such comfort in the arms of a parent. But an impundulu's loyalty to Wake was rivaled only by their commitment to family.

An already breath-stealing hug became bruising.

A bear hug from a bird shifter. If I hadn't been on the receiving end of bears' brutal attacks, I might laugh. But, no, all I want to do is enjoy this too-brief respite.

"Those bastards." A finger rimmed where a cuff dug into her skin. "Those MPs could've removed these before they left. Instead, they acted as if you were a threat."

"I did confess to killing several people."

Raicho's scoff sounded like clouds trying to muffle thunder. "Pieces of shit Sunhung. Soldiers aren't supposed to shoot and kill children, especially unarmed ones."

How did he . . .? "You weren't permitted to attend my hearing, but you know the details of what happened at the Namju-Tikala border."

Although she knew Raicho wouldn't hold her as long as he had when, as a girl, she would run into his room after a nightmare, having him release her so they could sit at the sole table in the room felt the same as the day he'd led her to the Tree of Karasi.

Unlike that day, he'll be the one to leave me behind.

"There are ways to get around gag orders."

"It's called having a courthouse spy."

"Not a spy but a good friend."

"I wanted to call and tell you myself. I didn't want you learning the awful truth from anyone other than me." Permission had been denied, first by Belay Njeri then by the arresting officers. Fayola hadn't liked their decision, but military protocol dictated no family contact until duty to the Wake concluded. Her arrest and fortieth mission hadn't made her any less the property of the military.

"You've grown into a beautiful woman."

"Dad, I . . ."

"It's the truth. You don't have a mother, so I get to claim everything good there is about you."

"What about the bad?"

Raicho moved his chair beside hers. "I would never use that word to describe you. You may have changed, just as I have, but the caring heart of the girl I raised never would. From what I was told, you saved nineteen children and a doctor."

When Fayola slept, she saw Peng, not as he'd been in life—a vibrant, brave boy—but an orphan defiled by violence.

"I lost two."

"You said that with the regret it deserves but also with guilt. Both are normal and, with time, the proper one will fade."

I don't think a day will come when I'll cease feeling guilty about Peng and Orion. The sure way Dad spoke, no doubt from experience, it must be true.

"Your eye looks better than I thought it would have." As if he were a physician, Raicho scooted closer, tilted her head back and examined her left eye. "Modern medical technology is a wonder."

"Your spy told you about my injury too?"

"Jelani had Durah call me."

"I should have guessed."

"He was always a good boy. He's grown into an even better man. I'm glad the two of you had each other. And that is the closest we'll ever come to discussing your sex life." Lips kissed the brow above an eye she feared forever damaged. "I've missed you."

Fayola had missed him too. "The judges made me wait five months before sentencing."

"I know. But not in a military prison. You've been right here on base. In solitary confinement, I'm sure, but still not in a prison cell. That must mean something."

"My judge advocate agrees that the handling of my case is abnormal bordering on illegal."

"He's right. You pleaded guilty. No trial required. The tribunal could've handed down your sentence that day. If not then, no more than a month later. Instead, they've kept you here. Under arrest and guarded but without a judicial judgment, much less a punishment. Although," he leaned back in his chair, brows furrowed and fingers laced in his lap, "the tribunal did send me a personal invitation to today's sentencing hearing. In contrast, they'd banned me from visiting you before."

Green lightning flickered in her father's eyes. Almost as quickly, the sparks faded, leaving his irises clear but his anger intact.

"You think they want something from me?"

"Maybe." Fingers twitched as if they could unlock the cuffs and steal her away.

He can't protect me. Will alone isn't enough. So many years in service to the Wake, but it took the death of a young bear shifter and a human teenager for me to accept such a basic fact of life.

"I don't have anything of value."

"Untrue. The Rashidi Tribunal lives for the Wake. Every decision they've made has been in what they perceive as the best interest of our nation. You broke Wake law, but you also completed your mission. Not stealthily, the way we are trained. Not without casualties which, let's be real here, the tribunal doesn't give a damn about you killing a few bears. What they do care about is the spotlight your action has placed on ops we complete in non–pact countries."

"I hear you, Dad. But I was charged with several crimes, the most severe being three counts of second-degree murder." Fayola refrained from staring down at the cuffs—a physical reminder of her criminal status. "I'm sorry," she whispered, as if barely speaking the words would lessen the impact on them both. "I thought of you, home and the Namju mission being my last. All I wanted, for as long as I can remember, was to sever military ties as quickly as possible."

No mission ever mattered. They were all inconsequential except as the most direct route to retirement. Then a small human girl held my hand and looked at me without an ounce of fear but with pounds of faith.

"When I formed my pact with the children, I knew it would end with either my death or my imprisonment. I chose the children over you. I'm sorry."

Raicho stared at her. Stared, as if she were a jigsaw puzzle with missing or worse, broken pieces.

A single bang on the door preceded its opening. The same military police officers from earlier entered. When they'd left her alone with Raicho, their lips and eyes had been turned down in a too-familiar scowl. Fayola had witnessed the same look of judgment on every MP assigned to her. She had ignored them all. Yet their current expression was one of . . . contrition?

Fayola did not understand.

Raicho jumped to his feet, bumping into the table and knocking his suit jacket onto the floor. "You assholes put her cuffs on too tight. They're cutting off her circulation. Loosen them. Now!"

To her surprise and further confusion, the forty-something MP with a pencil mustache best left in the 1930s, rushed to . . . remove her cuffs?

"That's right," Raicho said, as if the might of his command had moved the MP into action.

No matter how forceful his words, MPs do not take orders from civilians. If they've come to take me into the courtroom, where in the hell is my judge advocate?

Blood and feeling rushed to her wrists and fingers, a painful surge of relief.

"Come here." Raicho engulfed her in another hug. "Now we can do this properly."

The way she'd wanted to earlier, Fayola lifted her arms, squeezing while being squeezed in return.

"Whoa, you're stronger than you look."

"I had a growth spurt when I turned seventeen. I grew three inches."

"Wow, a whole three inches in two decades. It's like I'm hugging a sequoia."

Fayola laughed so she wouldn't weep. "I missed you so much."

"All right, Diello Fayola, let's get going."

Strange. Why the honorific when I've been stripped of my rank?

Raicho slipped into his suit jacket with the fluid grace of a shifter as comfortable in his human form as he was in his animal body. "No matter the tribunal's judgment, know that I am proud of both the soldier and the woman. Blood pacts matter. But sometimes, Fay, the pacts that matter most are the ones formed from the heart and forged in trust. I'll see you inside the courtroom." Raicho strolled from the attorney-client conference room with a final scowl to the MPs. His declaration was no less impactful for him not being a tribunal judge.

"Sorry about the handcuffs, ma'am. We didn't know."

"Know what?"

The second MP, who'd stationed herself by the door, shook her head. "Not our place to say, ma'am. We were told to escort you to the first-floor courtroom. Your father obviously knows the way."

Raicho had indeed known the way. Their eyes met when she'd entered the courtroom. They slid from Raicho to Jelani, who stood beside her father.

They could be father and son with their matching frowns.

From between Jelani's and Kwame's broad shoulders, Durah waved, a tentative hand movement Fayola returned with a brisk nod. Retired Diello Madana and Belay Njeri completed the row.

They must've received a personal invitation too. But why? I went from being alone at my hearing to having a gallery of family and friends at my sentencing.

Seated behind Fayola's loved ones were two full benches—ten people on each bench.

I don't know them. Despite minor design differences, they're wearing the standard black, gray, and white uniform of kettle law enforcement officers. Why are they here? A lesson on how not to end their service to the Wake?

"Good morning, Diello Fayola."

She snapped to attention at the sound of Kamau Audre's dulcet voice.

The Rashidi Tribunal—two women and one man—reclined in black leather chairs behind a twenty-foot wooden desk that looked more like a CEO's executive conference table than a military judge's bench.

As she had five months earlier, Fayola stood at the defendant's table, her court-appointed judge advocate beside her. Except for the service ribbons and badges decorating their dress blacks officer jackets, Fayola wore the same uniform as the kamaus. In her barrack prison, she'd prepared for the day by donning a crisp long-sleeved white shirt she'd tucked into black pants, a pair of dress black shoes shined to perfection, and a black neck tab that invariably felt as if one were being choked by a grizzly bear.

"Good morning, ma'am."

"I see we've quite the audience today." Kamau Audre inclined her head to those gathered. "Welcome. Thank you all for accepting our invitation." The kamau paused, and Fayola did not dare look behind her to see how Raicho and Jelani responded to her loose interpretation of the word *invitation*. "Very good then. Order in all things, in this courtroom. Shall we proceed?"

Judge Advocate Nikosana was a soft-spoken man whose kind eyes and reassuring smile would've had Fayola turning him away if she needed a shark by her side to mount a ruthless defense. She hadn't. Then and now, Fayola most needed Nikosana's sweet nature.

"Yes, ma'am. My client has waited patiently for this day."

Not a shark, but Nikosana has bite.

"Despite her presence in the courthouse, I've been held in this room and kept from my client."

Nikosana's "Why" was implied, but the man could have no more expected one of the kamaus to reply than Fayola could have anticipated what would come next.

"You are excused, judge advocate." Kamau Audre had spoken to Nikosana, but her narrowed gaze held Fayola's.

"W-what? But I'm—"

"No longer required." Kamau Audre, a woman who appeared as if she'd spent her century on Earth Pact lifting weights with her face, scratched a chin as unyielding as marble. "You've served your purpose." The kamau waved her hand as if shooing a fly away from her picnicked lunch. "Go. We appreciate your service. No doubt, so too does Diello Fayola."

Fayola thought Nikosana would scurry away, afraid of the tribunal's wrath if he didn't take his dismissal in obligatory silence. Instead, he took his time collecting his possessions—a mobile, laptop, and folders. All the while, he spoke, not in mumbles or whispers but in a strident voice of a shark he'd hidden from them all.

"You've kept her confined to an empty barrack twenty-three hours a day for five months. You barely gave her time to recover from her wounds before holding her hearing. Unethical. You've denied her access to her attorney on the day she's supposed to be sentenced. Illegal. You accepted her guilty plea before granting me permission to meet with her. Also illegal."

Shoving his folders under an arm, and his mobile in his pants pocket, Nikosana snatched his laptop case from the table.

Despite being the one whose future hung in the balance, Fayola found herself reaching a hand out to the older man, wanting to soothe his ruffled feathers. "I'll be fine. Thank you for everything."

"You would've found yourself here without me because we are all the Wake's tools." Leaning in close, he lowered his tone to the one she'd mistaken as kindness only. "They want something from you. I didn't want to believe it, but there is no other reasonable explanation for their misconduct. They'll want you to believe they have all the power. Let their arrogance be your strength."

Unsure what, if anything, she should say, Fayola shook Nikosana's hand.

"Good luck, Diello Fayola."

She didn't watch him walk away, but she did hear the opening and closing of the courtroom door.

Kamau Thulani, the sole male on the tribunal, tsked. At one hundred fifty-one, Thulani was also the ranking member of the tribunal. "Nikosana is a good servant of the Wake, Audre."

That's as close as one kamau will get to chastising another in public. Which leaves only me. I wasn't allowed to say goodbye to Jelani and the others before being arrested and escorted from the hospital. The arresting MPs shackled my wrists and ankles, not that I would've tried to flee.

Kamau Thulani granted Fayola a sparkling, white-toothed grin that sent frissons of wariness up her spine. "You have been a delight to get to know." Thulani nodded to the piles of gold folders in front of the tribunal. "Using so much paper is a wasteful act of a bygone era. Still, I enjoy the feel of paper between my fingers. But not as much as I do this visual. Have you counted the folders?"

"Forty."

"Quite right."

"Forty missions. Forty folders. A lot of wasted paper."

Kamau Thulani tsked again, dimming his unreadable smile. "That's not what I meant by wasteful and, after reading your mission reports—very carefully, I might add—I know you understood me quite well."

Kamau Haseena removed a folder from atop a pile directly in front of her. "The first thirty pages include every test you've ever taken—from basic training to years of mandatory in-service. Perfect scores. I would claim that an impossible feat, but I've spoken with every one of your former commanding officers, and they share the same opinion of you. Curious?"

Not even a little. I know what people think of me, particularly those who don't know me well but think they do.

"Ah, yes, there. I saw it at your hearing, but it's more defined now. Intelligent to the point of ennui. Respectful but with a hint of disdain. Strategic and hardworking, but in pursuit of a single goal. One consuming mission."

Kamau Audre pushed a pile of folders, sending papers flying. "A perfect, imperfect soldier."

"I followed orders. Served the Wake."

"Yes, you served. We all serve. But hollow actions aren't true service."

Fayola considered swallowing a retort. Her entire adult life had consisted of silent but false agreement. The military did not care for anyone's opinion other than their own. So, Fayola had stayed both quiet and the course. No matter how she felt inside, voicing her thoughts wouldn't change the fact that every impundulu served the Wake. The Wake came first. Except . . .

"Risking my life, over and again, was not hollow acts of service. The Wake has my body and my loyalty. Everything else belongs to me. I won't give you more."

Kamau Thulani grinned at her again, brown skin folding in on itself with the lifting of lips capable of sentencing her to decades in prison. "You could have left the orphans at the clinic, but you did not. You could have lied to Belay Njeri, but you did not. Between both of those decisions, there were many others you could have made that would have protected you from this tribunal. You were aware Tikala had security cameras at their borders, correct?"

"Yes."

"But you left them intact. Proof. Evidence that could be used against you in a court of law or court of public opinion. Are you that honest, or are you only smart on paper?"

Fayola could still feel where the cuffs had bitten into her skin. But she could no longer hear the rotating click of the gears that lowered her body temperature. She hadn't shifted since finalizing her mission with Dr. Pérez-Soto. In her human form, Fayola had ridden on Jelani's back. Her left eye had bled blood lightning the entire flight.

Jelani had rushed her to the nearest Wake hospital. A skilled surgeon had saved her eye, while three days' worth of nanite injections had restored her sight.

I survived all of that. I will not permit the kamaus to perform a public autopsy on me.

"Permission to speak freely?"

As if expecting her request, maybe even pleased by it, if she interpreted their smirks correctly, they inclined their heads.

"By all means," Kamau Thulani added to his physical assent. "We have waited five months for you to say something as interesting as what we watched on the Tikala border security footage."

Fayola assumed they had viewed the recording. The Tikala government, as far as she knew, had no reason to deny the tribunal's request for evidence in a criminal investigation. They would have also requested an interview with Dr. Pérez-Soto. Like the Tikala government, the pediatrician would have had no reason not to cooperate.

A few of the older children may have also been interviewed. With so many obvious avenues to obtaining the truth, why would

I risk compounding my actions with lies? Yet they seem intrigued. I don't trust them. "Sentence me now or release me."

Kamau Thulani's grin faded to faint reproach, while Kamau Audre pushed to her feet, sending her chair rolling. But it was Kamau Haseena's reaction that garnered the most attention.

The woman threw her head back and laughed. "You are a delight." Kamau Haseena wiped away the laugh tears with the back of her hand. Then, just as effectively, she swiped a pile of folders onto the floor. "Tell this tribunal the name of someone you've rescued during one of your missions." Before Fayola could part her lips on a reply, Kamau Haseena lifted a finger. "And don't say Dr. Teresa Pérez-Soto."

"Then I don't have an answer."

"What about the twenty-one orphans? Do you recall any of their names?"

A flutter of guilt began in her stomach, drifted to balled fists then spread to a face heated from anger.

Kamau Haseena raised the same finger, wagging it at Fayola. "The answer is right there. Controlled fire doused by cold guilt. Two young ones died."

Kamau Audre retrieved her chair, returned it to the bench, and sat. "We saw them. They worked as a team. They fought. They tried and, for most, they succeeded in escaping the Sunhung soldiers and crossing into Tikala. Bear and elephant shifters and humans."

"Tell us," Kamau Thulani said. "Tell us what you told them."

Kamau Haseena's finger remained pointed at Fayola, and her voice held no residual humor. "Tell us what you did to earn their trust in such a short time."

"They cried when you were hurt," Kamau Audre said, as if Fayola could so easily forget the sound of broken sobs punctuated by distressed breathing.

"They screamed your name," Kamau Thulani added.

Kamau Haseena snorted at the hand she slowly lowered to the table as if she'd forgotten the appendage. "They called you Dela Eden. Their savior. A powerful but ultimately weighty title."

Kamau Thulani pulled a folder from a stack. Opening it, he flipped through a few pages before stopping on one. "We know the training you received, beginning with Retired Diello Madana. She will work you until you drop, then slap you awake and have you begin again. She sent a letter of request to the Mokal City Police Department, asking them to accept every member of your basic training team. Did you know?"

"I suspected."

"Do you know why she would make such a request?"

Fayola glanced over her shoulder. She hadn't dared before. However, she now understood why the tribunal had forbidden her friends and family at her hearing but commanded their attendance at what should have been her sentencing.

Jelani and Raicho appeared as if they'd been forced to drink elephant blood. Their distaste for the odd proceedings tightened their jaws and darkened their eyes. Kwame's grin, cheerful and bright, was a refreshing rainbow in a gloomy sky.

Durah's wink and exaggerated pouty lips, from which she blew Fayola kisses, reminded her of life before special ops missions. Then, it had been a life when friends could hang out, gorge themselves on blood desserts and pretend the world wasn't horrible for far too many people.

Finally, Fayola's gaze settled on Retired Diello Madana. Her long braids cascaded down her front, gathering in her lap like yarn awaiting a knitter's skillful touch. There were times, during basic training, Fayola had wished for a less demanding, less perceptive trainer. But those had been naïve complaints from a girl who would grow into a grateful soldier.

Unlike the cuffs, Diello Madana never sought to dampen her pupils' spirits. Instead, she expected us to fly in ways other than in the sky.

Diello Madana's curt nod delivered its intended message.

Fayola turned back to the tribunal. Instead of answering Kamau Thulani's question, she simply said: "Wake law can never govern the heart."

"So you choose to disobey," Kamau Thulani said.

"Peng, Orion, Jwahir, Huan, Mei lien . . ." One by one, Fayola named each of Dr. Pérez-Soto's children. "Because of Wake law, I had every intention of leaving those children to their undeserved fate. Because of our pact with Dr. Pérez-Soto's brother, no room existed in the scope of my mandate to include the children. One impundulu was dispatched for a solo rescue. An emotional war should not have waged within me—my mind versus my heart. Rules and regulations versus empathy and ethics. Death or disobedience."

Kamau Thulani flipped to another page in the folder. "Death *and* disobedience."

"Unfortunately, yes."

"You would make the same decision, would you not?"

She shook her head. "No. If I could do it over again, I would slaughter every one of those Sunhung border guards instead of sparing their lives at the business park. If I had, Peng and Orion would still be alive. If I had, I would have protected the minds of children from the trauma of that night. Murder is rarely the best recourse. That day, it would have been."

"For the children?"

"Yes, Kamau Audre. On that night, the children were the only innocent souls at the Tikala border. The rest of us had blood on our hands long before our fates collided. We all know I fulfilled my military obligation to the Wake with the fortieth mission. Just as we all know I broke Wake law while doing it. I request a proper sentence or a dismissal of all charges. Having my loved ones here, no more than keeping me locked on this base, will alter what I've already accepted in my heart."

"Which is?" Kamau Haseena asked.

Fayola glanced over her shoulder again. A sharp, claw-like pain stabbed her heart and punctured a lung, making breathing difficult when she said, "I take solace in that our people are long-lived and that my love for my family is as deep as theirs is for me. Whatever your sentence, it will not alter that fortifying truth. Now," she refocused her attention on the kamaus, "send me to prison or set me free. Either way, this case ends today."

As if she'd hadn't given the most powerful people on the planet, second only to the Wake president, an ultimatum, the Rashidi Tribunal stared at her with eyes so piercing she readied herself for three lightning attacks.

None came.

But her heart still pounded in her ears like a drummer on the battlefield, sending messages to her brain. Fight or flight.

"We have no intention of sending you to prison," Kamau Thulani told her. "But you also aren't free to begin your civilian life."

"I don't understand."

"You will. There's a recording we want you to see."

A grainy holographic image appeared in the space between the defendant's table and the judge's bench. A human girl with eyes a lighter shade of golden-brown than her hair blinked at whatever screen she'd used to record the message.

Matted, unkempt hair. Sunken eyes rimmed black. Protruding shoulders. This can't be right. She can't be the same little girl who—

"Please, Dela Eden, I need your help . . ."

9: It Feels Just Right

2123
One Month Earlier
The People's Democratic Republic of Tikala
Zakot Mountains
Balo Creek Canyon

"It's time for your medicine, Ms. Seager." Jwahir shook the pill bottle, hoping the sound would draw the old woman's attention away from the squirrels outside of her window. But, unfortunately, her voice alone rarely had any effect, so she moved closer, a glass of water in her other hand. The one that held the pill bottle maintained a rhythmic rattle as if it were a rumble shaker filled with beads or pebbles.

Jwahir had learned not to stand directly behind Ms. Seager's electric wheelchair, so she stopped to the woman's right. She had also discovered that old people—or maybe only this particular elderly person—could not be rushed.

She stares out this window every day. There's nothing to see but that huge tree with yellow and orange leaves. Squirrels too. They climb onto the windowsill. Probably because I used to open the window for Ms. Seager, who would feed them her food. I didn't know I wasn't supposed to listen to her. She is an adult. When an adult tells me to do something, I do it. But listening to her got me into trouble, so I don't do that anymore. I'm still expected to listen to adults, though, but only to Mr. Seager.

"So pretty." Ms. Seager raised an arm covered by a white rose print cotton robe. She pointed at the scenery beyond the window but, for several seconds, all Jwahir saw was a thin, pale arm with sagging, wrinkled skin soft to the touch. She had no more desired to see Ms. Seager's naked body than she'd wanted the responsibility of washing her. "I used to have a garden right there."

"Oh, okay."

Jwahir could never tell if Ms. Seager's stories were real memories or false ones; not that it mattered because whereas she mostly ignored Jwahir's voice, she expected Jwahir to listen to hers "with respect."

Sensing the shift from what should have been a five-minute chore to one of Ms. Seager's long-winded stories, Jwahir placed the pill bottle and glass of water on the nightstand. Then, not bothering to return to Ms. Seager's side, she sat on the floor, wedging herself between the nightstand to her right and the wall to her left. Drawing her legs upward, she lowered her chin to her knees and pretended to give Ms. Seager her full respectful attention.

"My husband planted a rosebush for our first anniversary. For our second anniversary . . ."

What felt like an hour later, but may have only been twenty minutes, the crisp sound of Ms. Seager's mindless chatter turned into harsh wheezing. Still, Jwahir stayed put instead of dashing from the room.

One.

Two.

Three.

Tear droplets fell like rain weighing down a flower's silky petals.

Drip.

Drip.

While Ms. Seager is asleep and her son is working up at the Forest Center, I must try again. He should be busy checking in the group of human tourists visiting. Today might be my last chance to get inside the cabin house again. Even if I have to wait all day for the right opportunity, and risk Mr. Seager's wrath for being outside without permission, I have to try.

Moving quickly but quietly, Jwahir rushed to the bedroom door. With a final look to Ms. Seager, her head of snowy hair hung low. The rough, grating sound of snoring confirmed she'd drifted into a deep sleep.

Jwahir took off—out of the bedroom, through the Seagers' private cabin and into the bright light of day. Jumping over downed branches and slipping on wet leaves, she ran through the forest, stopping when she reached the forked trail.

Sugar Maple Ridge homes are to my right. Cedar, Hemlock, and Birch houses are to my left. I'll run into the Beech row houses and Balo Creek if I keep going straight. The Beech houses have bunk beds. I always wanted bunk beds, but Mommy and Daddy said one child didn't need two beds. I should've asked for a brother or sister first then bunk beds.

Jwahir turned left, sprinting down the hiking trail and between tall trees with wide, flat colorful leaves so large and plentiful they protected her from the worst of the sun's heat. Then, spotting the cabin rental she sought, a three-story single-family log cabin home with a wraparound porch built between three reddish-brown cedar trees with clusters of blue-green needles, Jwahir darted to a cedar tree across from the house.

From her hiding spot behind the 160-foot tree, she waited. But the wait wasn't like her time in Ms. Seager's bedroom. The woman's disjointed stories were irrelevant but gave Jwahir a little extra time between chores.

Only fifteen minutes passed before the front door opened, revealing a bear shifter family of three. A little boy, chubby cheeked and full of energy, squirmed in his father's arms. Laughing, the father set the boy on the porch, only for the child to lunge for the steps.

"Oh, no you don't, you little speed demon." The mother, a woman whose big, kind smile reminded Jwahir of her own mother, caught the little boy around his waist. "Slow down before you fall down the damp steps."

"Won't fall."

"Yeah, you say that now."

As he'd done with his father, the boy twisted this way and that. "I won't fall, Mama."

Ignoring her son, the mother carried him down the porch steps before setting him on grass still wet from last night's rain shower. "Now you won't fall."

"Say parents the world over until their child trips over air." The father, as tall as any bear shifter she'd seen, kissed his wife's cheek. Then, dropping to his knees, he bent forward. "Climb on, Kadeem. The view will be better from up here."

With a big *whoop* from such a little kid, Kadeem scrambled onto his father's back. Legs hung over shoulders and down the chest, while his hands were held safely in his father's grip.

"Ready?"

"Yup. Let's go, Papa. All the way to the creek."

"Then lunch," the mother said in an unnecessarily loud voice. "I fixed a pot of chili."

"Mine is better," the father boasted.

Kadeem looked in the direction of the cabin. "Nope, mine is the best."

"Yours?" the parents asked in unison.

Kadeem nodded. "I mixed Mama's and Papa's."

"Oh, did you, my baby bear? I thought your papa was the one who filled your bowl. That explains the mess on the countertop and kitchen table."

Kadeem growled, and Jwahir understood the feeling. "Mama, I'm not a baby. I'm a whole four."

"Oh, I see, a whole four, hmm. Okay. Well, we will have to see who has the best chili this side of Balo Creek Canyon when we return." She swatted her husband's butt. "Off with the two of you then. Less talking and more hiking."

Father and son took off toward the path she'd come up, but the mother paused, glanced over her shoulder toward the . . . Jwahir shifted, making sure the tree hid all of her.

Holding her breath, she waited. Listened.

Did she see me? Hear me? I was quiet, but shifters' hearing is better than humans'. Please, don't let her have heard me.

"Come on, Nita."

"Yeah, yeah, I'm coming. We'll be gone for about two hours."

"Why did you just yell that? Oh, never mind. Yeah, we'll be back in two hours. Plenty of time."

Jwahir didn't dare look, but her heart raced faster than she could run. Faster than . . . *crunch, crunch.*

I think she's walking away. I can't hear her boots on twigs as much now.

Knees pulled to her chest, she shivered like the rabbit she'd found last week.

Drenched and afraid, Jwahir had tucked the cute little forest animal into her jacket with the broken zipper. Unfortunately, she didn't have an umbrella, hat, or hood to keep her dry. But she offered what protection she could to her new friend. It hadn't been much and, the next day, she couldn't find the rabbit, but she'd been given a piece of meat that night for dinner. Too late, she'd figured out what she'd eaten, but hunger had dulled her disgust.

I don't have friends anymore. No mommy and daddy, like little Kadeem has. Jwahir's throat tightened, and her eyes slammed shut. *I don't want to cry again. I'm not a baby. I'm not. I have to keep trying. I must be brave, like Dela Eden.*

Jumping to her feet, Jwahir glanced around the tree. *They really are gone. But they'll be back in two hours. Gotta hurry.*

Slipping on twigs and wet leaves, Jwahir dashed toward the cabin. Reaching the front door, she grinned when the knob turned easily.

They always leave their door unlocked. Wherever they're from, they must live in a safe neighborhood. No mean soldiers. No terrible war.

Jwahir made sure to close the door behind her in case a guest noticed it was open. She didn't think that would happen since only Cedar House had occupants of the three lodgings in this part of Balo Creek Canyon. Jwahir had already paid the cost of carelessness. She wouldn't make the same mistake twice.

The cabin opened into a common area—shiny wooden floors throughout. A single bear-sized sofa, thick cushions and wide pillows, occupied the center of the room. A three-panel fireplace screen with a leaf design covered the fireplace in front of the overstuffed sofa. Having lived at the center for almost half a year, Jwahir knew the signs of a fireplace that had been used. However, this one had not, probably because of the young bear in residence.

I should hurry. I know where the cabin's computer is kept. But something smells really good, and they said they'd be gone for two hours. I have time.

Led more by her growling stomach than her thinking mind, Jwahir pretended this was her home, the nice couple with the cute little boy was her family and the bowls of chili on the kitchen table had been left for her.

She slid into the chair in front of a pink metal bowl with a lid. A spoon and napkin had already been laid out beside the bowl, waiting to be used by her, Jwahir reasoned, as she snatched up the spoon and removed the bowl's lid.

Inhaling the strong, sharp scent, her body lurched forward in a desperate, unconscious plea.

I'm so hungry. I know it's wrong to steal, but I don't know what else to do. The last two times, I only took fruit and nuts. Nothing the family would miss. If I eat this chili, they'll know someone was here.

Swiping at a rogue tear, Jwahir's grumbling stomach ended her internal debate. She dug into the bowl of chili. One spoonful. Two. As if her butt was on fire, instead of her mouth, Jwahir jumped from the table. Rushing to the refrigerator, she swung it open, grabbed a carton of milk and drank.

Too many chili peppers. Yuck. Why would someone use so many? Is it a bear thing?

Bringing the carton of milk with her, Jwahir returned to the table. This time, she sat in front of the green bowl.

Maybe this one will be better. The other one had beans and ground beef. I like both. This one also smells good. Looks good too. It even has melted cheese on the top. Yummy.

Jwahir downed more milk, took a deep breath, and then used the clean spoon beside the bowl.

She ate. One spoonful. Two.

Not spicy. There are no chili peppers and whatever else adults put in chili to make it taste good. Where is the flavor? Is it supposed to be watery? The other one was thick with lots of stuff in it. But it was too hot. This one is too . . . boring. I'm not sure if that's the right word.

Carton of milk in hand, Jwahir made her way around the table to the third and final bowl. Pink was her favorite color, so she'd first tried the chili in that bowl. Of the three colors of the bowls, green was her second favorite. Many of her former classmates liked blue—mainly the boys—but she never understood their preference. At least with green, there could be lime green and pear green—her favorite fruit.

As long as it isn't hot like the first one, I'll eat it, even if I have to force myself. I don't have the right to complain. I'm not even a guest. None of this food was made for me.

For the third time, Jwahir removed a lid from a metal bowl, picked up the spoon meant for the person whose food she was about to eat, and scooped out a big spoonful of the chili.

Thicker than the second one but a little thinner than the first. That strong, sharp scent is back. But maybe a little less strong. I can see beans, ground beef, and onions. Cool, there's a smiley face made from shredded cheese.

Jwahir shoved the spoon into her mouth, prepared for disappointment, but determined to eat her fill no matter the taste. If possible, her stomach and tongue did a happy dance.

This is good. Not too hot. Not too boring. It's just right. Blue is my new favorite color.

Jwahir tore into the bowl of chili, eating so fast she bit her tongue. The pain didn't stop her, though. She swallowed every drop. Jwahir knew better. Her parents had taught her manners but

. . .

Dropping the spoon to the table, she wet her first two fingers then used them to clean the inside of the bowl, seeking every drop of the chili.

Is there more, like this one? The chili must be in those pots on the countertop. Kadeem said he'd mixed the two. I'll try doing that too. I'm taller than him, so I won't need that stool over there. I won't try what he did yet, though. I should use the computer first.

Wiping her mouth on the napkin left beside the blue bowl, Jwahir forced away the thought of the last time she'd had a decent meal.

It's not fair. Why are some adults so mean? I'm not a bad girl, no matter what Mr. Seager says. He's the bad one. I want to go home. Finishing off the milk, she threw the carton in the trash can. *But I don't have a home anymore. That's not fair either.* Jwahir returned to the common area. Her stomach clenched as she trudged along, spirit dimmed. *I don't have anything. Nothing belongs to me except for my hunger and fear.*

Jwahir eyed the two brown leather recliners and the small rocking chair. The recliners were situated under windows, making them perfect locations for reading. However, a rocking chair sat beside an open chest of toys in the corner of the room.

Knowing she shouldn't, but doing it anyway, like her detour to the kitchen, Jwahir skipped to the other side of the room.

I haven't seen toys since my seventh birthday. Daddy and Mommy took me to the mall instead of buying my presents online. I built a stuffed bunny rabbit. Rainbow with a pink nose, yellow ballerina slippers, and a pink and yellow tutu. So pretty.

Jwahir tried to take her birthday bunny with her, even crying when her father refused to return to their burning home to retrieve the stuffed animal.

I was such a baby back then. Daddy was trying to keep Mommy and me safe. I cried and made him feel bad for leaving most of our stuff behind.

Jwahir removed a handheld video game from the chest. Grinning, she hopped across the room, jumped onto the largest of the recliners, and . . . frowned. *Too hard.* She shifted, searching for the perfect spot in the big chair to play the game. *Still too hard. And big. I thought it would be great to sit in this big chair. Everything I'm given now is too small or not enough.*

Sliding from the hard chair, Jwahir clutched the game in one hand as she darted to the recliner under the second window. She could tell this would be a better spot than the first. The window had been left ajar, letting in a warm breeze and the spicy scent of cedar.

This is much better. Softer. Really soft. Jwahir turned on the game. She'd played basketball at school, so she knew the rules. *This game is going to be so much fu . . . Why am I sinking?* Jwahir felt like she'd fallen into a trap for humans with little butts. Digging her elbows into the arms of the recliner, Jwahir heaved upward until she pulled herself free. *The chair tried to eat me.* Stomping back to the toy chest, she glared at the rocking chair she knew was meant for a kid as small as Kadeem. Jwahir sat, disliking how perfectly it fit her, despite turning eight two months ago.

The first chair was too hard. The second was too soft. But this rocking chair is just right.

Jwahir had learned how to tell time in the first grade. So even though she saw no clock in the room, the handheld sports game had an internal clock. She'd spent longer downstairs and in the cabin than planned, but she still had plenty of time. Besides, if she couldn't figure out how to find her online, she didn't know if she would have another chance to sneak back there.

I just want to play for a little while. A few minutes. Is that so wrong? I'm not a grown-up, no matter how many chores I'm given. I just want to play. Be a kid. Ten minutes. That's all.

Of course, Jwahir played longer than ten minutes and more than basketball on the video game. "Yay, touchdown!" She leapt onto the chair, forgetting it wasn't a recliner like the others. True to its name, the chair not only rocked backward but crashed to the floor. The video game went flying. Jwahir did not. She fell with the chair, the heels of her hiking boots striking an armrest and snapping it in two jagged pieces.

Oh no, I'm going to be in so much trouble. Maybe I can fix it. Will glue work?

The girl who used to earn high marks in school knew glue would not be enough to repair the damage she'd done, so Jwahir dragged herself to her feet and left the mess she'd made.

I'm so stupid. None of this is mine. Not the food and toys. Not even that small rocking chair. I have to focus. Act older. Be smarter. Orion and Peng died. No, they were killed. They did their best to help us reach the border. They tried their hardest. I must do the same.

Jwahir pushed open the door to a spacious bedroom. Sun blazed through the windows that covered the top half of the walls. She could see the path the family of bears had taken from this level. Face pressed to a window, she searched for signs someone neared. Then, hearing and seeing no one, Jwahir claimed the desk chair.

Only the luxury cabins were supplied with a personal computer and Wi-Fi. Of those three, only this one was occupied, and the Wi-Fi turned on.

I know the password. It's just the name of the cabin. Cedar House. But what should I search once I'm logged on? I know her real name, although I wasted thirty minutes searching for Dela Eden the first time. But Diello Fayola didn't come up either. So I searched impundulus and found the name of their country. But I don't know what to do. How can I find her with just those two names? Will she remember me? Will she come? She didn't ask for blood the last time. But she got hurt trying to help us. I don't want her to get hurt again.

Jwahir typed in Benekal and Tikala, grateful the internet corrected her spelling. She had no idea what she was looking at or should be looking for, but opted to click on the first link in the search results.

"The United Wake of Benekal Embassy in The People's Democratic Republic of Tikala," she read aloud.

The site had a lot of words she either couldn't pronounce or didn't know the meaning of, but she'd shopped with her mother online enough to know what Contact Us meant. So she clicked the hyperlinked words.

A blank form appeared. She followed directions, typing in her first and last name. The box underneath asked for an email address. Unfortunately, she didn't have one except for the student email assigned to her last school year. Jwahir no longer recalled her password, but her email was her full name followed by the name of her school.

"Jwahir Hall at Shaw Howard Elementary School dot education. What else do I need? A message." She stared at the empty message box. "I could type it or . . . yes, this form accepts a recorded message. That has to be better than writing it all out. Maybe seeing me will help her remember. I should think of something to offer as my side of the pact. She won't accept blood from a kid. What else do I have to offer Dela Eden?"

She pushed the red record circle beside the message box, knowing this would be her final opportunity. She'd made a mess in the cabin, eating food that would be missed, and the renters would likely report what happened to Mr. Seager.

He might not know it was me, but I'll still get into trouble for leaving his mother alone for so long. She's asleep, but he won't care. I'm not supposed to do anything other than what he tells me to do. No going outside without permission, no talking to the guests, and no using the computers.

"Please, Dela Eden, I need your help. I mean Diello Fayola. I know that's your name. I remember. I hope you remember me. Jwahir. I . . . umm, I'm sorry. I know you already saved me and the others. You were hurt because of us. Your eye looked really bad. I hope it's better."

Jwahir slid her hand into her pants pocket. She couldn't dare let Mr. Seager know what she had. It was hers . . . well, not exactly hers, but it was given to her for safekeeping.

"I've tried to be brave like you. I do my best every day. I follow the rules most of the time. But I can't stay here. Mr. Seager is mean. He . . ."

Jwahir clamped a hand over her mouth, trying but failing to contain her sobs. But the surge of tears poured from her like bathwater overflowing a tub.

"He says I should be grateful that he took me in. That only a selfish brat wouldn't be. I'm not selfish, Dela Eden. He's just . . . he's just a terrible person. Will you help me, please? Take me away from here? Maybe back to Dr. Pérez-Soto, so she can find me a better home."

Jwahir bit her tongue when it started to form the second part of her request.

If I ask her that, she might not come. But Dela Eden protects kids like me from bullies.

"I know you won't take my blood." She removed the item from her pants pocket. "Will you accept this as my pact payment? I forgot to return it. It's special to you. I could tell. I've kept it safe. I still will, even if you don't come."

Jwahir relayed all she knew about where Mr. Seager had taken her after Dr. Pérez-Soto's husband had handed her over to a man whose smile lied.

He's worse than those soldiers. With them, I knew they were dangerous. They didn't pretend they were good people.

She stopped the recording and submitted her message with a weary sense of relief.

I did my best, but I'm so tired.

Tempted by the king-size bed with big, fluffy pillows, Jwahir checked the time on the computer.

I have forty minutes. Time enough for a short nap. I'll be gone before the bear family returns.

She climbed onto the bed. *Come on. Not again. Too hard.*

Rushing from the room, she ran to the bedroom across the hall. A bed, a little smaller than the one she'd just been on, called to her.

Jwahir answered the call only to find herself shifting in a weird wave motion. The bed appeared normal enough—a box spring on a metal frame—but it felt less solid than a regular bed.

Not too hard. Not exactly too soft. But kind of like floating in water. Maybe I shouldn't risk taking a nap here. I've eaten and played. Best of all, I sent a message to someone who might know Dela Eden.

More curious than cautious, Jwahir entered the third bedroom. She wasn't surprised to see a twin-size bed in the smallest of the three rooms. Like the rocking chair, the bunk beds were meant for a small person.

Yawning, Jwahir lay on the bed. After what happened in the kitchen with the chili and in the common area with the chairs, Jwahir suspected this bed would be . . . *Not too hard. Not too floaty. It feels just right.*

With dreams of freedom in her head and a prayer on her lips, Jwahir drifted off to sleep.

10: Help is Coming

2123
The United Wake of Benekal
Fort Kumelo City
The United Wake of Benekal Military Courthouse

Talons formed, scratching the hardwood flooring's finish like a beaver stripping bark from the base of a tree. Wings and feathers replaced skin and clothing. Gold lightning sparked from Fayola's eyes, going off like a silent firecracker.

She turned away from the tribunal. *I don't know how this could have happened, but I'll find out after I get Jwahir out of that place.*

"We haven't given you permission to leave," Kamau Haseena said, her objection like freezing rain on overheated flesh.

What patience remained for the tribunal's unorthodox hearing evaporated the second she saw a malnourished Jwahir.

"I'm going to her. I assume you've done nothing to help the child since learning of the recording. Why else would you show me her message, if the situation had already been resolved?" Fayola took another step toward the courtroom door but stopped.

The two military police officers from earlier and six others stationed in the courtroom shifted into their impundulu form.

Fayola hadn't paid the other MPs any attention earlier, deeming them inconsequential.

Jelani jumped to his feet, shifting on the upward movement. Raicho did the same, followed by Durah and Kwame.

Snap. Snap. Gallery benches broke into pieces, the wood no match for the might of impundulu wings in fluttering, forceful motion.

Madana swore the way she had during basic training—loudly and with creative vulgarity.

As if removing shrapnel from a bleeding wound, Belay Njeri plucked bits of the destroyed bench from her curly frohawk updo with care. Frowning, she glanced between the shifted impundulus to her right and the MPs to her left.

Scrambling away from Fayola's father and friends, the twenty young soldiers looked torn.

"Stay neutral," she told them at the same time Kamau Thulani said, "Everyone, stand down."

No one moved, which, for people trained as soldiers from the age of fifteen, was as close to surrender as any impundulu would come. Still, Fayola would plow through the MPs if they didn't step aside.

"Order them to move."

"You're too emotionally invested in that child's welfare," Kamau Audre said, but Fayola sensed an undercurrent of primal satisfaction. "We didn't show you her video message to set you off like a deer fleeing a burning scrubland."

"I disagree." Shifting on her taloned feet, Fayola turned to the tribunal, careful to keep her wings at her sides and her sparks of lightning confined to eyes turned golden. *"You wanted to see my reaction . . . and theirs,"* she said, referring to everyone in the

gallery. *"Now that you have, now that you've seen we have a pact stronger than blood and duty, please have the MPs step aside so I can go to Jwahir."*

Even during her training, fighting her own kind had not appealed. But Fayola prided herself on learning as much as possible, perfecting her skills, and challenging herself. She didn't believe in competing against others—measuring her worth and growth by someone else's standards. But military protocol overruled her personal beliefs, so she had battled her peers, just as they had fought her. They had neither been enemy combatants nor friends, but allies in a cause greater than themselves.

"I did not fulfill my end of the pact. I failed to keep her safe."

Kamau Haseena stood, brandishing a black folder. "Forty-one, not forty." The older woman arched a dark eyebrow, daring Fayola to contradict her lie.

She didn't know where the black folder had come from, but it hadn't been among the others. Fayola remained quiet, impatient to begin her rescue mission but grateful the tribunal hadn't viewed her action as a threat to their safety.

Kamau Haseena's laughter cut through the thick tension in the air behind Fayola. Without having to look, she knew no one had returned to their human form.

Just because the tribunal has overlooked my transgression, that doesn't mean the MPs are willing to grant me and my friends the benefit of the doubt.

Fayola shifted to her human form, a belated attempt at de-escalation.

"Very good." Kamau Haseena opened the folder but never took her eyes off Fayola. "When you return, there is much we need to discuss, beginning with your rejected unit proposal."

She had no idea what her proposal had to do with her hearing. Worse, she did not like the implied connection.

Kamau Audre also rose but with none of the angry force from earlier. "I can see your brain working in eyes so bright gold one would think you weren't still in your avian form. We will grant you leave, but you must return here in forty-eight hours."

"With the human child," Kamau Thulani added, accepting the black folder from Kamau Haseena as if the woman had handed him a freshly conjured impundulu egg. Holding the folder to his chest, he repeated Kamau Haseena's words: "There is much we need to discuss. You have proven you are willing to waste away in prison, foregoing a civilian life with your loved ones, if it means not extending your term of service. At the same time, you have also demonstrated an honorable commitment to your goodwill pact. Fitting for an impundulu whose name means one who walks with honor."

Goodwill pact. The same words Jelani used to describe my proposal. Although I hadn't used the term in my paper, he was correct. What I viewed as a rogue mission had, in truth, been a goodwill pact. I was blind long before that bullet threatened to claim my sight. What else did I fail to see during my fortieth mission?

"The Rashidi Tribunal grants you permission to complete your goodwill pact." Opening the folder that obviously contained her rejected proposal, Kamau Thulani tsked, a sound he either didn't care was annoying or hadn't noticed. "You do love your data." He flipped several pages. "A lot of it too. Brutal, disturbing numbers I cared not to read, much less think about."

The older man paused, a shadow creeping into dark, wizened eyes that had seen yet not seen the details of her proposal.

Why is he choosing to truly see them now? Why are any of them now concerned about a document almost three years old? I assume that's part of what they want to speak with me about.

"I'm free to leave now?"

"Such a rude, impatient young woman." Kamau Audre waved her long hand with bluntly pointed fingernails in her direction. "Yes, yes, go. Save your little human friend."

"Thank you."

"You might want to reserve your appreciation until after our conversation. Do put away those wings," Kamau Audre said, still waving her hand as if it were one of her black and white wings capable of swatting a charging bear off course.

Telltale signs of shifting, flutters, and groans sounded behind her.

"That's better, but look at what you all have done to the poor gallery."

"And to the unfortunate floor," Kamau Haseena added.

"Don't mock me."

Raising her hands, as if in defeat, a smiling Kamau Haseena retook her seat. "I wouldn't think of it."

Kamau Thulani thumbed through more pages, his tsks growing in volume and intensity. "Retired diellos Raicho, Madana, and Durah, the tribunal appreciates your presence here today. However, we request that you not interject yourself into her goodwill mission. Belay Njeri and diellos Jelani and Kwame, you are ordered to do the same. As for you, Belay Fayola, we have taken the liberty of forming your new unit."

"My *what*?" she gritted out, voice a low, dangerous pitch the kamaus ignored as they would a drainage flow wind caressing their wings.

Kamau Haseena laughed, a raucous sound Fayola was tired of hearing. "Which word ruffles your feathers the most? Belay or new unit? Well, technically, new and unit are two words." Leaning elbows on a pile of folders, she sat forward, enjoying Fayola's predicament the way predators did their prey's fruitless whines. "On your flight to rescue your human, think what it would mean to be a belay of a unit whose sole purpose is to save children like your little Jwahir Hall. Then think back to all those data points you included in your proposal. 'Prevent, suppress, and punish.' Your words, *Belay* Fayola."

"But . . ." *Shit. I did write those words as the opening to the purpose of a new special forces unit.*

Kamau Thulani closed the folder with a reverence they hadn't shown when she'd offered the proposal for consideration years earlier. "The Criminal Exploitation Unit—an uncomplicated name for a spider's web of crimes that span countries. Your unit is young, skilled, and intelligent. We used your character profile guide as a basis for selection." Kamau Thulani paused. Either realizing he'd started a discussion they were to have tomorrow or sensing Fayola's lack of interest in anything other than the awful knowledge of her latest conscription.

Hands balled into fists and eyes burning lightning hot, Fayola turned and marched toward the closed courtroom door.

The MPs moved out of her way. One MP even opened the doors for her to exit.

Not just for me. For us. I hate this so much, but . . . The Criminal Exploitation Unit. Important. Needed.

Fayola bolted into the sky. Blue light scattered from east to west, brightening her field of vision to golden pinpoints of purpose.

Hold on, Jwahir. Help is coming.

The People's Democratic Republic of Tikala
Zakot Mountains
Balo Creek Canyon

"You've been out again." Mr. Seager stalked into Jwahir's bedroom, thick waist protruding over a black belt with a roaring bear head buckle.

She backed away from him. Her trembling legs and sweaty back were still sore from the last time he had stormed into her bedroom—eyes as wild and dangerous looking as the bear image on his silver buckle.

"I didn't go anywhere," she lied, pushing out the words through dry, cracked lips she sucked into her mouth, using her saliva to soothe the pain.

"You lie, little girl." A meaty hand larger than her face reached back and slammed the white door with a painted sun smiley face on the back closed with a terrifying *thud*. "You know the rules."

Jwahir's eyes lowered, watered. *I had to try again. She didn't come. I don't know what else to do. There's the butcher knife I stole from the kitchen.*

"But you insist on breaking them. Disobeying me at every turn."

I thought I got it to protect me from him. Using the heel of her hand to wipe away tears, Jwahir spared a glance to her neatly made bed and flat pillow, under which she'd hidden the butcher knife. *But I didn't. Not really. I'm not strong or brave enough to hurt Mr. Seager. Am I strong or brave enough to hurt myself?*

"I see another lesson is in order. Take off that dress and get on the bed."

As if someone had sewn her bare feet to the smooth wooden floor, spikes of sharp pain began at the tips of her ice-cold toes, gouged its way up thin legs, spread across narrow hips, and to a flat stomach that clenched and clutched, searching for stability as much as it did satiation.

She didn't move. "I-I'm sorry. I w-won't do it again."

He laughed, a cruel, inhuman rumble of thunder. "You need to learn, girl." A finger as wide as three of hers released the latch on his buckle.

Her eyes flashed to her pillow. *Can I do it? Will it hurt? Stupid question. It's going to hurt, but I can make it quick . . . I think.* She lifted her hand to her throat, pleased she'd managed the small feat. Then, sliding a finger from one end of her neck to the other, she felt the warmth of skin not meant for a knife's sharp, deadly touch.

"I said get on the bed."

His harsh, husky voice jolted her into movement. She ran for the bed on the other side of the room, jumping on it and reaching under the pillow. She despised everything about living with the Seagers except for one thing—the placement of her bed near a wide window. At night, she would lay in her bed counting stars and remembering life with her parents. Between chores, she would escape into her room and stare out of the window for a different reason. But for all the birds that had flown overhead, their wingspans short, beaks small, and feathers unimpressive, none of them had been the bird of her prayers.

Jwahir grabbed for the butcher knife, fearing she would have too few seconds to get the job done before Mr. Seager attacked— adding more scars and bruises to a mind and body incapable of surviving much more abuse.

If I'm going to die, I won't let it happen slowly and over years, my spirit beaten into submission, my body overworked. I won't die a slave. No choices. No freedom.

Steady fingers gripped the knife's black handle, warm from a pillow that had caught many of her tears—cotton soft and the closest she'd had to a comforting hand.

"What are you doing, you little . . ."

Jwahir pressed the tip of the knife to her throat. She had seen Mr. Seager use the twelve-inch stainless steel knife to cut slabs of steak into thick slices he slathered in olive oil before dipping them in a bowl of spices and putting the meat on his grill.

A hard, rough hand pinned her arm to the bed, holding it down by her elbow. "I wondered where that blade went. You are a sneaky one. Small and fierce too. I like that. I got you for Mom, but she won't be around forever, no more than you will stay a skinny, flat-chested girl. In two or three more years . . ." Leaning his weight on her elbow, she released the knife, afraid he'd break her arm if she didn't obey. "That's good. With time, patience, and a reminder of who is in control, anyone can be broken." The cool of his silver buckle, a raised bear face design with fangs, pressed against her upper thigh. "I paid good money for you, girl. I won't let you steal from me by killing yourself. The only thing that's free in my house is lessons."

Mr. Seager rose, and Jwahir wasted no time scrambling away from him and against the white bookcase headboard. When Mr. Seager had first brought her there, opening the door to this bedroom and shoving her inside with a, "This is your room. Fresh paint, and used bed and clothes left here by the guests' children. You be a good girl, do as you're told, and we'll get along just fine," she'd almost been hopeful.

He paid for me? No, he's a liar. A big, mean liar I wish would drop de—

"Not your face, though. Mom gets upset when she sees bruises on your face."

The sunny, midday sky that, when she pulled the white drapes with yellow stars to the side, the way they were now, lit up her room like glowworms illuminating a dusky campsite. As if she'd snapped the drapes closed, darkness swallowed the sun.

"Your back and thighs. She won't see all the trouble I have to go through to keep you in line. You'll learn your lesson this time or . . . What in the hell are you looking at?" Following her gaze, Mr. Seager twisted in the direction of the double-pane window.

She watched as the darkness drew nearer, a rhythmic swell of black between which white danced with the sun, the *boom*, *boom*, *boom* of thunder the opening score.

Mr. Seager rushed from the bed to the window. Curses flowed from him with stuttering exhalations, leaving him gulping for air. "S-so many." His gruff voice quavered as if someone had clamped their hand around his vocal cords and squeezed. "Ho-how? H-how?"

Boom.

Boom.

"You did this." Mr. Seager whirled on her, thin, pink lips pulled back, revealing bright white teeth that could rip out the throat she'd planned on slitting.

Boom.

Boom.

Bolts of gold lightning invaded the sky like meteoroids entering Earth Pact's atmosphere, a flurry of blinding light flashes and raging thunder.

He snarled. Lunged.

She screamed, knowing she stood no chance of getting to the closed bedroom door before he caught her.

Jwahir screamed and screamed, filling her lungs and releasing a great siren of sound that hammered against her invisible shackles.

Smack.

Her head smashed into the headboard. Ears rang, lips bled, and mouth filled with blood but still yelled the only two words that mattered.

"Dela Eden!"

Mr. Seager reared his hand back to strike her again. His fingernails lengthened into claws sharper than the butcher knife she'd stolen but hadn't tried to use before today because her parents had given their lives to save hers.

Suicide had been no way to honor their sacrifice but . . .

Smash. The wooden door crashed to the floor, shaking the room as if an elephant rampaged, lashing out at an ivory poacher.

No elephant shifter had broken down Jwahir's bedroom door, but the person who had was no less formidable for her smaller size. The last time they'd been in the same room, red blood had stained her all-black shirt and pants. Some of the blood had been hers but most belonged to the bears and elephants she'd fought. Her left eye had dripped blood lightning, while the other scanned first Jwahir then the other children with the same look she'd seen on her father's face when he'd checked her for injuries after their house fire.

Now, dressed in a formal white shirt, black suit jacket and pants, left eye healed and both trained on a stunned Mr. Seager, Diello Fayola oozed controlled menace.

"Who the fuck are you? Get out of my hou—"

"Binta."

A young woman, who wore a police officer's uniform, jogged into the room. Dimples framed her unsmiling cheeks, while pecan-colored eyes shifted from Diello Fayola to Jwahir, then settled on a snarling Mr. Seager.

He still loomed near. His razor-sharp claws were capable of killing her with one well-placed swipe.

"Yes, ma'am?"

"On the way here, you boasted of your speed."

"Yes, ma'am."

"Be faster than me."

"What are the two of you talking ab—"

In a blur—gold streaks of warped light—Diello Fayola and Binta moved.

Before she knew what was happening, Jwahir was snatched from the bed and cradled in Binta's protective feathery arms.

Oomph. Mr. Seager lay pinned under a fully shifted Diello Fayola. Jwahir's twin-size bed had collapsed under their combined weight. Curved talons Jwahir had seen rip into thick elephant hide caged Mr. Seager against the bed. Diello Fayola's long beak grazed his wide, flushed neck, a silent threat to slice him open and drink his blood.

"Th-this is a mistake. One big mistake. I-I have a sick mother. Elderly and sick. I needed help taking care of her. There's nothing wrong with that. I gave the human a home. Food. I took care of her. I . . ."

Jwahir wrapped arms around Binta's neck, realizing she hadn't shifted into her complete impundulu form. Instead, tall and lean, smooth black feathers covered an upright body not much taller than her human form. Her grayish-white beak led to a pointy head a shade of black lighter than the rest of her.

On the way out of her bedroom, Jwahir caught a glimpse of Diello Fayola's raised wing connecting with Mr. Seager's face.

For the first time since arriving there, Jwahir left the Seager cabin without the fear of having to return or the dread of failing to send a distress message while away.

Placing Jwahir on the ground outside of the Seager cabin, Binta then proceeded to shift into her human form. When finished, the transition of breaking and reforming everything, more spectacular when viewed close up, Binta smiled down at Jwahir, bringing her deep dimples to life. And while Jwahir could appreciate, maybe even envy the young woman's beauty, especially her enchanting brown eyes flecked with gold, she couldn't help but stumble backward. She fell to the hard grassy ground.

I saw their black wings. But . . . but . . . Mr. Seager was right. There are so many of them.

Binta lowered to a knee, her pretty eyes becoming browner, softer as she patted Jwahir's shoulder and wiped the blood from a lip she'd forgotten still bled. "You're safe. We won't hurt you, and neither will that man. Not ever again."

One of the police officers behind Binta, a male with cropped curly hair and as tall as Mr. Seager, but with none of the weight around his middle, removed his gray uniform jacket. Then, as if she were a helpless toddler, he assisted her into the garment, rolling up the sleeves to her elbows.

She winced at the slight pressure of his hand on her throbbing right elbow.

"Belay Fayola will make sure no one hurts you like this again," he told her.

The group of impundulu shifters nodded, sharing the same certainty as Jwahir in Diello . . . Belay Fayola's protective nature.

"By the way, I'm Cassius." Then, with the same tender care he'd used to help her into his jacket, Cassius lifted Jwahir to her feet.

"I'm Dominique," a young woman with eyes that reminded her of a delicious ripe plum said. The officer's head reminded her of the juicy fruit, too, considering it lacked a single lock of hair.

"Hi, I'm Jendayi, and this is my best friend, Marcel."

One by one, the impundulus introduced themselves. They had also surrounded her, twenty rescuers when she'd prayed for one.

They all pretended not to hear Mr. Seager's screams or his mother's repeated cries of, "Caedin, what's wrong?"

Fifteen minutes later, both sounds ceased. A minute later, the blockade of bodies parted, shifting to the left and right to form a straight line behind Jwahir. The woman she'd risked her life to contact stood in front of a cabin house that had never been her home.

Grabbing a fistful of Cassius's jacket, Jwahir lifted it past her knees and ran. Skidding to a halt, she stared up at her savior. "Dela Eden, you came."

"Of course I did." Belay Fayola bent to her level, eyes the same dark brown as the sweeping bangs with specks of blood splatter. "How else did you think I would retrieve my father's lishan medal?"

"Oh, yeah, your coin. I get it." Lifting Cassius's jacket again, Jwahir unbuttoned the side pocket of her favorite dress. Too tight across the shoulders and too short at the knees, the ivory dress with a rainbow-colored flying horse, wasn't so much pretty as the image on the dress was inspirational. Pulling out the coin, she showed it to Belay Fayola. "Thank you for saving me."

Instead of taking the coin . . . the lishan medal, Belay Fayola frowned. "You're thinner in person. I don't like it."

"Yeah, I . . . umm . . . yeah."

"You need fattening up, but the only food Jelani keeps in the fridge is blood desserts. Not exactly human friendly. A grocery run is in order."

I have no idea what's going on. I showed her the medal, but she didn't take it.

"Twenty of you, one of him," Belay Fayola said, speaking to the police officers she'd brought with her. "Not much of a meal to go around, but the flight was long, and we left home without packing B-rations. Leave some for Marcel and Eldrick."

"Ma'am, what are your orders for us?"

"There is an elderly woman inside. Main level, second bedroom on the right. She fainted when she saw me. Take her to the nearest hospital." Then, to Jwahir, she asked, "Do you know her medical condition?"

"Ms. Seager forgets a lot. She also tells me stories that don't always make sense."

"Medications?"

"Yeah, three pill bottles in the empty fruit bowl on the kitchen island. She also uses a wheelchair, but she can manage short walks with her walker."

"Secure her medicine and walker. Relay everything Jwahir said to the ER nurse and let them know the Wake will pay for the woman's palliative care."

"Yes, ma'am."

Who Jwahir assumed to be Marcel and Eldrick dashed past her and Fayola on their way to the cabin. Marcel's almond-shaped eyes had twinkled down at Jwahir when he'd introduced himself. He'd removed the metal headband that held his shiny black hair out of his face, handing it over to Eldrick with a, "You have a little sister. You'll probably do a better job than I would."

Eldrick had combed gentle fingers through hair tangled in parts and matted in others. He shared the same dark brown coloring as most other police officers. But where their eyes held a hint of repressed youthfulness, Eldrick's shimmered with a maturity beyond his years.

"Binta, I'm leaving you in charge."

"Yes, ma'am."

"Ready?"

Before Jwahir could reply, Belay Fayola scooped her into her arms. "Where are you taking me?" *Probably back to Dr. Pérez-Soto. Our pact is finished. Her mission is complete. There is no room in a soldier's life for an orphan.*

"I told you, we're going on a grocery run. After that, home. I haven't slept in my bed and next to Jelani in too long."

Home? She's taking me home with her? But what about Dr. Pérez-Soto, and who's Jelani?

"That bear shifter will die, but I need to know how painfully he'll meet his end." Then, as if a switch had been turned on in her eyes, golden flickering lights filled her orbs. "Did he touch you in a way an adult should not lay hands on a child?"

Jwahir's mind went to the beatings, some with Mr. Seager's belt, others with a "switch" he would get from the tree behind the cabin. But then she recalled conversations her mother had with her about "good" and "bad" touches. "If someone, anyone, touches you in a place that makes you a girl or wants you to touch them in a place that makes them a boy or girl, come to your father or me right away. Do you understand?"

Jwahir had not. But her mother had hugged her too tight and said, "If someone hurts you, it is never your fault. *Never.*"

"Bad touches?"

"Yes, bad touches. Did he?"

She shook her head, and the same coiled tension she'd felt in her mother's embrace eased out of Belay Fayola's eyes.

"Good. I'm late reaching you, but not as late as I could have been. Binta."

"Yes, ma'am?"

"You've seen some of the injuries on our friend here, repay her abuser in kind then drain the bastard dry."

"Yes, ma'am. We're all golds, you know."

"I noticed. The tribunal isn't funny."

"Maybe a little," Dominique said, "particularly Kamau Haseena. Our unit needs a name."

"It doesn't."

Dominique clapped her hands. "What about—"

"No."

"Damn, ma'am, that was cold, but you'll warm up to us."

Without replying to Dominique or releasing Jwahir, Fayola shifted into her complete impundulu form. Somehow, she ended up on the shifter's back, in a crevice perfect for . . . sleeping.

She closed her eyes, feeling the last of her shackles break apart and disappear.

Free. Safe.

"I paid good money for you, girl." Jwahir's eyes snapped open. *What if Mr. Seager didn't lie? What if Dr. Pérez-Soto and her husband are the real liars?*

11: She Chose You

The United Wake of Benekal
Kettle of Silesse City

Jelani sized up the enemy, taking their measure and deciding on the best course of action. He'd never failed a mission, and today would be no different. Yet this encounter had his pulse racing unlike any other. Squaring his shoulders and slowing his breathing to a calm, regulated trot, he stormed inside, determined to conquer the beast and win the war.

"Good afternoon, sir, welcome to Children Know Love." Two salespeople stood to Jelani's right and behind a see-through counter with colorful beads, bracelets, and baubles in various sizes and shapes. The taller of the two, the seventy-something woman who'd spoken, had blond bangs that covered an eye. The eye that he could see was ocean blue and observant. The saleswoman wore a long-sleeved red collared shirt with the store's name written down the right sleeve and a stitched white heart with a child's smiling face in the shirt's center. The woman's name—Calista—was stitched in white calligraphy letters above the heart image.

According to his uniform shirt, the man beside Calista, Lennox, was younger than his colleague by a decade and shorter than her by five inches. Lennox appeared no less taken aback by the sights and sounds of the store as Jelani.

Pandemonium reigned. Children were everywhere—running in circles, jumping into ball pits, climbing rock walls.

And screaming. They laughed, too, but they screamed like the store had a ban on conversational tones.

"What have I gotten myself into?"

Lennox tugged at the lobe of his ear the way a child would with an ear infection. "This is my third week on the job, and I've asked myself the same question every morning."

Jelani backed up, more frightened of being run over by preschoolers with a full tank of post-nap energy than he'd been facing down an active shooter.

"Where in the hell are the parents?"

Lennox strolled from around the checkout counter. At five-eight, the man's hickory thick hair was cut shorter on the sides than on top. His goatee with random strands of early-onset gray gave him a distinguished look incongruent with his bright red shirt and choice of post-retirement employment.

"New dad?" Lennox patted Jelani's shoulder like a reassuring father he'd never had. "Shopping for the young one, for the first time, can be scarier than flying into a hostage situation." The solid hand eased off his back, pointing to the store's second level. "You can't see it from here, but there is a relaxation room for parents in the back. While their kids play, they chat and drink and then shop. Everyone goes home happy."

Jelani rubbed his ears, not a single lobe, as Lennox had done, but a full ear massage.

Lennox chuckled. "I used to do that too."

"You still do. Stop scaring the poor man. Can't you see he's already shell-shocked?" Calista joined them on the opposite side of the counter, effectively flanking him. "This kind of place isn't for everyone. I'd be the first to admit that it can take some getting used to. Newborn or toddler?"

"What?"

"How old is your hatchling?"

Jelani thought back to the little girl's video message for Fayola. During his time in the military, he had seen all manner of vile crimes. Still, none cut deeper than ones committed against children and the elderly. Black circles had rimmed golden-brown eyes. Fatigue and sadness had punctuated every word she'd spoken, and her slight frame had delivered a silent message.

Jelani had faith Fayola would rescue the child. However, his concern for her did not fall in those quarters.

How will she handle the tribunal's dictate? What will they do if she refuses to lead the new unit? What will any of this mean for the rest of us?

Neither Jelani nor Kwame had been assigned a mission in the months since Fayola's imprisonment. Months often did pass between missions, with the Wake expecting soldiers to use that time to build the skills and knowledge necessary to lead productive and happy civilian lives. For some, that meant studying a trade. For others, like Jelani, Fayola, and Durah, it meant attending college online and earning multiple degrees. Some doubled down on their law enforcement training, becoming specialists in their chosen unit of study. Kwame fell into this category. Illicit drug trafficking was his field of expertise.

I wondered why neither of us had received a new mission. After today's ridiculous hearing, I think I have my answer. Those short-sighted, arrogant kamaus. Holding Fayola's friends' retirement hostage will not make her compliant. If anything, she'll become more resistant. Or, to their frustration, do things her way.

"Watch out," Calista warned, ducking and covering her head with her arms.

Too late, a herd of children ran down the stairs, feet thudding, screaming, of course, and wielding gray plastic . . . bazookas?

Jelani grabbed a fistful of Lennox's red shirt and dropped to the floor.

Tiny tot terror reigned above, while experienced soldiers cowered on their bellies. Plastic projectiles flew, connecting with squealing, delighted children. War raged under the swelling sound of laughter, and *Tag, you're it.*

Jelani rolled onto his back, giving in to the lunacy of it all . . . and laughed. Why not? He might not know what tomorrow would bring, but tonight would see the return of his Fayola.

I've missed her so much.

They hadn't spoken since the final time he'd seen her in the hospital. But everything in Jelani knew Fayola wouldn't return to the base or even to her father's house.

She'll come home to me. When she does, I'll have everything ready for her and for our guest.

"I need the works for a small but brave seven- or eight-year-old girl."

Calista peeked blue eyes out from under her arms, her smile half-pleased, half-terrified. "Then you've come to the right place. But . . . umm, let's wait until Team Bazooka runs out of ammo."

Considering the swimming pool-sized ball pit in the middle of the first level, Team Bazooka had chosen their weapon and battle location well.

"Where's that parent room again?"

Lennox grinned at him, a halo of red, blue, and green plastic balls on the floor above his head. "Smart man. Up the stairs. Keep straight until you reach the frozen treats vending machines and smell the nutty scent of whipped almond coffee wafting from the parent room. I'll come to get you when the coast is clear."

"Frozen treats?"

Lennox laughed like a man content with retirement life. "Those two words are like magic. Strawberry shortcake is my favorite."

"Mine is chocolate pudding." Calista caught two balls but missed the third, her eye paying the price for her slow reflexes. "Kids," she laughed. "A small seven- or eight-year-old girl. Got it." Calista vaulted to her feet, silky blond bangs shifting out of her eye with the fluid movement. "Lennox, you're on escort duty."

"What about you?" Lennox asked, getting to his feet and offering Jelani a hand.

"We've practiced this drill. I'll lay down fire, while you get our customer to safety."

With a swiftness typical of impundulu, Calista darted behind the counter. Bending, she disappeared for several seconds but returned with a kid's fire hose. A blue hose attached to an orange nozzle, she twisted the nozzle to a spray function and attacked.

Bold and bright fuchsia bubbles flowed from the hose, filling the play area with countering ammo.

"Go!" Calista yelled.

Jelani took off, following Lennox's red shirt.

I am getting one of those for the house.

"I may have gone a little overboard."

"A little?" Fayola and Jelani stood in the doorway of their second bedroom—an area they used more as additional storage space than they did for overnight guests. But the room had standard amenities—bed, dresser, nightstand, desk, and chair. Impundulus preferred natural wood furniture. Fayola and Jelani were no exception. Made of solid wood oak, they'd ordered the bedroom set from a local crafter, never imagining they would have a human child using the bedroom.

Gone were the storage bins and overflow clothing in the closet and armoire. In their place was kid-sized everything—colorful clothing in print designs and with cartoon characters, shoes and outerwear for every season, and enough hairbrushes, bows, and barrettes for a set of triplets. Then there were the toys. Beside an armoire filled with little girl clothes, Jelani had stacked boxes of toys—some educational, but most were designed for hours of silly, entertaining fun.

She pointed to two rectangular white boxes opposite the bed. Propped against the wall, the branding and picture facing away from her, Fayola couldn't tell the contents. "What are those?"

"Toy chests. An easy do-it-yourself project."

Easy? Perhaps, but he's never put anything more complex to-gether than a peanut butter and blood sandwich, and he almost forgot the peanut butter. "Jwahir has one body and two hands. What is she going to do with all of this stuff?"

"She has one belly and mouth, but our fridge and pantry are filled with human food. If you continue to give her two plates at every meal, the way you did for dinner, she'll burst."

"With all of those stuffed animals on the bed, where will she sleep?"

They looked at each other, stared really, and Fayola felt every day of the time they'd spent apart in the eyes that held hers with a matching love and desire.

"I've missed you more than I thought possible."

An arm snaked around her waist, pulling her to him with effortless charm. "I've missed you too. When I awoke this morning, I had no idea how this day would end. If I would be able to bring you home or if I would be forced to watch you taken into custody. I'm sorry I wasn't at the hospital when the MPs came for you. I didn't think they would—"

She kissed him, silencing his words of guilt. He owed her none, no more than she would apologize to the Rashidi Tribunal for breaking Wake law to rescue Jwahir and the other children.

Mmm, Jelani tasted good—a chocolate-strawberry mix she wanted to feast on all night.

Not yet. Not here. "We can't."

Full, soft lips slid down her neck that pulsed with need too far north to satisfy her craving. He kissed her there, mouth supple and bites tender. "I have plans for you."

Fayola gulped, as much from the deep timbre of Jelani's tantalizing voice, as she did from the thought of the physical recommitment of their relationship.

Peeling herself from him, his north pole a magnet to her south, Fayola's breath all but left her. Jelani's eyes, a sexy shade of scintillating red, bore the majestic color of his lightning. It was a blatant yet natural arousal response.

Licking her lips, while imagining his on hers again, Fayola's insides heated, and her sex throbbed. Animal instinct had them closing the short distance between them, mouths hungry, hands greedy, and—

"Dela Eden. I mean Belay Fayola. I've finished my bath."

They hadn't discussed parenthood beyond the notion of having children "after we retire." Five years or a dozen, they hadn't decided. By impundulu standards, they were still young, certainly young enough to put off having hatchlings for a couple of decades. And while both of their parents had opted for parenthood soon after retiring, Fayola and Jelani hadn't shared the same rush to become parents.

Fayola eased out of the kiss, realizing the many ways a child would alter their lives. "I have no idea what I'm doing with her."

"You have no idea? I spent hours in a kids' amusement park fronting as a children's department store."

"And spent a month's salary."

"About, yeah."

Taking her hand, Jelani led Fayola away from the bedroom, down a hall with walls painted a sterile white, and to a tiled bathroom with mirrors over the double sinks and a solar-powered skylight above the bathtub with a wet, waiting child.

Fayola entered the bathroom, but Jelani did not.

"I bought her a robe. It's on the hook on the back of the door. Give me a few minutes to clear her bed. When you bring her in, she can pick whichever toy she would like to sleep with her. A stuffed animal, a doll, a soccer ball. It's her choice, as long as it makes her happy." Lowering his voice, Jelani said, "You saved her life twice. That makes her yours, which means she's also mine. Unless you can think of a better, safer home for her than ours, we're keeping her."

"Jwahir is a person with a mind and the right to make her own choices."

"She did make a choice, and she chose you. If her video message wasn't clear enough, ask her." Kissing her cheek, a sweet, quick peck, Jelani condensed a potentially complicated situation down to three simple facts. One, Jwahir was an orphan. Two, she trusted Fayola. Three, Fayola and Jelani would care for Jwahir as if they'd created her from their lightning.

But there was a fourth fact, one that wasn't as simple as the others. No humans lived in the Wake, no more than elephant shifters did, and certainly not bear shifters, because a nation of "bloodsuckers" would never make it onto the World's Best Places to Live list.

"But you might want to rewash her hair. Her decision to leave her plaits in wasn't a good choice. See you two in a few. Jwahir?"

"Yes, Mr. Jelani?"

"If you like bubbles, I have a wicked fire hose I want to show you. We'll do that tomorrow. How does that sound?"

"Like fun."

"Yup, so much fun."

Winking at her, the way Durah often did, Jelani preened as if he'd won a prize then sauntered away from the bathroom and back down the hall.

"He's nice."

The "unlike Mr. Seager" went unsaid. However, it had been there in the way Jwahir used her gray striped washcloth to cover the bruise on her elbow still red from where her oxygen-rich blood had pooled under her skin.

Fayola knelt, still wearing her uniform's white shirt and black pants. She'd ripped her tie off at a grocery store in Tikala but waited to divest herself of her shoes and socks until she'd reached home. A puddle of bathwater soaked into the knees of her pants.

"Let's ice that down again before bed."

Jwahir nodded, and Fayola waited, wondering if the child would speak of her obvious abuse. Not that many, if any words, were required. The constellation of healed and healing bruises on the landscape of her fragile body told the story of her six-month captivity with the Seagers well enough.

"She's my domestic servant," Mr. Seager had told Fayola. "It's legal to have one of those."

True, but not when that service was forced or involved a minor. Fayola hadn't bothered to argue the lack of merits of his defense. She'd broken every finger and toe instead. By the time she'd finished with his hands, he'd answered all her questions—who, what, when, where, and how. She'd moved on to his feet, not because he'd withheld information she sought, but because he'd smirked through the telling of selecting and buying a child to fulfill his needs while denying Jwahir hers.

"It's all business. Money in exchange for a good or service. A simple transaction. The girl had no home. Her sorry-ass country saw to that. You know what they are doing over there, right? Burning people out of their homes, forcing them to take a side, and killing those who don't. So I did the human a favor. I fed and clothed her. I would've gotten around to sending her to school, too, because that's the kind of bear I am."

Fayola had repaid his sense of privilege and entitlement with matching cruelty.

"After today, you won't need these teeth," she'd told him. "But there is reason to smile. Just think, if you were in your bear form, there would've been ten more teeth for me to rip from your bleeding gums."

"If you like, I can take out your plaits and wash your hair."

"Yeah, thank you." Jwahir scooted until her back faced Fayola. Her spine was visible under delicate light brown skin.

As shifters, we know how much stronger we are than humans. Physically stronger, anyway. But whereas Caedin Seager had cried and begged, pleading for mercy, this human child stood her ground against a bully. Her body is weak, but her mental fortitude is mighty. Still, her trauma runs deeper than the bruises I can see. She needs more than food, clothing, and protection. Those Jelani and I can provide. But we'll need to seek expert help with her social and emotional well-being. All of that will come in time, though. Let's just get through tonight and tomorrow.

By the time Fayola finished washing and blow-drying Jwahir's hair, the little girl had fallen asleep on the bathroom floor. Seated between Fayola's legs and wrapped in a white robe with a spiraling unicorn horn on the hood, Fayola maneuvered Jwahir into her arms and off of the floor.

Jelani had put the lengthy time Fayola had spent in the bathroom to good use. He'd unpacked the rest of the bags of clothing, hanging some in the closet and storing others in drawers. He'd even had time to finish his DIY project. He'd removed the pile of toys and stuffed animals from the bed and placed them in the two wooden toy chests with white and gray polka dot cushions.

If we really are going to keep her, I need to learn how to drive. Maybe Dad will teach me how to create a few braid hairstyles he used to put my hair in when I was Jwahir's age.

Jelani had left a pastel tie-dye pajama short set—yellow, pink, blue, purple, and orange—on the bed into which Fayola placed Jwahir.

The child didn't stir. Her faith in Fayola was as frighteningly absolute as her exhaustion was real. One should have left her feeling relieved, but both added a weight of responsibility that extended beyond a single child.

Smiling at Jelani's choice of sleeping toy, Fayola grabbed the stuffed crochet impundulu from the foot of the bed. Like a real impundulu, black, white, and gray, the toy had yellow button-jointed arms and legs. Fayola placed the soft toy beside Jwahir, then covered them with the warm smoke blue comforter.

Taking a page out of Raicho's parenting handbook, Fayola kissed Jwahir's forehead, turned on the nightlight, and left the bedroom door ajar on her way out.

Fayola returned to the bathroom, cleaned up Jwahir's mess, and then took a quick shower, unwilling to climb into bed with Jelani smelling of Caedin Seager.

"You look fresh, supple, and"—Jelani slid from the bed, meeting Fayola at their bedroom door and closing it behind her—

"eatable, kissable." Warm, tantalizing lips sucked an earlobe into his mouth. "Fuckable," he whispered, sending electrical currents of need sizzling down her body.

She hugged him, overcome with love and fear because her next meeting with the Rashidi Tribunal would mark a watershed moment in their lives. Despite their heavy-handedness, their denial of visiting privileges had helped Fayola ease into her psychological acceptance of living apart from Jelani for the foreseeable future. Imprisonment did not appeal, of course, but, like ripping an adhesive bandage from a wound, it was best to make it quick.

The MPs arresting her at the hospital and taking her away to Fort Kumelo to await her first hearing amounted to ripping off an adhesive bandage. Moreover, the unexpected arrest hadn't afforded Fayola time to say goodbye to Jelani, which would have been equivalent to a slow removal of an adhesive bandage. For six months, she nursed her regret at not having had an opportunity to say goodbye. Tonight, however, they had time to speak parting words; yet none would suffice. So, she held him to her, soaking in his unforgettable scent.

"It'll be fine," he reassured. "We can plot now or later. The choice is yours. Whatever you want, I'm here. As always." Jelani drew her away from the door and to their bed.

"How could I have missed all of this?" First, the sweet, creamy scent of coconuts tickled her nostrils, whereas the flickering flames from the white scented candles drew her eye. Situated on both nightstands, the candles added an aromatic, romantic flavor to the room. Next, her gaze traveled from Jelani's bare, bronzed chest to a scrumptious pair of blue, white, and black pouched plaid lounge boxer trunks that accentuated his very nice package. "Those are new."

"Glad you finally noticed. Strategize now or later?"

Fayola snapped the band of his boxers. "Testing the elasticity."

"Uh-huh. I guess that means I can test this knot." Deft fingers untied the waist tie closure of her robe—a black silk garment with side slits at the hem and a hand-painted peacock on the back.

Iridescent green and blue plumage led to elongated upper tail coverts. The peacock's metallic blue and green eyespots were visible on the fanned tail.

Fayola wore nothing underneath. *Nothing but skin in need of his touch. Hands, mouth and more.* "Six months," she said, her voice a sultry whisper of repressed need.

"Yeah." Sweeping her into his arms, Jelani deposited her in the center of their bed. "This bed and house were lonely without you. I don't want to go back to that, so whatever we come up with must involve us staying together. Whatever that looks like, we'll work out before you see the tribunal. But for now"—his right hand slid down her stomach, teasing the sensitive flesh with a thumb that went farther still—"let's blend gold with red."

Sucking on his index and middle fingers as if they were the aching nipples she wanted in his mouth, Jelani left a trail of moisture down her stomach, stopping at the apex of her sex then sliding his fingers inside.

The thick digits, wet from his mouth, met ready slickness. "Nice and wet. You feel good. Your walls are clenching my fingers. Yeah, just like that."

Wrapping her hand around the nape of his neck, Fayola pulled Jelani down into a sloppy, wet kiss. Tongue parted lips, slipping inside with swirling licks over gum, teeth and against his delightful tongue. Busy and eager, their tongues embraced, rolling over each other in the same way Jelani's strong, big thumb slid over her sensitive, engorged clit.

Pressing.

Flicking.

Caressing.

His fingers found the delicate ridges inside her sex. Found the folds and flesh, and made her squirm and shiver for him with each swipe, with each slide, with each mind-numbing back and forth motion.

Eyes slammed shut, grip on nape tightened, and mouth pulled away, sucking in gulps of air.

"I'm going to make you spark and sizzle for me."

Fayola had never doubted his skill. Stars danced the minuet behind her eyes, gliding in straight steps—forward, backward, sideways. She wanted to kiss him again, to moan her pleasure in a mouth that crooned her name like a nightingale singing at dusk—whistles, trills, and gurgles. But Jelani, dark, curly hair and bright, intense eyes aglow in candlelight, kissed and nipped his way down her body.

Not too fast, nor too slow, but just right.

The mouth she'd had other plans for took mercy on her breasts. Sucking a nipple into his mouth, Jelani played, flicking his tongue over the pert tip and leaving a swirl of pebbled skin in his wake, only to switch breasts and begin anew.

Heart pounded like a marathoner, working hard and running fast to catch the leader.

Heated mouth and exploring tongue glided below her waist.

Fayola fisted the comforter, feeling the rise of heat and the snap of electricity everywhere her body met his.

Jelani did not rush. He'd once told her oral sex was a "slow makeout session," where "pulling hair and scintillating talk" were required.

Applying gentle pressure to her pubic bone, he kissed her quivering stomach, her trembling thighs, and her waiting, unhooded clit. "You taste like ripe berries sprinkled with salt. Do you want me to stay here? Keep kissing and licking?"

"Y-yes. R-right there. Oh, ooohh."

"Good, more tongue-touch. It makes you wetter." Lick. "Hotter." Lick. "Wilder for me." Lick. Lick.

All true. Shit, he's looking right at me. Watching my response. Enjoying my pleasure. Reading my body for clues.

Softening the pressure, slowing the pace, Jelani entered Fayola with his tongue—a teasing, probing tongue thrust.

Whatever nerve endings that hadn't yet come to life went off like colored sparklers at a winter light festival.

Fayola moaned, a deep, guttural sound that echoed throughout her flushed body.

"Message received." Palms pressed to her thighs, holding her legs open, he went back to work, thrusting in and out.

The speedy tempo of hips that couldn't stay still were silent demands for *more*. Jelani gave without reservation, increasing his pace to match her moans.

Heated magic overflowed her cells, igniting her organs and electrifying her hair. Sparks crackled up and down her spine, a roiling wave of charges searching for a ground source. They found it in Jelani's sturdy body, a balancing landscape of hips, legs, and chest.

Surging forward, Jelani shared the fullness of his masculine length, joining them. Their union was a primordial thunderclap of rippling curses and transcendent grunts.

Electricity filled her eyes, a sheen of gold snaps and hisses that didn't flow down her cheeks but formed a twisting bridge of lightning that grew with each of Jelani's hearty thrusts.

His own lightning formed in his eyes—a brilliant crimson.

Gold and red touched, twined, sparked.

Exploded.

They produced a cascade of electrostatic discharges, a supernatural orgasm unique to impundulu shifters.

"I missed you," Jelani said in her ear, a ragged, breathy sound that touched the heart she'd given him years ago.

I can hear the unspoken pain of our forced separation. If it's within my power, I'll never put him through that again. Tonight, Jwahir was our priority. Tomorrow, we'll decide how to deal with the Rashidi Tribunal, the Sotos, and the Criminal Exploitation Unit.

Snuggling under the covers, Fayola's head on Jelani's moist chest and his heartbeat slowing, she spoke the most potent truth between them. "I love you." Kissing his chest, she added four more words because fortune favored the prepared mind. "We need a plan."

12: Just Once, Baby

The Union of the Beloluga
Muliky County, Robinsk

"Come on, smile for me, sweetheart. No, not like that. Give me a sexy, I've-been-a-naughty-girl-and-need-a-spanking kind of smile." Viktor snapped shots in rapid succession, pleased with the setting but not with how much warp dust it took to loosen Katya up for these shoots. But the girl, when relaxed to the point of mindless compliance, made the most magnificent muse for his artist's soul.

Viktor had taken his time designing the bedroom, as he did with every shooting. But, if he had to pick his favorite themed setting, the Citrus Room would rise to the top of the list. Cheerful, bright, young, and innocent, the room exuded what his clients looked for when they logged onto his website—Sugary Sweet Treats.

The soft pink floral print wallpaper put one in the mind of a field of wildflowers blowing in the breeze on a warm spring day, and of a little girl skipping through the field, happy and carefree. He'd painted the lime green nightstands himself, knowing how perfectly the color would add to the room's cheeriness when combined with the retro silver bookcase, white comforter, and lime green, white, and fuchsia throw at the foot of the bed. When switched on at night, the two glass lamps on the nightstands shone with a protective glow capable of discouraging monsters from entering the mind of a sleeping child. But it was the bed's open design with scrolled detailing on the head and footboard that had proven a great source of boudoir photography inspiration.

"Grab the headboard, arch your back just a little and poke that cute little ass out some. Not too much. Tease. Tantalize."

Snap. Snap.

"Okay, good. Much better. Let's try the serpent pose. You remember. Lie on the bed like a snake. No, dammit, not toward the fucking foot of the bed. How in the hell am I supposed to get good shots that way? Twist around. Yeah, like that."

Snap. Snap. Snap.

"Let that gorgeous dark hair spill over the bed. Good, Katya. Show off your long, lovely neck. Give me an arched pose and close your eyes. My clients want to imagine you're thinking about them. That a girl like you is waiting for them after a long, hard day of work. That, when they fall asleep, you'll enter their dreams wearing that scrumptious schoolgirl costume."

Like the photo shoot setting, Viktor also prided himself on matching the ideal outfit with the perfect model, setting, and mood. Dark-haired, pale-skinned, and green doe-eyed Katya in a tie-front crop top with red trim, plaid miniskirt, and knee-high white stockings brought in the subscribers unlike any of Viktor's other girls.

He snapped away, anxious to have Lubov, his wife and assistant, upload the new batch of pictures to Sugary Sweet Treats.

"That's right, sweetheart. Yeah, yeah, good. Now, let's try the hangover. What I need for you to do is . . ."

The Commonwealth of Sunderton
Manbron City, Hingset
Lower East Side

"Are we gonna go back inside, Mommy?"

Emma clutched her daughter Elle's mitten-covered hand. Seated on a cold metal bench under a bus stop's domed roof, Emma was grateful for the little protection against the winter wind.

She shivered but not from the cold seeping through her mid-weight denim jacket and into achy bones.

I wish real life were as easy to wash away as the bathrooms I clean. I flush shit down the toilet, but I flushed my life away long before I got that custodian gig.

"I haven't decided, baby. But I . . . umm, I just need a little time to think."

"About what?" Eyes so green they reminded her of the emerald jewels Mason, Elle's father, used to give her stared up at Emma.

A teardrop necklace, an infinity bracelet, flower leaf earrings—Mason had given her so many trinkets of his affection. Emma had known the jewels were fake, but she'd taken the costume jewelry to the pawnshop anyway after Mason was sentenced to ten years for dealing drugs.

He said he would take care of our baby girl and me. I'm so fucking stupid for believing him. For getting caught up in his shit. I can't pay the rent and feed my little girl. I tried. But the eviction notices keep reappearing on my apartment door.

Emma pulled Elle's yellow and white ducky hat over red ears. "Nothing for you to worry about, baby. Mommy's gonna take care of everything."

Emma sat with Elle across from their apartment building. At eight in the morning on a Sunday, most people were still inside, recuperating from a long workweek or getting ready to attend church. A light dusting of snow still lingered on the cold ground from last night's teasing snowfall, adding beauty and innocence to a part of the city that hadn't been either for too many residents.

There's nothing beautiful or innocent about poverty. I might be a bear shifter, but that doesn't make me a natural-born bear who lives in a forest. Hibernation isn't even a real thing for bears. I can't find a den, fall asleep and wait out the winter. That's not how life works. Bills just don't disappear. There's no ignoring that harsh truth.

"I'm cold."

"I know, baby."

"And hungry." As if the daily admission had sapped the last of her energy, Elle slumped against Emma's arm. "May I have more jelly toast?"

A truck rumbled down the street, large tires dipping into and over stubborn potholes. What looked like streaks of tears flowing down a mud-caked face, was in fact melted snow that ran from the truck's roof down the side of the dirty vehicle and onto the neglected street below.

My life is like that fucked-up street. Walked on and trampled over. Patched in places, messily and without care, but ultimately to no lasting effect. I don't want that life for my Elle. But I can't keep her safe, if I can't keep a roof over her head. She'll begin kindergarten next year. When she does, I'll be able to look for a better job. One that doesn't have me leaving her in the apartment by herself for half the night while I clean toilets at a dive motel. Minimum wage and no health benefits. That heel of bread and the grape jelly packets I stole from the employee break room was the last of both. Not much of a breakfast for a growing child.

Emma's own stomach growled, loud and painful but not as heartrending as raising a four-year-old who confused starvation with mere hunger.

Emma had met a lot of men in her thirty years of life. She'd slept with too many but trusted few. Mason, Noah, and Lucas, she'd given them her body and her heart. But, in the end, they'd all abandoned and disappointed the little girl inside the grown woman who still cried for a father unworthy of her tears.

Emma pulled Elle onto her lap, sitting her sideways so she could lean against a heart slowly breaking into a thousand pieces of desperation. She breathed her in, a pointless fortification for the unforgivable act to come.

Emma had gone out there, hoping the frigid air would clear her head or a stroke of brilliance would give her a better idea.

One time. It'll only be one time. She's just a baby. Four. She won't hurt her. She promised. Just a little bit of company, she said. Company in exchange for letting us stay in the apartment this month. If I get in some double shifts, I should be able to scrape together enough money for next month's rent.

Except for their clothing, a few toys, and the television, Emma didn't have anything else left to pawn. Even if she were willing to part with what remained, the sale from their meager possessions would only be enough to feed them for a week. Rice, pasta, beans, cheese, and bread; Emma had learned to make inexpensive foods go a long way.

She hugged her daughter, recalling how she'd felt after her birth.

Having Elle, becoming a mom, nothing in my life mattered before that special day. Blond hair and green eyes, like Mason's, she was the most beautiful baby. I promised to care for her, to be a better parent than mine had been to me. But, in less than five years, I've already failed.

"Mrs. Snyder wants you to come over for a playdate."

"She's an old lady." Elle yawned, tucking her head under Emma's chin and wrapping her arms around her waist, seeking warmth.

"I guess forty-seven is old to you. But you like her, right?"

"She's okay."

"Older people who live by themselves get lonely. A playdate would be fun. Maybe you could stay with her while I'm at work. That way, neither of you will be alone."

"Don't want to."

"Why not?"

Elle shrugged shoulders that were too thin. "Don't know. Just don't."

Emma never pushed Elle to do something she didn't want to, no more than she scolded her child for acting out. But Mrs. Snyder owned the apartment building, taking over managerial duties, like issuing eviction notices, after her husband passed away and her daughter moved out. As far as she knew, the sixteen-year-old Ashley lived rent-free in a basement studio apartment but never ventured above the first floor to visit her mother.

Of course, rumors circulated about the mother-daughter rift like stale air in an old elevator. But pacts, like the bond of parenthood, could be broken if one party wanted out.

"Mrs. Snyder has lots of yummy food in her apartment."

Elle's little head leaned back, green eyes blinking up at Emma with a daughter's absolute trust in her mother. "Spaghetti and meatballs?"

"I don't know, but I'm sure, if you're nice to her, she'll cook you whatever you want."

"Cakes and cookies?"

"Maybe, if you're a good girl."

Elle grinned, showing off teeth as small as the white rice they'd eaten last night.

Boulders laced with acid settled in Emma's empty stomach.

What kind of mother uses her child's hunger as a source of manipulation? Will she grow to hate me the way Ashley despises Mrs. Snyder? Or will she understand I had no choice? That homelessness is worse than keeping a widow company. Just once, baby, I promise I'll only give you to her this one time.

"Will you do it? For me?"

"Tell her I like spaghetti and meatballs."

"I will."

"Good." Burrowing into her again, Elle sighed, the sound a soft huff of agreement.

Lava formed in Emma's lungs—thick, molten and choking.

Gravel filled her nostrils.

Sand her ears.

And while her eyes remained clear, unobstructed, her brain hemorrhaged. No tumor, stroke, or high blood pressure but a mother's soul-crushing guilt.

The United Wake of Benekal
Kettle of Silesse City

"Why are you sitting in the hallway at three in the morning?"

From her place on the floor, Jwahir looked up at Fayola. Even with how the bright white hallway light illuminated her full, round face, she still couldn't interpret her expression.

Is she mad? Will she yell at me like Mr. Seager did when I broke one of his rules? Will Mr. Jelani? He seems nice, but so did Mr. Seager at first. And Dr. Pérez-Soto. Did she really sell me?

Dressed in black pajama shorts and a white and black sleeveless tank top that highlighted toned shoulders and defined muscular arms, Fayola knelt beside Jwahir. "Couldn't sleep?"

"Nightmare."

Fayola nodded, as if she understood. Jwahir didn't know how she could.

She's big and strong. No one would dare bully someone like her. She didn't tell me what happened with Mr. Seager, but I saw her tackle him to my bed. Easy for her but impossible for me. I bet she never had a nightmare. I wanted to go home with her, but she and Mr. Jelani can't want a scrawny kid. What will two impundulus do with a human child? And why is she pretending she doesn't see the mess I made?

"You'll have them for a while." Fayola ran a hand over Jwahir's head, fingers combing through her riot of hair. "But not always. Not forever. When you're ready, when you feel safe in your own skin again, there is a person I would like for you to meet. She is someone you can talk to, a person capable of helping you work through what has happened to you since losing your parents."

Fayola's hand stilled at Jwahir's nape. Her caresses were so soothing in their delicateness she hadn't noticed she'd moved closer to the bird shifter, seeking something she was afraid to name.

"When I was a little girl, I used to have nightmares too."

"You did?"

"You sound so surprised." Fayola lowered herself to the floor, sitting cross-legged like Jwahir. "Family is everything to impundulus. Family and the Wake. We live for both. Will die to protect both."

"Kill?" Jwahir had seen Fayola at her worst, at her most violent. Even if her actions protected Jwahir and her friends, it was a frightening sight.

"Yes, when necessary." Scratching her own head, her short hair as bed mussed as Jwahir's, Fayola laughed, a soft, almost judgmental chuckle. "Not always necessary. Sometimes, a person's death feels earned."

"Like Mr. Seager?" She hadn't missed his screams when Fayola had been inside the cabin alone with the bear shifter, no more than Jwahir had failed to understand Fayola's directive to the impundulu police officers.

You've seen some of the injuries on our friend here, repay her abuser in kind then drain the bastard dry.

Fayola picked up the pink marker by Jwahir's knee, the first outward acknowledgment of her mess. "Life is a series of decisions. Options. Choices. The best that we can do, Jwahir, is make the ones that will do more good than harm. For you but also for others."

"Did your mommy and daddy teach you that?"

"I've only ever had a father. He's taught me plenty, and while no child would ever be left to fend for themselves in our kettles, I feared living in a world without my father in it."

"Your nightmare?"

"Smart girl." Rising to her knees again, Fayola traded the pink marker for the black one. Uncapping it, she surveyed what Jwahir had done, leaned forward, and added a name to the drawing. "This plain white wall needed something. I never knew what. Thanks to you, I now do."

Confused, Jwahir asked, "You aren't mad?"

Fayola added another name to the wall. "No. Was this a test?"

When she'd awoken in a strange yet wonderful room, filled with a child's greatest desires, Jwahir had wept. Even before her parents' murders, she'd never had so many material possessions. The couple had gone overboard, and Jwahir had felt undeserving of their kindness. She supposed a part of her doubted their sincerity. So, when she'd seen the three-tier pink metal art cart between the two toy chests, she'd gathered up paint, paintbrushes and markers and carried them into the hallway.

"Dr. Pérez-Soto was nice to me, too, but Mr. Seager said he bought me from her and her husband. He was a mean man. He tricked me into thinking he was nice, but he wasn't. Now I think Dr. Pérez-Soto tricked me too. Me and my friends."

Again, Fayola wrote a name on the wall—inside Jwahir's drawing. "How many are we missing?"

Jwahir's eyes moved from one name to the next—counting. "Twelve."

"I think you're right." Fayola stood, thighs thick with muscles, bare feet long and toe and fingernails as free of color as the hallway walls. "I'm far from the tallest impundulu you'll meet, but I have enough height to help you make this heart bigger." Reaching down, she lifted Jwahir to her feet. "This is the pinkest heart I've ever seen. Favorite color?"

"Yup. What's yours, Belay Fayola?"

She pointed to her black shorts.

Jwahir wasn't surprised, although she half expected her to say blood red.

"Just Fay or Fayola. Ms. Fay is also fine, since you seem to have been raised to place a title before an adult's name. So, about this heart. Bigger?"

"B-but I made a huge mess in your clean hallway."

"True."

"A-and I painted all over your pretty white wall."

"Also true. Your point?"

"I-I . . . I don't know."

"You won't provoke me to anger. I also won't permit you to do whatever you want because you're just now realizing that asking an impundulu to save you is not the same as living with and fully trusting one. I drink blood. Bear *and* human. That will never change. You trusted me to save you from Seager. You agreed to come home with me but, in fairness, you're young and probably couldn't think of any other place to go. But, understand this, Jwahir, I can and will find you a good home with human parents, if that is what you want. You owe me nothing except your happiness."

"Our pact was my safety and your coin . . . I mean your lishan medal."

"True, but your happiness was implied in our pact." Hands on her hips, Fayola returned her attention to the pink heart. "Bigger, right? We want to make sure your heart is large enough for all twenty-one names. I'm thinking, if we bring the arch of the heart up here" —she pointed to an area on the wall far above Jwahir's head— "we could add Peng's name on one arch and Orion's on the other. What do you think?"

Jwahir had no idea. She hadn't expected any of this.

I did want to stay with her. I trusted she would protect me from Mr. Seager. But I didn't know how it would feel to be in her home. I don't care that she drinks blood. I just . . . I just don't want her to regret taking me in.

"Yeah, bigger sounds good. You know all of our names?"

"I asked Dr. Pérez-Soto." Turning, she leaned her back against the wall, Jwahir's heart to her left. "She lied to me, too, I think. I'll get the full truth out of her."

The way she said that—emotionless bordering on arctic—reminded Jwahir of the diello she'd met at the clinic. But she'd sensed a warm, caring heart inside the stoic impundulu on a mission.

Mirroring Fayola's position on the opposite wall, Jwahir asked the one question that had kept her from falling back asleep. "Were the others sold too?"

Closing her eyes, Fayola's head fell against the wall. Her mouth opened but closed without making a sound. But fingernails lengthened. Not by much. Yet Jwahir swore the air in the hallway heated.

"Let's finish your heart painting. I have a busy day ahead of me." Eyes still closed, Fayola inhaled, retracted her claws, and then knelt. Opening her eyes, she grabbed one of the clean paintbrushes. "I'll take the top. You get the sides."

"What about me?" Mr. Jelani, pulling a white T-shirt over his head and wearing a pair of navy blue sweatpants stumbled into the hallway, blinking sleepy eyes at them both. "The party is out here, and I wasn't invited."

"Not exactly a party, but since you're here, you can take the top. I'll add the names, and Jwahir can paint everything at her level."

"Wait, that's going to be a lot."

"Complains the girl who vandalized my wall."

"And interrupted the best sleep I've had in six months."

Fayola and Jelani looked at Jwahir, wearing similar expressions—neither smiles nor frowns but a slow lifting of a single dark eyebrow.

They're playing with me, I think. Ms. Fay said I could decide. Stay with them or move in with a human family. I trust she would find me a kind, loving, human family to live with.

As if reading her mind, Fayola ruffled Jwahir's hair. "One thing at a time. Right now, that is finishing your tribute to your Namju friends. When the time comes, *my friends* will take care of the rest."

The adults shared a look Jwahir did not understand—brief but serious and followed by—

"Whoa."

Jelani scooped her onto his big shoulders, the top of her head inches from the ceiling. "Now you can help me paint up here, and Fay can do everything down there. Sounds good?"

"Yup."

"Traitors." Fayola walked down the hallway. "I'll open the crepe maker Jwahir picked out and try my hand at pancakes while the two of you paint that wall."

"You don't know how to cook human food," Mr. Jelani said. His deep voice rippled with humor.

"I'll learn."

Jwahir believed she would.

13: A Long-Ass To-Do List

Fayola halted at the threshold of her living room. She didn't suffer from claustrophobia, nor had she thought her home too small for entertaining. Yet as she watched the score of twenty-one-year-olds consume the space with their youthful energy, loud chatter and restless bodies better suited for outdoors, Fayola contemplated sending them home.

Jelani's big body pressed into hers, a silent, sensual reminder of his presence behind her. He whispered in her ear. His warm breath was a tickle of temptation. "They're here because you asked them. We talked about next steps. Addressing them is on our list."

Jendayi and Marcel had claimed the love seat, Binta and Eldrick the sofa, while Dominique and Cassius chatted near the balcony's sliding glass doors. The others either sat on the floor or leaned against the walls like redundant support beams.

"Only you can do this part. So while you are, I'll make the other calls then take our little guest to the playground."

"I already spoke with Dad and Njeri."

"Good, two fewer calls for me then." Kissing the nape of her neck, Jelani smiled when she shivered. "Nice to know I still have that effect on you. Last night was great. Tonight will be even better." With a gentle press to her back, Jelani encouraged forward movement. "Be nice."

"I'm always nice," she mumbled, but Jelani had fled, leaving Fayola in a suddenly quiet room.

They all bolted to their feet and to attention.

For a second, Fayola wondered if a commanding officer, Belay Njeri, for example, had paid her an unexpected visit and was standing behind her. Then, like an acorn crashing to the ground, Fayola recalled her new role.

They don't care that I'm not officially their belay. The kamaus forced me to take them with me yesterday. But no one compelled me to invite them to my home this morning.

"Relax," she told them. "I'm unsure if I'm your belay. Even if I am, I'm uninterested in formalities, especially in my home." She waved at them. "Sit. Stand. Just . . . stop looking at me like my words weigh more than the sun."

One by one, they resumed their position in her living room, effectively producing a low-grade headache in Fayola because they appeared no more relaxed than they had been standing at attention.

"That wasn't meant to be an order. I . . ." She gulped down her impatience with herself. "Let's try this again. Thank you for coming."

No one spoke, not even the chatty Dominique. But the young woman did smile at her, white teeth as bright as her personality. Dominique's bald head was a tempting lifestyle choice for the hairstyling-challenged Fayola.

But it was Binta, black-brown hair in a ponytail at her nape, eyes greener today than brown, who first spoke. "I'm glad you received my email. After everything that happened yesterday, I wasn't sure you would check your messages. But you did."

Fayola had indeed, but she did not know how they'd obtained her email address. "A single email from the group would have sufficed. One is polite. Two is thoughtful. Twenty is overkill."

Jendayi laughed as if Fayola had delivered the best joke. "Yesterday, you told us to do to that bear shifter what he had done to Jwahir, but you'd already beaten the shi . . . I mean crap out of him. He wasn't dead when we got to him, but I think that fits into the overkill category."

The others laughed, not all as hard as Jendayi had, but still with genuine lightheartedness.

Fayola found herself staring at them. Moreover, she wondered who in the hell had chosen them for the unit.

She didn't share in the good humor, not because she didn't find them entertaining, but because Fayola wasn't ready to commit to being their belay.

I don't appreciate the tribunal's strings. However, a part of me does want this. I don't give a shit about being belay, but these are a great group of young soldiers, and the charge of the unit is a worthy cause.

She strolled farther into the room, stopping in the center so she could address them all. "I'm a person who believes in transparency. I won't ever lie or mislead you. I'll talk, but I'll also listen. I'll always value your opinion, even if I choose to act on my own. I didn't ask you here today to tell you what I want and need, but to find out what you hope and expect from me."

"Umm . . ." Marcel, almond-shaped eyes, shiny black hair, bushy eyebrows, and a wide-set nose, scooted to the edge of the love seat. Finger scratching across a hole in a nostril where a nose ring should be, he stared at Fayola. "Our hopes and expectations of you?"

"Yes. It's only fair. You were assigned to a unit you've never heard of, headed by a woman who, until yesterday, was under arrest."

"All of that's true, but we also applied to be in your unit."

Fayola squinted at Marcel as if his revelatory sentence had taken him out of focus. "You what?"

"Five months ago," Binta said. "When applications were sent out for post–Wake Armed Police assignments, the Criminal Exploitation Unit was on the list. It's all confidential, as you know, so we couldn't tell anyone until we were chosen by the unit's belay."

Fayola understood the process well. Belay Njeri's unit had been Fayola's first choice. She'd felt honored the belay had selected her to join the elite unit.

"You all chose this unit?" She knew she sounded incredulous, but she couldn't help her shock. Three years ago, the tribunal had not only rejected her proposal. They had made a point of letting her know how insulted they had been at her audacity to raise the issue.

Yet, five months ago, they added the CEU to an application that hadn't changed in decades. They could've made that decision any time over the past three years, but they didn't. Instead, they waited until after my arrest. Why?

Cassius, brown cropped hair reddened by the sun, stood. He wore a pair of light wash denim jeans, a light blue button-down shirt rolled to muscular forearms, and a pair of minimalist gray sneakers. "The application process was different from the others. I thought all I had to do was submit my military record, an essay of intent, and four recommendations."

The others agreed with nods and verbal confirmations.

"I soon discovered those normal requirements were only the first part. To be honest, when I received an email about the other components of the application for the CEU, I thought about withdrawing my name."

Except for a few outliers, Binta and Eldrick among them, another round of nods followed Cassius's admission.

"What changed your mind?"

Zephan pushed through the crowd until he stood beside Cassius. Seven inches shorter than the six-one Cassius, Zephan's stocky frame filled out his fitness outfit—short-sleeved red shirt with crew neckline and knee-length shorts with a white vertical line down the sides.

Fayola didn't expect the leather flip-flops with the athletic attire, but they didn't detract from Zephan's relaxed, casual spring look.

"Everyone who had CEU as their first or second choice was invited to Fort Kumelo. Private. Confidential. At the time, we didn't know you were being held there. We didn't know any more about you or the CEU than what was included in the application. One page of information, just like the other units."

With Jelani's help, Fayola had written the unit's description. When formulating her proposal, she had wanted to make it as simple as possible to implement—meaning providing the kamaus with the necessary details to make adding the new unit an easy lift for the belay of their choice.

"Three hundred five applicants, ma'am," Binta said, her dimpled smile secondary to the pride radiating from her eyes. "From three hundred five to a unit of twenty."

"We were shown your fight with the soldiers at the Namju-Tikala border," Eldrick said.

"Right." Cassius grinned. His crooked smile was boyish, and his dipped head was a telling sign of the young man's embarrassment. "That's when I decided."

"Because of a fight? You've spent the last few years with the Wake Armed Police. You've witnessed that and more, no doubt."

"Fights, yes. But not for that kind of cause. Not even to that level of brutality and self-sacrifice. After the video, we were given your proposal to read. The cause was clear. The need is more so. I want my time in the military to matter beyond feeding the Wake. I don't mean to imply that's not important, it's just . . . there has to be more to serving than blood pacts. Until seeing your rescue video and reading your proposal, I didn't know what else I could do."

This time, the grin Cassius granted her was that of an adult impundulu proud of his sound reasoning.

Few things in life had left Fayola stunned. Leaving Raicho and Aradi City had, hearing Jelani confess his love for the first time had, and now, listening to soldiers with years of military service ahead of them explain why they joined the CEU had stunned her into silence.

I meant every word of my proposal. I spent weeks researching. But the harsh truth is that I wrote that paper never believing the Rashidi Tribunal would approve my proposal. Was that a lack of faith in them or in myself? Three hundred five applicants? Such interest. I would've never imagined. Likely, neither did the tribunal. All of this raises many questions. If the tribunal followed my selection protocol, this group should include people with specific skill sets.

"We have the entire day ahead of us, most of which will not be spent in my living room."

"You have a nice, big backyard," Jendayi said, already getting to her feet. "Dibs on the hammock."

Marcel touched the hem of Jendayi's white blouse with ruffle sleeves. "We'll share."

"It's meant for one."

"Your point?"

Jendayi plopped back onto the love seat, where she'd been seated beside Marcel.

Fayola had no interest in wading into those murky waters of young yet blind love, so she asked, "Who are the hackers on the team?"

Neville, Sula, and Chikondi raised their hands from their places on the floor.

Sula, a perfect pear shape with sloping shoulders, slender waist, wide hips, and thick thighs pulled her mobile from a peach leather shoulder handbag with white straps. "In your report, you used the term 'skilled computerist.'" Sula chuckled. "What you just said is what I knew you meant."

"Me too," Neville said. "You got a job for us?"

Fayola did. She had two laptops in the house—hers and Jelani's—but three hackers. Considering Sula already had her mobile out, waiting for Fayola's directive, the number of devices would not be a problem.

"I want to know what the kamaus knew and when."

Neville and Sula gaped at Fayola, but Chikondi vaulted to her feet—her vibrating excitement strangely endearing.

"I have my mobile, like Sula, but I'd rather work on a computer." Onyx eyes glanced around the crowded living room.

"None are in here, but I do have two. One for you and one for Neville."

"You actually want us to hack into the most secured network in the Wake?" Neville had posed the question but with none of his earlier shock.

"If you can."

Neville ran a hand over a full beard that added years to his appearance. "We could be court-martialed."

"Or find ourselves locked in a barrack for six months," Sula said, looking at Fayola and smirking.

Who in the hell chose them? If I didn't know better, I would swear I had. They are all different. Quirky. Likable. Damn smart.

"I have a plan but no approval from the tribunal. What we do together, beginning today, could result in your imprisonment. I want to make this clear, you are not under my command. You owe me no allegiance. You chose the CEU, but I did not select the twenty of you. However, that does not mean that I would not have if I'd been in a position to do so. When in service to the Wake, we are given too few choices."

Fayola walked toward the threshold of the living room, stopping and turning when she'd crossed into the hallway. "I'm going upstairs to retrieve the two laptops. Use that time to make your decision. Stay or leave. The choice is yours."

Fayola left them alone to determine their immediate future. Once in her bedroom, she sat at her desk for fifteen minutes, giving them time to think, discuss, decide and, for some, time to leave without the perceived shame of her seeing them fly away.

Gathering both laptops, she returned to the living room. Unlike the last time she'd entered, the room was nearly vacant.

They'd claimed different parts of the open space, Neville the love seat and Sula the sofa. Chikondi sat on the floor and at the rectangular glass coffee table like it was her personal desk.

Fayola handed Neville and Chikondi a laptop each.

Grateful for their assistance, Fayola was surprised at her level of disappointment. She'd assumed some would leave but she thought even more would choose to stay.

What did I expect? They joined the CEU thinking they'd have a belay who would guide them in sanctioned missions. Instead, they are saddled with a woman with no clear objective save for righting one awful wrong.

"Passwords?" Neville asked.

Fayola rattled off hers, then Jelani's.

"Cool," Chikondi said, "we're good. Sula is ahead of us, but we'll catch up."

Sula, shoes off and feet under her, hadn't looked up from her mobile once. Thumbs tapped away, moving at an impressive speed.

Fayola pulled out her own mobile. Just because the others had chosen to leave, that didn't mean she would forgo her plan. It would be more difficult without them, a lot more, but not impossible.

Still typing, Sula glanced up from her mobile. "Why are you in here with us,"—she canted her head toward the balcony doors—"when everyone is waiting for you out there?"

They're what? Striding to the closed balcony doors, Fayola opened them. Sure enough, in her backyard, and as quiet as scheming mice, were the other seventeen members of the CEU.

The part of Fayola too afraid to want to be these young soldiers' belay, smiled. Then she leapt from the balcony to the grass below, ready to get to work.

"The kid gave you a long-ass to-do list." Kwame pulled Fayola close for a one-arm hug. "With all of these missions, we might as well call the kid Kamau Jwahir."

Squeezed between Jelani and Kwame, they stood opposite Jwahir's big pink heart.

"She didn't mean it that way."

Kissing her cheek, Kwame held her tight but not long.

Fayola had missed him, too, although neither had uttered the words.

"I'm sure she didn't, but that doesn't change the facts. Omitting Jwahir and the two deceased boys, that leaves eighteen unaccounted-for children."

Despite her guilt, Fayola refused to soothe herself by entertaining the possibility that Jwahir's situation with Mr. Seager was an anomaly.

In the face of my wrath, Seager admitted to purchasing Jwahir from the Sotos. As despicable of a person as he was, the man told me the truth.

Jelani's hand slid into hers. The back and forth caress of his thumb was a silent reassurance. But no words or actions could minimize her regret.

"The truth was right in front of me, but all I saw were twenty-one obstacles to completing my fortieth and final mission."

"You saved them," Jelani said.

"Not all." Her gaze rose to two names on the heart design—Peng and Orion. "After everything the children went through to get across the border, I turned around and returned them to a woman as dangerous as the soldiers they'd fled."

"You didn't know." Hands going to her shoulders, Jelani turned her to face him. "Anyone can be deceived, even a veteran soldier. Criminals like Dr. Pérez-Soto perfect the art of deception. That, more than anything else, is how people like the Sotos earn the trust they don't deserve."

Kwame rested his chin atop her head, an annoying reminder of their height difference. "Skilled liars and manipulators, those kinds of criminals are the hardest to discern. But once we do, once we take away their advantage, they go down just like any punk on the street."

Jelani's hands slid from Fayola's shoulders to her cheeks, cradling her face. "Kwame is right. We have all been victims of con artists. It doesn't feel good. But I won't offer you a bullshit pep talk because I would feel the same if I was on that mission instead of you. This is what I know. That was the first and last time you'd be deceived by the Sotos. Our job is to guarantee they aren't allowed to trick others into trusting them."

Warmth radiated from her, filling the small space between them like convection currents rising from a hot pavement—shimmers of heat.

"Umm . . . when did you guys become a threesome?" Durah cleared her throat, too late, if interrupting an intimate moment.

Laughing, Kwame removed his chin from Fayola's head but gave her a quick squeeze around her waist before stepping back. "Tried that once five years ago. It works better when two of the three aren't already a couple going in."

"Spilling secrets," Fayola said, feeling more like her pre-incarcerated self the longer she stayed in her friends' company. "People we know?"

"No."

"Liar," she accused with the same lack of conviction as his quick one-word reply.

"She's a smart girl." Durah joined them, leaning against the opposite wall and crossing arms over her chest. Dressed in dark wash, high-waist skinny jeans, brown soft suede flats, and a short-sleeved white V-neck T-shirt trimmed in blue, Durah appeared every bit the casual retiree with nowhere to be or people awaiting her arrival. "Jwahir told me how she managed to send that message, including how many times she tried. A lot of times, if you're wondering."

"Anything else?" Fayola asked.

"She stopped talking every time I neared the topic of verbal and physical abuse. Mom will have a better chance of getting Jwahir to open up. She has three decades of child psychology experience, while I haven't had a chance to use what I learned in graduate school. Mom told me the family practice will be there when I'm ready to join. She says I need to become acclimated to civilian life before venturing to help others with theirs."

There was no one Fayola would trust more with Jwahir's mental health than the mother of one of her best friends.

"The conversation we had amounted to a half-hearted preliminary exam. Despite her intermittent bouts of silence, I can tell she does want to talk about what's happened to her. With a bit more time, she'll be ready to speak with Mom. In the meantime, meeting her basic needs will go a long way in helping her feel safe and stable. From the looks of her room and how much food you two piled on her lunch plate, I'm not worried about her basic needs."

"That frown you're wearing says you're concerned about something." Fayola glanced to her right and toward Jwahir's bedroom. Durah had closed the door when she'd exited, and Fayola could hear the high-pitched laughter of cartoon characters. Combined, she felt confident Jwahir couldn't hear their discussion.

We could switch to Onya instead of speaking in Arcadius, but I don't want to risk alienating Jwahir by speaking in a language she does not know. This house is her safe place. Part of that is being able to understand what is being said. Jelani and I decided that last night, and I think we made the right decision.

Shoving hands into her front pants pockets, Durah's nonchalant shrug contradicted her serious expression. "What are the two of you going to do with a human kid? I mean, good intentions aside, her room looks like a day care center on steroids. I'm pretty sure once the novelty of having grilled cheese and chocolate for lunch wears off, Jwahir will want actual food that won't rot her teeth. Why in the hell did you put chocolate on grilled cheese, anyway?"

Three sets of eyes settled on Jelani, who rolled his own as if insulted by their silent judgment.

"Come on, chocolate is delicious. Of course, it's better when mixed with bear blood, but I'm not looking for converts. Besides, she ate every drop." Raising his right hand, palm out, he gave himself a high five with his left. "I'm the best Mr. Jelani ever."

"You're ridiculous. Cute and, thankfully, taken by someone stranger than you, but you made my point."

"You're wrong," Fayola said, careful to modulate her tone so Durah would know she appreciated her concern despite disagreeing. "When her parents died, Jwahir lost more than a mother and father. Yesterday, when I took her shopping, I let her choose whatever she wanted. When she awoke early this morning, after what I imagine was an awful nightmare, she sought to soothe herself by drawing the heart behind you with the art supplies Jelani purchased for a child he'd never met. If she chooses to stay with us, we'll figure out all the little things that put those creases between your brows. Right now, though, it's more important for Jwahir to feel a sense of control, even if in small ways, than it is for her to have fruits and vegetables. She knows limitations exist. The last six months with Seager made sure she did. I won't deny Jwahir her hard-fought freedom, no more than that bully of a bear could strip away her agency."

Jelani lifted both of his hands, palms out, to Fayola. "Up high."

Obliging his silliness, she smacked his palms with hers.

"Sooooo," Kwame said, extending the word as if a precipice loomed before them, "you do realize that was Durah's preliminary examination of the two of you, right?"

Jelani reached around Fayola, shoving Kwame's shoulder while offering Durah a fist bump.

"I told Jwahir I would find her human parents who would love and care for her. She knows I will keep that promise. My word . . . Jelani's word is Jwahir's superpower."

"Very good. I told Mom as much but . . ."

"She needed to be certain of us. Dr. Thando is everything you said she was. I have no reservations Jwahir will be in safe hands with her."

Durah nodded to Fayola and Jelani. "She's already in safe hands."

Beep.

Beep.

Beep.

Beep.

Four sets of alarms went off. Even Durah had worn her tactical watch.

They looked from one to the other, but it was Fayola who stepped forward. "Durah, Dad is expecting you and Jwahir in Aradi City. Her overnight bag is already packed."

"I saw it at the foot of her bed. She also showed me Raicho's lishan medal."

"She thinks I returned to her side more for my medal than for her. I'll rectify that faulty thinking, but she knows I'll always come for her as long as she has my medal. For now, that will have to be enough for us both."

"So, boss," —Kwame slung an arm over Fayola's shoulder— "are you ready to fight the power?"

"Don't call me that." Shoving his arm away, she tried to muster a proper glare. But she found herself grinning instead—an inappropriate response to what the next few hours and days could mean for them all. For half a year, Fayola believed she wouldn't see her father and friends—her family—for years after her sentencing. She assumed they would visit, just as she had decided to refuse them when they did. Selfless, she had told herself, even if it was painful for them all. Yet seeing them gathered, willing to challenge their system of military governance for a pact of friendship and love, Fayola understood her selfless desire to spare them pain from seeing her behind bars, would have been a selfish response to her own heartache.

"If not boss, then Belay Fayola."

"That's worse." She sighed, tired from the forecast of blood and violence in their future. "Maybe I shouldn't take them."

"You gave them a choice," Jelani reminded her. Then, tucking her against his side, he hugged her.

Two powerful arms wrapped around Fayola and Jelani. "Let's get all of this feel-good shit out of the way. Come on, Durah, get your cute little retired ass in here."

"No, thanks, I'm not into foursomes."

Kwame pulled Fayola and Jelani along. His arms a lariat of flesh and bone, he shifted them across the short hall. As if sprouting a third arm, Kwame added Durah to the group hug.

"You're such a spoiled, stubborn—"

"Handsome feast of a man, I know, I know. No need to laud my many fine traits." With a loud *smack*, Kwame kissed Durah's forehead, then squeezed them like a human would a lime into water.

Fayola swore she saw stars.

But no one moved, and no one complained, not even Jelani.

Fayola felt the weight of the eighteen names on the wall behind her, more than she did the combined love of her friends. However, without the latter, reconciling the former would prove even more difficult.

"Thank you," Fayola said. Her heart was as full of gratitude as helium in a balloon—lightweight and uplifting. "Ready?"

"I could eat," Jelani said.

"Yeah," Kwame said and released them, licking his lips as if anticipating a great meal, "so could I."

In unison, they turned to Jwahir's pink heart.

Fayola recalled Raicho's words from long ago. *"Know this, Fay, the color of our lightning means little without a good cause to justify its use. This truth will become murky when you are in service to the Wake. You may even forget. However, when it matters the most, you'll remember. When you do, you'll use your lightning, regardless of its color, for something or someone greater than a blood pact."*

"Our goodwill pact begins, my friends. Let's go."

14: We Must All Do Our Part

The United Wake of Benekal
Fort Kumelo City
The United Wake of Benekal Military Courthouse

"You aren't the belay we were expecting." From his place at the tribunal bench, seated between Audre to his right and Haseena to his left, Thulani tempered his irritation. Folding hands on the table before him, he nodded to Njeri who stood at parade rest. Her arms were clasped behind her back, feet twelve inches apart, shoulders straight and deep brown eyes on him.

Dressed in the all-black uniform of Wake special operations soldiers—waist-length jacket, scoop-neck shirt, fitted pants with three zippered pockets from mid-thigh to knee, ankle boots, and a wrist-to-elbow vambrace used to control electrical discharges while in human form. Njeri looked nothing short of a soldier ready to depart for a mission.

"Fayola sends her apologies."

"Does she," Thulani said, lacing his response with enough disapproval the belay would understand he hadn't posed a question.

Her eyes remained on his, holding his gaze with the unblinking confidence of a soldier firm in her conviction.

Never one to take a perceived insult sitting down, Audre shoved to her feet. "What of the human child?"

"Rescued."

"And the brown bear who held her captive?"

Thulani tsked, too late to have prevented Audre from revealing too much.

Njeri's expression remained unchanged even as she replied with another single word. "Dead."

"I assume the kill wasn't caught on video."

"No, ma'am, it was not."

"There is that, but you are a poor substitute for Belay Fayola."

"Am I?" Her dark brow may have arched, yet Njeri's respective tone revealed no emotions.

As usual, Haseena laughed. The woman was seemingly incapable of letting an opportunity to annoy Audre pass without comment. "Perhaps it would be best if we did not antagonize the one person in possession of information we seek."

"She hasn't said anything of worth. She's just standing there, waiting for one of us to dismiss her so she can run along and do Fayola's bidding. Isn't that correct?"

Interested in Njeri's response, Thulani nodded for her to answer. Even Haseena sat up straight. Her joviality was more strategy than it was personal amusement.

Njeri, still at parade rest, stared for a beat too long without answering. But when she did, any hope the tribunal had of controlling their new belay died with the utterance of four words. "She knows what you did."

"Ahh," Thulani said. There was no better response.

"None of this had to have happened."

"Hold your tongue," Audre spat. "We did not give you leave to speak freely."

Haseena waved for Njeri to continue. "No, we did not but go on."

With a glare at Haseena, Audre sat.

Unperturbed by the divergent responses of two kamaus, Njeri brought her hands from behind her back, linking them in front of her. "Annually, this tribunal mandates a proposal submission from each special operations unit. The purpose is to offer evidence-based recommendations for amending practices of a current unit or for establishing a new unit. We all know which avenue Fayola went down."

"We rejected her proposal," Thulani said, uncomfortable with the impetus to justify their decision to a lower-ranked officer.

"Not because the content lacked merit."

"You overstep," he scolded.

"Not me. The three of you. Now, two children are dead, and eighteen are missing. Add those numbers to the ones in Fayola's proposal. The Wake can't solve the world's problems, but we could've saved those twenty-one young people from the Sotos and their buyers."

This time, it wasn't Audre who stood but Haseena. "War, political corruption, poverty, and natural disasters. They have always existed."

Njeri, as self-composed as any unit commander, growled. "Sexual exploitation, forced labor, domestic slavery, benefit fraud, debt bondage."

Haseena pressed the palms of her hands to the table, leaning forward as if Njeri's list of criminal exploits were an unsheathed blade that threatened to fell her. "Yes, child trafficking."

"Calling it what it is leaves a nasty aftertaste, doesn't it, Kamau Haseena?"

"Vile."

"Like blood past its shelf life," Thulani added.

"One hundred fifty-two million children are victims of forced labor. Was it the section in Fayola's report on the estimated number of poor and neglected children used as blood donors for our pacts with some nations that you decided to reject the truth? Or was it the number of children and exploited adults who've died in blood camps?"

Haseena returned to her chair, a quiet retreat. "It is for each nation to determine how and from whom they harvest their blood donations. It isn't for us to inquire."

"But we should have," Thulani said, tired of making excuses. *Three years' worth of excuses. Longer, if I'm being honest with myself.* "We should have."

To Thulani's surprise, Audre agreed. "There is no place in this world for modern slavery, yet the act has returned in grotesque, overwhelming fashion. So now we have a rogue belay on the loose, trying to right a wrong that belongs to us. Is it safe to assume her junior unit is with her, as well as diellos Jelani and Kwame?"

"I'm unsure of their current location, ma'am. I—"

Thulani tsked, halting Njeri's creative dodging of Audre's implied question. *She might not know where they are at this very moment, but she does know where they will be in the near future. Probably because, based on her attire, she's planning on joining them.* "When you next see our MIA belay, remind her that the Rashidi Tribunal is not her enemy and, as leaders of the Wake military, we do not wish to be pulled into a war."

"With all due respect, sir, every time we consume blood from a child donor—a blood slave—we have included ourselves on the wrong side of the war against child trafficking. This tribunal could have feigned ignorance until Fayola's proposal but not afterward. But our eyesight is better than others. It is certainly more acute than human and shifter hotel employees who fail to notice a string of men entering a hotel room occupied by a young female. Dozens of men a day," Belay Njeri said, her eyes hardening. "Shall I state the appalling number of males, police officers, doctors, lawyers, even religious leaders, who visit hotels and motels for the sole purpose of raping a minor? Or how many times those pimped-out, drugged-up girls are forced to have sex in a day? A month?"

Audre lifted her glass of water to her mouth and gulped the liquid like a woman freed from the perils of a desert's unforgiving heat. "It's all very shocking."

"No more than turning a blind eye to the truth."

Thulani understood that Njeri meant more than the tribunal. But he stood firm in his position. It wasn't the role of the Wake to police other countries, even over a crime as amoral and sickening as child trafficking. Yet had they not formed the Criminal Exploitation Unit to challenge what was quickly becoming the status quo in too many countries?

"For once, kamaus, let us impundulu lend our might to those who offer us nothing in return but their heartfelt gratitude. No blood pacts, but deliberate acts of kindness. I know Fayola outlined a detailed approach to addressing this serious global issue in her proposal, but we aren't there yet. Where we are today, where we will be tomorrow and the immediate days afterward, is dealing with two known child traffickers and their most dangerous buyers."

"Is there a request somewhere in your monologue?" Haseena asked, pushing to her feet again. "Considering you're here instead of Belay Fayola, it's obvious we have more than a single rogue soldier."

"Not rogue, ma'am. We are predators."

"The natural way of our people." Haseena laid a hand on Thulani's shoulder. "We are not without empathy."

"Or regret," Thulani added, admitting to an inconvenient but a dogmatic shame. But, despite his admission, only Fayola was entitled to the rest. "Your hunt is but a droplet of blood in an ocean of sins."

A beatific smile graced Njeri's face. "I will pass along the challenge, sir."

Audre's hand appeared on his other shoulder—a physical display of unity.

We are three, but we are also one. Unity above all else. It is how every tribunal has ruled the military side of the Wake since the adoption of blood pacts—a balance between us and those whose blood we need to survive. Yet a diello who sought neither leadership nor reward revealed the shortsightedness of our nation's single-minded pursuit of blood before honor. Because no honor exists where a Wake soldier is forbidden from offering humanitarian aid to persons beyond the scope of their mission parameters.

"Be safe, Belay Njeri. You are dismissed."

"Thank you, sir." She nodded to Haseena and Audre. "Ma'ams."

Thulani watched Njeri march past the unrepaired gallery and out the courtroom where an unassuming soldier had reminded them of their purpose.

"I did not fulfill my end of the pact. I failed to keep her safe." No, young belay. It was the tribunal who failed to keep you safe.

Haseena plopped into her chair, blowing out a breath. "Were we ever that young?"

"Or that idealistic?" Thulani said.

"Or bold?" Audre added simultaneously.

Haseena swiveled her chair to face Thulani and Audre. "Young, bold, and idealistic. I would like to think, at some point in our long lives, we possessed the second two."

So did Thulani. But all he could think to say was, "We unfairly punished one of our dedicated soldiers. Manipulated her. Used her. Are we any better than those child traffickers Fayola is hunting?"

The United States of Delcanos
Belcara County, Esnel

"This asshole is going to make a run for it." Jelani perched beside Kwame on the roof of what had to be a half-million union dollar home. Located south of El Cecari Mountains, Belcara County was one of those communities formed by upwardly mobile people with enough education, money, and aspirations to move away from the harsher realities of urban living but didn't quite possess enough of the second to insulate themselves from everything and everyone they thought beneath them. Changing zip codes altered much in a person's life, including the types of crimes committed by its residents.

No open-air drug markets.

No grand theft autos.

No strong-arm robberies.

But for every type of crime committed by the "least desirable" in society, there were others—less talked about in news outlets or by government officials—committed by those with high social standing and influence.

For the past hour, Jelani and Kwame waited for the asshole who'd just pulled into his driveway. After landing, they'd shifted into their human form and seated themselves on his roof as if it were a chair atop a sturdy floor.

Expensive-looking cars and important-looking people came and went. Everyone was too busy going about their day to notice two people seated on a roof—legs dangling off the side like a kid on a swing.

Almost no one.

"Guilty people look up." Jelani stood. "Innocent and naïve ones look straight ahead."

"Yup, that piece of shit saw us the moment he pulled into his driveway."

The front half of Castel Soto Herrera's white SUV was in his driveway. The moment he'd seen them, the man had slammed on the brakes, and his eyes had met Jelani's.

Soto still watched Jelani, just as the SUV still idled. The trafficker's hands gripped the steering wheel like it was the neck of the person he probably thought had ratted him out. No one had. Fayola's hackers were gifted. They'd uncovered many secrets, including the Sotos' new residence. The two-story home sat on 200 wooded acres next to a flowing stream and waterfall.

Kwame linked his fingers, pushed his hands out in front of him, and cracked his knuckles. "He's going to make this hard."

Jelani agreed.

"Worse for him, if he does, but more fun for us."

"We aren't here to have fun. But, yeah, this asshole deserves to be fucked up for all the shit he's done. Fay wants him alive and able to talk, though."

Rising to his booted feet, Kwame flipped the scowling Castel off. "Alive and capable of speech is a low bar. You know how much damage we can do to that punk-ass bear for him to still be able to answer Fay's questions." Patting his pocket with the hand not giving Castel the middle finger, Kwame tapped his mobile. "She texted us her questions. So I say we drag his sorry ass out of his pimped-out truck, drop him in the tallest tree in this state, and interrogate him with our lightning until he tells us where we can find Jwahir's friends."

Jelani had zero fucks to give for people like Castel Soto Herrera.

I bet every one of my lishan medals he and his wife used their ill-gotten money to buy this luxury home and that expensive-ass truck he's cowering in. What kind of man can sleep at night knowing he's responsible for the rape and enslavement of children? He'll get what's owed him but not a second before we've wrenched every last detail of his trafficking operation out of him. There is one minor issue with Kwame's excellent plan, though.

"Put your hand down and take a look in the back passenger seat."

Kwame did and swore. "Where did that kid come from? Isn't he supposed to be in school?"

Pablo Soto Pérez attended Belcara Private School for Boys—an 800-acre residential campus with streams, woods, ponds, fields, and a school farm. For the lower school students, like nine-year-old Pablo, the annual tuition was 31,300 union dollars.

Jelani considered himself flexible, even on a mission. But children had a way, as Fayola's fortieth mission reminded him, of interfering with the best-laid plan. "I think he was lying down."

"He's wide awake now. How do you want to play this?"

"The bigger question is how much that papa bear loves his baby bear. He clearly doesn't give a damn about other people's children, but that me-first attitude might not extend to his flesh and blood. Let's find out."

Leaping off the roof, arms out to his side as if he'd sprouted his wings, Jelani landed with an electrifying *crackle* to the cement walkway that led to the front of the Soto home.

Kwame landed beside him a second later—white lightning mingling with Jelani's red.

"You stay here," he told Kwame. "He knows what we're capable of. There's no need to threaten him more than our presence at his home already has."

"I still think he's a flight risk."

Jelani didn't believe in ruling anything out. Castel had spent years lying and deceiving. So why would Jelani think the bear shifter would meekly turn himself into them.

Yet he hasn't made a move. Not forward into his driveway but also not in reverse. He's sitting there. Thinking. Weighing his options. Deciding what he's willing to risk for his freedom. Or maybe he's wondering if his wife sold him out. If she didn't, if he could bargain with us for her capture in return for his leniency. Perhaps he's thinking we've captured, maybe even killed his wife, leaving him with only his son to protect. Whatever is on Castel Soto Herrera's mind, the small window to make a run for it has nearly closed. It wouldn't take much for us to catch him if he tried to speed away now.

Jelani walked down the path toward the end of the driveway. Holding his arms up and palms out, all he could do was assure the bear shifter that he had no gun in his hand. Of course, everyone knew impundulus did not require conventional weapons to be deadly. Still, if he wanted to minimize the probability of the situation escalating, a show of nonviolence was needed.

Two body lengths from the SUV's grille, Jelani stopped, hands still raised. "You know why we're here," he said, voice pitched just loud enough for Castel to hear through his closed windows.

At seven in the evening, most residents on that block had returned home from work while Jelani and Kwame waited for Castel's arrival. Since then, some had come out for a run or walk. Most had kept about their business, even if taking a long double look at Castel's poorly parked SUV. But others, nosy or inquisitive, had stopped and stared. No doubt, even more neighbors watched from the safety of their homes.

"What happens next is up to you. There is no going back from this. No reclaiming this life or starting a new one." With his finger, Jelani gestured to the small but growing crowd across the street.

"What's going on?" he heard one of the onlookers ask.

"Are those impundulus? I think they are. I've never seen one this close before. Shit, and now I've seen two in one day."

"They jumped off the Sotos' roof. The wife is rarely at home. They must've done something awful, if the Wake sent those two men after them."

On and on the whispered gossip went. Jelani could see at least four of those gathered had pulled out their mobiles.

Good. This is why we came during the day. Fayola wants to send a message. Let the world see. Let traffickers and their clients tremble with fear, afraid they'll return home one day to find an impundulu waiting for them too.

"We officially have an audience," Kwame said. "I wish the kid weren't here, though. See if you can convince the piece of shit to let me take the boy to his uncle. At least he has one upstanding member of society in his family."

"Let's keep this simple and quick," Jelani said to Castel. "You know why we're here. But you also know there's no getting away from us. So the question becomes, what is the last image you want your son to have of his father?"

"Don't threaten me," Castel yelled.

"Not a threat. It's a reality check if you are too stubborn to grasp the magnitude of what can happen here."

Jelani couldn't hear Pablo, but he assumed the child said something because Castel turned toward his son in the back seat.

"What did he do?" asked a teenage boy in a T-shirt that read: I Kick Balls, written above a burning black and white soccer ball careening into a goal. Despite his shirt, the teen held a skateboard in his hand. In his other one, he trained his mobile on Jelani and Castel.

"My boy's sick. He still gets that way sometimes."

Now wasn't the time to have the conversation about the irony of Castel wanting Jelani and Kwame to give a care about Pablo's medical condition. They did, of course. Thanks to Fayola's trio of hackers, they'd read details about Pablo Soto Pérez's medical condition, just as they had about the all-boys school he attended.

"Your neighbors want to know what you've done to warrant a visit from the Wake." Jelani lowered his arms to his sides. "I have no problem revealing your dirty secrets. Maybe some of them won't be surprised. Do you have any clients in the crowd? Someone my partner and I should visit next?"

Castel lifted Pablo from the back seat, securing him in the front passenger seat beside him. "Is my wife safe and unharmed?"

"Yes."

"For how long?"

Smart man. But we didn't come here to answer his questions.

"We have a pact to fulfill. A mission to complete. The only question is whether we do it in front of your son. Put him first. My partner will see to Pablo's safety."

"He has an uncle in—"

"We know. We've already spoken to Mr. Javier Pérez Ramos."

A lie. Fayola had tasked Durah with that assignment but hadn't made it a priority since Pablo Soto Pérez was supposed to be at school taking summer remedial classes.

"He'll be in good hands. For once, make the right decision for a child." Jelani didn't have to, probably should not have, but he added, "It shouldn't be hard. You've put his welfare above others before. This time shouldn't be much different. His good health in exchange for someone else's freedom . . . *your* freedom. It was worth it before. It should be worth it now."

"Shut up, I'm trying to think."

Kwame snorted. "Trying is right. While that asshole is jump-starting his questionable brain cells, I'll be across the street."

"Don't forget, whatever we say or do will fall back on Fay. So keep to her script."

"For her to not want to be belay, she sure is bossy."

"Particular. Precise. There's a huge difference."

"Okaaay, and I'm off."

Jelani didn't watch Kwame make his way across the street, but he knew when he'd reached the crowd. Within seconds, he was peppered with questions. Two minutes later, Kwame's free press had tripled.

Suave and outgoing but with a sizzling undercurrent of danger about him, Fayola had made the right choice of Kwame as CEU's unofficial spokesperson.

Unlike every other special ops unit, the power of the CEU will not be their work in the dark but in the light. Casting a spotlight on the ugly, underground world of child trafficking begins today, on Lost Souls Square. The street name is too ironic for my taste.

"Give your son the security code to the front door, then tell him to go inside and call his uncle. Then, if it'll put your mind at ease, my partner will stay outside until your brother-in-law arrives. A sixty-minute drive from Los Sanvo County. Forty-five, if he speeds."

"Papa? What is going on?"

"It's fine."

"But that man . . . What is he talking about? I don't want to go to Uncle Javier's house."

Kwame's self-assured voice spoon-fed the crowd Fayola's script. "People, mainly young women and girls, who are victims of sex trafficking, are often sold over and again to different traffickers."

"Listen, Pablo, I know I said I would take care of you then return you to school, but I need to go with that man out there."

"The world is full of predators ready to swoop in to offer false protection, a better life, even a grand adventure to those seeking to escape a life of hardship."

"But why? I don't understand. You never leave me when I'm sick."

"Runaways and kids from unstable homes, their situation makes them vulnerable to traffickers. Poverty. Neglect. Who is looking out for them? Who cares if they disappear?"

"Uncle Javier knows what to do when you're sick, and so do you. You have your medicine. I didn't have to take you out of school. We both know I didn't."

"Yeah, but Papa, I don't want you to go."

"Human trafficking affects most countries in the world, including this one. And don't fool yourself into thinking most victims are kidnapped by strangers. On the contrary, the majority of them are trafficked by someone they know—a friend, family member, lover." Kwame paused, and Jelani knew his friend's next words. "A trusted physician and her business owner husband."

Questions exploded from Kwame's captive audience.

But not from the teenage boy with the skateboard. Pushing dark, wavy hair out of his eyes, he dropped his skateboard and jogged across the street and right up to Castel's driver's side window. Rearing back like a snake ready to strike, the teen spat on the window. "Lowlife. Do you sample the little girls before selling them to your pedo friends? Is that what gets you off?" He repeatedly spat before giving Jelani a thumbs-up and jogging back across the street. Then, jumping onto his skateboard, the teenager rode up the street, disappearing around a corner.

"Papa, why was that boy angry?"

"It's nothing. Everything is fine." Castel ruffled his son's dark hair and kissed his cheek. "Everything is going to be fine. Isn't it, impundulu?" he said, voice pitched louder as he shifted his attention from Pablo to Jelani. "Tell my son everything will be fine."

Jelani had no interest in lying to the boy, no more than he relished the thought of the child losing both of his parents. Pablo would, though, which did not mean Jelani would serve as the bearer of bad tidings.

Having moved closer while Castel spoke to his son, Jelani laid a hand on the truck's hood.

I think he's fully committed to letting his son out of the truck. If he tries to flee after that, I'll send a surge of electricity through his vehicle. But I don't think it'll come to that, thanks to Pablo. Whether Castel knows it or not, Pablo spared him a pointless chase that would've ended badly for him.

"My partner and I need to speak with your father. He has important information we require."

"You mean grown-up talk?"

"Smart young man. Yes, very important grown-up talk. Your father is going to help us capture bad people."

Pablo looked from his father to Jelani. A thin smile formed, and he offered Jelani a nod. "I don't know why that boy was so mad at Papa. He shouldn't have spit. That was nasty. Maybe, after you talk with my papa, you can find that boy and talk with him too. Explain that Papa is helping you catch bad people. Criminals, right?"

"Yes, criminals. You know about impundulus?"

"Bird shifters. Blood pacts. My teacher said impundulus help people so they can eat . . . I mean drink blood without having to kill people for it." His hand lifted to his neck, and Jelani supposed Pablo's teacher had also passed along that enduring myth.

The truth, unfortunately, was far deadlier than impundulus drinking blood from a donor's neck like a fanged vampire from paranormal stories.

"Papa, you're going to help the impundulus catch bad guys. That is so cool."

"Yeah," Castel said and hugged Pablo to him, his forehead on the top of his son's head, "it's the coolest." He whispered something in the child's ear, and Pablo nodded again.

"Got it." Happy at the thought of his father doing his civic duty to aid law enforcement, Pablo bounced in the front passenger seat. His action revealed no sign of the illness that had Castel retrieving him from a school that no doubt had the finest health center tuition money could fund.

"While girls and boys can and are trafficked for the same purpose, there are differences based on their gender. For example, boys are most often used as labor. In contrast, most girls are used for sexual exploitation and forced marriages."

The crowd had swelled, as did the number of mobile devices recording Kwame's every word. Each disturbing fact had come from Fayola's proposal.

"Domestic servitude, organ trafficking, forced prostitution, child soldiers, all of those fall under the category of forced labor."

"Okay, impundulu, on your word of honor, I'm sending my son into the house. He has the security code. I told him to call his uncle after taking another dose of medicine. Your partner has a lot to say. I don't need him to wait for Javier to get here. Pablo is a big boy. My son is capable of waiting in a locked house without a guard." Castel glared at Kwame's back but offered no greater threat than his disapproval.

"Traffickers use emotional, physical, and sexual abuse to control their victims. They also use drugs to keep them compliant and dependent on them for their next high."

Lest Castel think he planned on holding Pablo hostage, or worse, hurting the child to punish the father, Jelani opted to stay put instead of moving toward the front passenger side door.

"Traffickers can work alone or in small groups."

The passenger side door swung open.

"They can also be part of a medium-sized trafficking ring. Compared to the large criminal networks, the medium-sized groups recruit, move, and exploit on a small scale."

Castel hugged his son again, holding him close for long seconds.

"The large criminal networks operate internationally. Those rings involve more than child exploitation. They also launder money and are in partnership with high-level officials. Because of both, these kinds of networks produce victims on a global scale."

"Remember what I told you."

"I love you too, Papa." One small leg appeared at the door's opening, then the second. Pablo jumped from the SUV. He was dressed in chocolate khaki shorts and a white collared shirt with his school's crest on the right pocket—a four-quadrant shield with brown background, laurel leaf wreaths, and a burgundy symbol inside each quadrant: a key, tree, stars, and bear paw print.

He's small for his age. Thin and pale, yet a strength of character radiates from young Pablo. If raised with the right role models around him, he'll grow into the type of man he believes his father to be.

With a final wave to his father and one to Jelani, the little bear shifter rushed up the walkway to his house.

Jelani watched Castel track Pablo's progress from the SUV to the front door.

"To stop criminal exploitation, we must all play our part. Sharing what I've said today is a good start but not the only action you can take."

"My son is inside the house. You could've arrested me in front of him, but you didn't. He left thinking I'm a hero because you made him think I was going to help you send criminals to prison."

"Raising awareness, like posting the video and pics you've taken of me, will help shed light on this international travesty."

"You will help me send criminals to prison, but you're not the hero of this story. That distinction belongs to a brave human girl with golden-brown hair and a penchant for the color pink. Now move into the passenger seat; I'm driving."

"Recognize the signs," Kwame said. "Report suspicious activity and be an advocate for victims."

Jelani hustled to the driver's side of the SUV. Most of the teenager's saliva had rolled down the window to settle in the crevice where the glass met metal. Opening the door, he hopped inside.

Castel stared out the window at the door Pablo made sure to close behind him. "He's a good boy. Sweet and smart. He's been through a lot in his young life."

"Thanks to you and your wife, he's going to go through even more."

"Yeah."

Regret, but only for his son and his family. I hope the big bastard chooses silence. I'll enjoy beating the answers out of him. I didn't lie to Pablo. His father will help us capture criminals. Thanks to the baby bear, we already have one in custody.

Jelani backed the rest of the way out of the driveway.

"Don't forget—increase your knowledge, recognize the signs, report suspicious activity, raise awareness, and advocate." Kwame glanced over his shoulder to the approaching Jelani, then back to the dozens of neighbors who'd filed onto Lost Souls Square.

Jelani slowed the SUV enough for Kwame to open the door and jump in behind Castel. "Text Fay a progress report."

"On it. Nice work."

"You too." Jelani drove out of the now bustling neighborhood and onto a highway with stop-and-go traffic. "How many?" Jelani asked Castel.

Stubborn chin held high, Castel sat with a rigidity that did not bode well for him keeping his blood inside his body or sparing his bones from being broken without a shift to accompany the act.

"Belay Fayola sends her regards," Kwame said.

Jelani understood the message wasn't for him but for the heartless trafficker beside him. He knew one other thing the lowlife did not.

Kwame grabbed Castel around his neck, yanking him into the back seat.

Surprised by the attack, Castel was slow to react. It wouldn't have mattered, anyway, because Kwame was fast, strong, and fierce.

White sparks of lightning sizzled.

Castel screamed.

And Jelani turned on the radio, not to drown out the beating Kwame gave Castel but because his friend liked listening to heavy metal music while he worked.

Intense.

Virtuosic.

Powerful.

15: Those Who Request a Virgin Are Charged More

2123
One Month Earlier
The People's Democratic Republic of Tikala
Zakot Mountains
Balo Creek Canyon

Nita shook her head, amused as Kadeem rushed past her and Emmett, heading for the downstairs bathroom. "I've never known a male bear shifter who disliked peeing outdoors, regardless of his form."

"You really mean all males."

"I don't believe in stereotyping."

"Yeah, whatever you say, Ms-Give-Me-A-Minute-I-Need-To-Tinkle-Behind-That-Tree." Emmett closed the cabin door, kicked off his boots, then sniffed. "You smell that?"

"The moment I stepped on the porch."

While not all humans smelled the same to bear shifters, for some reason, young humans, twelve and under, smelled like sassafras trees, sweet and spicy. In contrast, older humans' scent reminded Nita of allspice—a blend of cinnamon, cloves, and nutmeg.

"The scent is stronger in here, though." Nita had recognized the same scent, sweet and spicy, when she'd exited the cabin two and a half hours earlier. Standing in the expansive foyer with her husband, hands on her hips, she scanned the main living area. "We haven't seen a human while we've been here."

"This place caters to bear shifters but isn't an exclusive resort. Some humans enjoy the great outdoors almost as much as we do. Still, it is odd for the cabin to smell like a human and us not having seen one during our week here."

"I'm hungry," Kadeem declared, hands wet, shoestrings untied, and face upturned.

Nita patted the crown of her son's head. "I'm glad you remembered to wash your hands. Next time, dry them too."

"Yup." Kadeem promptly used his pants to dry his hands in typical little boy fashion. "All done." He grinned up at her with such pride she didn't bother correcting him. "Chili, chili, chili," Kadeem chanted.

"Finish with your shoes first."

Kadeem's eyes lowered to Nita's boots. His lips quirked up and, before he could say anything, she dropped to a knee.

"Race you, kiddo."

Emmett strolled toward the kitchen. "I'm hungry too, and our chili does smell great."

Nita eyed Emmett as she untied her right boot. *He's going to check out the house first. Neither one of us sensed whatever human had been in here but, with Kadeem, Emmett won't take any chances.*

"So slow, Mama. I'm done." He dropped his boots in the shoe basket in the corner of the foyer.

"Wait for me."

Kadeem bounced on his toes, glancing from Nita to the direction Emmett had gone.

Taking her time, and giving Emmett more, Nita added her and Emmett's boots to the basket.

"Mamaaaa," Kadeem whined, "my stomach is growling." He stumbled as if he would collapse to the floor from hunger.

Laughing, she picked him up, tossed him over her shoulder, and softly swatted his behind. "Come on then."

"Unfair."

She swatted him again. "I'm bigger than you."

"Bully Mama."

"Yup." Nita marched to the kitchen, holding Kadeem's squirming body tight and peppering his behind with tender smacks. "What's wrong?" she asked Emmett, joining him in the kitchen.

Her husband stood beside the kitchen table, holding his bowl of chili. "Someone has eaten from my bowl."

Nita placed Kadeem on his feet, who then ran to the opposite side of the table where he'd left his lunch. She lowered her gaze to her own bowl of chili. The pink bowl had a clear top, which she'd used to cover her food before leaving on the family hike. But, like her family's bowls, hers was no longer covered with a lid. "Someone has eaten from my bowl too."

"Hey, someone ate my lunch." Kadeem climbed into the chair in front of his place setting—frowning. "And they ate it all up. So unfair. The person didn't eat all of your food."

"From the looks of things," Emmett said, clearing the table of used spoons and placing them in the sink, "the intruder tried all three but liked Kadeem's the most. I guess you were right; your chili is the best."

Instead of being placated, Kadeem huffed and puffed. Then, crossing arms over his thin chest, her baby bear glared at his empty bowl, as if doing so would have the miraculous effect of returning what the intruder had eaten.

"Want to help me check out the rest of the house?" Emmett asked Kadeem. "Let's see what else our visitor liked best."

"Unfair." Kadeem slid from the table, giving his empty bowl a longing look before turning away and taking Emmett's offered hand.

"There's still plenty of chili left," Nita told her son. "That makes you a lucky little bear because you have two pots full of food."

"I know, Mama, but . . ."

"I know you were looking forward to your special chili mix." Nita knelt to Kadeem's level, understanding her son's disappointment, maybe even anger, but wanting him to comprehend the potentially larger issue. "I'm thinking the person who ate your food was very hungry. Much hungrier than you, Papa, and me. Maybe the person who ate your food doesn't have any of their own."

"No food?"

He sounded confused. Understandable, since he'd never gone more than a few hours between meals.

"That's not right. Everybody gets hungry. Food makes us strong." Lifting his free arm, Kadeem flexed.

Emmett mirrored their son's action, to greater effect, of course. "What Mama says is right. Some people have more than others. More clothes. More toys. More food."

At four, Nita did not expect Kadeem to grasp the fullness of society's inequities. Still, four was not too young to introduce the topic or encourage empathy.

"The person must've been really hungry. They didn't leave me any. But, yeah, I can make more. I remember how."

"Good attitude." Standing to her full height, Nita said to Emmett, "This is more than the fruit that went missing those other times."

"I know. I still don't hear anything, and nothing is missing from what I can tell. Let's examine the living area and upstairs before deciding whether we should report this to Mr. Seager."

They hadn't the last two times. Other than food, nothing had been taken then either.

If we file a report with Mr. Seager, he'll probably call the local police who will spend hours scouring the canyon for what is likely a runaway. Maybe we should've informed him the first time we realized someone had been in the cabin.

"I know that look. We'll talk later. Let's just search the cabin for any more messes before deciding what to do about them," Emmett said to Nita. Then, to Kadeem, he asked, "Ready?"

"Yup."

Off they went, with Nita trailing behind the males.

Entering the main living area, they parted ways, each of them moving to a different area of the room.

"Someone has been sitting in my chair," Emmett said, tapping the side of his nose.

Nita didn't need to imitate her husband's actions, despite the scent of sassafras wafting from her favorite chair in the room. "Someone has been sitting in my chair too."

"Come on. So unfair. Someone has been sitting in my chair." Kadeem stomped his feet and balled his fists. "And they broke it. Look, look, someone broke my rocking chair."

Sure enough, the small chair lay tipped on its back, bits of wood on the floor beside it.

Emmett closed the toy chest with one hand while tapping the side of his nose with his other.

Nita understood, for she had also detected the same scent around the toy chest.

Kadeem slid his hand into Emmett's. "What now, Papa?"

"We check the bedrooms."

"Eat, play, and sleep?" Nita said. "Do you really think the young human is still here?"

"I don't know. At first, we thought it was a hungry, homeless teen. Now, I no longer think that's the case. There's plenty of stuff lying around to steal and pawn. But all we've seen is evidence of a kid being a kid. No vandalism. No theft. Not even an attempt to cover up their presence."

Nita agreed. Neither she nor Emmett had much growing up, despite the long hours their parents worked. However, what they did possess was a strong sense of morality and justice.

Some too many kids go to bed hungry every night. By not going to Mr. Seager, I thought we were doing the right thing. Now, I'm unsure if we did.

Before she'd reached the upstairs landing, Nita knew the human had taken the same path. A little stronger than downstairs, the sweet scent of sassafras tickled her nose.

Emmett and Kadeem entered the master bedroom first. "The bed is a little ruffled." Emmett ran a hand over a small area of wrinkled comforter. "A little thing. Bigger than our Kadeem but still small. I was hoping we were wrong about the scent. That the human was at least a teenager. What do you have there?"

The desk chair and laptop on the desk had caught Nita's attention while Emmett had been examining the comforter and Kadeem the space under the bed.

"Nothing under here, Papa. I'm gonna find the person who ate my chili and broke the rocking chair."

Nita couldn't tell if her little bear meant his statement as a threat or as a youthful intent to help someone in need.

"I pushed this chair in." Grazing the top of the closed laptop, Nita was again struck by the feeling of wrongness. "The computer isn't exactly where I left it either."

"This isn't just about a hungry child, is it?"

"It no longer feels that way." Nita turned to Emmett, whose dark brows were drawn together. "What are you thinking?"

"That we should check the other two rooms, then this computer for clues."

"Search history?"

"That's the easiest way to—"

"Hey, someone's been sleeping in my bed."

Nita hadn't noticed Kadeem leave. She and Emmett rushed from the master bedroom, down the hall, and to Kadeem's room.

"And she's still here." Kadeem stood at the foot of the upper bunk bed, finger pointing at a girl as stunned by their presence as they were by hers. "Hey, you ate my lunch."

A little girl, a human with golden-brown hair, sat up. Sleepy eyes widened, growing big as she took in the three bears before her.

"I'm sorry. I'm sorry. I'm sorry. I didn't mean to . . . I didn't . . . I'm really sorry."

"It's okay." Nita lowered Kadeem's accusatory finger. "We aren't upset."

Emmett settled a hand on Nita's shoulder—a nonverbal gesture of agreement. "We have plenty of food for you and for us. Don't we, Kadeem?"

"Umm, yeah. Plenty. And two beds. One for me and one for you."

From her spot on the top bunk, the little girl stared down at them through glassy eyes. This close, the scent of sassafras wafted from her like a sweet-smelling perfume that threatened to override the stronger smell of fear.

"Do you need help?" Emmett asked.

"I can get down by myself."

"That's not what I—"

As if she carried more in her genes than normal human DNA, the girl leapt from the top bunk to the bottom one, then darted past them and out the door.

Nita gave chase, overtaking the girl before she reached the front door. "We won't hurt you."

"I gotta go. Please, let me go."

"We can help. If you let us, we can help you."

Emmett and Kadeem hovered on the stairs behind Nita.

The human child shook her head. "I'm not supposed to be here. I'm sorry, I didn't mean to break the rocking chair." Then, backing closer to the front door, wild, wide eyes filled with tears, she added, "I sent her a message. She'll come for me. I'll be fine. She'll help."

"I'm sure whoever you messaged will help later, but we can help you now." Moving slowly to not add to the child's anxiety, Nita removed her boots from the shoe basket.

"Let Mama help you. She's a good helper."

Eyes consumed with a fear she hated to see because it meant the girl suffered from more than hunger, she nodded, almost imperceptibly, to Kadeem.

"I'll be fine," the girl repeated, clutching a jacket that smelled of musk, cinnamon, and a bear scent she knew but couldn't quite place. "Dela Eden will come for me. She'll come. I know she will."

Such certainty. Faith. What kind of name is Dela Eden?

"I'm Nita. Emmett is the big bear behind me, and the little bear next to him is Kadeem. We won't hurt you. We only want to help.

Please, tell us how we can help." Dragging on first the right boot then the left, Nita let her words hang between them, unwilling to rush a child who had no reason to trust strangers.

Nita glanced over her shoulder to Emmett, hoping he had a better plan. But his pinched brows revealed nothing new, certainly not a plan to calm the human.

Emmett shifted down two steps. A shake of his head had Kadeem halting instead of following.

Nita finished lacing her boots.

"This is our last night here," Emmett said, his deep voice as soft as a man his size could make it. "Before we leave, we could take you to the resort's owner. His family has run this place since its building. Mr. Seager knows almost everybody in the nearest town. I'm sure he can—"

As if she'd seen her mortal enemy, the girl squeaked, then bolted from the cabin.

Nita raced after her, convinced she would catch her as easily as she had before. She would have too, if not for the . . . Nita jerked to a stop like a driver slamming on brakes.

A group of fifteen-plus people, *a human tour group for fuck's sake*, from the smell of them, was led by a bear shifter guide.

Dressed in khaki everything, including her hiking books, the thirty-something tour guide with red curls dangling from under her wide brim sun hat with drawcord, smiled tightly at Nita. "You're on vacation, my friend; what's the rush?"

Nita disliked passive-aggressive people, almost as much as she did to lose her prey. Not that the human child had been prey, but she had gotten away from her all the same.

With so many human scents mixed in with the smells of outdoors, it'll make tracking the girl harder. Why did she run? I thought we were getting through to her.

"Did anyone see which way a little girl went?"

Some glanced around at the children who were part of their tour group, while most chatted as if she hadn't uttered a word, including the tour guide.

"The log cabin in front of you is the . . ."

Nita jogged into the cabin and slammed the door behind her. Emmett was gone but Kadeem sat on the bottom step.

"She got away?"

"Unfortunately."

"You were right, Mama."

Nita sat beside Kadeem, her disappointment a heavy load needing relief. "About what?"

"I don't think an adult is taking care of her. I think she would make a good big sister, if she wasn't so hungry and sad."

Scooting closer, Nita took hold of her son's hand, curious. "What makes you think she was sad?"

He leaned against her, his head on her shoulder. "I would be sad if I had to steal food to eat. You and Papa take care of me. Buy me stuff. Keep me clean. Cook me food. She's sad, Mama. I know she ran away, but she needs help. Can we help her?"

"We?"

Big, brown eyes met hers, followed by a squeeze to her hand. "I don't mind sharing my food and toys. Even my bed. But I don't have bunk beds at home."

Nita hugged Kadeem, feeling every bit like a proud mama. "We'll do our best to help her. Where's your papa?"

"He said—"

"The United Wake of Benekal." Emmett appeared at the top of the stairs. "Our guest went to one site—The United Wake of Benekal's Tikala embassy."

Nita jumped to her feet. "Why would a kid do that?"

"No idea. Come on up. We have a long-distance call to make."

Nita went, hoping someone at the embassy would know who in the hell Dela Eden was, and that the person could help. If not, then Nita and Emmett would have no choice but to speak with Mr. Seager and file a report with the sheriff's department.

No matter what, we must do something to help the child.

2123
The Kingdom of Yokka
Northern Hona City

Teresa shook Hadiza's hand. "We have a deal."

They sat at the bar of a restaurant of the hotel Castel had chosen for what she hoped would be a short stay, a few weeks, maybe less. Neither fancy nor a dive, Hotel Kiko, named after the nineteenth-century rebel leader who'd led the people of Yokka to freedom against an ever-worsening stream of despotic rulers, catered more to budget-minded international business travelers than locals wanting to reminisce about the "good old days."

Nature hadn't been kind to the Yokka. From wildfires and droughts in the north to mudslides and torrential rain in the south, the elements had proven a more despicable ruler of their lives than any past warlord.

"We have a deal," Hadiza agreed. Her accented Arcadius was far better than Teresa's mangled Nokro.

Usually, Teresa limited her business transactions to countries where she spoke the language. However, doing so meant she spent time in countries too close to home and visited them far too often than was prudent.

After this last job, I'll retire. I'm tired of being away from my family. But the money is so good. So maybe one more job after this one, then I'll be done.

"And the juju?" Hadiza asked, eyeing Teresa over the top of the drink she sipped. "The ritual is important."

"It's a waste of time."

The restaurant sold nothing stronger than water with lime and too-thick coffee at seven in the morning. Teresa ordered water, no lime; Hadiza coffee, two sugar cubes, and no cream. They had the place to themselves except for two other early risers. A young man sat beside a window, using a fork to push the food around on his breakfast plate, while an equally young bald-headed woman perched on a stool at the opposite end of the bar. Her fingers tapped the scarred dark wood finish in a melodic one-one-two cadence, while her other hand held a mobile up to her ear.

The young man and woman could've been a feuding couple for all Teresa knew. They certainly hadn't looked in each other's direction, much less at Teresa and Hadiza.

Hadiza lowered her coffee cup. Her dark brown eyes had hardened at Teresa's statement. "Your ignorance of the Yokka culture is as appalling as your choice of beverage and clothing."

"You find drinking water appalling?" She didn't bother taking issue with the other insult. *These business trips aren't about impressing the locals with my sense of fashion but getting them to trust me with their children so I can make money for my family and future.*

Hadiza placed the blue and white striped mud cloth design coffee cup on its matching saucer. At five-ten and over two hundred pounds, Hadiza, a local spiritual leader and healer, wore her weight and makeup well. If not for her sweet, spicy human scent, Teresa would've mistaken her for an elephant shifter. The woman wore high heels with a hip-hugging, knee-length black skirt and a light gray blouse with dark sweat stains under the armpits.

Like the mediocre hotel, Hadiza possessed neither great beauty nor unflattering appeal. However, both the hotel and the human served a purpose, so Teresa retreated from a stance that would yield nothing but animus from her temporary business partner.

"Have your juju ritual. Use the girls' hair, blood, and clothing to bind them to you."

"You speak as if you understand. You do not."

"You don't need my understanding. That's not our business arrangement. We both have connections the other does not. So let's stick to what we both do best."

Despite Hadiza's influence in her small town of Gomar, her reach ended there. On the other hand, as a humanitarian doctor, Teresa's reputation opened many doors closed to the average Yokka woman. At the same time, no one would have reason to question the business relationship between two physicians, even if Hadiza had bestowed herself with the title of *healer*.

Despite Teresa not holding her glass of water and Hadiza having finished her coffee, the human clinked their cups. "I've already told my girls about you. Specifically, your work in Namju with the orphans. They're excited to begin working. They want to make money for their family. Lots of job loss in the city and too few opportunities for decent, stable employment."

Same story. Everybody's looking to make money. To start life over someplace new. Thanks to Castel paving the way for me, I already have clients. All I need are the girls, and the exchange of money for workers can begin. "I'll need to examine your girls."

"I know."

"Gynecological exams."

"I said I know." Hadiza glanced around, an eyebrow arched. "Four customers but no bartender."

"Do you want to order breakfast? Another coffee?" Teresa was expecting a call from Castel. The time zone difference meant one of them was either ending their day or beginning a new one. But she hadn't eaten and, considering she didn't have to be on guard with Hadiza, the human would make a tolerable breakfast companion.

"I want nothing but the bill for my coffee."

"I'll have the bartender put it on my tab. Are you leaving then?"

"All my girls aren't virgins."

"That truth rarely matters. As long as they're disease-free and not pregnant, my clients won't know the difference. Most don't care, but those who request a virgin are charged more."

"During the ceremony, I can link the spirits to your exam."

Teresa rolled her eyes. "Do not tell them the exam involves me inserting an evil spirit into their vagina."

Hadiza shrugged broad shoulders confined to a silky top. "Speculum, evil spirit, most are too inexperienced to know the difference. After they're sold, you'll be gone. But I'll still be here. Having them go through the juju, believing there is a bad or evil spirit inside of them, ready to strike them dead if they don't obey their oath, will keep them compliant and your clients happy."

"Forever in your debt for helping them find employment."

"They're supporting their parents and younger siblings. It's their duty to help."

Teresa didn't require the spin, but she could appreciate Hadiza's unique approach.

When the bartender returned, smelling of cigarette smoke, Teresa ordered breakfast, then waved goodbye to Hadiza, with a promise to, "Talk again after the juju ritual." By the time she'd finished eating, more people had filled the empty tables. Two waiters had joined the bartender, and the young man and woman had disappeared without her having noticed.

Teresa pulled out her mobile to call Castel again. She joined a man in an elevator dressed in a navy suit and white shirt. He wore no tie, leaving the top three buttons of his shirt open, revealing a teasing swath of hairless brown skin.

Why isn't Castel picking up? It isn't that late at home.

Teresa considered calling Pablo, but she would have to go through the residential hall's resident advisor. The pain-in-the-ass student was a rule-following seventeen-year-old senior who took his responsibilities far too seriously. He'd once told her, "There's a reason why the younger kids aren't permitted to have a mobile in their room. How will they adjust to being here if they can call and receive calls from their guardian whenever they like?"

Teresa's hand had twitched, and she'd wished she possessed the ability to give the RA a long-distance slap. But that power being beyond her, she'd grumbled something unkind then hung up.

Dammit, Castel, answer your mobile.

As she exited the elevator, Teresa smiled at the man who'd been kind enough to push the button for her floor. Unfortunately, he wore too much cologne, which had ensured she stayed on the opposite side of the elevator.

"Have a good day, ma'am."

The door closed, but the last word he'd spoken lingered.

Compared to him, I guess I am ma'am. Is there a job fair being held at the hotel? Are they recruiting twenty-year-olds to replace older and more skilled but higher-waged workers? Either that or the three kids I've seen this morning are vacationing on their parents' credit cards.

Teresa closed and locked the hotel room door, removed her flats, and plopped onto the couch. Mobile in hand, she was primed to call her husband again. But the device rang, lighting up and revealing the caller as someone other than Castel.

"This is an unexpected surprise. How are you doing, Jav—"

"What in the name of our dead parents have you done?"

Five years her senior, Javier had a terrible tendency of reminding Teresa that while they may have become adults, he still viewed her as his "baby" sister.

"What are you talking about?" Deciding to take whatever scold her brother was about to unleash, Teresa reclined on the couch, legs crossed at the ankles.

"I'm at your house with Pablo. He called me."

She sat up, swinging her legs over the side of the couch. "Why? Where's Castel?" Her stomach suddenly felt empty as one awful possibility after another had it tightening.

"According to Pablo, Castel left with two impundulus. He's under the impression his father is helping them catch criminals."

It felt like all the blood in her body pooled in her heart, freezing on contact.

"Did you hear me?"

Teresa sank to the floor, every breath forced through constricted lungs.

"There were neighbors and news crews outside when I arrived. I had to fight my way past them to get inside the house. But not before some woman shoved a mobile in my face, hurling crazy accusations."

"W-what was on her mobile?"

Raising knees to her chest, then lowering her head between them, Teresa breathed in through her nose and out through her mouth. In through her nose and out through her mouth.

"A recording of two impundulu soldiers like the one that was sent to retrieve you from Namju. I should've known then that you and Castel were into something illegal. But not this, Teresa. Tell me you aren't involved in what those people have accused Castel of doing. He stayed in his truck the entire time the nosy neighbor recorded everything she could. So, I didn't see or hear him admit to any wrongdoing. But he did leave with the soldiers without a fight."

"He had Pablo with him. Why would you expect Castel to fight two soldiers?" *Pablo should've been at school. I don't know why he wasn't. But Castel's capture explains why I couldn't reach him.*

The thought of never speaking to or seeing her husband again had Teresa bolting to her feet and dashing into the bedroom.

"Impundulus are honorable soldiers. They don't harm children."

"As far as you know." Grabbing her rolling suitcase from the closet, she dropped it onto the bed. "They drink blood. You have no idea what else they are capable of doing." She pulled open drawers and scooped out her clothing and dumped it into the suitcase. "You can't trust people who feed off other living beings."

"You can't be serious. If even a third of what I've seen on the news and social media is true, you and Castel are the true bottom-feeders."

Yanking the suitcase from the bed, she ignored her brother's hurtful words. "I'll be on the first flight home."

"Don't."

The single word, spoken softly, halted her hurried movement to the door.

"There's a warrant out for your arrest. I'm doing my best to maintain the lie Castel told Pablo, but I can't keep him in a bubble. Come tomorrow, whatever neighbors haven't heard will have. The same with the students, faculty, and staff at that expensive school. I looked the other way when you and Castel made purchases above what you should've been able to afford. None of

Castel's business ventures went far, and a doctor who floats from one disaster-ridden area to the next accumulates little but frequent flyer miles." His voice softened again. "No matter what you've done, you're my sister, and I don't want you to go to prison. Or worse, if impundulus come for you too."

Teresa slipped back into her flats, touched by her brother's concern but knowing she had to leave the hotel and city, even if she didn't return home.

I don't know how they found Castel or how the Wake discovered our secret. Not that it matters now. My Castel is likely dead because nothing short of a threat to Pablo would have him leave our son by himself. And he would never betray me, just as I would never turn against him. Even so, I'm on my own, which means I can't assume the Wake isn't after me too.

Teresa wanted to fling herself onto the bed, curl into a ball and cry until the pain of losing her husband and life faded to dull, throbbing aches, replacing the sharp, relentless stabs slicing her heart.

"Go somewhere safe. Let this die down. When it does, I'll bring Pablo to you." Javier paused. "Tell me it isn't true. About you two being child traffickers."

He wants me to lie to him, to assuage his guilt for offering to turn Pablo over to his criminal mother. I could lie to him. I've been doing it for years. What would one more matter?

"Castel and I did some things we shouldn't have but nothing so awful as to be wanted by the Wake. Of course, we aren't perfect, but to do good in places like Yokka, I've had to work with questionable people. In the end, though, Castel and I have secured homes and employment for hundreds of needy kids. Did we break a few laws to do it? Yes. Do we peddle children? No, and I'm disgusted anyone would define our humanitarian work that way. Do you think I'm guilty of what you've heard?"

Hand on the doorknob, Teresa remembered what she'd forgotten in her haste to leave.

"If that's all you two did, then no. Helping children in need could never be a crime. But they're saying you sold children. I don't want to believe them, but the money for this house, Pablo's medical bills and private school had to come from somewhere, and it wasn't from me."

"Look," Teresa said, hoisting her retrieved pocketbook onto her shoulder, "we can discuss those slanderous rumors later. But you're right, I shouldn't return home. Once I'm settled, I'll seek legal counsel, so I can begin righting this awful wrong. I also won't tell you where I am or where I'm going. That way, you won't have to lie for me." *As much as I love him, Javier is a horrible liar. I won't risk my life on him keeping my whereabouts to himself, especially if an impundulu comes calling.* "I must be going. Put Pablo on."

"He's asleep, and I'd rather not wake him until it's time to leave. Find a safe place, get a new mobile, and then call my private office line in a couple of days."

"You're a good big brother."

"I'm doing this for Pablo."

"I know. Thank you." Teresa ended the call, grateful for Javier and already missing Pablo and Castel. *I'll see my son again soon. As for my husband, I can't think about him now. I can only afford to think of myself. And what I need to do right now is get the hell out of this hotel and city. Hadiza will just have to find her own clients. With a bit of ingenuity, she'll manage.*

Pocketbook on her shoulder and fingers wrapped around her suitcase handle, Teresa opened the door.

Stopped.

Frowned.

A woman leaned on the closed hotel room door across the hall. Not just any woman, but the same bald-headed young female from the restaurant.

She smells like the man from the elevator. The same strong, cloying scent. I thought it was cologne. I hadn't paid much attention to her at the bar beyond thinking she and the man not eating his breakfast would make a cute couple.

"How long have you been watching me?" Teresa risked a glance down both sides of the hallway. To her left, the man who'd ridden the elevator up with her waved. At the opposite end of the hallway, the man from the restaurant licked his lips and winked at her. His shoulder was propped against the door that led to the east stairwell.

Now I know why he hadn't been interested in his breakfast.

Teresa snatched her gaze from his, returning it to the woman a mere ten feet in front of her. "How long?" she asked again, proud she'd kept the tremor from her voice.

The woman's grin was beautiful yet frightening for the eyes that flashed golden. "How long is inconsequential."

"What did you say?"

More lightning formed, skittering from one side of her eyes to the other. White teeth against dark brown skin, her grin widened—unnaturally and with deliberate intent to evoke fear.

The male impundulus hadn't moved. So even if she managed to overpower the female, the men blocked the only two avenues of escape. Unlike them, she couldn't fly. Any route to the first floor from the fifteenth would end either in her death or a trip to the emergency room.

"Inconsequential," Teresa said, knowing only one person who used that word as a substitute to answering questions she deemed unimportant. "Inconsequential." Teresa staggered backward, feeling the weight of each syllable. "Did she tell you to say that to me?"

"No, but Cassius, Eldrick, and I have a bet. Not that you would figure out who sent us and why but"—she pointed to Teresa's face—"how fast your heart would race when the truth hit you."

Teresa's heart, no longer frozen in mourning, rampaged in her chest like a herd of wild horses. "She didn't wear a scent disguise when she came to the clinic. With what should have been a simple grab-and-go mission, it's optional."

"W-what do you want . . . and d-don't you dare say inconsequential."

"But it is. We want nothing from you, doc. Think of us as your silent partners." She tapped her fingers on her cheek, the same one-one-two rhythm Teresa noticed at the bar. "Well, partners isn't the right word."

"Bodyguards," the man from the elevator said, reminding her of impundulus' acute hearing.

"Wrong," the other man said. "Both of you are wrong." Pushing from the stairwell door, as if he barely had enough energy to keep himself upright, he shoved hands into his pants pockets. "I didn't eat breakfast, and I'm starving." He winked at Teresa again. "You smell delicious but aren't on the menu, so you can stop gaping at me like you're an open vein and my mouth is an empty glass."

"Go feed," the young woman told the man. "I caught her in the parking garage. She's in the trunk of our car."

"Alive?"

"Alive . . . ish."

He shrugged. "Good enough."

Then he was gone, leaving Teresa with an unsettling suspicion of who the impundulu female had captured.

"I'm Dominique, by the way. Think of us as walls you can't go over, through, or around. Not bodyguards or partners. Cassius was right. We're more like prison guards."

"I'm under arrest?"

The man from the elevator . . . Eldrick, approached. "You wish it was that simple." With a jerk of his chin, he gestured to her hotel room. "You're allowed room service. We wouldn't want you dying of starvation before our belay comes for you."

"I'll call the police."

"And tell them what?"

They had her, and they knew it.

There's no one I can call for help. Not Javier, and no longer Castel. For the first time in my life, I'm at the mercy of someone else. It doesn't feel good. But I suppose that's what Diello Fayola intended. I don't know what belay means in their language, and I don't need to. She is behind what happened to Castel and what is happening to me. She knows I lied and used her. She sent these young soldiers here instead of coming herself. Why? Where is she?

Moving with an ennui that didn't match the woman's age, she stood from where she'd been leaning against the door. "We were ordered to not harm you except in self-defense."

Eldrick moved even closer. "Or if you tried to flee. I wouldn't recommend doing either."

"So go back inside. Lock the door behind you if that'll make you feel safer."

Teresa had seen Diello Fayola break down her clinic door in Namju with appalling ease.

They're playing mind games. How long will Fayola make me wait? Should I take my chances with local authorities?

Teresa slammed the door, then promptly locked it before storming into the bedroom. She crawled onto the bed, curled into a tight ball, and burst into tears. Whether she cried for her deceased husband, their innocent son, or for herself, she didn't know. What Teresa did know was that she did not want to end up like Hadiza—stuffed in a car's trunk then fed on by a hungry impundulu.

She shivered.

And cried harder.

16: You Mentioned Bait

Three Days Later
The State of Namju
East Tousaki City

"Is she still there?"

Mobile clutched in one hand, her reliable rifle in the other, Matriarch Moshi stomped to the window. Planting her feet like the roots of an ancient tree, she snarled at seeing the same damn sight she'd witnessed for the last twelve hours. From a height of seventeen hundred feet, the Zuungat Trade Center was the tallest building in Namju, the tallest in the Western Hemisphere, and the sixth tallest building on Earth Pact. She claimed the historic tower as her base of operations, the local government falling to her Sunhung herd of soldiers.

Every day, since securing this city, a coup unrivaled by any other matriarch in the history of Namju, Moshi would come to this window on the ninety-fourth floor and stare down at the city below. The sight pleased her, but she would not be satisfied until all of Namju was under her rule.

Moshi's hand gripped her mobile tighter. "She hasn't moved off that roof since I first noticed her presence. Not to piss or eat. Not even to sleep. She stands, sometimes kneels, but she always watches. Waits."

On sunny, cloudless days, the Zuungat Trade Center afforded Moshi an unobstructed view of the city.

One day, Zuungat Trade Center will bear my name.

Moshi tapped the wide, tall window with the barrel of her rifle. "She's mocking me. Reminding me that, no matter how tall and impressive Zuungat is, the structure was not only modeled after the tallest building in Benekal but that it pales in comparison to their Autry Clock Tower's thirty-five hundred feet."

"You're fixating on the wrong thing."

Moshi agreed with Matriarch Etsu, not that she would admit as much to the young, ambitious woman.

Without my help, she wouldn't have secured Fuxing City. Even now, there are small but growing pockets of rebels Etsu's soldiers haven't extinguished. She is loyal, though, and brave. I'll need matriarchs like her in my new regime.

Moshi lowered her rifle, the weight heavy for the rounds she wouldn't dare yet release into the troublesome impundulu's body.

"I'm focused on an impundulu soldier who has no legal authority to be in our nation. I haven't seen more, but I doubt the brazen bird would dare enter my city alone."

"Is it the same one from the border skirmish?"

More than a skirmish. That impundulu attacked and killed several men under my command. The remaining Namju-Tikala border guards spent days in the hospital—most with life-altering injuries. A couple of the more prideful ones returned to their unit—angry and vengeful—but ultimately useless. Fear carries a stench worse than death.

"Perhaps it is. I would enjoy putting a bullet through that particular impundulu's brain. But I'd rather know the extent of the threat than whether the female impundulu watching my every movement is the same one who stole my property."

"There is one way to find out who she is and what she wants."

The steel in Etsu's voice reminded Moshi of how the thirty-one-year-old had risen to the rank of a matriarch.

Unyielding strength, yes, but also a cold, hard strategist.

"Test her resolve. Dangle bait before her and see if she bites. If she does, then she's likely the same impundulu from the border. If she isn't . . . hold on, I have a call on my landline."

Moshi heard the tacky sound of boots on tile flooring, then parts of a one-sided conversation.

"Where?" Etsu asked. "Are you positive? No, I don't have binoculars on me. Okay, okay, calm the hell down. Just the one? Okay, good. Get the snipers in place. Good idea. Ground-to-air missiles too."

Moshi divided her attention between listening to Etsu's voice shift from calm to concerned to dangerous, and watching the impundulu stand, stretch, and then nod at Moshi with such confidence that left no room for doubt.

She sees me as clearly as I can her, but she doesn't require the aid of a telescopic scope to do it. What do you want, little bird? My blood? Shoving her mobile in the pocket of her baggy BDU pants, Moshi raised her rifle to the window, took aim, and then lowered her eye to the scope's eyepiece. *Nine times the magnification. I can shoot the sweat off your arrogant nose, or . . .* Moshi shifted up and to the right. Just a hair. *Take out your right eye. That's your vulnerable spot. One bullet from this distance to the center of your eye and bye-bye bird, hello brain splatter. An easy kill shot. Too easy. What will happen if I give the order for my snipers to take you out?*

"We have another problem." Etsu's voice, intrusive in the quiet room, did little to draw Moshi's attention away from the impundulu.

Whether you're the same impundulu who killed Captain Seifu, you'll serve as my message to the rebels, the Wake, and the entire fucking world. Namju belongs to Matriarch Moshi and the Sunhung herd. Defy my will, and you will die.

"Moshi, are you still there?"

Retreating from the window but not from her intent to see the impundulu female dead, Moshi propped her rifle against the side of the rectangular glass desk. Maps of the nation filled most of the space. Areas circled in red were under Sunhung's control. Those in blue were held by the Taepo herd. While regions marked in brown, some entire cities and counties, others random neighborhoods here and there, were still controlled by the former government. To Moshi, those areas constituted battles yet to be won.

Wars aren't won in weeks or months. The government might still have control of the air force. However, as long as they care about the welfare of Namju civilians, they won't send their planes and fighter pilots into the areas under my command. They won't risk murdering thousands of innocents to route us from our hiding holes. The people are our best shields and, as long as we have them, our victory is guaranteed.

Moshi smirked, withdrawing her mobile from her pants pocket. "Let me guess, an impundulu has been spotted in your territory."

"A male. Perched on a building like it's a fucking tree branch."

"They do like their heights. They think it's an advantage, but history has proven that even the mightiest, highest-flying bird can be brought crashing to the ground if provided with the right incentive. You mentioned bait."

"The Wake has never shown much interest in Namju. Until last year, we thought they upheld our non–blood pact agreement. Thanks to that brawl at the border, we know differently."

Snatching up her rifle, Moshi left the executive suite. She didn't bother looking over her shoulder at the impundulu. Nothing would change on that front until either Moshi forced the issue or the Wake soldier revealed whatever plan lurked behind her stoic golden eyes.

She stopped in front of an elevator but didn't push the button to bring it to her floor. "I'm going to give her more than bait."

"What do you mean?"

Moshi returned to the executive suite, placing her rifle atop a map of Ballur County—her next target. County Executive Chidike Umburter had defied Moshi at every turn, thinking his police officers were a match for her herd. But, like the bold but foolish impundulu on the rooftop, the county executive would soon learn how far Moshi would go to achieve her goals.

"I'll take care of our pest problem here then. If you need support dispatching with yours, I'll send reinforcements. But, for now, keep that impundulu in your snipers' crosshairs. I'll call you when I'm done here."

Moshi ended the call with Etsu only to dial someone else. "Bring the newest recruits to the roof," she said the moment Captain Jomo answered his mobile.

"Ma'am?"

"You heard me."

"The roof, ma'am?" Jomo cleared his throat, and Moshi allowed his questioning of her order to go unpunished in light of her odd command. "I mean . . . yes, ma'am. All of the new recruits to the roof."

Moshi spared another glance at the impundulu.

Who will you try to save this time if it really is you? One or two of them? Or yourself?

Moshi laughed, knowing whatever decision the Wake soldier made wouldn't end well for the impundulu.

"Ma'am?"

"Nothing, captain. You're right. I don't need all the new recruits. Only Dr. Pérez-Soto's last batch. Perhaps, after six months, not so new anymore, but they still carry a scent and look of innocence. You have ten minutes to get them to the roof. Make sure you're the only one who is armed."

"Yes, ma'am."

"Take your mobile and wait for my call."

"Yes, ma'am. Ten minutes."

Moshi didn't place more calls, but she did send a group text message to the current shift of snipers. Within an hour of spotting the impundulu on the rooftop, Moshi had established two rotating teams of snipers. The six-soldier teams had secured locations on buildings nearest the impundulu.

Their presence and the silent threat had little effect on the Wake soldier. She had simply cataloged their presence, nodded, and then knelt as if meditating.

I'll teach her to take my herd and me seriously.

Moshi returned to the widow, her rifle hanging from a strap on her back and her thumbs typing away.

When she shifts, light her ass up.

No return texts, but Moshi knew her snipers had received her order.

She scanned the sky. There were calm, bluish-white clouds for miles and not a black and gray feather in sight. No thunder. No lightning. No other impundulu.

"You're all alone, little bird. Just you, me, and my snipers. If, by some act of extreme luck, you manage to survive, my herd will finish off what's left of you. I'm going to enjoy feeding you to my bear shifter soldiers. There is no better builder of morale than devouring the enemy."

Moshi called Captain Jomo.

"We're here, ma'am."

"Good. Listen to me carefully. I want you to walk them to the edge of the roof. The side facing the impundulu."

Moshi waited for a beat. Jomo had lost his twenty-one-year-old son in the war. The young man had fought bravely by his father's side. Jomo had found what was left of his namesake after a fierce exchange between the Sunhung and Taepo. The brief but hard-fought battle ended with the detonation of a bomb. Jomo had returned home with his son, delivering the only part of him he could to the boy's mother— Junior's upper torso. Jomo's wife had spat on him. Cursed. Raged. Then collapsed to the ground, not in a fit of hysterics but with body-wracking sobs. A day after the funeral, Jomo's wife disappeared. No great loss, as far as Moshi was concerned. But the woman had taken the couple's two daughters with her—one fourteen, the other seventeen. If the Sunhung were to win this war, they needed strong, brave soldiers of every age. What they could not afford were softhearted soldiers and mission-driven impundulus.

My snipers know what to do if Jomo proves himself as worthless as his wife.

"O-okay, ma'am."

Moshi could hear the young soldiers in the background. Their curses and sniffles meant they'd both heard her directive to Jomo and understood her intention.

"We didn't do anything wrong," one of the boys said.

"Keep walking. You heard the matriarch. She wants you over there."

"No."

The too-familiar voice belonged to a mouthy female who, if Moshi had been a less tolerant matriarch, would've had her throat slit instead of her hair hacked off as punishment for questioning orders.

"Her first."

"Ma'am?"

"Set an example with her. Throw her off the roof or shoot her where she stands. Either way, rid us both of that tiresome girl."

"B-but . . . but . . ."

"You or her. Which will it be, Captain Jomo or Mei lien?"

The calm, quiet sky, perfect for both picnics and murder, seemed to take a deep inhalation, held its breath, and then blew it out in rumbling waves of thunder.

Bluish-white clouds darkened, not by slow, building degrees but in harsh rampaging crackles.

Thunder.

Lightning.

Moshi's gaze darted to the impundulu. *She's still in her human form. So who's causing the thunder and lightning? Wait, can she manifest both without shifting?*

No longer concerned with the impundulu overhearing her directive to her snipers, Moshi grabbed the walkie-talkie from her hip. She held the push-to-talk button. Instead of a brief static response followed by a quiet, empty space into which she could deliver her command, the crackle of static continued. It grew in intensity, mirroring the lightning storm outside her window.

Unnatural. Contained.

Golden flecks of light, and sharp bursts of electrical discharges filled the sky.

Jagged. Blinding.

"Do it now!"

On the other end of her mobile, Moshi heard Mei lien scream. The girl probably fought too because Dr. Pérez-Soto had an eye for talent. Fortunately, the good doctor only sold brave yet malleable products, smart yet naïve, strong but no match for an older, well-trained soldier like Captain Jomo.

A gunshot sounded, followed by a second scream. But the howl wasn't from the person she'd expected.

Another shriek.

Another.

More.

The sound of booming thunder and the hiss of lightning mixed with the awful *thwack*, *thwack*, *thwack* of bodies under ferocious, relentless attack.

Even if Matriarch Moshi could give the order to "Kill the fucking bird," there was no one on the other end to follow through.

A shout and a scream blasted from her mobile. Seconds later, a body tumbled past her window. Long, straight black hair whipped in the wind, smacking against a face gone ashen.

Huan. Not the mouthy twin I preferred to see meet her end, but I'll take the tactical advantage.

Moshi swung her gaze back to the impundulu, wanting the female to see her best "Fuck you, you lose" grin before she went scurrying after—too late—a dead Huan.

The impundulu was not only still on the roof and in her human form, but leveling a finger at Moshi. The other hand was pointed at the dark clouds that had formed above her.

"The rest of them." The order rushed from her like rats seeking higher ground during a flood. Moshi hoped Jomo had time to kill the rest of the child soldiers before . . .

Crackle.

Crackle.

The sky split like skin under a champion boxer's hammer fist. Clouds didn't so much part as succumb to the undeniable might of a superior force of nature.

The Wake soldier leapt from her perch.

Fell.

Fell.

Forehead plastered to the window, Matriarch Moshi watched the impundulu's fast, spiraling descent. Then . . . shit . . . then a change so swift, a shift from falling human to soaring bird occurred so unbelievably fast, Moshi barely had time to back away from the window.

Up the impundulu flew.

Not one. Not two. Not even three.

Too many to count.

Long beaks and longer wings beat against the air, unleashing a torrential shower of gold lightning on the city below.

Crackle.

Crackle.

Crackle.

Crackle.

Unnatural. Contained.

Instead of flying down, Moshi watched as an impundulu flew up, slowing as she reached her window. Unlike the others, this bird carried cargo on its back. Huan flipped Moshi her middle finger. As if the message needed repeating, her second middle finger joined the first.

Moshi retreated from the window. One step. Two.

Thank you for the confirmation. County Executive Umburter told me you warehoused child soldiers in this tower. An unverified rumor, he told me.

Moshi shook her head, disliking the impundulu's voice in her mind. But she was no more capable of preventing the intrusion than her snipers had been able to avoid being struck by lightning.

Gunfire sounded below, and Matriarch Moshi grinned.

Once my herd takes care of you Wake soldiers, I'll do the same to that traitor county executive. Umburter should've known better than to invite outsiders to a family fight. He'll pay.

She wasn't sure if her internal thoughts could be heard by the impundulu who'd spoken in her mind. It didn't matter if she could because Moshi's soldiers fought below. Their gunfire was a staccato affirmation that they lived.

My Sunhung herd won't lose any part of Tousaki City to Wake soldiers. Not a single block, and certainly not Zuungat Trade Center.

Ground-to-air missiles exploded.

Golden lightning followed, raging bright and multiplying.

The impundulu Huan rode atop flew upward, likely to the roof where, if Matriarch Moshi was lucky, Captain Jomo still lived, and his gun was at the ready.

Matriarch Moshi raised her rifle and took aim—right eye pressed to the eyepiece.

One impundulu remained. Her eyes were as golden as the others'. But not identical. Moshi had seen those eyes, sometimes brown, other times gold. Yet, despite her shift, the stoic eyes she saw on the other end of her telescopic lens had not changed with the alteration of the Wake soldier's form.

She hovered outside her window, black wings flapping with predatory grace.

Moshi fired. The bullet escaped her rifle, smashed into the window, and crushed in on itself.

Thick layers of pane. Bulletproof.

She could've sworn the bird smirked. So, too, did Moshi.

Satisfied the windows would keep the impundulu at bay, she turned toward the door. The young soldiers were kept locked in the basement. Too many had tried to flee or kill themselves for Moshi to trust leaving them unguarded and armed. She would see them all dead before turning a single one over to the Wake.

So, she ran toward the door, her rifle clutched in both hands.

Smash.

She turned. Gaped. Growled.

The glass fell inward but also out. Then, between the sharp shards, a cutting explosion that had Moshi taking cover behind a sofa she'd used for napping, and the occasional fuck, a black, gray, and white bird flew.

She rose, aimed, and fired. One chance.

Moshi's bullet landed in the center of the impundulu's head. Of course, that would've been a kill shot for any other creature on Earth Pact.

The crushed bullet bounced off the impundulu's head like a pebble hitting the side of a moving train.

Moshi scrambled to her feet, bolted toward the door, and . . . *thwack, thwack, thwack.* Lightning bolts sent her crashing to the floor. Intense, burning heat began in her back, radiating down her ass and to her legs, across her arms and up to her shoulders, then to her neck and head and out eyes that threatened to melt like cheese in a frying pan.

She thought the impundulu would turn her over, maybe even drag Moshi to her feet so she could interrogate her. But she wasn't afraid of torture. And while the tower might never be named after her, Matriarch Oratile Moshi would never be forgotten.

So, she prepared herself for what would come next. If given the slightest opportunity, she would shift into her elephant form. The change would not be as quick as the female impundulu's shift, but her thick elephant hide would fare better against lightning attacks than her fragile human skin. Moshi's mind whirled with possibilities, as much as her body screamed from the heat still coursing through her.

This doesn't have to be the end. I can still make it out of this alive. I can hear my soldiers on the street below. Still fighting. But so are the impundulu. Their damn lightning is nonstop. But I can still win this battle. I can—

Not do a damn thing but shut up and die.

The impundulu's beak latched onto Moshi's ankle. Latched, lifted, and swung her into the air.

Into the air . . .

And out the broken window.

Moshi shrieked on her way down in a way Huan had not.

She screamed.

And screamed.

And . . .

Thud.

17: A Victim of Circumstances

The State of Namju
Fuxing City

Gold lightning lit up the sky, miles away but clear as a full moon at midnight. Jelani had waited almost thirteen hours for the signal.

That's our cue. Snapping his wings and pushing against air currents, Jelani dodged a ground-to-air missile.

A second.

A third.

They exploded on contact, careening into the building Jelani had claimed while waiting for Fayola's signal. He'd abandoned the hotel's rooftop just in time. The upper levels of the building began to crumble.

People on the lower floors, Sunhung military, ran from the building. Guns out, curses foul, they searched the street and sky for the enemy.

Soldiers in the surrounding buildings flooded the area, jumping into trucks, yelling orders, and shifting into bears and elephants.

Jelani rose higher into the sky. And waited. He didn't know how many soldiers had settled in Fuxing City since Fayola's last mission there. Nor could he be certain which areas contained civilians. But he didn't need those details because he had eyes on the ground.

He waited.

Red smoke. One block up.

More red smoke. Two blocks east.

Four blocks west.

Two more signals came from the north. They weren't Fayola's gold lightning but Fuxing City's freedom fighters' flares.

That's our second signal. We protect those areas. The others are our feeding grounds. Let's go.

Jelani bolted through a corpse of cloud cover. Kwame followed him out, then Belay Njeri and her entire Rescue and Recovery Unit.

Fifty strong, Jelani had never seen so many impundulu galvanized for the same mission. Not working in the dark or solo. Not for blood or a lishan medal. Not out of duty or even for honor.

Half of Belay Njeri's unit flew toward the areas with red smoke. Then, they split further into smaller groups, dividing themselves between the civilian areas.

Jelani led the charge into the heart of the Sunhung occupancy of Fuxing City.

Red, green, white, and gold lightning attacked. Lethal barrages of electricity surged from wings, slicing through the air and striking bodies too slow to avoid the onslaught.

The Sunhung soldiers defended themselves, shooting at the impundulu with high-powered weapons.

Jelani would show the enemy the same mercy they'd given the citizens of the areas they'd claimed in their pursuit of power and control.

None.

For the first time in his life, Jelani fought for a cause of his choosing. He drank until full, and then coated his beak and belly with even more blood. He didn't question or wonder about the source of his meal, for he looked each soldier in their eyes before stabbing them with his beak and ripping open their chest.

Not blood from a slave, a child, or even from a convicted felon but from men and women who'd terrorized their own people. Burning their homes. Killing nonjoiners. Starving survivors. Turning children into soldiers . . . into murderers and rapists.

Jelani fed.

Feasted.

They all did.

Not from a bloodlust. Not even from hunger. But because they could. Because even if elephant blood was too salty or too sweet, bear blood was just right. Jelani finally understood why the Wake instituted blood pacts, why the Rashidi Tribunal compelled military service, and why Fayola's proposal, on its face, threatened the balance of Earth Pact.

Jelani swallowed. Drank. Dead Sunhung soldiers laid at his taloned feet.

Others still fought, unleashing bullets at impundulu capable of withstanding the onslaught.

Fayola's controlled fight with the border guards had given the Sunhung matriarchs a false sense of security. They hadn't understood how much she had held back or how unforgiving an impundulu could be when fighting for a worthy cause.

For there was no greater cause than the protection of children. And while vengeance sounded like wings snapping and lightning crackling, it tasted like blood.

Fresh.

Warm.

Filling.

The State of Namju
East Tousaki City

Blood.

Death.

Too much of both.

Fayola landed on the tower's roof, her talons touching down with a gentleness she had not granted Matriarch Moshi. The scent of blood perfumed the air. It was a mouthwatering, stomach-growling smell that should've had Fayola seeking her next meal instead of shifting into her human form. She'd gone without food for too many hours. Despite her self-imposed fast and the rich, flavorful scent of bear blood wafting from the battlefield below, Fayola ignored her hunger in exchange for a different instinct.

Huan vaulted off Binta, falling in her haste but recovering with a fortitude that no doubt had served her well since Fayola had last seen the elephant shifter.

But it was her twin, Mei lien, who'd reached Fayola first. A little taller than she remembered, perhaps a tad muscular too, the dark-haired teen slammed into Fayola like a wrestler gripping an opponent for a hard takedown. No throw followed the embrace, but tears did.

Over Mei lien's head, Fayola watched the other children approach. Huan reached her first. She wrapped one arm around Fayola's waist and the other across her twin's shoulder. Within seconds the other children added to the group embrace.

Eight of them. Only eight. I promised Jwahir I would find all her friends. Where are the others? Did Castel lie to Jelani and

Kwame? No, they wouldn't have ended the interrogation until they were positive they'd gotten every truthful detail out of him. What happened to Mei lien's hair? Someone must've done this to her. If the person isn't already dead, they soon will be.

Whimpers and cries overshadowed the heady scent of blood and vengeance, dimming her hunger for both.

What do you want me to do with him? Binta held a Sunhung soldier by the back of his BDU jacket in her long, strong beak. *The girl I caught said he tried to throw her sister off the roof. There was a scuffle with him and the girls. The other one went off instead. He deserves to die, and you haven't eaten.*

"Thank you." Mei lien's dark, watery eyes stared up at Fayola. Red nose sniffled. Twitched. "I tried to keep everyone together and safe. I really did. I-tri-tried . . . but . . . but—"

Mei lien's hiccuped sobs sealed the soldier's fate. But it was the misguided guilt Fayola detected in the teen's broken voice that condemned everyone involved in her heartache, up to and including Fayola herself.

"I'll eat later. You can eat now. But not here. Not in front of them."

The soldier, who had been lax in Binta's deadly hold, probably thinking his calm compliance would have them spare his worthless life, now screamed and fought. "No, no. I wasn't going to kill them. I swear. It wasn't my call. Matriarch Moshi ordered me up here, but I would never hurt children."

More screaming.

More fruitless pleas.

Binta lifted into the air. *Resistance is waning down there. It won't be long now. The city will soon be ours.*

No, not theirs, but the good people of Tousaki City. Even if Binta did not, Fayola grasped the fullness of what they and the other units had done that day. Nothing pretty. Maybe not even good and righteous, depending on one's perspective.

And they weren't yet done.

Fayola nodded to Binta, whose lightning preceded the opening of her beak and the sliding of the soldier from her grasp. Perhaps the sight and sound of terrorized children had ruined her appetite as well.

"I'm sure you did your best, Mei lien. In fact, I'm certain." Fayola used the back of her hand to wipe away Mei lien's tears. She was sick and tired of having too many reasons to seek justice, although mainly vengeance, on a child's behalf. "No matter what happened, know you were a victim of circumstances beyond your control. Yet you are also a survivor." One by one, Fayola touched the children's heads, reassuring them and herself that they had indeed survived when others had not. "You are all survivors, and I am very proud of each of you."

Fayola stayed on the roof with the eight brave souls of the Sotos' child trafficking scheme. Words could not erase their pain, but time, patience, and safety would help facilitate their healing. So, Fayola lowered to the graveled roof, sitting in the center of the children while knowing much more needed doing.

Besides the time she'd spent with Jwahir, Fayola had little reference point for interacting with children. Impundulus were either soldiers or parents. They were never both at the same time. She'd blurred the line between the two, leaving a murky blend of competing responsibilities and of dual-bladed priorities.

Fayola accepted a hug from Ursel, a stocky eleven-year-old bear shifter whose name she'd learned from the woman who'd sold him to the Sunhung herd. Now, though humbling the moment, Fayola had the privilege to match the names on Jwahir's pink heart to the children who surrounded her.

They were not hers. Not eggs formed from her lightning. She barely knew them, and they knew even less about her. Yet, when they wept both tears of sadness and relief, her heart clenched with protection and pride.

No, they were not hers. But she was all they had, which made their mental health, as much as their physical safety had been earlier, Fayola's priority.

Not justice. Not even revenge. Both would be waiting for her after she tended to the children.

"There are others." Mei lien stood. Her black hair, cut in messy, spiked layers, gave her a youthful, worn look that blended as well as impundulu and elephant blood. "In the basement. There are more like us."

More child soldiers, she means.

Fayola joined Mei lien. "Lead the way."

Justice and revenge can wait, and so too will Dr. Pérez-Soto. But not for long. Not for long at all.

18: Survived to Tell Her Story

A Week Later
The United Wake of Benekal
Kettle of Aradi City

"I should've known I'd find you out here."

Jwahir hadn't heard Raicho enter the bedroom; she never did, but she did sense his presence at the balcony door behind her.

She lifted her gaze to the night sky, spying a crescent moon and flapping wings. Even after a week and a half of the same sight, Jwahir hadn't become used to seeing so many impundulus. Tall buildings stretched high into the sky from which impundulus took off and landed.

She leaned against the wrought iron balustrade, white and gray and in the shape of bird wings. Despite the balcony's height, the metal enclosure didn't frighten her the way the thought of never seeing Fayola again did.

"Have you been watching the international news again?"

Jwahir nodded, then waited to be scolded for her disobedience. When it didn't come, she chastised herself for thinking of Raicho in the way she had Mr. Seager. "There's still a lot of fighting go-ing on over there."

"As I told you, it's to be expected. But that's not what brings you out here every night. Do you want to talk? I'm a pretty good listener."

She kept her eyes cast to the sky, enjoying the aerial display as much as she did staying in a bedroom that once belonged to Fayola. But both left her feeling anxious and abandoned.

"Ms. Fay hasn't called to check on me." Jwahir didn't mean to sound ungrateful or even needy. She hadn't been prepared for how she would feel about the separation and subsequent silence. She knew she had no right to expect so much. Jwahir also knew Fayola and the others were off fighting a war because Fayola had promised to rescue her friends. She trusted her, she really did, but her father had left an underground parking garage where they'd been living to get food one day and never returned. Her mother had cried for days, so too had Jwahir. After that, Jwahir and her mother joined a group of other women and children displaced from their homes. That's how she met Mei lien and Huan.

"Contact with family isn't protocol while on a mission. But know, if something were wrong, we both would know."

She didn't understand, but Raicho always spoke with such calm certainty that Jwahir believed him. Still, one after the other, a mother was taken by Sunhung and Taepo soldiers—beaten and shot but not before having other things done to them. She'd overheard the older kids talking after her own mother had been dragged away by a small group of soldiers. Jwahir had hidden the way all the children had been trained to do when soldiers were spotted close to where they'd made camp—an abandoned warehouse, a dilapidated barn, a roach-infested motel. So when she'd fled with the twins to their hiding spot, Jwahir didn't know the fleeting glimpse she had of her mother would be her last.

Mom didn't cry or scream, not even when that mean soldier punched her for refusing to tell him where to find the rest of us. She was brave. I can see that now. Mom was very brave.

Jwahir turned to Raicho and let him draw her into his arms as if she were his granddaughter instead of a burden he'd agreed to take care of in his daughter's absence. Jwahir wept, not because the flapping overhead wasn't Fayola, but because she was too afraid to believe her streak of bad luck had ended.

"Let me show you something." Raicho lifted Jwahir into his arms, carried her through Fayola's old bedroom, down the hall and into his bedroom, where he placed her at the foot of his bed. Then, flipping on the ceiling light, he moved to a wooden dresser.

In the mirror, she could see him grab something from the dresser before turning back to her.

He held a rectangular glass box trimmed in gold, which he handed to her. "Open it."

Securing the box on her thighs, Jwahir cracked open the lid.

Kneeling in front of her, Raicho nodded to the box's contents. "You recognize these?"

"They're all gold. The one Ms. Fay gave me is green."

Raicho's eyes flashed the same color green as the medal she had in her pocket. "All of these gold lishan medals belong to our Fay. Thirty-nine of them." He patted her head, his smile like a warm breeze in early autumn. "I guess, in a way, her sending you here to me is her fortieth, although having a child in my home again is a much better gift." He removed a medal from the glass box. "Each time I received one of these in the post, I knew my daughter was one mission closer to fulfilling her promise." He searched through the medals. "Here it is. This is Fay's first lishan medal." Lifting it eye level, he pointed to a date. "She was only twenty-one when she received her first medal."

He sounded so proud, the way her own father had when Jwahir met with success, like learning to ride a bike and receiving high marks in school.

"If these gold ones are hers then"—she removed the green medal from her pants pocket and showed it to Raicho—"is this one yours?"

Like he'd done with the medal in his hand, he pointed to the year on the medal she held. "Fay's birth year. I couldn't wait to become a father, to have a mission in life that mattered on a deeply personal level. Service to country and kettle might be honorable, just as blood pacts are essential to our way of life. But little in this big world is more rewarding than a child's trust, a child's unwavering faith. That's why, my sweet, golden-hearted Jwahir, our Fay will not return to us until she's not only dealt with those who betrayed your trust and faith, but those who did the same to your friends."

Jwahir examined the medal as if she didn't already know every word and scratch on it. "She let me keep your medal."

"She did. Do you understand why?" Before she could think of an answer, Raicho returned the glass box to his dresser, patting the lid the way he had the top of her head.

He didn't press her for an answer, no more than he objected when she returned to the balcony instead of climbing into bed.

"Fay's old things are in storage. It took me a while, but I finally admitted that keeping her room the way she left it didn't mean my little girl had stayed that way. She grew up and went away because that is the nature of things. But she never forgot me, never once let me go, no matter where in the world she went. Do you understand?"

The crescent moon shined just as brightly. Impundulus still flew to and from. And Jwahir still waited for the return of her Dela Eden.

"Yes, Mr. Raicho, I understand."

The Kingdom of Yokka
Northern Hona City

As much as Teresa wanted an end to the nauseating waiting, the chilling dread of the unknown, nothing compared to the thrumming beat of fear at seeing Diello Fayola again evoked. Like most everything else with this trip, little of what Teresa thought would happen actually occurred. Despite Fayola's arrival, an hour earlier, and Teresa's certainty the soldier would kill her on sight, she still lived.

Standing on the suite's bedroom threshold, her dinner steak knife in hand, Teresa watched the rise and fall of Fayola's chest. Black booted feet on the floor, head reclined against the couch cushion, mouth slightly parted and palms resting on thighs, the damn impundulu slept like an EMT who pulled a double shift—crashing on the first soft surface after returning home from work.

While being held prisoner in her hotel room, Teresa had little to do but watch television. She'd consumed hours of news programming, hoping to learn more about Castel's fate. But, in light of the war raging in Namju and the unexpected support of Wake soldiers giving the beleaguered local military air and ground support, the tide had turned. Every major news outlet covered Namju's civil war, which relegated Castel's story to temporarily forgotten news. If not for the broader implication, Teresa would've been grateful journalists had turned their attention to a meatier topic than a husband-wife child trafficking team.

But the two news stories were indelibly linked even if the reporters had yet to make the connection. And while Teresa hadn't seen Fayola in any of the news footage, she had surmised that only another blood pact had kept the impundulu preoccupied and her alive.

Fighting elephants and bears would more than count as pulling a double shift for a Wake special operations soldier.

No blood stained her all-black clothing. Instead, her smooth skin and short hair smelled of soap. This mild lavender fragrance complemented her less than intimidating human form. In repose, one could easily mistake the bird shifter as harmless, perhaps even as a victim-in-waiting.

She isn't either, and I no longer have the assumption of innocence on my side. At the clinic, I'd managed to tap into the kindness I'd glimpsed around the edges of her armor, using the character flaw to my benefit. At the time, I thought myself fortunate, clever even to have outsmarted a Wake soldier.

Teresa dropped the steak knife to the carpeted floor. She knew, even if she shifted into her sun bear form, she stood zero chance of winning a physical battle against an impundulu. So, where did that leave her?

Underneath the scent of lavender is a smell she can no longer conceal. Empathy. She's been chasing demons, I'd wager. Guilt demons in the form of orphans she didn't save, children she failed to recognize as the actual victims. Instead, she thought first of her precious mission, her sanctimonious blood pact, making her blind to the truth right in front of her. I hope the orphans' fate has given her nightmares. It would be a comfort to know what I did to her disrupts her sleep as much as what she's done to my family has ruined mine.

"Plotting my death?" Fayola's voice reached across the divide, like a giant octopus's tentacle, slapping Teresa across the face with its sharp wakefulness. Fayola's eyes remained closed, although Teresa no longer mistook her relaxed posture as sleep.

"More likely, you're wondering what you can say or do to dissuade me from my mission." Then, with languid grace, her eyes opened as the rest of her sat upright. Neither grogginess nor sluggishness clung to Fayola the way an outbreak of sweat suddenly materialized on Teresa's back.

Swallowing nothing but spit, certainly not the fear Fayola's intense glare evoked, Teresa shoved one hand into her dress pocket. The other she hid behind her back, hoping Fayola hadn't detected the way it trembled.

"I wondered how exhausted a person would have to be to fall asleep in a place they weren't sure was safe. How hungry to eat the food of strangers? Or how afraid of being beaten that when offered help, instead of taking it, the person runs away and back to their abuser."

Fayola paused, and Teresa knew better than to think she'd done so expecting her to fill the space with her own words. So she remained silent in the face of a monologue that could end in her death depending on the outcome.

I'm not ready to die. But I also don't want to spend the rest of my life in a prison cell. I wouldn't survive. I'm not built for that kind of life.

"I haven't eaten or slept in too long." Fayola pushed back against the couch cushions, as if testing their level of firmness. "Good support. Soft upholstery." She frowned. "But I couldn't get comfortable. I couldn't convince my brain to shut down long enough for me to rest. Your pacing before deciding to watch me didn't help. I think I even heard your deceitful mind whirling about your head like a hamster on a wheel—running hard but going nowhere."

Fayola sighed, an exhale with all the punch of a deflated balloon. "I have a B-ration in my pants pocket, and you over there smelling sweeter than any bear shifter ought. But I'm still not hungry enough to lay down my burdens, even if for a few minutes to enjoy the meal due me."

Perspiration rolled like a snowball down Teresa's back, picking up speed as it descended into her panties, over buttocks, and down the back of knees that threatened to buckle.

Teresa swallowed again, tasting the sour film of fear that had formed on her tongue.

"My entire flight here, I went over what I would say to you. Would I relay the terrible stories told to me by children you'd sold into slavery? Their physical, emotional, and sexual abuse? Would I recount the names of those who'd died in skirmishes, killed by Taepo soldiers who saw enemies instead of children forced to do the bidding of adults? Or maybe I would describe the sight of grave pits where Matriarch Moshi had her dead buried, tossed in like garbage instead of buried with dignity because they had once been people with hopes and dreams."

Fayola slid to the edge of the couch, forearms on her knees and fingers laced between parted legs. "Or about a little human girl, overworked and underfed. Braver than me." Fayola nodded to Teresa. "Smarter than you. But still a kid. Hungry. Tired. Afraid. So she ate, played, and then slept in a cabin rented by a bear shifter family. A mama bear, a papa bear, and a baby bear. Just like your family. Three black bears. One golden-brown-haired human girl. She ran away but survived to tell her story."

I can't recall the details of every child I've sold. How am I supposed to remember which one had golden-brown hair? After too much effort, I finally sold my batch to Matriarch Moshi. At a huge discount because of the soldiers she'd lost at the Namju-Tikala border. Those kids I do remember. She is here because of them.

"I helped you." Pointing her finger at Fayola's face but meaning an eye that should be no more but watched her with perfect vision, she added, "I also called your friend. I didn't have to do either. I did because I was grateful. You saved my life."

"Is that how you sleep at night? Massaging the truth? Twisting the facts? I won't argue either with you. But, as I said, I'm tired and hungry." Fayola stood, uncoiling her lean frame like a snake. Her dangerous nature was on full display. Golden eyes. Taut body. "At some point, you decided to wage a bidding war between the Taepo and Sunhung herds, treating your so-called children like any other good that could be bought and sold. If I hadn't been there to save you, those soldiers would have paid you nothing and taken what they wanted. There is no honor in war and even less among those who think themselves civilized to everyone else's barbarism."

Fayola took a single step forward. Her movement was predatory, but her boots were silent. "You're afraid."

Back, panties, and legs were coated with sweat. Teresa's heart pounded in her throat, a raging rhythm she felt in her eyes. "Of course I am. You want me to be. You're punishing yourself by not eating and sleeping. But hurting yourself won't make you feel any less guilty. And killing me won't banish that feeling either."

"You're correct, Dr. Pérez-Soto." A second step. "I do feel guilty about the children." A third step. "I will for too long." Fayola rolled her neck, stretching muscles with the rotation. "But you're also wrong. I'm not going to kill you, no more than I ordered your husband's death."

Teresa sank to her knees, collapsing under the weight of the knowledge that Castel still lived. She'd prayed but held out little hope that God would answer her pleas. When God had failed to heal Pablo, Teresa and Castel had no choice but to take matters into their own hands. They did whatever it took to guarantee they had ample money to pay for the best doctors and medical care.

Not a massaging or twisting of facts. Pablo would've died otherwise.

"He's broken and bruised but otherwise unharmed. He'll never see the outside of a prison again." Fayola bent and lifted Teresa's chin with a hand that glowed golden. "And neither will you." The same hand that held her chin with gentleness reared back and struck her in the chest.

The palm strike sent her flying into the bedroom, her body stopping when it slammed into the foot of the bed. The impact jolted her forward, but it was the surge of electricity from the attack that had her doubling over and spitting up blood.

"I'm stronger and faster than you." A hand grabbed her by the back of the head, her hair caught in an unbreakable grip. "Meaner."

Another surge of electricity bolted through Teresa. As if the tendrils of hair Fayola held were an extension of her, she sent waves of controlled lightning from her fingers, down Teresa's locks of hair and into her scalp. Her brain.

She screamed.

"But not as callous, and certainly not as selfish." With a hard yank, Fayola forced Teresa to her feet. Her hair and scalp protested; so too did the teeth that clattered, biting her tongue and drawing more blood. "It shouldn't matter. But what makes me want to electrocute you into a sizzling mass of nothingness is that you are a female who sold girls, knowing sexual abuse awaited them at the hands of merciless, amoral adults. Mainly men, but women too. Women as despicable as you."

The hand in her hair lowered to her throat—squeezing, shocking, and then lifting Teresa off the floor. Her feet dangled as if she were tied to a tree with a hangman's noose around her neck.

"Druggings, beatings, rapes. For some, death was likely a prayed-for relief. I rescued only nine."

Teresa was shaken with such force that stars swam across her vision, blurring her sight.

"Nine out of twenty-one. Forty-three percent. I enjoy statistics, but not those numbers. You're going to add to those facts, however. You're going to add to numerical truths you've cataloged as less important than your son's health."

Considering two Wake soldiers had tracked Castel to their home, Teresa should not have been surprised Fayola knew about Pablo's illness. Instead, the knowledge made her sick to her stomach. However, the queasy feeling could've been the low-grade pulses of electricity Fayola kept shoving into her body through fingers that hadn't yet shifted into talons.

She said she wouldn't kill me, but she clearly isn't above torture.

Teresa's insides heated. Body hair curled in on itself then burned away, a hissing exposition of future horrors.

"You're going to answer all of my questions. You'll provide names, dates, and locations. I want to know everything you do about the children you've sold and to whom. If you have records, I want them. Pictures, mobile numbers, email addresses, everything. Hold nothing back."

Is this what those Wake soldiers did to my Castel before dragging him to jail? Forced our greatest secrets, our most humiliating sins from him on threat of physical violence? Am I being used to corroborate what my husband has already revealed, or does she think he withheld information?

Teresa tried to think it all through, but cogent thought was made difficult when each breath burned her lungs. "C-can't breathe."

"You can. I've just made it painful to do so." Then, as if she were a ball and the bed a puppy wanting to play catch, Fayola tossed Teresa.

The landing didn't hurt nearly as much as the threat she saw coursing through Fayola's eyes. Lightning flickered at the corners like sparklers.

"Impundulus survive on the blood of others. We can't help or change the way we were made and what we must consume to live. But what we can do, what we have done, is create a system that keeps us fed and others safe. Because, Dr. Pérez-Soto," Fayola loomed over her, eyeteeth descended, "we aren't vampires of lore. We don't drink from veins with fangs, neither discretionary sips nor greedy swallows."

Like she'd done in the doorway, Fayola knelt, placing them at eye level.

Tears tracked from Teresa. She wanted to wipe them away, but really, what would be the point when more would soon follow?

"We can't eat without killing our food source. Blood pacts made it possible, though, a veneer of civility in a world of users and abusers. Victims and their survivors. Exploiters and the exploited."

"W-which of t-those are y-y-you?"

Teresa flinched at the approaching hand but could do nothing when it settled against her face. Neither a slap nor a punch, but Fayola's hand felt dangerously hot.

"Right now, I'm more of an unrepentant bully than an avenging angel. The worst version of a Dela Eden. I won't lose sleep over what I'll do to you. In fact, once I'm done, I'll place an overdue call to a little girl. Then I'll drink my B-rations and fall asleep in my own hotel bed after having Dominique, Cassius, and Eldrick turn you over to local authorities. The Hona City police are waiting in the lobby. But no help will come from those quarters. They weren't happy to learn of your plans with Healer Hadiza Bah."

Teresa detected no joy in Fayola's eyes, not even in a voice that sounded too weary to hold either gentleness or malice.

I guess I'm one of her data points now. A statistic to join the others. I did it all for Pablo. Can't she see? Everything Castel and I did was for our son.

The first shock repudiated her excuse. The second and third called her a liar. The tenth and eleventh mocked her bear shifter strength, while the twentieth shock loosened her bowels.

Teresa didn't recall much after Fayola had "softened her up for the interrogation," other than a litany of questions followed by responses that condemned the Sotos and their buyers.

Flinging her head off the side of the bed, she dry-heaved. Her empty stomach clenched into corded knots, seizing over and again but expelling nothing but blood and bile. Teresa's limp body followed her pounding head, and she tumbled off the side of the bed, landing at Fayola's feet.

The impundulu stepped back, her voice sounding as if she spoke to her through a train tunnel. "After hearing all of that, you have no idea how much I want to kill you. I've never been this hot without making the change. I feel the pull of my hunger, hear the whispers of my ancestors telling me that taking blood directly from the source is my birthright."

Through swollen, bloodshot eyes, Teresa watched Fayola's booted feet retreat. She didn't return either, not even when the three young Wake soldiers who'd served as her guards entered the bedroom.

The bald-headed woman, Dominique, whistled. "Your screams did not do our belay's work justice. Damn, she fucked you up good and sweet. Her lightning marks are etched into your face, arms, and legs like body art." Dominique snorted. "A talented tattoo artist could duplicate the reddish fern-leaf pattern of a lightning strike but not the excruciating pain that accompanies the skin's reaction to the attack. Want to know something truly frightening."

She didn't, but speech was beyond her, even if the posed question hadn't been rhetorical.

"Belay Fayola is more sad than mad."

Cassius lifted her into his arms, and Teresa tried not to howl. "Disgusted, I think." He jostled her, sliding sweat-sticky clothing against her sensitive skin. "You must be a real piece of work to have gotten under Belay Fayola's skin the way you did. There is a special place in Hell for people like you."

Dominique grinned down at Teresa, with the same emotion she detected in her snort. Disdain. "But hell on Earth can be worse. The Wake will make sure you experience it to the fullest."

Eldrick snapped a black zip tie around her wrists. Tight. "Belay Fayola didn't spare you. If anything, she spared her stomach the taste of your spoiled blood. No impundulu would dare taint themselves on the likes of you and your husband. Foul."

"Let's go."

Teresa was tossed over Cassius's shoulder and marched out of the suite and toward a truly distasteful future.

19: Caring Can Be Painful

The United Wake of Benekal
Kettle of Silesse City

"The bathwater is getting cold."

Seated between Jelani's raised knees, her back pressed against his chest and her head on his shoulder, Fayola shifted so she could graze her lips across his stubbled jaw. "I know, but just a little longer. It feels nice to be like this again."

Arms tightened around her waist, holding her firm and sending a silent message of agreement. "You need to sleep."

"We both do. We've been going full throttle for days."

"If you want, I can be the one to say it."

Fayola kissed Jelani's jaw again, twisting but still not enough for her to reach his lips.

As always, he met her in the middle, giving Fayola what she needed. Jelani turned his head to the left and lowered his face to meet hers.

They didn't so much kiss as sip from each other, drawing in the sparks of electricity that formed on their lips. Tendrils of gold and red hung between them, binding lips that had yet to touch. Then Jelani surged forward, swallowing her gold at the exact moment his luscious full lips seized hers.

Despite them having spent over a week in a war zone, killing and trying not to be killed, their kiss reflected none of the brutal, bloody harshness that fighting in Namju had brought to their lives.

Tender lips met, sliding against each other in a languid caress that had Fayola shifting upward to deepen the kiss. They stayed like that for long, tranquil minutes, their kissing more about connecting and grounding themselves in each other, than it was an arousing prelude to lovemaking. That bonding would come. But the glide of their tongues in each other's mouths, the twirling, the sucking, it all had less to do with building them up to a place where only a physical joining would alleviate the driving demand for carnal pleasure and more to do with reminding themselves they weren't monsters.

They were, however, top of the food chain beasts of prey. No matter how long Fayola kissed Jelani, that fact would never change.

"We killed a lot of people," Fayola said, her words a balmy withdrawal from their warm embrace. "I keep feeling as if I should regret our actions. I've been waiting for remorse to creep up my spine and burrow into my heart. But it hasn't."

"Because it won't." Raising her pruned hand from the bathwater, Jelani placed the palm over his heart. "This works fine. So too does our minds. I understand what you're feeling. We've never let loose like that before. It was . . ."

"Freeing," she finished. The word had settled in her brain like a benign tumor—its presence worrisome for the threat it could pose in the future.

Holding her hand flush against his damp, muscular chest, Jelani nodded. "Every mission is controlled might. It's how we've been trained. I didn't fully understand why we were uprooted from our family and kettle at fifteen. I mean, I know what we read and what we were told."

"But that's different from having an actual experience." Sliding her hand from chest to throat and around his neck, she held his nape, her thumb caressing. "When I left home, my single desire was to return as soon as I could. I had no interest in serving the Wake or ensuring the continuance of blood pacts by helping those who wouldn't invite us to their country during the bright light of day."

"And now?"

Pressing her lips to his, she admitted, "I still want to go home. Except for you, this kettle has never felt like that to me. At least not in the same way as Aradi City."

"Impundulu attachments run deep." Jelani pulled back, but only enough for their eyes to meet. "I also want to return home. I miss my mother as much as you do your father. There is nothing wrong with seeking the completion of your heart. Family, friends, Wake. The Wake forced us to place it first for most of our lives. We don't have to anymore."

Considering neither of them had been released from service, Jelani's claim amounted to wishful thinking.

With the Rashidi Tribunal promoting me to belay, I had every right to request Jelani's and Kwame's assistance from their belays. With all they did in Namju and the nonviolent capture of Castel Soto Herrera, they fulfilled the last of their forty mission requirements. So technically, they've earned their retirement. Unless the tribunal objects, nothing is preventing them from returning home. But Jelani won't leave without me.

A thumb slid across her brow. "You're thinking. Worrying. This isn't furrowed, but it might as well be. Come on." Taking her hand, Jelani helped her out of a bathtub that had been filled with hot, clean water and vanilla-scented bubbles. It was a refreshing end to a grisly week.

They drained the bathtub and dried themselves with thick white towels. Each action, done in silence, reminded Fayola of Jwahir's first night in her home. The little girl had also enjoyed a long soak. Warm water had the miraculous effect of soothing both the body and the mind. At least temporarily.

Towel wrapped around her from chest to knees, Fayola forwent cleaning the bathtub in exchange for the call of her soft bed and Jelani's hard body.

Fayola halted in front of Jwahir's painting on her way to her bedroom. With their night vision, neither had bothered to turn on a light, so she stood in a dark hallway in front of a child's painting she didn't have to look at to see. The image was burned into her brain—each name a hot poker to her heart.

Beginning at the bottom, she touched each child's name, speaking the ones aloud she'd been too late to save.

"You did your best."

"I know. A part of me wishes I could go back to caring for nothing but you, Dad, Kwame, and Durah. My missions were important in only how each of them got me closer to a one-way trip home and the beginning of a life I really wanted to live." Fayola stepped back and right into Jelani's embrace. He held her snug around her waist, his chin on her bare shoulder. "But if you'd asked me what that life would look like, I wouldn't have been able to tell you. I couldn't envision the one thing I wanted so desperately beyond having Raicho in my life again. So what does that say about me?"

Chin lowered and a hot open mouth pressed against her shoulder—kissing and licking.

She shivered.

"It means you're normal for wanting what was taken from you. I don't just mean your father. Your freedom to choose, Fay. *Our* freedom of choice. Caring can't be dictated. That emotion played no role in how well we executed our missions. Caring comes at a price. We're paying that price now." Jelani's kisses spread across her shoulder, up her neck, and to the lobe of her ear. He pulled the soft flesh into his mouth, sucking then letting it go with a wet *pop*.

"Caring can be painful."

"Absolutely, but it can also be rewarding beyond measure." Sliding from behind Fayola, Jelani smiled at her. "Wait here."

She watched him stroll to the guest room they'd given to Jwahir, his fisted hand keeping his towel from falling free. Pity, Jelani had an applause-worthy ass.

Fayola smiled, not a transformative shift in her mood but a reminder that all their choices hadn't been denied them. The most important ones—like who to love and trust—undergirded Wake society in a way often forgotten in the shadow of blood pacts and military service.

Jelani returned to her side and handed her one of two black markers he held.

"Why did you grab these?"

Jelani pointed to the right side of the wall. "You take that side, and I'll take the other one. We can meet in the middle at Jwahir's heart."

Fayola had a good idea of Jelani's intention, and she couldn't love him more for how well he tended to her soul's garden. She removed the marker's cap.

Mei lien had led Fayola to a room in Zuungat Trade Center's basement. Filled food crates, half-drank water bottles, and sheet-covered mattresses occupied most of the floor space, around which forty-seven children huddled. Aged nine to sixteen, they watched Fayola enter their domain through hooded eyes. She hadn't known what atrocity they may have been forced to commit, and while she cared, Fayola hadn't judged. Matriarch Moshi had seen to their basic needs, making sure she kept her young soldiers well-fed. But for every stocked food crate, for every warm blanket and fluffy pillow, she'd stolen chunks of their childhood and innocence. The herds had taken pieces of the children no one, no matter how well-meaning, could return. For now, acknowledging their wounds and accepting the aid of allies were two pivotal steps they could take to begin their journey of healing and growth.

Unlike Jwahir, she couldn't bring them all home with her. But that did not make them less of her responsibility.

Fayola wrote a name on the wall. A second. A third. More. She hadn't met the people Jelani added to his side of the wall. Their missions had been separate, but their overall goal was Namju's freedom. Much still needed doing, but those particulars would come after meeting with the Rashidi Tribunal. Fayola didn't imagine the kamaus would be happy with her first mission as belay. In fact, she suspected, after Njeri's and her units' public display of impundulu military force, the kamaus would find more charges to file against her.

As she added more names to the wall, civilians caught in the middle of feuding herds, government officials and news reporters held hostage, fatigued but determined Namju soldiers and police officers, Fayola's gratitude grew, as did her hope.

Instead of sleeping or making love, Fayola found contentment in the simple recording of names of the people their combined caring had helped.

So, they wrote in companionable silence, eventually adding names of dead Sunhung and Taepo soldiers beside those of the living because no one began life as an abuser of children, a denier of rights. And while suffering was part of the human condition, preying on others did not have to be.

An hour later, they were in bed with Jelani curled around Fayola.

I could stay like this for the next twenty-four hours.

"When we move back to Aradi City," Jelani said, "I'm taking that wall with us."

Unfortunately, her meeting with the tribunal was in seven hours. She suppressed a groan, not wanting Jelani to mistake the sound as a response to him.

"An entire wall, as opposed to having its image made into a large decal?"

"Not the same."

"I suppose it isn't. But an entire wall, Jelani. That's a bit extreme."

"Says the woman who raided a country."

"When put like that, it sounds so bad." She turned in his arms, satisfied when red eyes stared back at her. "Since you were part of the raiding party, if the kamaus send us to prison, we can request a shared cell." She kissed him. "They might even allow you to bring our wall."

Jelani laughed, a soft, sexy sound that had Fayola pulling him atop her. "A quickie," he suggested. "You need your rest before meeting with the tribunal."

"I do, but I need you more."

20: Uninspired but Inspiring

The United Wake of Benekal
Fort Kumelo City
The United Wake of Benekal Military Courthouse

Unable to stifle her yawn, Fayola broke the parade rest to cover her mouth with her hand. "Excuse me."

Kamau Haseena's dark eyes glinted with good humor. "The yawn reflex is hard to deny. Tell me, what or *who* kept you from getting a restful night's sleep?"

Fayola locked both hands behind her back again and, instead of averting her gaze from the kamau in embarrassment, she hardened it, which Kamau Haseena must've found amusing because the older woman chuckled with a heartiness that had her snorting.

Kamau Audre glared at her colleague, while Kamau Thulani tsked.

Unconcerned with the other kamaus' silent judgment, Kamau Haseena shook her head and rolled her eyes, then grinned at Fayola with so much warmth she didn't trust her words of, "It is good to see you again, young belay. And in one piece. Do sit,

Fayola. I have no desire to look up at you the entire time you're here."

"Yes, yes, sit," Kamau Thulani said. "And relax. You're stiff enough to serve as an airplane runway. No doubt you would balk if we assigned you such a mission."

Kamau Haseena, seated to Kamau Thulani's left, patted his shoulder. The gesture was an unsubtle acknowledgment of the ranking member's attempt to assuage Fayola's tension.

Pulling out the chair across from the kamaus, she successfully followed orders and sat but failed at relaxing.

They must've commanded someone to put this chair here for me. I've never seen anyone sit at this bench other than them. Kindness is generally appreciated, but it feels weird coming from them. Well, not all of them. Kamau Audre hasn't spoken. But her arrogance is more grounding than Kamau Thulani's awkward attempt at humor.

Kamau Thulani's hands rose from his lap to rest atop the gold folder in front of him. "You have made us wait for this meeting."

"Rude. Impertinent. It was an audacious act to send Njeri here instead of coming yourself."

Fayola almost grinned at Kamau Audre's predictability. Fayola knew where she stood with a person like her, which made responding to her personality type simple.

She ignored her. But not the equally gold folder in front of her laced fingers.

A third gold folder doubled as Kamau Haseena's coaster. Her half glass of water had a warm pink lipstick stain on its rim. The color was of lesser potency than her red lightning.

With a single finger, Kamau Audre tapped the folder in front of her, revealing she'd seen the path Fayola's gaze had taken. "Always so observant. Yes, it was entertainingly audacious to see Njeri walk through those double doors instead of the belay we were expecting. Did the thought of our displeased expressions bring a smile to your too-serious face?”

“I apologize if you found my actions, since leaving this court-room, as disrespectful. That was not my intent.”

Knowing she wouldn’t allow her response to go unremarked, Fayola shifted her attention to Kamau Audre a second before the older woman parted her lips in rebuttal.

“*If* we found your actions *disrespectful*? You are disrespect wrapped in a discrete package. Not a shiny gold star that screams: ‘Look at me, I want everyone’s attention.’ You genuinely do not. You actually couldn’t care less what people think of you.” Kamau Audre opened her folder and glanced at the top document. “Your spirit pleases Haseena because you’re the unwritten, unplanned-for heroine in a fairy tale meant as a cautionary tale. Don’t trust strangers, steal, run away, or enter a place you do not belong. No author would have written you, certainly not me, if my talents laid in that direction.”

Kamau Audre’s dark gaze raked over Fayola like fingers through tangled hair.

Thorough.

Patient.

But with an air of irritation for having to engage in the act at all.

“Yet there you sit—unbought by blood pacts and unbossed by this tribunal. I’ve never known a more distasteful combination, not even in Haseena. She enjoys anything I find headache induc-ing.”

Headache inducing as opposed to a pain in her ass? Consid-ering the source of the insult, it could’ve been worse.

Kamau Audre’s flipping of pages in her folder rang out in the quiet room like microexplosions. Fayola might as well be an airplane runway, as Kamau Thulani had joked, because she sensed Kamau Audre was about to make a hard landing atop her.

"Earlier, Haseena skirted the edges of a vulgar innuendo about your obvious fatigue. Despite her crass state of mind, we know you have earned your exhaustion."

Kamau Thulani opened his own folder, nodding as he read. "A thorough report. I must admit, I did not expect to receive one before this meeting. Our summons afforded you less than a day's notice. You continue to surprise me. This mission report must've taken you hours."

After leaving Dr. Pérez-Soto in the care of Dominique, Eldrick, and Cassius, Fayola had flown home. The empty house afforded her quiet time to record her mission reports. She uploaded both the oral recording and a typed version the Rashidi Tribunal could read on any mobile device or print a hard copy, which seemed to be their preference.

Kamau Audre flipped a few more pages, her intense expression like that of an exacting diello during basic training. "Kamau Thulani does not impress easily." Lifting her gaze from the folder, her features flattened. "He not-so-secretly enjoys it when he is, though. It happens infrequently, but he tries his hand at humor when it does. His attempt normally fails, but Haseena tends to take pity on him, while I refuse to encourage such mediocrity."

A shadow of a smile flittered at the edges of Kamau Haseena's lips, while a frown pulled down Kamau Thulani's.

The man in question cleared his throat. "Since you've decided to lay us bare, we await your own divulgence."

Raising her glass of water but not drinking, Kamau Haseena winked at Fayola, then extended the glass in Kamau Audre's direction as if in a toast. "Yes, my friend, we await your confession with bated breath."

Perhaps she'd fallen asleep and into a dream, but nothing about this meeting felt real. While she hadn't known what to expect, Fayola thought she would be called upon to explain her actions in Namju, to account for every life taken and Wake law broken. But, instead, the tribunal gave her a seat at their table, treating her as a welcomed guest in their home.

"No confession. I am neither impressed by her actions nor do I view her as anything other than a soldier who has lived her life encased in a bubble of nonchalance. Now that her bubble has burst, she wants everyone to care about the very things she'd ignored."

That truth may have sent Fayola rocking on her heels had she still been standing and hadn't heard firsthand accounts from both a child trafficker and her victims. Seated as she was, though, and not one afraid of criticism, she accepted the assessment as she would any other.

Fayola cataloged the feedback, deemed it valid, and then vowed to never retreat to her bubble again. Too much of life had passed her by. Until her fateful fortieth mission, Fayola had been unconcerned about anyone other than Raicho and her small band of friends and allies.

"To be fair," Kamau Audre said, her voice not giving an inch, although it seemed her words soon would, "there is little in our society that teaches, models, or even rewards actions that do not directly impact Wake or kettles. Except for how their actions affect our blood pacts, we couldn't care less what happens in other countries."

"Except," Fayola said, venturing to speak without having been asked a question, "we should."

"Why?" Kamau Thulani asked, not in challenge, she sensed, but with genuine curiosity as to her reasoning.

Taking a slow breath, she finally granted herself permission to relax. The chair's stiff wooden back didn't aid her efforts, but the plush leather seat made speaking her truth less uncomfortable.

"There are several answers to your question. Caring about and helping others is simply the right thing to do for some of us. If we can be of assistance, then we should. For others, caring and helping adds meaning to our lives that have nothing to do with obligatory service. Our actions are ours alone. Our choice. Our decision to make because we're thinking about *all* people, not only those who look like us."

Kamau Thulani's closing of his folder felt like a question mark at the end of a sentence instead of a period Fayola hoped her response had been. "You're a smart woman. You know that's not enough for the average citizen. Soldier or civilian. Tell us how caring and helping others will benefit *us* because, at the end of the day, rescuing poor and orphaned children will not put blood in impundulu bellies."

They watched her, their collective years of experience an intangible but heavily felt weight on shoulders that had begun a slow ascent to her ears.

Fayola willed calmness into her body. She scanned the face of each tribunal member, assured she'd made the best decision for most involved. "The needs of the Wake are never far from my mind. Going into Namju on a humanitarian mission, driven by empathy and justice, if not outright anger and vengeance, our non–blood pact actions will humanize impundulus in the eyes of the world. Even though we slaughtered and sated our hunger on the enemy, we will be viewed as heroes because of who we saved and why."

"What else?" Kamau Haseena asked. Her glass of water was as empty as her focus on Fayola was full.

"Humanitarianism breeds trust. Gratitude. The international community will come to view us as a nation of people instead of a country of predators. Political allies instead of hired mercenaries. By showing we care about them beyond their blood, goodwill for the sake of doing good, the international community will, in turn, care about us. And in caring about our well-being, as we care for theirs, blood donations will increase. Not organized by self-serving government entities or impersonal conglomerates, but willingly given by individuals."

Placing her elbows on the table, Kamau Audre leaned forward. "Are you so naïve as to believe that acts of impundulu kindness will erase the monstrous vampire image everyone has of us?"

"No, ma'am. The people we want to fear us will because they should." She shifted forward in her chair, fingers steepled in front of her and between parted knees. "I want them to be very afraid, as much as I want to embolden everyone else to live with their eyes fully open. No more looking the other way. No more not knowing what to look for or what to do when we see it. That's what people like the Sotos rely on. They hide in the bright light of day because people don't want to believe . . . to admit that the face of human traffickers, pimps, rapists, and enslavers are not horned monsters from nightmares but the widower next door, the flower shop owner, the retired police officer, the newly hired first-grade teacher."

Fayola slid back in her chair. She hadn't planned on voicing so much, no more than she thought the kamaus would be more interested in her *why* than in her *what*. Namju wasn't an irrefutable success story, but it was the beginning—a violent start, true—to a positive change in Wake international relations.

Again, the tribunal stared at Fayola, but she was too tired to give it any more weight than that of a water droplet. So she closed her eyes, inhaled deeply through her nose, and released it out of her mouth.

"I wondered what she saw in you."

At the sound of Kamau Audre's voice, Fayola opened eyes she hadn't realized were still closed.

"Your unit proposal was factual but emotionless. Your basic training grades were exemplary, and your special operations missions were completed with near robotic precision. No reprimands in your evals. Perfect scores. Not a blip in your military record that would raise any red flags. Successful by all counts but uninspired. Yet not uninspiring, it turns out."

Fayola wanted to ask who the tribunal had spoken to about her but decided knowing wasn't more important than learning what the tribunal had decided about her future.

Kamau Thulani reopened his folder, pulled out a sheet of white paper, and slid it across the table to her. "Go on."

Retrieving the offering, Fayola read. *It's a list of special ops units. Covert Pursuit. Salvage. Strategic Reinforcement. That's Jelani's unit.* "There are ten units here. I don't understand."

Kamau Thulani slid several more sheets of paper to Fayola. "These are emails that were sent to my personal inbox. While Audre prides herself on being the smartest person in the room, her bar for what she believes impresses me is insultingly low. Not a well-written and honest mission report but . . ." He nodded to the small stack of papers in her hands.

Dozens of emails. Brief but clear messages. The same four words are repeated. Criminal Exploitation Unit and . . . transfer.

Fayola's head jerked up, as if commanded to attention by a bolt of lightning to her spine.

Kamau Haseena's chuckle was like beams of strident light beating back the fog of Fayola's mind. "Unit requests to finish off what's left of the rebels in Namju. Your and Njeri's units nicely handled the Sunhung herd and a few Taepo squads, but most of the Taepo herd remains intact and a threat to the fragile reinstated government."

"Unprecedented," Kamau Thulani said. "No special ops unit has ever requested a mission. They complete them because they are commanded to do so. They know only as much as is required to meet their mission parameters. They serve the Wake for blood and survival. Everything else is—"

"Inconsequential," Fayola said, her voice a soft interjection of sound that reverberated between her past and present selves.

"Yes," Kamau Thulani agreed. "But not this time. They want this fight . . . this . . . goodwill mission. Just as the soldiers in those emails want to transfer to the CEU. Again, unprecedented."

"As I said, uninspired but inspiring. I thought the record number of applicants for your unit was a fluke." Kamau Audre tossed her gold folder onto the floor beside her rolling chair. "More of a curiosity because of its newness rather than a true interest. Even with the rigorous application criteria, I was certain the pool would thin." Tapping fingernails on the table, her eyes squinted, and her nose flared. "I really do not see the appeal. But there is one. I will no longer deny that annoying but obvious truth. Whether the cause, you, or both, many of our soldiers are intrigued and moved to the point of action."

The finger tapping ceased but not Kamau Audre's scrutiny. Dark eyes peered at Fayola, as if doing so would help the kamau solve a puzzle visible only to her.

Fayola remained unmoving, permitting Kamau Audre to take her fill. She had no solutions for the kamau, no answers other than the ones she'd already provided. Admittedly, Fayola had asked herself similar questions.

Why did I care? Why would I risk everything for strangers? For children not mine? For a country not the Wake? For people not impundulu?

"Here." Kamau Haseena tossed something to Fayola, which she caught with one hand. "Your fortieth lishan medal. You earned it months ago. We should've ordered its release long before now. We also should not have accepted your guilty plea without the aid of counsel, nor should we have kept you in a barrack prison. We had our reasons. At the time, we thought them important enough to justify our decisions. They were not."

If I had ventured so far as to assume a tribunal member would come close to apologizing, it would've been Haseena. Maybe Thulani but never Audre.

Fayola wondered if the kamaus would also admit to knowing about Jwahir's message months before her sentencing date and choosing to do nothing about her predicament until it served their purpose.

They should've sent someone to rescue the child, even if not me. Instead, they used her as a pawn.

Kamau Haseena's hand disappeared under the table again. When it reappeared, likely from her pants pocket, she tossed Fayola three additional lishan medals—one red, two white. "For diellos Jelani and Kwame."

Everything she'd done for two and a half decades coalesced to this very moment. Every mission. Every lishan medal she sent home to Raicho. Every urge to disobey orders and return to Aradi City.

To her surprise, Kamau Audre stood, walked around the table, and up to her.

Reflexively, Fayola pushed the chair backward, granting Kamau Audre space to stand in front of her.

Kamau Audre placed a palm on each of Fayola's shoulders. "You have served the Wake with distinction. When I look at you, I see a future I do not recognize but one that is inevitable. Perhaps that is why I dislike you." A hand slid from Fayola's shoulder to her chin, cupping and lifting her face. "But I respect your loyalty and dedication."

Stepping away, Kamau Audre returned to her place at the table. However, instead of retaking her seat, she remained standing.

The other kamaus joined her. Their dress black uniforms were as crisp as their expressions.

Unsure what to do, Fayola pushed to her feet, placed the printed emails Kamau Thulani had given her on the table, and then stood at attention. Realizing this would not be the moment she'd dreaded since her arrest and confession, her body didn't tense, or her mouth dry out. Her heart did not pound, or her hands sweat.

But her skin did tingle from growing anticipation.

Kamau Thulani smiled, his white teeth prominent on a face aged with thin lines. "It is my honor, indeed my privilege, to grant your discharge from The United Wake of Benekal Military. I also grant the same to Jelani and Kwame of the Aradi City Kettle. You are free to return home, Fayola, with no other expectations from this tribunal."

Free to return home. Free to return home.

The words swirled about her head and heart. The news of her freedom was too new to be absorbed by either. Neither her vision nor hearing was impaired, so her senses continued to feed her information from the kamaus.

Their nods and smiles. Their voices telling her, "We'll appoint someone else as belay of the Criminal Exploitation Unit. Thank you for your stellar service."

"Go home," Kamau Haseena said. "Don't keep Raicho waiting."

As if wading through waist-high sand, Fayola turned, struggling to align finally obtaining her wish with a sudden sense of loss. But when she reached the courtroom's double doors, her world shifted on its axis again.

"Oh," Kamau Audre said, "we nearly forgot. We will approve your citizenship request for your human, of course, but we've received several emails from the Newtons. They've offered to adopt the child."

"Her name is Jwahir," she gritted through a mouth primed for her shift.

"Yes, well, Jwahir and the three bears. We've already ordered background checks on the Newtons. I'll personally email you the final report. From initial findings, though, Nita and Emmett Newton are upstanding citizens, if not painfully dull. They'll make good substitutes for the child's deceased parents. You're welcome. No need to thank us."

Fayola wouldn't. Didn't.

Flinging open the doors, she staggered forward. Dizzy. Tired. And more than a little sick to her stomach.

Jwahir and the three bears. The Newtons can't have her, but I promised to find her a safe, loving family. Dammit, I promised.

21: Selfishness is Allowed

Two Weeks Later
The United Wake of Benekal
Kettle of Aradi City

"Which tie?"

Jwahir turned to see Raicho in her bedroom doorway. His hands were extended in her direction. From each, four ties hung—one navy blue, another dark green with thin white stripes, and the third and fourth were both black. Jwahir squinted, trying to see the difference between the two black ties.

"Which one do you think Fayola will like best?"

Jwahir lowered her gaze from the two black ties to the three pairs of shoes at her bare feet. She wiggled her toes.

Raicho's laughter, a tender sound for such a strong man, had the wondrous effect of easing some of Jwahir's nervousness. "You too, huh?" Lowering his arms, Raicho joined her in the room. "We're being silly."

"Yeah." Still, Jwahir wanted to look her best for Fayola. She hadn't looked good at the clinic, where they'd first met, and her appearance had been worse when they'd reunited at Mr. Seager's cabin. Jwahir tapped Raicho's left hand. "Ms. Fay's favorite color is black."

"Good point. Which one, though?"

Jwahir had no idea, but with Raicho closer, she could tell the difference between the two black ties. "The skinnier one, I think."

Raicho's wide grin added brightness to an already sunlit room. "Nice choice. All four are gifts from Fay. She knows how much I like ties. Since completing basic training, she has sent me two every year."

"That's a lot of ties."

Raicho bent to a knee. "These are cute. Did Fay buy these shoes?"

"Mr. Jelani. The right size and everything, though I don't know how he knew."

"Soldier," Raicho said, although Jwahir did not understand the connection, nor did his reply help her make a decision. "Which pair do you like best?"

Jwahir first considered the pair of red sneakers with silver-colored glitter on the soles and then the white-trimmed purple sandals with ankle straps shaped like butterfly wings. But it was the high-top black sneakers with white laces that drew most of her attention, not because she favored black but because she knew exactly how to spice them up.

"That smile tells me you've made a decision." Raicho slung the skinny black tie over his shoulder. The other three he folded before sliding them into his pants pocket. "Which pair?"

"The black ones."

"That doesn't sound like you."

"I'm going to add the charms Ms. Fay sent me last week. They're colorful, fun, and really cute."

Raicho stood with a grin and nod. "Now that sounds like the Jwahir I've come to know. You put them on the laces while I finish dressing. Meet you downstairs in ten."

Jwahir rushed to the dresser and found the bag of charms she'd placed in her sock drawer.

Ms. Fay thought about me while she was away. She called. Not a lot because she was busy. But she's coming home today. No more missions. Where will she and Mr. Jelani live? Will she still want me to live with them? Will we be a family? I don't speak much Onya, but I could learn. I could be a good daughter, even though I can't fly. I can't shift into anything. I'm just a human. I'm . . .

Jwahir ended the negative train of thought. It wasn't fair to Fayola, who had only ever treated Jwahir as an equal. So, she snatched the high-top black sneakers off the floor, jumped onto her bed, and opened the clear bag of charms.

She withdrew her favorites—a "Human Girl Magic'" charm written in pink cursive letters, a "Human Lives Matter" charm in white block letters with black trim, a charm of a brown-skinned girl with goddess braids, a gold lightning bolt charm, and what had to be a custom-made dangle charm that read: Golden Lady. Taking her time, she placed each one on her black shoelaces. Then she plucked a few more from the bag—a yellow crown, a pink diamond, and another dangle charm. She placed the *J* dangle so it would hang on the side of her shoe, moving when she walked.

Satisfied she'd done all she could to liven up the boring black sneakers, Jwahir yanked on a pair of socks and pulled on her shoes. Grinning at herself in the full-length mirror on the wall nearest her bed, she liked the way her charm sneakers looked with her light blue jeans and short-sleeved yellow shirt with a blue dolphin jumping over a rainbow.

"They're here," Raicho yelled to her from downstairs. His deep, loud voice sounded every bit as exuberant as Jwahir felt.

So why did she not rush from her bedroom and down the stairs? Why had her knees stiffened, and her ankles locked? Why did the creak from the front door opening and Raicho's ebullient "My Fay is finally home" have Jwahir breaking into a sweat?

"Dad, you're squeezing too tight."

"Deal with it. Tell her, Jelani."

"I know how she feels. I think Mom broke a rib. Ow, yeah, definitely a rib."

Raicho's laughter reached Jwahir the same way his announcement of Fayola's arrival had—with joy and unspoken relief.

Feeling like an outsider eavesdropping on a family reunion, she remained unmoving.

"You got off lucky, Jelani, because I'm not letting my Fay go until I've filled up on two and a half decades of hugs."

"Come on, Dad, we talked about this. You said you wouldn't make a big deal about my homecoming."

"No party. That's all I promised. That, and not calling the kamaus to give them a piece of my mind. I should . . . wait, what is taking her so long? The only thing she had to do was put on socks and shoes."

As the conversation unexpectedly shifted to her, Jwahir's heart pounded like a drum slipping in and out of tune. But nothing she did, nothing she told her body to do, got her moving toward a woman she'd clung to in her dreams and pined for during the waking hours of the day.

"You gave her my old room, right?"

"Unless she's in the bathroom, she should still be in there. Go see what's taking her so long. That'll give me a few minutes to speak with Jelani."

"Dad, come on."

"It's fine, Fay. You escaped it today, but you have one coming from Mom too."

"We've lived together for years. We're adults."

Fayola's voice sounded closer, although Jwahir heard no footsteps.

Feeling incapable of doing more than stand there, Jwahir waited for Fayola to come to her. Fayola already had twice before—once when she'd returned to the clinic and the second when she'd stopped Mr. Seager from hurting her. Both times she'd saved Jwahir's life. Now, the third time, Fayola stood on the threshold of a room that once belonged to her, and all Jwahir could do was stare.

Fayola wore fitted black jeans and a snug V-neck red shirt that showed off a shiny gold necklace on which hung an equally gold charm. Watching her in return, Fayola removed her black flats then entered the room with none of the hesitancy that kept Jwahir rooted.

Like Raicho earlier, Fayola bent in front of Jwahir. Removing the gold necklace, she held it out. "Let's trade. Mine for Dad's."

Jwahir had no good reason to keep Raicho's lishan medal on her as she'd done while living with the Seagers. But every night, she slept with it under her pillow, and after dressing each day, she would find a safe place to keep it on her person. Sometimes that meant in her shoe. Other times, like today, she kept the green medal in her pants pocket.

Jwahir pulled it out, opened her palm, and showed it to Fayola.

"You kept it safe. Thank you."

"Y-you came back." Jwahir could've bitten her tongue for the stupid statement. This was Fayola's home, and Raicho was her dad. Of course, she returned.

"Are we starting over? Have I been gone too long?" Fayola blew out a breath and, with that single gesture, the soldier in civilian clothing looked like any other adult worried they had disappointed a child. Obviously undeterred by their mutual bout of insecurity, Fayola granted her what she now knew to be Raicho's tender sweet smile. "Turn around so I can put this on you."

As if the soft request melted the ice that had formed like a mountain rising from the sea around her body, Jwahir complied.

"Your hair is beautiful. Triangle box braids. Dad made yours a little chunkier than the ones he used to create for me. They look good on you." Turning Jwahir to face her, Fayola smiled again. "So does my fortieth medal. Dad has the others. He won't mind that I gifted you with this one. Besides, gold is a better color on you than green. May I have my medal back, please?"

"Oh, oh, yeah. Sorry, I forgot." Jwahir returned the medal that had kept her company for more than half a year. In many ways, it had been the closest she'd had to a friend. Its silent presence had given her hope, even on days when fear of never being rescued had her crying until her stomach cramped and her voice broke.

"May I hug you?" Fayola's question was spoken even softer than the deep brown eyes that met Jwahir's.

Patient.

Hopeful.

And a little sad.

Jwahir had no explanation for what she thought she saw in Fayola's gaze, but she did not believe she'd misinterpreted her.

Taking a step forward, Jwahir allowed herself to fall into an embrace that came straight from her dreams. But apparently sadness was contagious because the longer Fayola held her, the more Jwahir wept.

She cried for her deceased parents and friends, for the enslaved child who'd lived in fear with the Seagers, and for children who didn't have someone like Dela Eden Fayola to rescue them. She wept and wept because behind her sadness, her bone-deep grief, was a heart slowly sewing itself back together with the strongest of threads.

Trust. Want. Affection.

So much of all three formed the delicate lining of Jwahir's heart that she collapsed against Fayola. Her forehead in the crook of Fayola's neck and her bottom seated in her lap, Jwahir's stream of tears felt like standing under a spray of warm shower water.

Soothing and safe.

"I have you. I always will."

"I-I don't want to be a burden."

"You aren't. You never could."

"B-but . . ."

"I didn't expect tears today. Well, maybe from Raicho but not from you." Picking her up, Fayola settled them both in a bed big enough to accommodate Jelani too. "We can stay here, if you like. No rush to go downstairs."

Leaning up on an elbow, face wet and in need of a good wipe, Jwahir touched the medal that dangled from her necklace. "The Newtons called. They are the bears whose cabin I broke into to use the computer to contact you."

"I know. I gave them permission to speak with you and told Raicho to expect their call. They are good people. They found your search history on their computer. Saw you pulled up the Wake's embassy in Tikala."

"They told me."

"Did they also tell you they contacted the embassy?"

She nodded.

"Their call started a monthslong investigation. The details don't matter now, but I wish I had them back then. I would've . . . well, I would've reached you sooner."

Releasing the medal, Jwahir used the same thumb and forefinger to rub between Fayola's eyebrows. "This moves when you're mad."

"Only when I don't care who knows how I'm feeling. Did you have a nice conversation with the Newtons?"

Jwahir now understood why she hadn't joined Raicho downstairs. The inevitable conversation she wanted to avoid had found her anyway. She plopped onto the bed, back on the firm mattress, and eyes to the ceiling instead of on Fayola. "I don't want to talk about it."

"Neither do I, but we will because we must."

"We don't."

"Yes, we do. Tell me."

Jwahir could protest more, but nothing about the Diello Fayola she knew would waver in the face of a child's petulance. So she sighed, shifted onto her left side, and took hold of Fayola's right hand. "The Newtons are nice."

"I agree. What else?"

"They asked me questions. Let me talk. Accepted my silences."

"Okay. Anything else?"

"You know what else."

"I do, but it's important for you to speak the words."

Jwahir didn't see why, but she couldn't deny the empowering feeling of being allowed to speak her truth without fear of retribution.

"They said I could visit. Stay longer than a visit if I want." Jwahir waited for one of Fayola's patented brief responses, but none came. She pushed up on both elbows and looked down at a woman who, with each passing minute, appeared less like the hardened diello she'd met last year. "Do you not want me anymore?"

Fayola squeezed her hand, a tender gesture Jwahir felt in her heart as much as she did on her skin. "You know better than that. But I won't be selfish, and neither will Jelani. We want the best possible life for you, even if that life is with someone else."

"They aren't fully human. You said you would find me a human family if I wanted."

"You're right, and I did. But the Newtons live in a diverse neighborhood and a multicultural city. They also have full-human members of their family. With them, you would not be an isolate. You wouldn't lose your age-mates when they turn fifteen and go off to basic training. It's a Wake cultural norm, but the impact on a human would be greater than on an impundulu. I hadn't thought of that when I offered you a home with Jelani and me, although I should have. Every friend you'll make will eventually leave you. One year, then the next, and another year still. Gone."

"But you'll be here. You, Mr. Jelani, and Mr. Raicho."

"Yes, we'll be here, but you'll need more than us. Just as I needed more than Jelani and memories of Dad when I went off to basic training. I would not be the person I am today without Durah and Kwame as my friends. I want to deny you nothing, especially not lifelong friendships. Or even the chance at motherhood. You're only eight, so that's something you won't have to consider for a long time, but I need to think about that part of your future now. Do you understand?"

Jwahir reclined on her back again but kept her fingers laced with Fayola's, a grounding connection to a woman who seemed further away than she had before returning home. Yes, she understood but . . . "I wouldn't like losing any friends I'd make. And I guess, eventually, when I'm a woman like you, I'd like to have a kid like me or even like Kadeem. He's cute and kinda funny. But impundulus don't have babies the way bear shifters and humans do, right?"

"Correct."

"Yeah, that's what I thought you meant." Jwahir sat up. With her second hand, she held Fayola's between both of hers. "Is it selfish to want both?"

"Selfishness is allowed. I only need you to tell me what you want. Then, if it's within my power to grant, I will."

Jwahir had never known anyone to treat her as if her opinions and feelings mattered on a scale beyond what she could envision.

"I would like to visit the Newtons. To get to know them and maybe stay for a while if they are as nice as they seem. I wouldn't mind having a brother. Being a big sister. That would be fun, right?"

"I think so, yes."

Clutching Fayola's hand to her chest, as if it would turn into a wing and she fly away, Jwahir said very carefully, "But I also want to be a part of your family. I'd like to think of Mr. Raicho as my granddad. Maybe he'd let me call him that."

"He would be honored."

"What about you, Ms. Fay?"

"Impundulus are long-lived. I look forward to watching you grow into the best possible version of yourself. Your happiness is the best tribute you could pay your parents." Touching the medal she'd gifted her, a sliver of gold bled into the brown of her irises. "When you look at me, you see the soldier who saved your life. When I look at you, I see the girl who saved mine."

Jwahir shook her head, a visceral reaction that had her dropping Fayola's hand and sputtering, "I-I'm only a human. Weak and young and nothing compared to you and bear and elephant shifters."

"Young, yes. Weaker in physical might to shifters, also yes. But any other perceived weakness ends there. I can see you're wearing the charms I sent. 'Human Girl Magic' and 'Human Lives Matter' aren't trite sayings. At least not to me."

Jwahir couldn't fathom how she'd saved Fayola. When had her life been in danger? When she fought the soldiers at the Namju-Tikala border? Even then, all Jwahir had done was cry and scream Fayola's name. Neither had helped, despite her eventual win.

Mirroring what she'd done to her, Fayola rubbed between Jwahir's eyebrows. "You're thinking too literally. You're also eight, which puts the onus of your comprehension on me. Just know my life lacked depth, a true passion and purpose I hadn't realized were missing until you held my hand in that clinic and stared up at me with unearned faith. There is a power, Jwahir, a rare mighty strength capable of generating a power grid of caring, introspection, and eventually action. Until that moment of unexpected energy, an electrical transmission connecting you to me, amplified by a singular, unchanging goal, I thought myself whole."

Jwahir still did not understand, which did not prevent her from nodding as if she had. Knowing they hadn't finished their conversation about the Newtons, but happy at the prospect of having two families, Jwahir settled against Fayola's side. "Are you going to take a nap?"

"No, we're talking."

Jwahir peeked up at Fayola, who rested on her back, a hand covering a yawn. "Your eyes are closed."

"Means nothing. Tell me about your time with Dad."

Jwahir did, but the longer she spoke, the quieter Fayola became. Her short responses turned into even briefer "Mm-hmms," then into intermittent nods and finally into a long silence.

"Fay, what's taking you and Jwahir so lon . . . oh . . ." Three strides had Jelani in Jwahir's bedroom and beside a sleeping Fayola. "I wondered how long before that would happen." Jelani flicked Jwahir's *J* dangle charm. "The *J* is for Jelani."

A giggle bubbled out of her. "Is not."

"I was with Fay when she bought it. *J* for Jelani not Jwahir."

"Nope. You're wrong."

"I'm always right." Leaning close, he kissed her forehead. "Missed you, kiddo."

She'd missed him too. It felt good to miss someone who was alive and well and capable of returning to her.

"Fay drove all the way here. She hates flying in a plane, which meant us in our car following behind our moving truck."

"But Ms. Fay told me she doesn't know how to drive."

"Yup." Jelani rubbed the back of his neck, wincing as if he'd pulled a muscle. "If I didn't love her so much, that twenty-hour road trip would've ended things between us for sure."

Jwahir was far too young to have ever been in love, but she'd seen the emotion between her parents, and she witnessed it again in the way Jelani stroked Fayola's hair and kissed her cheek, all without disturbing her rest.

"Would you like to go with me while Fay sleeps and Raicho watches over his sleeping beauty?"

Careful not to wake Fayola, Jwahir scooted off the bed. "Where to?"

"The ice cream shop for cones, then to Mom's house. She wants a grandhatchling, but she's not getting one any time soon. I already told her as much. She thinks, more like hopes, she'll get a different answer from Fay. She won't." He kissed her cheek again. "You're the cutest. Better, you're smart, polite, and tough. Mom never had a daughter so, between you and Fayola, I'm the best son ever. Impundulus are not above bragging about our families. With your help, I'll give Mom something to brag about that may not be a grandhatchling but is better because you're a fully realized person."

Jwahir didn't mind the thought of having an impundulu as a grandmother, especially if Jelani's mother was as kind and funny as her son.

"The ice cream cone is a bribe." She placed her small hand into his big one, feeling safe and happy.

"Bribe? Who taught you that awful word?" He chuckled with a youthfulness that made him fun to be around. "Fair warning, Mom is a hugger like Kwame. Two ice cream cones then. One today and another tomorrow. Are you in?"

"With rainbow sprinkles." They stopped at the bedroom threshold. "And a cherry."

"We've got a deal. I can already taste my chocolate ice cream cone."

"Strawberry for me."

In unison, they looked back to Fayola. She'd moved onto her side. Her back was to them, and she curled in a ball.

"I don't want to forget my mommy and daddy."

"You won't. They'll forever hold a special place in your heart. The heart has an endless capacity."

"That means I can love new people without losing the old ones, right?"

"That's the great thing about our hearts. It gives us endless possibilities for happiness. Old and new loves can exist beside each other in our hearts for as long as we choose to keep them there. No one could ever replace your parents."

Comforted by his words, she held his hand tighter.

"When the time is right, you can tell her. No rush, though. You'll find there's a perfect time for everything."

"Like ice cream and chocolate?"

Jelani led her away from the bedroom. "I stand corrected. Every minute of every day is perfect for ice cream and chocolate."

With a final glance over her shoulder, Jwahir assured herself Fayola would be there when she returned. As for her heart, it thumped with anticipation and joy.

"How long did I sleep?"

Fayola joined Raicho on the balcony. As a child, she would keep the door open throughout the day, letting in the sounds of the outdoors as much as she did flies, the heat, and the cold. She would dream of taking flight back then, no longer relegated to the mundane ground but elevated to the limitless sky. Now, all she wanted was the warmth of home.

Dropping her forehead against her father's back, Fayola wrapped her arms around his waist. Hugging him, breathing in his honey scent, hearing the loving way he spoke her name, Fayola never needed much to be happy. But this, having her father in her life again, an enduring, transcending bond of love and re-spect, this reunion had been a daily prayer.

"Today is my second favorite day."

"What day is your favorite?" Fayola knew the answer, but she'd posed the question because selfishness was allowed, as she'd told Jwahir. On this day, above all others, she very much wanted to be selfish.

Raicho removed his hands from the railing and covered hers with his. His thumbs stroked her knuckles. "The day you hatched is my favorite. No other day compares to the day of your birth. Your little gray beak broke through first, then one leg followed by the other. It took you several tries, but you managed to get the rest of yourself out. Small and tired, you stumbled then fell into my waiting hands. You've only slept an hour. On that day, you slept for five before you opened your eyes again. Brown, like most newborn impundulus. No red, green, white, or gold. No electrical pulses to strengthen you but a hunger that needed feeding."

"My first blood meal."

"Small drops every two or three hours. By the second month, I awoke to find a chubby human baby in the nest I'd built and placed beside my bed. The same brown eyes stared up at me from a face I would watch grow until it was my turn to escort my only child to the Tree of Karasi. Jelani and Jwahir are visiting Zintle. They'll be back in time for dinner. I've become quite good at cooking human food, if I do say so myself."

"Thank you for taking care of Jwahir. She looks wonderful. Healthy. Happy." Sliding around Raicho, Fayola stood beside him at the railing, her shoulder touching his. "She wants to visit the Newtons."

"And that saddens you?"

"More than it should. She's seeking the familiar, even if she doesn't yet realize that's what she wants. The Newtons, while not fully human, are closer to what she had with her parents in Namju than any life we can give her here."

"That's what you think, but I doubt that's how Jwahir feels."

"She's a child."

"With a keen mind and a strong sense of self. What else did she say?"

Fayola turned her face upward, enjoying the receding summer heat on her exposed skin. "She said she wants to call you *granddad* and to have two families."

Though she wasn't looking at Raicho's face, Fayola could hear the happiness in his voice. "Granddad, huh? I like the sound of that. I might have to drive over to Zintle's and get our Jwahir back before she charms the girl into staying with her."

Raicho's hearty laugh had Fayola lowering her gaze to him. As she suspected, her father sported a big, beautiful smile.

He's as overjoyed as I knew he would be. Of course, I'll give him a grandhatchling one day, but Jwahir is more than enough of a grandchild for him and Zintle to love and spoil.

"While shared parenting doesn't exist in the Wake, it is practiced in other countries. We aren't losing her. She'll be a short flight away."

"I know.

Raicho bumped her shoulder with his. "Tell me why your mobile buzzes with near-constant notifications. It kept going off, so I had to go digging through the purse you left downstairs to switch the thing to mute."

Fayola refrained from groaning. Instead, she leapt onto the railing, balancing herself as if it were a tree branch, and she was in her avian form. "Part of my proposal for the Criminal Exploitation Unit included the suggestion of a dedicated website. Human trafficking hot spots. Myths versus facts. Ways to help fight human trafficking." Turning to face her father, she added, "A trafficking hotline. I created a shell website as an example. Apparently, one or more of the CEU's computer geniuses finished the site, made it live, and routed the hotline to my damn mobile."

If Fayola wasn't so proud of the unit's ingenuity, especially Neville's, Sula's, and Chikondi's, she would've tracked each of them down and tagged their brazen asses with her lightning.

"Unimpressed by boundaries of authority," Raicho said, grinning but with a twinkle of something else in his eyes.

Fayola rolled her own eyes, knowing what her father was thinking. *I respect authority and boundaries just fine. More or less. One of these days, I'll figure out who in the hell selected members of the CEU. That person is not funny. Wait.*

"Dad, you said a trusted friend told you what happened during my Namju mission. Who is the friend?"

Instead of replying, Raicho eyed Fayola, and she wasn't sure if he found her balancing act amusing or impressive. Then, leaping onto the railing with the grace of a much younger man, Raicho grinned down at Fayola with a wink. He then . . . shoved her off the wrought iron railing.

Shock turned into laughter just as quickly as her human body shifted into her bird form. Black feathers sprouted, replacing soft, warm skin. Wings pushed through her widening back, catching heated air currents and drawing her upward.

"You're even more powerful looking than you appeared in the courtroom. You're no longer my hatchling fresh out of her shell. No wobbly legs or blurred vision." Lifting his hands, he stretched his arms in front of him. "Too big to be cradled in Daddy's hands. A grown woman. A force of nature. What will you do now, my mighty Fayola? Settle into quiet retirement? It is your right. You've earned the privilege of peace and solitude. But is that your heart's true desire?"

Wings flapped a steady beat, so too did her heart. But her mind, her thoughts, were like an amateur orchestra, a discordant ensemble of individuals.

Peace and solitude. I want to have both with my family and friends. For so long that has been my dream. Home. Dad. Jelani. But also Durah and Kwame, and now Jwahir. My old dream is now my new reality but is it my only desire?

"We've never flown together." As quickly as Raicho had displaced Fayola from the balcony, she was just as fast as she sent a lightning bolt his way.

Reflexes as sharp as the talons that formed, Raicho avoided being struck. His full-body shift was quicker still. He'd pivoted out of the way, transforming his lower half to manage the feat, then his upper torso. Raicho's all-black avian form was as rare among the impundulus as a black spinel gemstone among the precious gems of the world.

"I always wanted to fly with my daughter. Shall we?" Shiny black wings caressed hers, a show of affection.

"You said Jelani and Jwahir will be back in time for dinner. So that gives us a few hours."

"You want to race, don't you?"

"To Autry Clock Tower and back."

"That's three kettles away."

"I know. Have you traded in your stamina for a chef's apron? As slow as I sent that bolt at you, an impundulu new to the change could have avoided its touch."

"Shit starter."

"Yes, sir. I'm your daughter through and—"

Raicho took off, leaving a shower of green lightning in his wake.

Not to be outdone, Fayola sped after him.

She was happy to be home and in a loving relationship with Jelani. Her goodwill pacts were complete, and her friends were free to live their own lives, just as she was. So why did Fayola feel something stronger than the wind push against her wings?

22: What Justice Would Look and Sound Like

A Month Later
The Union of the Beloluga
Muliky County, Robinsk

Pulling out his desk chair, Viktor slid onto the suede seat. He sank most comfortably from the perfect, well-worn fit. At ten thirty in the evening, the household had finally quieted, affording him un-interrupted time to update his website. The laptop was already opened and on his website, so Viktor typed in his admin username and password. He licked his lips, excited to upload his new photos to Sugary Sweet Treats.

Creating a pirate-themed bedroom had been a good idea. But putting the twelve-year-old blond-haired, blue-eyed Adrian in a pirate costume had been a stroke of genius. When Viktor had handed Adrian the black eyepatch that would complete his outfit, the boy had mumbled something stupid like: "I wanna go home."

Viktor had ignored him, of course. With his dimpled smile, ocean blue eyes, and alabaster skin, Adrian was like catnip to his clients who preferred boys aged ten to thirteen. Besides, what twelve-year-old boy didn't like having his dick sucked as part of their job duties? Hell, Viktor had to go off to college before tickling his first tonsil.

With that groin-tingling trip down memory lane, Viktor added a new website page, titling it, The Bone Hard Pirate. The page name was a little on the nose for his creative taste, but the simplistic wordplay would offer his clients the right amount of teasing temptation. He'd taken about a hundred shots of Adrian, most of which wouldn't make it onto the site. But he only needed two dozen to create next month's subscription package. Choosing each month's feature image always left Viktor excited. This time proved no different.

Opening the electronic file labeled: FavPirate082123, he examined each photo again. The featured image would serve two purposes. One, to reward current subscribers for their continued business. Two, to encourage buyers of individual pictures and videos to upgrade to one of Sugary Sweet Treats' subscription packages. Viktor's wife, Lubov, created four subscription tiers. From expensive to economical, Lubov guaranteed their services were affordable to all, while also rewarding those at the higher price point with access to curated photos and videos like the one Viktor made of Timofey prepping Adrian for his pirate shoot.

I like this picture as the feature image. Flushed and wanting release after I ordered Timofey to pull off, Adrian is bone hard like my perfect title. He wanted to come so badly. The shame at having another boy get him off was long forgotten when pleasure joined them in bed. Working himself the rest of the way, Adrian messed his pants and hand. He also gets all red when I have one of the girls work him up for a shoot. I don't get the complaint.

These pictures are fire, especially this one. I think I have a winner. But I also like the one with the boys kissing under the wooden rudder wall art. Hmm, the choice is harder than I thought it would be.

"Harder," Viktor said aloud, laughing at his own unintended double entendre. "I need a second opinion. Perhaps Lubov wouldn't mind—"

"How did you get in here? No, no!"

Viktor jumped from his chair, tripped over the laptop cord, and landed on the hardwood floor.

"Stay away. I said . . ."

Splayed on his stomach, whatever adrenaline surged in him at his wife's scream, fear in every word, drained away when a figure loomed in his doorway. Lubov no longer screamed or sputtered, and he could see why.

Held off her feet and by her throat, his wife dangled from the clawed hand of an . . . impundulu? The creature who'd invaded his home and was choking his wife wasn't any impundulu he'd ever seen. But it had to have been one because its half-human, half-bird form stood at over six feet. A human-looking face with black feathers for hair and skin pulled dark wings around itself as it dropped Lubov to the floor.

His wife gasped and he did too, despite the tightening of his throat.

"Come on, kids. We're getting you out of here."

Viktor didn't recognize the male's voice, but he did the ones that followed. Katya, Adrian, Timofey, Maxim, and Gennady were all the kids who had bedrooms on the first level. Sofia, Inessa, and Mila shared a room on the second floor, while Daniil and Yuri slept in the basement.

"There's more up here," a second male yelled. "I'll bring them down as soon as they dress. Check the rest of the house, peacock."

"Now is not the time for jokes."

The female impundulu stepped over an unmoving Lubov. Golden eyes lowered to him, and a snarl lifted lips that would have made for a great feature image for a horror-themed shoot for his clients with darker fetishes. "Shift."

"W-what?"

Reaching down and behind her, she shoved Lubov across the floor to Viktor. "You're both polar bears. Large and strong. None of the children you keep here is a match for either of you. What do you do with them when they are too old for your preferred demographic? Sell them? Toss them out on the street? Hooked on drugs and with nowhere to go. Some, I'd wager, were too afraid and ashamed to return home."

Using one of her wings, she slammed the office door shut.

"We don't have time for this," one of the men yelled from the other side of the closed door. When she didn't answer, he swore. "Make it quick. Kwame and I swept the entire property. The tip was good. The intel gathered from our surveillance was better. Ten children. MCPD will be here in seven minutes. They prefer for us to be gone before they arrive. So I'm giving you five."

"I'll be out in three." Lightning sparked around the edges of her eyes like a dangerous ring of fire. "Last chance to shift."

With none of Viktor's caution, Lubov lunged at the impundulu. But her transformation was incomplete. Bones broke and lengthened. Sharp teeth and claws pushed from a body unused to a quick shift. Lubov roared, her reforming throat a painful transition he could hear as clearly as he could see the impundulu duck his wife's wild claw strike.

Countering, the impundulu attacked with a crackling fist of electricity to Lubov's chest.

Slam.

What human parts of the impundulu he'd recognized as female changed with the speed of a literal blink of his eyes. One moment he watched his wife crumple to the floor, her white fur smelling of burnt hair; the next, a fully formed impundulu barreled down on him.

The top of her head skimmed his ten-foot ceiling. Beak long and deadly, wings dark and dangerous, Viktor gaped at the predator who'd felled his wife with a single blow.

You should've shifted when you had the chance, she spoke in his mind.

Sparks of electricity flickered from golden eyes, spread to flawless wings and down a chest triple the width of his own. Snapping electrical pulses slithered between sharp talons like snakes cutting through ankle-high grass.

The ceiling bulbs exploded, descending the room into treacherous darkness.

This is going to hurt. Badly.

Gold lightning filled his office, chasing away the darkness with its threatening light.

Thunderclaps sounded and *zap, zap, zap*.

Viktor shrieked. Piss and shit soiled his boxers, a runny, foul mess of a response to lightning strikes to his stomach and groin. Three minutes should not have felt like an hour, but the more the impundulu filled his body with electrical surges, the louder he screamed and the more he feared the torture would take him from this world.

Stepping on his hands, she sliced arteries and crushed delicate bones.

Viktor shrieked even more, but only hoarse gurgles met the brutality leveled against him.

Thirty more seconds. What will I do with the balance of our time together? Oh, I know.

Slash. Slash.

You won't ever use those hands to brutalize children again.

Viktor couldn't hear the vicious impundulu over the explosion of pain ripping through his body or see his severed hands through his torrent of tears.

Three Weeks Later
The Commonwealth of Sunderton
Manbron City, Hingset
Lower East Side

"I-I swear I didn't touch her." Fran Snyder rushed from her bed. Her bare skin was cool yet sticky from the sudden outburst of sweat. She halted at her bedroom door, seeing a shadowy figure standing at the end of the dark hallway that led to her apartment door.

How did they get into my home? I didn't hear anything. One minute I was asleep, the next . . .

"Elle," the woman behind Fran said, voice a low, kind timbre, "my name is Fayola. I protect children from bad adults."

"Y-you do?"

"Yes."

The figure in the hallway stepped forward, leaving Fran with no good options, so she planted her back against the wall beside the open door.

Every time Emma allowed Elle to stay the night, Fran turned the nightlight on the girl's side of the bed. Fran couldn't tell much about the intruder with no other light on in the room except that she was female, with a tapered haircut, and wore all-black clothing.

She swallowed, afraid she knew what the woman was, who'd contacted her and why.

Even if she is a detective from the Special Victims Unit, she and her partner have no right to break into my home. There are laws against stuff like that. I'll call a lawyer. The press. I'll have their badges. I know my rights.

With her back to Fran, she couldn't see the detective's face, but she did see when she reached into her jacket. "I once helped a girl a little older than you. She's smart and brave. I bet you are too. In fact, I know you are."

Elle sniffled, the way she often did when afraid and unsure what to do. Fran had to put up with that a lot, especially when Emma first allowed Elle to stay the night. The child would whimper, then outright cry. With patience and time, however, she'd settled into quiet compliance. Fran liked when they were docile. It made her time with them more enjoyable.

"I-I'm not brave."

"Trust me, you are. Here, this is for you. The little girl I mentioned gave this to me to give to you. Do you know what kind of stuffed animal this is?"

Elle didn't give a verbal reply, but she must've done something in the affirmative because the detective said, "Smart girl. It's my goodwill promise. I have a friend. He's waiting for you in the hallway. Where are your clothes?"

Again, Elle did not speak, but she saw her hand point to Fran's pillow.

After undressing her, Fran had folded Elle's pajamas and placed them under her pillow. Fran had learned, that first night, that Elle was less likely to run from her if she stripped her down and hid her clothes and shoes.

The SVU detective dressed the child in silence but forewent the girl's slippers because Elle hadn't seen where Fran had hidden them.

"Come on, my brave girl. My friend, Jelani, will take you to your apartment and help you pack a bag."

"What about Mommy? She's at work."

"Don't worry about your mother. I'll take care of her after I'm done with Mrs. Snyder."

Fran did not like the sound of that.

If I go down, I'm taking Emma with me. But I'm not confessing to a damn thing. They can't make me.

"Tell me, Elle, how many times did you ask your mother to not leave you with Mrs. Snyder?"

"Don't know. I don't count too good."

"It's okay. You should've never had to ask. Ready?"

"Yes."

"Close your eyes." The detective lifted Elle into her arms, encouraged her forehead against her shoulder, and told her, "You won't ever have to see her again."

Her. She means me. But I think she also means Emma. No matter what I said about not touching Elle, the detective knows the truth. She . . . shit, is that a stuffed impundulu bird Elle is clutching? Long gray beak and black feathers. It couldn't be anything else. Fuck. She's not a detective from the Special Victims Unit but a goddamn Wake special operations soldier. She said goodwill promise, not blood pact, though. What in the hell is a goodwill promise?

Fran bolted to the opposite side of the room. Her naked body did not prove her guilt, but it also did not support her lie. Retrieving her nightgown from the floor, Fran's hands shook like a person diagnosed with essential tremor disorder. Fran pulled on her nightgown despite the rhythmic tremors, while keeping her eyes on what she now knew was an impundulu in human form.

"Don't forget she's human," she heard the person in the hall-way say.

Not her detective partner but another Wake soldier. They've been all over the news. All of a sudden, everyone's kissing their damn feathered asses. Has the world gone crazy? They drink our blood, but now they're the fucking heroes.

Arms outstretched, the male soldier relieved his partner of Elle. "That's a cool stuffed animal you got there."

Elle remained silent, which did nothing to discourage the man from initiating a one-sided conversation. His voice eventually faded to silence.

The *click* of Fran's closed apartment door had the remaining impundulu whirling to face her. She supposed the woman ex-pended all of her softness on Elle because she looked at her like she was a demon spat from hell.

"You started with your own child. Many pedophiles do. You left an indelible mark on Ashley, as you have on Elle and whoever else you've abused over the years. Perhaps you were also a victim of abuse—sexual, emotional. You obviously need help. I suppose that's true for every rapist, child molester, and child trafficker. But I'm neither a therapist nor a religious leader willing to hear your confessions and absolve you of your sins."

Snatching the nightstand's lamp's cord from the wall, she held the lamp in front of her like a medieval lance.

The impundulu's eyes glowed golden, but she stayed beyond Fran's reach.

"You, like others, won't serve enough time in prison for justice to be truly served. In a few years, you'll be back on the streets, hunting for your next victim. But I'm going to make that vile hun-ger you have inside of you for little girls a bit harder to feed. I asked your daughter what justice would look and sound like for her. Do you want to know what she said?"

Fran tightened her grip on the lamp. Her heart galloped at a pace that would soon have her hyperventilating. Sweat dripped into her eyes, causing stinging pain that had her blinking hard and fast.

"Ashley said, 'Justice looks like fingers that can't touch, legs that can't chase, and lips that can't kiss. It sounds like silence. No tongue to tell lies. No tongue for . . .' I don't need to say the rest because you know. You. Know."

Yeah, Fran knew. Her ungrateful daughter had turned on her. The bitch.

The impundulu removed her black gloves and cracked her knuckles. "No lightning. No shift. Just you, me, and your daughter's list of hurts. Your crimes. Your punishment. I'll begin with your lying tongue."

23: The Fine Art of Finally Giving a Shit

Two Months Later
The United Wake of Benekal
Kettle of Aradi City

"The Tree of Karasi." Fayola held Jelani's hand as if they were the same fifteen-year-olds who'd had no choice but to converge atop the very wall they now stood. Their lives had forever changed at this tree. For years, she'd resented much about that fateful day, but meeting Durah and Kwame had proven an unexpected gift.

"You should jump in." Kwame's big, strong hand slapped down on Fayola's shoulder. "Or maybe I'll push you in."

Fayola reared back and shoved her elbow in Kwame's stomach.

The hand on her shoulder fell away as he doubled over with laughter. "I guess all of that ass-kicking has worn you out. That elbow strike felt like a tickle."

Durah pushed Kwame aside, wedging herself between the two of them. "Leave her alone, or I'll be the one kicking your ass and tossing you down there."

In unison, the four friends looked into the fountain of blood. As dark as night, hundreds of gallons of blood filled the fountain, covering a third of the towering tree.

Durah was the first of them to lift her head. She craned backward, taking in as much of the tree as she could. "I thought the tree would look smaller. I'm older and bigger, and I'd like to think I'm a whole lot wiser than I was at fifteen. But look at it. It's as huge as ever." Reaching out, Durah plucked a blood-filled green leaf from the tree. "We've all felt it, right?"

Kwame snatched the leaf from Durah's hand, sucking the blood from the veins before Durah could do more than scowl at him. "I'll walk down one street, and it's as if time has frozen. I turn a corner, and it feels like I've stepped into a different city. It's a surreal sensation to feel both at home and a tourist in your hometown." Removing three leaves from the tree, all white like the color of his lightning, Kwame handed one to each of them.

Instead of eating her leaf, the way the others had, Fayola held it up. "These are our leaves because this is our tree. Every mission we completed was a blood pact fulfilled. Our sacrifices helped to feed the citizens of this kettle. Our family, friends, and neighbors, they all relied on us to do our part for the Wake."

"The way our parents before us did," Jelani added. "The night before we were to meet here, I struggled to fall asleep. I couldn't stop thinking about everything and everyone I would leave behind." Bringing their joined hands to his mouth, Jelani kissed the back of Fayola's hand. "What finally helped me sleep was knowing I would see you here. Somehow, with hundreds of other kids on this wall, I knew you would find me. And you did."

"Oh, come on. Don't make me gag on my blood leaf." Kwame's soft chuckle revealed the depth of his heart before his words of, "I've always been able to be myself around you three. Accepted and accepting. As much as we disliked being torn from our families, I sometimes think we wouldn't have become friends otherwise." Reaching around Durah, Kwame plucked Fayola's earlobe. "You're right. This is our tree."

Durah fingered a gold leaf but did not remove it from the tree. "Blood is our past, present, and future. So are pacts. This time around, however, we choose." Durah nodded and grinned, her contentment with her decision obvious. "We have already chosen."

"Indeed the four of you have."

Fayola did not bother searching for the source of the voice. She hadn't managed to see her in the tree the first time they'd all been there, and she doubted she would this time. But Durah had, so she looked to her friend, whose eyes scanned the tree.

"Nothing," she whispered. "How can she still be this good?"

"Am I the only one who feels fifteen again?" Kwame asked. His own gaze shifted from one part of the tree to another. "Peacock, you got eyes on her?"

"Still with that peacock shit. Get a new joke. And what makes you think my sight is better than yours? If Durah can't find her, what chance do we have?"

"I can't believe any of you finished basic."

Fayola focused on the direction the voice came—to her right and way the hell up. "Considering you were our diello and trained us, what does that say about you?"

Kwame's laughter rippled through the cool air almost as loudly as the sudden rustling of leaves.

"So irreverent. I see you've stopped pretending otherwise."

Kwame plucked Fayola's earlobe again, and she swatted his hand with a bit more force than she'd used with the elbow strike.

"Not irreverent, Madana," Fayola said, following Jelani's lead when he moved to the right. "We didn't expect you so soon. You're as stealthy as I remember."

From her trajectory, Madana intended on planting herself in the center of their group, so Fayola and Jelani moved even farther to the right.

Wide, long wings fluttered then snapped out on Madana's landing. The movement whipped up a face-smacking breeze that pushed the quartet farther away from the newcomer. Madana's red eyes glowed in her hybrid form with the same look of long-suffering Fayola remembered from her time in basic training.

Hand still holding Fayola's, Jelani offered Madana a proper welcome. "It's good to see you again. I hope you had a pleasant flight."

A feathered eyebrow arched, and a lip curled into what a stranger would think was a snarl. But the look Madana gave Jelani before turning it on Fayola, then on Kwame and Durah, spoke of the line she often walked with them between exasperation and pride. Madana lowered wings whose hybrid form span was an impressive seventeen feet. Stepping back, she positioned herself so she could address them all.

Fayola squelched the temptation to ask Madana how long she'd been in the tree. Instead, she thanked the ancestors that the older impundulu was an ally and not a foe.

"Despite recent actions, you're all intelligent, which means you know the definition of the word *retired*."

"We are," Durah agreed, "and we do."

"Nice." Kwame raised his hand, prepared to slap Durah on her back, but her push to his chest was quicker. "Okay, I get it. High five?"

Durah ignored Kwame but said to Madana, "Retirement means having the right to decide who we help, where we'll go, and when we'll arrive and leave."

"In your fantasy world where freedom of choice rules all, where does accountability factor?"

Fayola stepped forward. "Before each raid, we confer with the local police chief and municipal leader. Mayor. County Executive. We share surveillance duties, but we conduct the raids, and they make the arrests."

"Interagency collaboration. A first for the Wake. I would be more impressed with the employment of that strategy if not for the defendants' claims of assault before their arrest. Was corporal punishment your idea or Kwame's?"

"If you're going to scold us," Kwame said, "you shouldn't have trained us in the fine art of kicking ass and not giving a shit afterward."

"Unhelpful," Durah said. "But, umm, yeah, he's right. The tribunal has rarely cared how we completed our missions. I can't see that changing for a bunch of sex offenders and human traffickers. We want to send a message, and so do local authorities."

"That crimes against children will be met with brutal force?"

Jelani's single step had him standing beside Fayola again. In this, as in life, they were partners. "Yes, but not only that. Our blood pacts have evolved to include goodwill missions."

Madana leveled a finger at Fayola and curled her lip. "The CEU does not follow orders, they won't take another belay, and the tribunal knows they've been feeding this unsanctioned civilian unit unauthorized intelligence."

Fayola laced her fingers with Jelani's, relishing the warmth he generated. "Yet you don't seem surprised by any of that."

"Or upset," Jelani said. "We asked to speak with you about the CEU. The fact that you agreed to the meet confirms Fay's suspicion."

"It took me longer than it should have to figure it out, although, once I did, you being the mastermind behind the selection of the CEU members made a strange kind of sense. Also, learning you were the person who fed Dad details of my battle at the Namju-Tikala border, despite the tribunal's gag order, made deducing the rest a simple equation."

Madana's curled lip morphed into a full-on shit-eating grin. She even fluttered her feathers. The act was an impundulu's way of tooting a metaphorical horn. "You should've seen your face when the kamaus promoted you to belay."

"I was angry."

"You were afraid of the weighty responsibility that comes with being a belay. You might think that's the wrong emotion for a leader to possess, but you'd be wrong. The right amount of fear in a leader promotes humility, cautiousness, and reflectiveness. Come here, please."

Much of Fayola's relationship with Madana was superior to subordinate. Yet there, in that sacred place where history and culture dictated their interactions, Madana did not command Fayola's compliance but extended a request.

With no ranks between them, no duties that separated them, and no obligations to kettle or Wake, they were, for the first time, equals.

Fayola walked to Madana, stopping within arm's reach.

"To achieve their full potential, some people require a small push, while others a large one. But you, stubborn, homesick, and apathetic needed a—"

"Swift kick in the ass," Kwame said with a laugh.

"It was tempting, but not even that would've worked." Madana swept a long bang out of Fayola's eyes, guaranteeing she both saw and heard her clearly. "You required a push off the tallest mountain I could find. Njeri helped by assigning you the task of writing the annual proposal for her unit."

Fayola should've felt manipulated, tricked. A tiny part of her did. But she'd known Madana and Njeri her entire adult life. She trusted them as soldiers, but she liked them as people more. They would no more act against her well-being than she would question their loyalty to the Wake.

"Except for the vile creatures you've been hunting, there is little worse than wasted potential."

Fayola took Madana's extreme statement and pointed judgment on the chin like the grazing punch it had been meant as.

"Why build an all-gold unit?" Jelani asked.

Madana aimed her fingers at Fayola's forehead, clearly intent on plucking it the way Kwame had done to her earlobe earlier.

She sidestepped the attack, leaving Madana with nothing but air.

"It's nice to see my training in action."

"Not all wasted potential."

"After that response, Jelani, do you not know the answer to your question?"

"We all know Fay's an undercover smart-ass," Kwame said.

The look she shot at him garnered her a shallow shrug and a slow batting of eyes.

Knowing Jelani was too polite to agree with Kwame in mixed company, he continued as if their friend hadn't interjected. "You wouldn't pass over excellent candidates to build Fay a unit of soldiers with similar personality traits as her own if they weren't also the best of the applicants. Or . . ."

Fayola glanced over her shoulder to Jelani. He'd paused, and she wanted to know why.

"You mentioned wasted potential, in reference to Fay. You also meant the members of the CEU, correct?"

"I did. Fayola," Madana said, garnering her attention, "I choose your unit in the most technical sense only. When the Rashidi Tribunal requested my assistance, I had no intention of accepting. The success of any unit is based on the foundational relationship between the belay and members of their unit. Each unit has its own synergy, and it begins with whatever the belay sees in the soldiers they select to join their team."

"What changed your mind?" Fayola asked.

"I recalled the specificity of your selection criteria. Not everything. It had been years since I'd last read your proposal. But I remembered how meticulous you'd been, how thoughtful you were about character traits, such as high values and wisdom." Madana pointed to herself and then to Jelani. "Reds are known for our determination and ambition. While whites," she said, nodding to Kwame, "can be creative and open. Then there are those with green lightning, like your friend Durah. They trend toward—"

"Equilibrium, renewal, and rebirth," Fayola interjected, recalling a long-ago conversation with Raicho. "Not stereotypes but thoroughly researched and documented personality patterns."

"You've surrounded yourself with people whose personalities and drives are different from your own. Wise. But even the most determined red would struggle to move a planted gold. Golds need a reason, a damn good one, to . . . well, give a shit about people outside of their tight-knit circle. That's what you outlined in the unit composition portion of your proposal."

Unsurprisingly, Kwame laughed. "The Criminal Exploitation Unit, the fine art of finally giving a shit. Classic. Perfect. That is so you, Fay."

Durah's giggle started soft but evolved into barking belly laughs. "He has a point. Your proposal was tantamount to a public display of your diary."

Crossing arms over her chest, Fayola harrumphed, as if offended. "I've never had a diary."

"You made my point. So, taken to its logical conclusion, you're responsible for . . ." Durah pointed to the sky behind Fayola. "Them."

Fayola's groan, unlike her harrumph, was heartfelt. She turned to see twenty stubborn and homesick but no longer apathetic impundulus flying toward her. Fayola lifted the palm of her right hand and extended it toward the approaching group as if it were a stop sign. "You're early."

Twenty sets of black wings beat against the cool midday air. Their brilliant minds were as deadly as the gray beaks that opened and closed as if capable of speech. Yet grouped together as they were, black and gray flowing into black and gray, telling them apart, from fifty feet, should've been impossible. As always, Jendayi and Marcel were beside each other, while Binta pulled up the rear despite her superior speed.

Even when in a safe environment, she protects her team's backs. One day, when she's ready, and if she wants, Binta could become the belay of this unit. But that's years into the future. Now, I need them to . . . "Tree."

But—

"Dominique."

Yes, ma'am. Parking it in the tree.

Between Madana and the unit arriving early, Fayola didn't know why she bothered with creating an itinerary. Fayola turned back to Madana, prepared to apologize for the interruption. "What's with the smile?"

"You sidelined them."

"They're early, and we are still tal—"

"Not now. For your goodwill missions. You sidelined them."

Fayola did not see why that decision warranted any special attention, certainly not from a woman whose status would soon change in a significant way.

"As you so eloquently reminded us, we're retired. I hold no military rank. I command no one but myself." Fayola's gaze darted to Kwame, sure he'd say something inappropriate about her "commanding peacock in bed."

Her friend remained silent, but his broad grin and nod to Jelani delivered his joke well enough.

"Yet there are twenty soldiers perched in the Tree of Karasi awaiting your next directive. What will it be?"

Fayola looked to Kwame and Durah, who understood her pointed expression meant for them to join her and Jelani. As a unit of friends, they faced Madana.

The older woman's smirk returned, while her eyes glowed crimson. "All right, then. You're finally ready to get to the heart of our meeting."

Jelani's arm grazed Fayola's. The subtle movement generated a frisson of electricity where their bodies touched. "We requested this meeting, but you selected this location."

"I wasn't informed of the CEU's presence at our meeting."

"As this meeting involves their future, I invited them," Fayola said. "But they're an hour early because they have an unforgivable tendency of hacking into my mobile unit. I should've taken Durah's advice and stopped adding my appointments to my virtual calendar." Instinctively, Fayola patted the pants pocket that held her mobile device. "I've had this new number for only two days." Fayola chuckled, partly annoyed but mostly amused by the CEU's persistence. "We're all here, even if a few more than you intended."

Madana shifted from her hybrid form to her human body with precision and speed. The transformation, shrinking of bones, withdrawing of feathers, realigning of organs, and recalibrating of electrical pulses to form hair, clothing, and shoes, occurred with a painless grace befitting an impundulu of Madana's caliber. Within seconds, a six-foot woman in dress black slacks, a pale green blouse with scooped collar, and a pair of high-heeled black shoes, which granted her an additional three inches of height, stood in front of Fayola. Black braids with red tips fell to her knees.

Fayola asked the question she'd wanted to know since they'd met. "How did you get away with having non–regulation length hair?"

A chorus of "Yeahs" came from the tree.

"That's a conversation for another time." Then, as if taunting Fayola with her unsatisfying reply, Madana flipped braids over her shoulder. "I would think you'd be more interested in why I accepted your meeting request instead of having the tribunal send PMs to haul each of you before them."

"We wouldn't have gone, if they had," Jelani said.

"I told them as much."

Jelani extended his right hand. "Is it too early to offer congratulations?"

Despite the vague sentence, a round of applause began with Fayola, Durah, and Kwame and continued with the CEU.

Madana's mouth did not fall open, no more than her eyes widened. The only telltale sign of her surprise was the return of her smirk and her words of "Well done." Extending her own hand, she shook Jelani's. "Thank you. The appointment won't become official for another three months."

"We know." Fayola nodded in the direction of where members of the CEU perched in the tree. "You gave me three hackers and two who are nearly as good. They enjoy a challenge. Boredom leaves them with too much time to go snooping, though. I did sideline them for our goodwill missions, but I'm not above acting on credible intel when provided. So, soon-to-be Kamau Madana, I'd like to negotiate the terms of our relationship with the CEU."

"Negotiate?"

"That's why you're here," Durah said, as bold as ever. "You wouldn't have agreed to meet us, if you weren't in a position to negotiate on the tribunal's behalf."

"Numbers don't lie," Kwame said from beside Durah.

Neville, Sula, and Chikondi rattled off stats from their goodwill missions as if zapped by each other's lightning. Voluntary blood donations. International news reports. Sex offender and trafficking hotline tips. Arrests, confessions, and guilty pleas. Number of visitors to the CEU's "How You Can Help Stop Human Trafficking," web page. Their verbal volcanic explosion of dates, people, and numbers also included illegal drugs confiscated from their raids.

By the time Neville, Sula, and Chikondi concluded their impromptu report, every member of the CEU had made their way down the tree and onto the wall. Like everyone else, they were in their human form. But, unlike everyone else, wariness had them maintaining their distance from Madana who'd swung in their direction.

They may be stubborn, but they're wise beyond their years. They aren't pets to be patted or children to be coddled. But I want to keep them. They'd be mine as much as I'd be theirs.

"That's a fine bit of cherry-picking of facts," Madana said, addressing the entire CEU. "Off the top of my head, I can list six laws you've broken to obtain the very information you casually spat all over me. Should I begin?"

No one from the CEU responded, which was the only reply Fayola knew Madana would have accepted.

"Very good. You have much to learn from the four behind me, just as they have much to learn from their elders." Returning her attention to Fayola, Madana's eyes shone with slowly receding red. "With each successful goodwill mission, blood donations have followed. Many non–blood pact nations have reached out to the president and Rashidi Tribunal. Human trafficking has no borders. But there are segments of the world population that are the most vulnerable, the most susceptible to that kind of crime. At this point, we all know who they are, just as we know the societal conditions that produce their vulnerability."

Reaching out, Madana slid the same lock of hair from earlier away from Fayola's eyes. In less time than it took Madana to lower her hand, the lock of hair fell back into place.

Madana snorted. "Even your hair is stubborn. State your terms, Belay Fayola."

Belay Fayola. I still don't like it, even though I knew the acceptance of the official role would be the tribunal's primary condition. They have every right to ask it of me, especially in light of my recent actions.

"Three belays," Jelani said. He linked his hand with hers. In turn, Fayola held Kwame's hand, who stood to her immediate left. "Three belays. Three CEU special ops teams. That should accommodate non-gold applicants, transfer requests, and re-up requests."

"My CEU unit," Kwame said after an unusually long quiet spell, "will focus on the drug production and distribution side of human trafficking."

"And mine," Jelani said, gesturing to himself with his free hand, "will be responsible for the coordination with local authorities in joint task force efforts."

"And you, Durah?" Madana asked in a conversational, inquiring tone but with an edge of predatory bite. "What is your role in this?"

Fayola watched as Durah dug into the jacket pocket of her warm caramel trench blazer. Then, pulling out her mobile, she showed Madana a screen.

"Your digital business card," Madana read. "Ah, you're the unit's personal physician. Very good. I had forgotten Fayola included a mental health therapist in her proposal."

"And professional development specialist," Durah added. "They're dealing with abused and traumatized children who also aren't impundulu, which necessitates ongoing skills training. We do not want to compound their abuse with a lack of emotional and cultural intelligence." Durah leaned around Kwame and said to Fayola, "Mom has compiled a referral list of mental health practitioners. The price of the list is a visit. So bring her by the house the next time she's in town. Mom has a little something for her."

"Between your and Jelani's mothers and my father, her bedroom is overflowing. And I refuse to take one more thing to the Newton home."

From beside her, Jelani laughed. "Jwahir has the biggest extended family ever. The girl is pure gold."

Inexplicably, the conversation shifted to Jwahir.

"When is her next soccer game?" Sula asked.

"She texted me one of her drawings." Marcel moved closer, showing everyone the image on his mobile.

Outlined with a squiggly white line, Jwahir had drawn a brown gingerbread man with three pink hearts as buttons. The gingerbread man's eyes and lips were colored a darker shade of brown, with her accenting the smile with red dots at the corners.

Jwahir had texted Fayola and Jelani the same image, along with a half dozen other drawings. Whether the drawing was of a person, place, animal, or object, Jwahir always added a pink heart somewhere on the picture.

Before Fayola knew it, everyone had lowered themselves to the wall. With their back to the Tree of Karasi and them facing a long, wide street buttressed by high-rise buildings, their feet dangled from the wall as they chatted away. Impundulus flew overhead, while others went about their day on foot and in vehicles.

"You've got to be kidding me."

Of the twenty-four people seated on the wall, only Fayola responded to Madana. She shifted to her right. "Why are you still up there?"

"We haven't finished our negotiation talks."

"Really? Huh, I thought we had."

Dark brows arched, and hands flew to hips. "You damn well know we have not."

Realizing she still held the white leaf Kwame had given her, Fayola handed it to Madana, who snatched it from her hand.

"I expect more respectful treatment after I'm sworn in as kamau."

"I'll pay you the same respect as I do kamaus Thulani and Haseena."

"Considering any terms of our negotiation must receive Kamau Audre's approval, I suggest you mind your manners while in her presence."

"Yes, ma'am."

"About those terms."

"Not many," Jelani said. He also shifted to see Madana, but to his left and after kissing Fayola's cheek. "No contractual term of service for any retired soldier who joins any of the three CEUs."

Balling the regifted blood leaf, Madana shoved it into her mouth. "Okay. What else?"

"A larger budget," Durah said. She raised her first three fingers. "Three units. Worldwide outreach. Mental health and professional development support services. There's also unit-specific supplies we'll require."

"All of that is possible. Make sure your budget proposal includes a detailed supply list of anything beyond what is traditionally provided to each unit. Is that it?"

"Nope," Dominique said. "Oh, sorry, Kamau Madana."

"Why are you even talking?" Binta said.

"Because Fay is dragging this out."

Kwame, seated beside her, smacked her shoulder again. "You really are. Just tell her already so we can get out of here and go to Open Air Sweets. A new one opened eight miles from here."

A chorus of "Yays" erupted.

"Who in the hell said anything about you brats being invited."

"Booooo."

Kwame laughed, and so did everyone else. Well, everyone except for Madana.

Fayola cleared her throat. "Considering the scope and breadth of the CEU's mission, I think its members, especially the youngest ones, deserve a boon."

For all that Madana had been a tough-as-talons diello, accepting nothing but the highest quality output from her cadets, she was a fair, kind, and supportive leader. Fayola did not doubt she would make an even better kamau. She couldn't think of anyone more deserving to fill Kamau Thulani's seat than Madana of the Kettle of Perahu City.

"Don't make me ask what boon, Belay Fayola."

"No, ma'am." Using Jelani's sturdy shoulder, she pushed to her feet. "I request that the CEUs be headquartered here."

"That's not much of a request. But you aren't a selfish person."

"I ask that you waive the non–family contact for current and future unit members. Our work saves lives and reunites families. Why then should these young soldiers be denied theirs?"

"That's a huge ask."

"I know."

"It goes against centuries of military protocol."

"Yes, ma'am, I know."

Madana's gaze traveled the length of the wall where a score of twenty-two-year-olds sat. She took them in, as if seeing the team she'd built through clearer eyes. Empathetic eyes perhaps, but she likely viewed them as the face of the military the tribunal could no longer deny.

"Kamau Audre won't like it, and neither will many others. We are a people of blood and traditions."

"First and foremost, we are family. We can have both. Do both. We shouldn't have to choose."

"Maybe, but I'll be a junior member on the tribunal. The position comes with an equal voice and vote but little bargaining power."

"Untrue." Fayola flung her arms wide, and everyone on the wall stood at attention. "You have us. Our accomplishments will be yours. Every reunited family. Every conviction. Every hotline tip. Every adopted victims of trafficking and violence protection law. Every new blood-pact treaty signed with countries who'd once shunned our presence in their nation. All yours to claim. New friends and allies. And enemies to fear our great Wake. Yours. The success of our goodwill missions will precede us. And that, more than anything else, will be both your bargaining power and your legacy. No wasted potential but an honorable legacy of freedom and justice.”

“Freedom and justice.” Madana removed a gold leaf from the tree. “Legacy.” Another gold leaf. Another. And another. Hands full of leaves, she began with Fayola. Madana handed a gold blood leaf to everyone on the wall. “Legacy is a powerful word but not as mighty as freedom and justice. You’ve grown, Fayola. You all have. I see no wasted potential before me.”

“A family,” Jelani said.

“The best one ever,” Durah agreed.

“Kickass,” Kwame said.

The CEU repeated the six-letter word with such loud exuberance that passersby stopped and clapped, and drivers waved and beeped.

“If the CEU is to be my legacy and the Wake’s future, then you need a name.”

“I’ve been telling her that for months,” Dominique shouted. “Finally, someone else gets it. I have a great idea.”

“No,” the CEU said in unison.

“Except for the kamau and belays, the rest of you are assholes.” Dominique stomped her way to Fayola, giving a playful gut punch to each friend she passed. “Hi, Fay,” she said, gutchecking her too because the boundaries between them that mattered existed in the field.

“That’s the reason they wouldn’t accept another belay.” Madana shrugged. “Your leadership style is your own.”

Fayola did not have a leadership style, at least not consciously. She simply believed in respecting differences and leaning into the strength of others.

“Hello, Dominique. I see you’re letting your hair grow out.”

Dominique's hand flew to her head, running over a short layer of black hair. "I can't believe you called me out on missing my weekly barber's appointment."

"Your skin is thicker than a bit of gentle teasing." Fayola chucked Dominique's chin. "Tell us, so we can finally lay the name of the CEU to rest."

Bouncing on her tiptoes, Dominique's sweet smile reminded her of Jwahir's. "Yes, it's about time." Sidling closer to Fayola, Dominique whispered into her ear.

"You've got to be kidding me," Binta said, throwing up her hands in feigned exasperation.

Even Madana seemed amused by Dominique's uncharacteristic bout of shyness.

But Fayola understood that even bold, confident people were sometimes gripped by moments of insecurity. So, she listened without judgment. Fayola didn't even poke fun at Dominique's cute, if uncreative, unit name.

"What do you think?"

Fayola had never seen the point of having a unit name beyond the original one. Every unit's name was descriptive of the types of missions they performed. When writing her proposal, Fayola had followed the same practice.

But we are unlike every other Wake special ops unit. So why then should we have a standard unit name?

Fayola raised the hand with the gold blood leaf from the Tree of Karasi. "A toast." She scanned the smiling faces of her friends and allies, beginning with a trusting Dominique and ending with a loving Jelani. From one person to the next, the crackling embers of fear snapped and hissed, a soft but persistent specter that taunted: You can't save them all. The world is too big, the problem is too great, and your unit is too few.

Yes, a healthy amount of fear could motivate but fear in the absence of skill, will, and action was tantamount to a bird flying into a headwind—halting forward progress and blowing it backward.

Impundulus aren't any bird. I'll gladly fly into any child trafficking wind type with this team. "Dominique has named us Bearly Gold, and so we are. Bear blood fuels. Strengthens us. It is a priceless gift. Its high value is predictable, stable, and measured in impundulu lives. We will triumph, not because we won't experience struggle and failure, but because the good people of Earth Pact want us to succeed."

24: Family and Friendship

Three Months Earlier
The People's Democratic Republic of Tikala
North Lagoba City, Santou

Jwahir had visited the Newton home on four previous occasions. Nothing about the three-story brick house had changed. A sturdy six-foot aluminum gate painted black still surrounded a backyard with toys perfect for a young active bear shifter: a saucer swing set Kadeem had vaulted himself from during her first visit, a geometric dome climber Kadeem had claimed as his mountain peak during her second visit, and an obstacle course with a rope ladder, monkey bars, and gymnastic rings Kadeem couldn't complete on her third visit but fared better with her help on her fourth.

The house still had a doorbell that sounded like a yapping dog, although it had taken a laughing Jelani to explain the Newtons' humor.

"Small yapping dogs have no fear, not even of bears hundreds of pounds larger than them."

Despite the Newtons' unique doorbell chime, they did not have a pet dog, but they did have a fifty-five-gallon glass aquarium tank on an upright wooden stand in their living room. Colorful fish swam through sculptured lava rocks and hideaway pipes, inside barrel ornaments and sunken ships, between multicolored silk plants and under stone bridges.

Nothing about the home had changed—not the furniture, bear shifter sturdy; not the smell, a lemon-scented cleanser; and not the residents, Nita, Emmett, and Kadeem Newton.

Nothing has changed, but everything is about to. I knew I would be nervous, but I didn't think my heart would pound so hard. My hands are sweaty, and I'm not even playing on Kadeem's monkey bars. I want this change. I really do. Fay said I could be selfish. But the more that is given to me, the more that can be taken away. I already lost Mommy and Daddy. Will moving in with the Newtons mean I'll eventually lose my impundulu family too? I've heard some grown-ups say, "Out of sight, out of mind." Will they forget about me? Will they be too busy to come get me when it's their turn? Shared parenting. Joint custodial parents. Fay and Jelani explained what those words mean. I'll spend the school year with the Newtons. But the summers, some holidays and birthdays, and every other weekend I'll stay in Benekal.

Seated on the Newtons' living room couch, Jwahir sat between Fayola and Jelani. Like an unnatural appendage, she clung to Fayola's arm.

Nita and Emmett sat on a love seat across the room from them, while little Kadeem seemed incapable of staying still or being quiet. He darted into the living room again, breathing hard. "That's a lot of stuff. The movers are strong. They said I was too small to help." Wiping sweat from his forehead with one hand, Kadeem brandished a familiar stuffed animal from behind his back with his other. "This fell from a box." Cocking his arm back like a major league pitcher, Kadeem threw the toy. Up it went, wide and high.

Chuckling, Jelani snatched the plush toy from the air before it sailed past his head. "Aim needs work, but your form is good and your throwing arm strong."

"Next time," Nita said, "hand it to her." Crooking a finger, she gestured to Kadeem to come to her. "There's no way anything fell out of the packed boxes. What have I told you about touching what doesn't belong to you?"

"Not to."

"And telling fibs?"

"Not to."

"That's right. Now," Nita lifted Kadeem and plopped him on Emmett's lap, "I know you're excited to have Jwahir move in, but I need you to take a deep breath and relax. Okay?"

"Yes, Mama."

Emmett wrapped an arm around Kadeem's waist and pulled him close. "I got him. We're excited too but we don't want to overwhelm the newest member of our family."

Jwahir pressed her face against Fayola's arm, unsure how to respond.

Mr. Emmett smiles at me the way Jelani does. He's just as nice and kind. I feel safe with them both. How can I have two sets of new parents when some of my Namju friends don't even have one? It's not fair.

"It doesn't have to be today," she heard Nita say. "If you aren't ready, you don't have to move in today."

"Yeah, it's fine, sweetheart. The room next to Kadeem's will still be yours. You can claim it whenever you're ready."

One sniffle turned into two, and two turned into an embarrassing bout of crying.

Strong arms wrapped around her waist and lifted. "Please excuse us."

"I'm sorry," she said to Fayola between sniffles.

"You're entitled to your emotions." Fayola carried her out of the living room, down a carpeted hallway with framed family pictures on the wall, past the open front door, and up a flight of stairs.

Jelani followed but stopped at the front door to speak to a mover with green dyed mohawk hair and eyebrows as dark as her mood.

Jwahir did not know whether the Newtons planned on having more biological children, but they'd given her their spare bedroom. The last time she'd seen the room, it looked more like a home gym than a child's bedroom. Bed, dressers, bookcase, desk and chair replaced free weights, a spin bike, and a rowing machine. The formerly beige walls were repainted a cheery yellow with white accents.

All of the furniture looks the same as it did online. Fayola let me choose then too. The sparkly pink and yellow comforter looks better in person.

"You aren't losing us." Fayola deposited Jwahir on a bed she knew, if she demolished her walls of guilt and released her grip on fear, would give her many years of peaceful slumber. Kneeling in front of her, Fayola held her hands. "And we aren't losing you. Isn't that right, Jelani?"

As if her question summoned him, instead of Fayola's acute hearing having detected his presence in the carpeted hallway, Jelani entered the room through a doorway wide enough for . . . well, a full-grown bear.

"Raicho and Mom will disown us if we miss a single weekend visit, parent-teacher conference, or birthday. So, no, we aren't going to lose each other."

"Has everything been unloaded?" Fayola asked.

"Yeah, I saw the movers off and thanked them for their hard work." One hand moved to his hip, the other held her stuffed impundulu; Jelani shifted to the right and left. "Emmett and Nita did a nice job setting up the room, but the walls are bare. Where's the decal?"

Fayola pointed to the desk in front of a bow window with a yellow and pink sheer draped curtain that let in a warm glow of natural light. "Check that storage bin under her desk. Unless I'm mistaken, I packed the decal, along with a tape measure, sponge, and rubber squeegee in that white bin. There should also be a spray bottle in there. You can get water from the bathroom across the hall." Then, to Jwahir, Fayola smiled and asked, "Where would you like Jelani to place your heart?"

When I moved into our new house in Aradi City, she asked me the same question. When I left their home in Silesse City to stay with Granddad Raicho, I didn't think I would see my pink heart again.

As gentle as ever, Fayola squeezed her hand when her inner thoughts kept her from answering. "The ceiling above your bed, like at home?"

No, that's a special place just for the three of us. "I think I would like it over there." Jwahir pointed to the wall above the white six-cubby bookcase.

"Done." Placing her stuffed impundulu at the foot of the bed, Jelani went to work. He applied the large decal in no time at all, bringing the wall to life with a brilliant splash of pink. "Looks good. You picked a great spot, kiddo. Morning or night, you'll be able to see your friends from your bed."

I hadn't thought of it that way, but he's right. Many of my friends are gone but seeing their names reminds me of them. So, maybe adults are wrong. Like Mommy and Daddy, my friends are out of sight, but they aren't out of mind. I still remember them. Jelani told me I always would, and I believe him.

Jelani kicked off his soft leather shoes, the way he did when they were home. "I'm tired, and that bed looks good. How about a nap?"

Fayola shrugged, then proceeded to remove her own slip-on shoes.

"Wait. What? I don't get it."

"What's there to understand?" Fayola unlaced and removed Jwahir's high-top black sneakers. Handing both pairs of shoes to Jelani, he stowed them in the closet.

My closet. Boxes with half of my stuff from home are in there. My clothing and toys are somewhere in these boxes. My laptop with a special GPS tracking system is in my book bag downstairs. Thanks to Sula, anywhere in the world Fayola's and Jelani's missions take them, I'll know where they are.

Fayola crawled into the bed behind Jwahir. "Change can be scary. Believing you deserve happiness and accepting it as truth are not the same. We're cuddling, so pick your spot before Jelani sprawls his big body over most of the bed."

I've lived with them for weeks. Their thoughtfulness and affection shouldn't still surprise me. I am happy. Yes, yes, I am happy. I deserve to be happy with them . . . and with the Newtons.

"Too late, kiddo." Jelani playfully shoved her until she lay with her back against Fayola's front. "I'm staking claim to the outside of the bed. Fay gets the wall, and you're in the unenviable position of being squeezed between us."

Sure enough, Jwahir's slow response left her wedged between the two.

She giggled, not minding the position and their special way of reminding her of what they'd told her many times. *"We're a family."*

Plain. Simple. True.

With a hand to her stomach, Fayola pulled Jwahir closer. "The new mobile we gave you this morning has everyone's contact information."

Jelani shifted to face them. "Memorize ours, Raicho's, and the Newtons'." Tapping a braid with three pink beads on the end, Jelani's eyes turned a serious shade of red. "You're not alone. Not anymore. Never again. Got it?"

I haven't felt alone since Fay rescued me from Mr. Seager. Sad and uncertain, sometimes, but never alone. "Yeah, got it."

"Good. We have dozens of mobiles like the one we gave you. When Fay and I visit Namju next week, we'll distribute one to each child trafficking survivor."

"Huan and Mei lien?" Jwahir asked with giddy excitement that had her heart pounding for a better reason than nervousness. "I'll be able to talk to them whenever I want. Or better, we can video chat."

Fayola kissed the back of Jwahir's head. "When I said everyone's contact information, I also meant your friends. Their device also includes your mobile number and home addresses. So when you receive your new student email, you can share that with them too." Fayola laughed, emitting warm, reassuring embers of heat. "Durah has included the purchase of mobiles in our budget proposal to the Rashidi Tribunal. Of course, they won't like it, but I'm confident we'll come to an agreement."

"Don't forget the stuffed impundulus."

"There's a line item in the budget for your and Jwahir's precious toy."

From where he'd left it at the foot of the bed, Jelani retrieved Jwahir's stuffed impundulu and handed it to her. "It was kind of you to give yours to little Elle. But it was the first toy I bought you, and I couldn't have you without your own."

"Now," Fayola said, her soft voice a prelude to sleep, "we give one to every child we help. The stuffed impundulu is meant as a reminder that they are still children, despite the grown-up acts they were forced to engage, while the CEU mobile is—"

"A promise," Jwahir said with absolute certainty in her correctness. Then, rolling onto her left side to face Fayola, she placed her palm on a cheek that was both hard and soft like the bird shifter. "Family and friendship. Not blood ties."

"No, not blood ties. Lightning and goodwill." Fayola turned her face to kiss Jwahir's palm. "We love you."

As if a sandstorm formed right in front of her, whipping golden granular particles into her eyes, Jwahir blinked. Fast and hard and . . . *How does she always say stuff I don't expect?* "Y-you love me?"

"Of course." Fayola glanced over her shoulder to Jelani, who laughed and mumbled something that sounded like, "The fine art of giving a shit."

Jwahir shot up in bed, her body suddenly as light as a springtime breeze. "I love you too. Both of you. A lot. I mean, a lot, a lot."

"We know, kiddo. You didn't have to shout it."

"You know?"

"You're loud." Fayola tugged her back down. "And obvious." She kissed her cheek with lips that had never lied to her but did, on occasion, poke fun. "Look at that, three bears."

Jwahir popped back up again, ready to call Fayola's bluff. But no, strolling through the wide doorway was the Newtons in their bear forms. It was a tight fit with the boxes, but Nita, Emmett, and Kadeem managed to squeeze inside.

Nita and Emmett reclined on the floor beside the bed with Kadeem's cute chubby bear form curled against his mother's side.

Feeling every bit entitled to her emotions as Fayola said, Jwahir took in the people gathered in her bedroom and grinned.

And grinned.

And grinned.

We are all here together because I ran away from a house in a forest with an abuser and to a cabin home with a kind mama, papa, and baby bear. Only one bowl of chili, a small rocking chair, and a child's bed was right for me. But here, with my new family, everything feels right. Just. Right.

THE END

Author's Note

In 2019, I wrote *Crimson Hunter*, an urban fantasy reimagining of *Little Red Riding Hood* for the *Promise Forever: Fairy Tales with a Modern Twist* anthology. As the title suggests, each contributing author shares a modern-day retelling or reimagining of a fairy tale. My participation in the anthology laid the foundation for what would become my Fairy Tale Fatale series. This series, like the anthology, presents reimagined fairy tales but with a focus on the heroine and set in the future and on an alternative Earth.

Bearly Gold is the second book in the series. It is a fantasy reimagining of *Goldilocks and the Three Bears*. While I purchased the book cover a year before writing the novel, I did not have a plot, much less defined characters, or a world for them to call home. Like many authors, I use research to help me brainstorm. To begin, there were two pieces of information I needed answers to, followed by one question that eventually formed the heart of *Bearly Gold*. One, what is the generally accepted theme or moral of the fable? Two, how old is Goldilocks?

British author and poet Robert Southey wrote "The Story of the Three Bears." This literary fairy tale, with an old woman who breaks into the home of three bachelor bears, where she proceeds to eat their food, break a chair, and sleep in their beds, evolved into the *Goldilocks and the Three Bears* tale we know today (Warick, 2016). It was writer Joseph Cundall who transformed the character of the little old woman into that of a little girl in his work, *Treasury of Pleasure Books for Young Children* (Warick. 2016). Yet, it was the author William Wallace who named the little girl Golden Hair, which evolved into Goldilocks by 1904 in Old Nursery Stories and Rhymes (House, 2012, Preceden, n.d.) While Southey's original story, with its female lead and three bachelor bears, is a perfect set-up for an author of reverse harem stories, that was not the direction I wanted to take my story.

I discovered that the version of the story that is most well-known today is considered, by some, a cautionary tale about the potential perils of trespassing. The moral of the story is that children should not enter places without an invitation, break other people's property, and take what does not belong to them. The fact that Goldilocks' fate does not result in more than a fright does not diminish the potential danger or illegality of her actions. Yet, the character does not fare nearly as well in other variations of the fairy tale, such as James Katzaman's account, where she is eaten by the bears (Pocono Record, 2012).

In "Goldilocks Mauled to Death by the Three Bears," she is identified as a seven-year-old who was 'fatally wounded following a brief scuffle after she was discovered breaking into the property of the Bear family' (Pocono Record, 2012, para 7). I asked myself: What would possess a seven-year-old girl to break into a stranger's home, eat their food and then fall asleep? To my way of thinking, most children of Goldilocks' age would not do any of the above. Yet hunger, brutality, manipulation, and fear can encourage even the most moral child to cross the line, engaging in criminal activities as an act of survival.

So, where did learning the moral of the popular children's version of the fairy tale and Goldilocks' age leave me for a plot? Why would my Goldilocks character mirror the most notable actions of Southey's old woman and Cundall's little girl? An idea struck me, as they so often do when I am not actively thinking about a story, but thoughts are still percolating in the back of my mind.

Child trafficking. Ding, ding, ding. That was it. My idea resulted in both happiness and anger. I had finally found an intriguing solution to a significant plot point. At the same time, child trafficking is a despicable crime I did not want to research because knowing is painful. Nothing in me wanted to read the horror stories of the trafficked victims, to learn the extent of their abuse, or even to discover their tales of resistance and resilience. With my Feline Nation duology, I experienced the same emotional reticence to engage in the kind of research necessary to write a compelling story based on real-life events. I researched child trafficking, of course, because even if told through the lens of a fantasy novel, more attention must be brought to this human rights tragedy.

CHILD HUMAN TRAFFICKING

The breadth and depth of human trafficking are as staggering as it is sickening. So, I encourage you to learn more about child trafficking and how to report a suspected child abuse crime. The National Human Trafficking Hotline, UNICEF, and the National Society for the Prevention of Cruelty to Children websites are good places to begin your research.

Heroes are needed in this fight. Not vampiric lightning birds of lore but informed and caring human beings. Child trafficking is not inconsequential but bringing the crime to its overdue end requires people to, like Fayola, engage in the fine art of giving a shit.

References:

House, T. P. (2012, July 13). *The history behind the story of goldilocks*. Owlcation. Retrieved January 7, 2023, from https://owlcation.com/humanities/goldilocks-and-three-bears

Pocono Record. (2012, August 28). *The many painful fates of goldilocks*. Pocono Record. Retrieved January 7, 2023, from https://www.poconorecord.com/story/lifestyle/2012/08/28/the-many-painful-fates-goldilocks/49440417007/

Versions of Goldilock Timeline. Preceden. (n.d.). Retrieved January 7, 2023, from https://www.preceden.com/time-lines/318470-versions-of-goldilock-timeline

Warick, M. (2016). Deeper Meaning of Southey's "Three Bears" (thesis).

Bonus Images

About N. D. Jones

N.D. Jones, Ed.D., is an award-winning author who has achieved USA Today bestselling status for her captivating Black Fantasy and Paranormal Romance novels. Residing in the heart of Maryland with her loving family, N.D. is a trailblazer in the literary world of Blacks in fantasy.

Driven by a passionate desire to introduce more positive, sexy, and multi-dimensional African-American characters as soul mates, friends, and lovers, N.D. embarked on a remarkable journey of her own. Determined to address this challenge, she took it upon herself to redefine the narrative.

N.D. has an impressive portfolio of series that reflect her dedication to bringing diversity and depth to the romance genre. Her works include the enchanting fantasy romance series "Forever Yours" and the contemporary romance trilogy "The Styles of Love." Moreover, she has authored three thrilling paranormal romance series: "Winged Warriors," "Death and Destiny," and "Dragon Shifter Romance," along with two captivating fantasy series: "Feline Nation" and "Fairy Tale Fatale."

One of N.D.'s distinctive strengths lies in her commitment to crafting in-depth mythologies within her novels, as well as seamlessly weaving paranormal elements into the fabric of her stories. When she creates a world of witches and shapeshifters, N.D. ensures that her readers not only witness their extraordinary existence but also gain a deep understanding of what it truly means to be a part of the world of these mystical beings.

In her novels, the paranormal is not merely a background feature; it takes center stage and is crucial to the plot, enriching the reader's experience with every turn of the page. N.D. Jones invites you to join her on an extraordinary journey where Black love intertwines seamlessly with the paranormal, creating a world where love, mystery, and enchantment reign supreme.

Other Books by N. D. Jones

<u>Winged Warriors Novella Series</u> (Paranormal Romance)
Fire, Fury, Faith (Book 1)
Heat, Hunt, Hope (Book 2)
Lies, Lust, Love (Book 3)

<u>Death and Destiny Trilogy</u> (Paranormal Romance)
Of Fear and Faith (Book 1)
Of Beasts and Bonds (Book 2)
Of Deception and Divinity (Book 3)

<u>Forever Yours Series</u> (Fantasy Romance)
Bound Souls (Book 1)
Fated Path (Book 2)

<u>Dragon Shifter Romance</u> (Paranormal Romance Standalone Novels)
Stones of Dracontias: The Bloodstone Dragon
Dragon Lore and Love: Isis and Osiris

<u>The Styles of Love Trilogy</u> (Contemporary Romance)
The Perks of Higher Ed (Book 1)
The Wish of Xmas Present (Book 2)
The Gift of Second Chances (Book 3)
Rhythm and Blue Skies: Malcolm and Sky's Complete Story
The Styles of Love Trilogy Complete Story Boxset

<u>Anthologies</u> (Paranormal and Fantasy)
AfroMyth: A Fantasy Collection, Volume 1
AfroMyth: A Fantasy Collection, Volume 2

<u>Fairy Tale Fatale Series</u> (Fantasy)
Crimson Hunter (Book 1)
Bearly Gold (Book 2)

<u>Feline Nation</u> (Fantasy)
A Queen's Pride (Book 1)
Mafdet's Claws (Book 2)

<u>Fantasy in Black Series</u> (Adult Coloring Books)
Spread Your Wings and Fly: Black Women Fairies Coloring Book (Book 1)
Be UnBound: Black Men Angels Coloring Book (Book 2)
The Beauty of Black Mermaids Coloring Book (Book 3)
Black Superheroes Coloring Book (Book 4)

<u>Resilience Series</u> (Nonfiction Self-Help)
The Color of My Resilience: A Guided Self-Care Journal for Black Men (Book 1)
The Color of My Resilience: A Guided Self-Care Journal for Black Women (Book 2)

<u>Create-A-Comic (Fiction, Comic and Manga Reference)</u>
Blank Comic Book Creator: Level Up Your World
Blank Comic Book Creator: The World is Yours

N.D. JONES
novels with soul